THE ΛPRICITY SERIES

C000165207

Starlight on the Snow is especially dedicated to my mom, Shannon.

Thank you for always showing me how to be strong.

I love you, momma.

Book cover photo and character illustrations by Amelia L. Carter
www.meialoue.com

Novel content, book design, cover design, typesetting, and manuscript editing by Mariah L. Stevens
www.starlightwriting.com

This is a work of semi-autobiographical fiction. It was taken from multiple separate experiences in the author's life and compiled into one narrative.

Some characters, places, and incidents are from real pieces of the author's personal life. All names are fictitious. Some characters, places, and incidents either are the product of the author's imagination or are used fictitiously. Some resemblance to actual persons, living or dead, events, or locales is inevitable yet coincidental. Any musical band names mentioned are real.

Novel Copyright © 2021 by Mariah Lynn Stevens
Cover Photo and Illustrations Copyright © 2021 by Amelia Louise Carter

All rights reserved. No part of this book may be reproduced or used in any manner without written permission of the copyright owner except for the use of quotations in a book review. For more information, e-mail:
starlightxwriting@gmail.com

Second paperback edition March 2021
ISBN-13: 9798703782033 (paperback)

TRIGGER WARNINGS

If you choose to read this trigger warning page, unfortunately it will spoil a bit! So be mindful and aware before you read the warnings.

This trigger warning is a blanket warning for the entire Apricity series.

If you are a minor reading this book, please understand that it is an 18+ book, as is the entire Apricity series. The characters are age 19-20. They are not minors.

The Apricity series contains trigger warnings for:

Sexual assault/rape *(**Book One – Chapter Eighteen: pg. 243-248**. Do not skip page 249 and onward unless you want to miss an important plot point.)*

Emotional and mental abuse

Eating disorder content *(Bulimia, purging, starving, etc.)*

Toxic relationships

Mentions of racism/discussions about race

Religious themes and absence of faith *(specifically Christianity)*

Adult content warnings:

Marijuana and drug use

Sexual content

Foul language

Things the author ensures:

Author's personal experience with all content

Tasteful descriptions of content

The end goal of recovery *(no matter how toxic the relationship gets, the end goal is recovery. The point of the Apricity series is to show the dark side of trauma and why the only solution is recovery and medical help.)*

THIS BOOK SERIES IS WRITTEN FROM THE MALE CHARACTER'S POV FOR A SPECIFIC REASON

This is to showcase the eating disorder and the way it affects the people who exist outside of the eating disordered individual's experience. It showcases how eating disorders affect those around you, and what happens when someone takes it upon themselves to "fix" something that can only be healed through medical intervention and recovery. It has nothing to do with race or skin color, though those things as well as the "white savior trope" are tackled in this novel.

This is a graphic depiction of struggles that the author has faced, presented in a way that can help others seek the first step towards recovery. The author has written this story according to her personal experiences with rape/sexual assault, a 10-year long battle with Bulimia, and a 4-year long abusive relationship, however the narrative itself is done to tell a story for the characters.

For example, the author's sexual assaults were not under the same circumstances as the main character, however the author has still written completely accurate to physicality, emotional turmoil, trauma, and thoughts.

This novel as well as the Apricity Series is written by a Black author to provide representation and healing for other survivors of both sexual assault and eating disorders. While it does have an overarching plot, this series is meant to encourage taking the first step to recovery to save your life. And while the main character is also a Black woman, it is not a novel meant to exploit Black trauma.

The Apricity Series takes a pro-recovery stance.

There is no sugar-coating and there is no pretending that things like abuse, racism, and trauma do not exist.

If you complete reading of this novel and feel that a trigger warning is missing from the page, e-mail the author at starlightxwriting@gmail.com to notify her, and she will add it to subsequent novels in the series.

THE APRICITY SERIES

STARLIGHT
on the Snow

BOOK ONE

written by MARIAH LYNN STEVENS

illustrations by AMELIA LOUISE CARTER

CHAPTER ONE

June 8th, 2017

Ash Robards thought eternity might feel cold.

He imagined the way it would creep by, slow and lonely as nothing existed around him in the dark. Eternity might stretch across the black space between stars, reaching empty corners of the universe that sunlight couldn't warm.

There were things he would never experience up there, floating in the shadows amongst the icy remains of cosmos that had died years before. And there were things he would never experience down on Earth, where the sun could bathe him for hours in the Winter and he would never stop shivering. Never stop fighting his desire to melt.

Sometimes, he wondered what it might be like to let himself freeze.

The night air felt chillier than usual to Ash, kissing his flesh and raising pebbles along his bare arms. His right bicep felt sore, the fresh gardenias that were tattooed there feeling raw from the way the Summer breeze brushed against the tender skin. He ran the fingers of his other hand backward through his messy, bleached-blond hair, heaving a sigh as his feet crunched over the underbrush of the forest.

He stopped for a moment, taking the joint from the back pocket of his skinny jeans and placing it between his lips. Cupping his hand in the air over the end of it to block out the wind, he used his right hand to press the button on his lighter. A tiny flame flared to life, flickering along the paper and lighting it.

Taking a drag, he felt the burn in his throat as the smoke filled his lungs. He held it for a few seconds and then coughed twice as he let it out.

Much better.

Due to the clear, starry sky hung with a moon that was full and bright, it wasn't as dark in the forest as it would have been had it been the Winter. Behind him, Ash could hear the other students in the Senior class who had decided to sneak out.

They chattered in an amiable manner, their laughter echoing into the branches of the thick fir trees as they trekked up the side of the mountain. It had been twenty minutes since they crept out of the school building and they were only a little ways away from their destination.

"I can't believe we're doing this," came the familiar voice of Keely Daniels, a girl he'd somehow managed to have the same English class with since ninth grade. "Like, this is actually hella out of control."

"For real," replied Ji Hyun Park, Ash's ex-girlfriend and one of his best friends. "If we got caught, you know we'd be like, expelled, right?"

"Oh my gosh, yes. That's why I'm so nervous."

"Ash, have you ever been out here before?" Ji Hyun skipped to catch up to his long-legged gait. At five-foot-three inches, she had to crane her neck to maintain eye contact. Her brown eyes seemed almost as black as charcoal through the shadows that the moonlight filtering down through the foliage caused.

Ash, who stood at six-foot-four inches, looked down at her with a slight smirk playing about his lips, a lock of his hair falling forward and brushing his cheekbone. His voice was hoarse from the weed. "I fucked Rachel out here, remember? Not this far up, but like, we were in the trees."

"When was that?" Ji Hyun's brows twitched together in confusion, then she gasped. Her eyes widened and she tossed her long black hair over her shoulder. "Oh, my God, no! I remember that. Hm. Well, you'd better not try to do anything tonight. I don't wanna have to deal with it."

Keely caught up to them, her crimson-red curls bouncing with each step. "The fact that you guys can talk so casually about... That... I just don't know."

"Why, because we go to a Christian boarding school?" Ash teased, his gaze washing over her.

She crossed her arms over the chest of her hoodie, casting him a wary look. "Well, when one goes to one of those, one doesn't exactly think of fucking people in the forest behind it."

"Call me a whore and get over it," he said, holding the joint

2

between his forefinger and thumb as he took another drag. His voice was strained as he spoke with the smoke building inside of him. "Unless you're wanting to —"

"Ash! Good God." Ji Hyun smacked him against the arm with the back of her hand. "You're so nasty. Why do you have to be so nasty all the time?"

His laughter choked off into a soft *hey* of pain as her knuckles grazed his new tattoo. He pulled the sleeve of his black V-neck up, glancing down at them as though she had ruined them. He glared down at her, feeling the pull of his brows as he did so.

"It's still sore. Be nice."

"I won't be nice," she said, turning her nose up into the air. "I'm staying on for the college pre-req program and since you are, too, you'd better just get used to it."

"To what?" he spluttered, the joint at his lips again. "Your bitch complex?"

She blinked against the smoke he exhaled in her direction and then grinned, her teeth flashing white. "Exactly."

In the time that they'd stopped to bicker, the others had caught up to them. There were about thirty students that had decided to sneak out, as the school had always had an underground tradition of sneaking up the mountain on the last night before graduation. If any of the teachers found out they'd done this, they knew they risked losing out on the privilege of being able to walk at the ceremony.

But that was the fun part.

Ash stood there in the center of the path, facing the trees but looking down the slope at everyone walking up towards them.

Half of the students who had come were on scholarship, and the other half were the students who weren't. It felt so strange seeing two sides of a nonsensical war coming together to do this. A war that had been going on since before any of them ever enrolled at Christ Rising Boarding School. The students with money disliking the students without. It wasn't exactly a new concept in 2017 society, and it definitely wasn't new for their boarding school.

Yet here they were, mingling together in conjoined conversation. He saw girls conversing who'd been at each other's throats for years. Guys on the football team talking to guys in the Robotics Club. Girls he'd slept with joking with guys he'd gotten into fist fights with during long-lost lunch periods. He saw his best friend Elijah Ires

3

walking backwards beside the girl he could never seem to get along with, Tayshia Cole. They were laughing.

Ash lifted the joint to his mouth, studying Tayshia. Scrutinizing her. Watching her.

Tayshia, with her catlike hazel eyes, never seemed to find any reason to turn a warm glance in his direction. Her skin was a tawny bronze in the sunlight, but the light of the moon paled her to khaki. She was shorter than Ash, standing at about five-foot-eight, but she carried herself like she stretched seven feet tall. Her hair normally spiraled out of the top of her head in short, coiling curls that reminded him of a cloud, but the past week she'd had it pulled back into rows of braids that were tight to her scalp with fake hair added to make the braids as long as her elbows.

As she traipsed up the path with Elijah turning at her side, it was clear that she was having a difficult time catching her breath. She wore all-black sneakers, black leggings, and an oversized navy blue tee shirt, however there were parts of her face that shone as though the temperature were still in the eighties.

She stopped before him with one hand over her heart and the other hand on her hip. Deep, gasping breaths escaped her mouth. Elijah skidded to a halt in the dirt next to them, grinning up at Ash. Before he could say anything, Ash spoke.

"Out of breath?" He took a drag, holding Tayshia's gaze as he did so. Without looking away, he blew the smoke out to the side. "Want me to carry you?"

"Why you all up in my business?" she snapped, the expression on her face contorting with irritation. "What, I can't walk up the same path as you?"

"That's not what I said," he replied with an incredulous half-laugh. "I asked you if you needed me to carry you."

"I'd literally rather die." Her voice was flat as she took one hand and held up a finger, using it to emphasize the *literally*.

"Damn." His head pulled back on his shoulders. "You can't stop being a bitch, even on our last day together?"

"It's not our last day. I'm coming back for the program, too."

He arched one eyebrow. "Aren't you like... Rich? Why would you need to do your pre-requisites here?"

"It's not about the money, not that it's any of your business how much money my parents make."

"Oh." Another drag, and he felt something pulling at the back

4

of his mind. Something akin to curiosity. A curiosity that he'd never felt when it came to her, beyond wondering when she was going to get out of his way in the hallway. This was the first time they'd spoken outside of an educational environment. It felt alien. Weird. Surreal. "Then why are you coming back for the pre-reqs?"

Tayshia opened her mouth to answer, then the words seemed to die in her throat. Her eyes fell to his arm, where they lingered on his new tattoo. She pulled a disgruntled face.

"Wait," she said. "How old are you?"

"What, because of this?" He glanced down at his bicep. It wasn't like it was the only tattoo. "I'm—"

Elijah interjected, slinging an arm around Ash's neck. The movement caused Elijah's wavy brown hair, cropped on the sides and long on top, to fall across his forehead. The two boys stumbled together as Ash hid his smile with the joint.

"He's almost nineteen. Five days to go," Elijah said, grinning at him. "What were we doing for your birthday again? Were we— wait—wasn't it the—"

"No, that got cancelled," Ash said, giving him the sort of look one gives their best friend when trying to speak using only one's mind. "Andre has to work. We can chill at my house, though."

Elijah grimaced, his brown eyes appearing concerned. "But... Like, your dad, though. Isn't he...?"

Ash tried not to cringe, hyper-aware of the fact that Tayshia seemed to be the one watching *him* now. Something about her gaze felt different. Less distasteful. Less cold.

Curious.

"So, do you live with your parents?" Tayshia said, her words pulling them both to face her, "Are they okay with you having gotten all those tattoos?"

Ash held the back of his right hand—which already had a black-and-red rose tattoo spanning the back of it—over his mouth.

"You serious?" he asked with an expression of mild amusement. "Do I look like I care what my parents think?"

"Not really. No."

It sounded like an insult.

He brought the joint to his lips and inhaled. Then, he reached down for the hem of his shirt, pulling it up to reveal his abdomen right as he blew the smoke out. She stared at the caged ravens and black feathers he had tattooed across the planes of his torso.

"My parents don't give a shit what I do," he said, the buzz of his high finally settling over him like a peaceful cloak. "They haven't since I was fifteen."

Tayshia's jaw dropped. "You got those when you were fifteen?!"

"No," Elijah said, and then he grabbed Ash's hip and jerked him around so his back was facing her. He felt Elijah pulling the collar of his shirt from the back. Pulling until the skin between Ash's shoulder blades was visible, he revealed the top of the dead tree he'd gotten with the first two paychecks from his first-ever job. "He got *this* when he was fifteen."

"You got a tattoo when you were *fifteen?*" She sounded horrified. "Do your parents not care about you?"

"What the—?" Ash felt a spike of anger lashing through his psyche like a crack in the Earth and he whirled around. "What the fuck is your problem?"

"I don't have a problem. I just don't—"

"Tayshia!"

Her back straightened like a lightning bolt had rammed into her spine from the top of her head. She looked past Ash, who turned to glance behind him.

A ways up the mountain path, standing at the back of the still-walking group, stood Tayshia's long-time boyfriend, football player Kieran O'Connell. His light brown hair was messy on his head from the breeze as he stormed back down to them. The perpetual dark circles that ringed the undersides of his eyes seemed to cast even darker shadows across his face as he glowered at her. His eyes seemed to crinkle at the edges whether he was smiling or frowning.

"Jesus Christ, why are you all the way back here? With *them?*" He grabbed her hand, yanking her forward. "I told you to keep up."

"Kieran!" she cried, appearing simultaneously alarmed and angry. She made an attempt to pull her hand out of his grasp. "Can you not?"

Ash sneered in spite of the insult she'd slung his way not minutes before. He couldn't help it. Kieran had always been an asshole. Ash had made sure he knew it when he punched him in the face one lunch period in tenth grade. As bitchy as Tayshia could be towards him, there was no reason for Kieran to be so hands-on.

"Maybe you should keep better tabs on your girlfriend," Ash said, blowing marijuana smoke into Kieran's face with intentional malice. "If she can't keep up, then don't you think you should—I dunno, maybe slow the fuck down?"

"Hey!" Kieran cried, his eyes blazing with rage as he staggered back, covering his mouth and nose with one hand. "Just because we're out here doing this doesn't mean we're trying to be like you."

Ash smirked.

None of the rich students liked the scholarship students, but it seemed that Kieran himself despised their group more than anyone else. Kieran was such a dick that he couldn't stand even being partnered up in class with Ash or any of his friends. Anyone at Christ Rising on scholarship was as good as trash to him.

"Let's just go, Kieran," Tayshia said, walking ahead of him with her hand still clutched in his. She tugged. "It's our last night. I don't really care to watch you get into another stupid fight."

Kieran gave Ash one more dark glare, looked Elijah up and down, and then turned. As he walked up the hill, he quickly overtook Tayshia. She could barely keep up.

"Such a fucking asshole," Elijah said. "I kinda hope you find a reason to punch him when we get to the cave."

"Bruh, shut up or I'm gonna do it."

"And you think I'd stop you?"

Ash bit his lower lip over a wicked grin as he passed Elijah the joint.

✧✧✧

The cave in question lay at the end of the path.

Nestled halfway up the mountain through a copse of trees, the opening loomed high over the heads of the Seniors gathered there. It was blocked off by signs from the town. To the right, nestled in the trees, was the large national park building. When the cavern was open during the day, tourists could go inside to buy souvenirs, set up tours inside, or eat food at the restaurant.

There was a sign that said *Closed* and listed the hours of operation. Another said *Warning: Cave floor is slippery!* The rest of the wooden signs listed information about Crystal Springs Caverns, from historical information about the cave, to geological information about how the mountain was an active volcano that caused the pools of water in its depths to be warm.

One sign in particular caught Ash's attention. It was large, propped high against the edge of the cave's mouth.

Crystal Springs and Soulmate Things: Have you ever wondered where the legend of the hot springs came from?

Long ago, when Crystal Springs settlers first built this town, they were surprised to find a glowing cave full to the brim with amethyst crystals of all sizes. Not only did they find crystals, but they found a series of large pools of water that had been heated by the magma chamber beneath the mountain for years and years! Through a strange hole in the roof of the cave, they saw that the constellation Centaurus glowed bright – right into the hot springs.

Over time, as more and more people settled in Crystal Springs, and people started coming to the hot springs to relax, strange things started happening to those who came at night. Some fell in love who hadn't loved before, and some fell out of love who thought they were meant to be. Legend grew. Myth faded.

Could it be that the stars above the cave were bringing magic to the waters? Was it the springs that brought these people together? The springs that tore them apart? Or was it just coincidence?

Right below the final line, in small print, it read: *Hot springs are off limits to enter! Please stay behind the barriers at all times.*

Fuck, the sign was so corny.

Ash had heard of it before, though. It was common knowledge at Christ Rising—gossip shared amongst students of all grades, from Freshman to Senior to pre-req program students. No one believed it, but the myth was the exact reason why the Seniors years before them had made it tradition to go to the cavern on the last night before they left the school forever. The tradition had begun long before the school introduced the program, but the theme behind it remained.

New beginnings and an eternity written in the stars.

It sounded promising. Promising and cold.

When everyone had gathered, Keely stood on a rock and counted heads. When she was satisfied with the number, she began to talk, her voice projecting outward.

"All right, everybody. It's midnight and we need to be back to the dorms before park rangers get up here for early morning rounds. Everyone needs to use their phones for light. If you didn't bring your phone for whatever reason, partner up with someone who did. The floor's going to be slippery, so we need to be careful. Once we get through the first part, I remember when I went here with my parents, the main cavern has algae on the walls that glows, so we'll be able to see when we get there. Ricardo's got the music, Britt and Jalissa brought the drinks, and I think Stephen said he's brought a speaker?"

One of the football players held both hands up. He used one to make a thumbs-up sign. The other held a speaker that could connect to a phone.

"Sick. Okay." Keely grinned and held her hands wide. "So... Let's do this!"

Everyone began to file inside. Ash had left his phone back in his dorm, so he stuck close to Elijah's side, both of them using the flashlight app to walk behind the group through the cave.

Ash had been here once with his parents when he was younger, so he remembered that the entrance cavern was moderately-sized. There were two tunnels that led to the same cavern, and then the main cavern was so large that an entire classroom could fit inside it.

The ground felt slimy, Ash's shoes slipping a bit even as he took ginger steps. Everyone talked and laughed, some of the girls clinging to one another and shrieking every time one of them almost toppled over.

Ash heard Tayshia and Kieran arguing, bickering like an elderly couple, and he rolled his eyes in the darkness. He never understood relationships. It was easier to fuck and duck, then text them when he was horny again. Even better when a girl smoked him out.

But there was something off about the way Kieran talked to her.

The group reached the main cavern soon enough. The laughter turned to gasps of awe.

Amethysts of all shapes and sizes lined the walls and ceiling, glowing with the algae that had gathered on the rock walls between them. Large and small amethysts were littered about the floor, some removed for park footpaths through the cave, placed near one another to create glittering displays.

At the back of the cavern, there were wooden barriers roped together that stretched across the distance from wall-to-wall. Carabiners bolted into the walls held the ropes taut. Behind those barriers lay the hot springs, a series of three interconnected pools.

The pools glowed opalescent, shimmering with the algae and the starlight coming from above. Steam rose from them, faint but present as the warm water existed in its own heat. High above, there was a hole in the ceiling — just like the sign had described. The hole was large enough to shine moonlight down across all three pools.

Ash wandered near, one hand in the back pocket of his jeans and the other pushing through his hair to get it out of his eyes. As he drew closer, he saw that there were small crystals adorning the back wall of the cavern where the moonlight shone. They almost looked like they could be plucked from the wall like roses in the snow.

It wasn't long before the music started echoing around the cavern, alcoholic beverages were passed around, and then the party began.

The bittersweet emotions that graduation had fostered amongst all of the students — the same bittersweetness that had brought them all together in spite of their differences and cliques — cast a somewhat somber pallor over the party. Though the music played and the teenagers drank, the overall atmosphere was as tranquil as it was sad.

Ash found a large boulder-sized amethyst with a flat face on the top. He turned to face the cavern, placing his hands on the rock behind him so he could heft himself up onto it. He pulled one knee to his chest and began to roll another joint with weed from his pocket. Then, as he licked the paper to close it, he watched his peers.

He could see people mingling even more than they had on the walk up. There was more laughter, less bickering. Kieran on one side of the room with Tayshia on the other.

Tayshia, laughing a melodic laugh that made Ash feel something a little less than annoyance toward her purely because she was acting like a normal person. Seeing her smiling, not worrying about the arbitrary rules that all *good girls* followed.

With the pools glowing to her right, casting light onto her face that made her eyes shine, he could deign to think she was pretty.

A little.

Many students wouldn't be staying on for the pre-requisite program. Many of their friends would be departing for universities across America and when they did, it was common sense to understand that they might never see each other again.

Ash was fortunate. He'd grown up in Crystal Springs. He wasn't a scholarship kid because his father worked his ass off to make sure that Ash's tuition was paid every year. When Ash turned sixteen, he started helping. It was just unfortunate, the things both he and Ash had to do to make the money necessary for him to go to Christ Rising *and* keep the rent paid.

That was why his parents didn't care if he got tattoos.

His mother was lost in a world of her own making and Ash was too busy worrying about *her* to worry about her opinion on tattoos. His father was a different man than he used to be, having gone from gardening roses to gardening other things.

Things that he liked to line his veins with.

An hour or two later, when Elijah was starting to get too drunk to care if he was talking to Ash or an amethyst the size of his entire body, Ash hopped down off of the rock and wandered over to the barriers by the springs. He crossed his arms over his chest and studied them, wondering if the things he'd read on the sign were true.

Not that he believed in soulmates or any shit like that.

He looked up at the sky through the ceiling, watching all the stars twinkling in their cold places. They looked so close together but he knew. They were as far apart as he and Tayshia, full of ice and holding no reverence for one another.

The stars simply existed.

After taking Astronomy for an entire year in eleventh grade, he could make out Centaurus with his naked eye. It stretched long and dim, with Crux tucked beneath its tail like a colt hiding behind its mother. The Hydra slithered along above it, aimed for Libra.

"Don't tell me you're about to jump in."

Ash rolled his head to the right and down, his gaze finding Tayshia through his lashes. She stood beside him, her hands on her hips like she was waiting for him to do it. To challenge her and prove her right.

As if he cared to prove anything to her, to someone who judged him and his family based on preconceived notions tied to her ridiculous need to be as good as possible. To be good and prove that everyone who did things the opposite was somehow bad.

"I was thinking about it," he drawled. "What're you gonna do?

Tell on me?"

She wrinkled her nose, her face souring. "No. But do you have to be so rude?"

"Me?" He scoffed. "Me, the one being rude? That's funny as fuck."

She was silent.

In his peripheral vision, Ash could see something clicking in her jaw. Her emotions were written in the lines on her furrowed brow. The conflict wavered there.

"I'm... Sorry," she said.

"For?" He cast a nonchalant glance down to his new tattoo, scratching an itchy spot with one black-painted fingernail. The silver and black rings he wore glinted as the starlight reflected off of them.

Why did he feel so breathless?

"For what I said about your parents," she muttered. After a roll of her eyes, she looked up at him. "It's not right for me to make assumptions."

"Tayshia Cole, Christ Rising's resident Good Girl," Ash said as though he were announcing it. He returned his attention to the hot springs. "You find it really difficult to be good when you're around me, though, don't you?"

"I don't mean to be rude," she snapped. "I just find you really fu — flipping! Flipping annoying."

"It's okay," he said.

"What?"

Their eyes met.

"You can say *fuck*."

She turned her face to the right, quick as a flash. He was so certain she was blushing that he'd bet his life on it. God, it was easy to rile the girls at this school up, but Tayshia was even easier. She was always angry. Ash's mere existence in their shared classes had her fuming. He didn't know if it was the tattoos, his refusal to follow dress code, or the fact that he was always late.

"Fuck."

"What was that?" he said.

They looked at each other. He saw her teeth sink into her bottom lip as she very slowly and carefully pronounced the one syllable word.

"*Fuck*."

Like sunlight burning, he felt like he was seeing her for the first time. Her mask had faded into embers, leaving him to gaze upon her face. Upon round cheeks and full lips, a wide nose and a sharp chin. Not for the first time, he saw that the thin, short hairs at her hairline had been styled into flat, swirling shapes that framed her square face in a way that almost made him think of ocean waves.

Fuck.

Those eyes.

They were more than catlike. They were sultry and they burned the same way the stars did. Watching, distant and far away, but as bright as though she were close.

Ash felt something familiar twisting its way through him—something he knew he'd never felt for her before. Something that felt as dangerous as the sin the school wanted to keep them from. Something that told him that no matter how much he couldn't stand her personality, Tayshia Cole was not the exception.

She was hot.

The back of his neck prickled. In a near-panic, Ash changed the subject.

"Did you read the sign outside?" he asked.

"Which one?" She cleared her throat, reaching up with one hand to lift a braid and play with it in an absent-minded manner. "There were like, thirty-five."

"The one about the legend."

She raised one of her feathery brows. "I know about the legend. Do you believe it?"

"Not really. That's like asking me if I believe in magic."

"Well?"

He looked at her again. "Well, what?"

"Do you?"

His eyebrows shot up. "Uh... About as much as I believe you'll get into the hot springs with me."

"We can't go into them. The signs—"

"Fuck the signs," he said, letting out a laugh. "We should just do it."

She gaped at him. "Are you for real?"

He stepped up to the barriers, grinning at her as he hunched over slightly to grip the top of one. Her gaze fell to his mouth again, where he knew she could see that his teeth were just as white as hers, and then she frowned.

"Don't," she said.

Ash smirked and swung one leg over the barrier.

Tayshia cast a quick glance over her shoulder, as though the other teens weren't too drunk to notice what they were doing. Her braids slipped down her back. She looked worried.

"Ash, seriously — don't."

"Why not?"

"Because — what if its toxic?"

"It's not toxic."

"The signs — "

"The signs are to keep you out of the water," he said with a scowl. He moved to the other side and took a step back.

"But what if they're true? Ash, wait!"

"Then I guess I die," he said, letting out an exasperated sound. "I mean, what the fuck?"

"We really shouldn't," she said. "You don't want to get in trouble — especially since you're coming back for the program."

"Do you ever break rules, or do you just lick the asshole of authority? Who cares? I'm going in."

Feeling a spark of glee in his chest, he dropped his tongue over his bottom lip, flipped her off with both hands, and hop-skipped backward. Her head tipped back in frustration right before he turned and kicked his shoes off on the rock near the water's edge. He removed his socks, stuffed them and his weed into the shoes, and then he walked back over to where she stood, the barrier between them. The rocks were cold underfoot and felt like they were covered in wet moss, but he paid them no mind.

"For your information," she said, her face illuminated by the glowing water, "I do like to break the rules. When it's worth it."

"It's your last night before Summer. The last night you have with some of your friends." Ash leaned down until his face was near hers. "Don't you want to know what it feels like?"

"What what feels like?"

"Being bad."

Tayshia's eyes flickered down to his lips. He saw her throat move as she swallowed.

Was she nervous?

After one more glance cast toward their drunken stumbling and laughing peers, she sighed.

"All right, fine."

"Yeah?"

Her lips pursed, her expression turning wary.

"Yes. I'll—whoa! What are you doing?!"

Ash paid her cries no mind as he gripped her by the waist and lifted her into the air. Her hands smacked down on the tops of his shoulders, her eyes wide as he hauled her over the barrier and set her down. It was normal, picking up a girl. But with her, it felt... Confusing.

It felt like they were in a dream.

They headed towards the nearest pool, surrounded in crystals that seemed to glow on their own. The water lay before them, still and shimmering. Ash could see the stars of Centaurus reflected on the unbroken surface.

"Ready?" he said.

"If it's toxic," she said, her tone one of warning.

"Then we die," he said, "but at least we die together."

She shot him a look, to which he responded with one in return.

"Did you not take the geology elective? Amethyst isn't toxic. The water isn't toxic. If it was, the temperature in here would be so high that we couldn't even come into the damn cave. And if it really *was* that toxic, they would put barriers at the cavern's entrance."

Tayshia said, "We live in Crystal Springs. The caverns are behind a Christian boarding school. They don't put barriers because they're not expecting anyone to break in just to go into a pool of rocks and algae."

"Did you bring your phone?"

"Huh? No, Kieran used the flashlight on his."

"Good. Get in the water."

"You're not listening to me. The water may not be toxic, but if we get caught, do you know what the school could do? They could keep us out of the program!"

"Get in the water." He took a step toward her.

She backed away, holding up one hand. "Boy, you better not try me. On God, I'll slap the crap outta you."

"Get in the water," he said through another smirk, "or I'm throwing you in."

"I will get in the water *myself*. Back up."

She walked past him, her shoulder brushing his chest. Sparks rippled, spreading outward beneath his shirt from where it did.

"This is ridiculous," she said. "It better not get on my hair. If I get even one drop on my braids, I'm making sure they expel you."

Ash's head fell back in laughter as he moved to stand beside her. Together, they lifted their feet and stepped into the pool. It was clear, the stars and algae lighting their way as they moved forward.

The water felt as warm as a fresh-drawn bath, instant in the way it soothed any aches Ash hadn't known he had. He felt it soaking through his clothing—his jeans, boxers, and shirt—but it didn't bother him like perhaps jumping into the Oregon coast would have.

It rose higher the further in they stepped. He could feel the amethysts, surprised that they weren't as sharp as he thought they'd be. They almost fell dull.

"Fuck," he said under his breath as he stopped to look around him. "This is the prettiest shit I've ever seen."

"It really is, actually. I didn't grow up here, so I've never been here."

"For real?" he asked, surprised.

"Yeah. I'm from Medford. I—*Ah!*"

Tayshia moved forward...

And touched nothing.

She gasped as her foot sunk into the depths. The water was so clear that the amethyst-speckled floor of the pool looked closer than it was. A small leap of his heart had Ash reaching to grab her under the arms and drag her back up before her head went under.

He moved back, pulling her with him as the water splashed around the lower part of his chest. She leaned back against him, her breaths coming in short, heavy pants. She seemed disoriented. Shaken.

"I'm sorry," she said, the words quick. "I'm sorry. I—I'm so—"

"Hey." Ash's hands moved, one to her back beneath the surface of the water and the other to her shoulder. He turned her to face him, brow furrowing. "Stop apologizing. This water is *hella* clear. I couldn't even tell that it was that deep."

She nodded, her eyes a bit wild.

"That must be—it must be why they have the signs," she whispered. "I knew we shouldn't have come in here. We should get out."

"We could..." His hair fell forward and he pushed a wet hand through it, painting it with water. "... Or you could just stay right where you are and don't walk forward again."

"Obviously, you jerk." She turned her back to him again. Her tone made it clear that she was upset. He didn't blame her—anyone with any knowledge of cave pools knew that when they were deep, then they were *deep*. "I think we should just get out. I don't think we should be in here. I don't like it."

"Calm down," he said, voice rough. "You're panicking over nothing."

"It's not nothing. I legit almost *died*."

"Hah!" He barked a laugh. "You think I would have just—what? Let you dramatically *slip away*?"

"We hate each other, so." Tayshia looked up at him, her back still pressed to his chest. "I wouldn't be surprised."

Ash gave her a bewildered look. "I'm an asshole, but I'm not a monster. I wouldn't let you drown—that's ridiculous."

She clucked her tongue and said nothing. Ash wanted to change the subject—to talk about school or go back to bickering—but something about her disposition bugged him.

Did she really think he was that bad?

"Look at me," he said, his tone commanding.

She did, the water sloshing gently.

"Do you honestly think I hate you so much that I'd let you *die*?" Ash asked. "Because I can't think of any valid reason why you would think that low of me."

Tayshia inhaled, almost as though she were preparing to yell at him, and then something shifted in her eyes. Clicked into place like puzzle pieces. Her facial expression fell.

"I'm sorry," she said. "I don't think I've been fair to you at all. Ever since we met, I've treated you like a criminal. No, I don't think you hate me that much. I don't know why I thought you would actually let me..." Her hand fluttered through the air in a dismissive motion, then slapped against the water. It sent droplets up into the air. "It's stupid. I'm stupid. And I'm sorry."

"It's fine," he said, even though it bothered him. She hadn't exactly explained what she *did* think. He didn't know why he cared. "Just—do me a favor and leave that shit here in Senior year. When we come back to school next year for the program, let's try *not* to bite each other's heads off, all right?"

"Okay," she said, averting her gaze for a second before lifting it to his face again. "As long as you promise to stop interrupting me with your snide laughs when I answer questions in class."

"Fine, as long as you stop telling the principal on me for every stupid little thing," he shot back. "I'm not about to be a literal college student having detention every day."

"I will if you stop smoking weed on campus—*even* if it's in the trees."

"Absolutely not." He looked her up and down. "You can get fucked on that one."

Perhaps it was just a trick of the starlight, or a flicker of shadows, but he thought he could see her blushing again.

"I won't tell, but you have to do something equal for me." She crossed her arms over her wet shirt. "It has to be the equivalent."

"What could *possibly* be the equivalent to getting high for you?"

She tapped her chin, the process of her thoughts visible on her face as she wracked her brain. "Do you have a car?"

"Yeah," he said. "I mean, it's my dad's second car, but it's essentially mine. Why?"

Her eyes lit up. "Next year, I want you to take me off campus for lunch sometimes."

"Off campus for lunch?" He spoke the words slow and drawn-out, his tone a bit scratchy. "*That's* the equivalent for you?"

She nodded. "I don't have a car and next year, I'll be in the program's apartments complex. I signed up for one of the two-bedroom roommate apartments."

"You're in luck," Ash said, remembering how he'd filled out the paperwork just the other day. The apartment complex was in town, right at the foot of the mountain. The school was, of course, placing girls with girls and boys with boys, but they'd all share the same apartment complex. "So did I."

"Then if we're in the same complex, this should work out perfect," she said, and then she smiled. Her eyes sparkled like the stars in Centaurus. "We can even try to be friends."

"Friends? With *you*?" He huffed. "Maybe this water *is* toxic. You sound like a lunatic."

"You said it yourself," she said with a shrug. "Let's leave the drama in the past and just try to be friends."

He gave her a nod. She exhaled, looking down at the water, and then over at the party.

"What if everyone else comes over here and wants to get in, too?" she asked.

He followed the line of her gaze.

The other students were plastered, singing at the top of their lungs and jumping up and down to the beat of the music. Several of them kept slipping on the glowing algae and falling over. That caused the peals of laughter to seem nonstop—it irked Ash. He hated when people weren't calm. That was why he preferred weed to drinking.

"Ash!" she said, her tone rising in pitch. "Are you listening? What if everyone else comes over here?!"

"Just chill the fuck out," he murmured, turning her back to face the pool and the wall of crystals. His hands found her waist again. "Here—I've got you."

Ash felt the fabric of her shirt clinging to her body, felt dips and curves that he hadn't even thought to look at on her before, and he felt the blood in his body flooding his face.

They stood there in a sudden silence that arrested Ash of all previous thought, the only sounds coming from the gentle ripples their bodies caused in the water, their raucous friends and peers, and the music that played on the speakers. She smelled good, the faint scent of her floral perfume wafting up from her skin to fill him with a pleasant, calm feeling.

God, she had the longest neck, didn't she? With a gentle slope that seemed to melt into her collarbones, it was the sort of neck that— if she were a hook-up and she wasn't Tayshia fucking Cole—he might want to kiss a little. To taste it and see how loud she gasped.

Once again, she leaned back against him, still remaining silent. Her gaze was trained on the pool and its amethyst-filled depths. Ash's fingers flexed against her abdomen, his thumbs pressing into her back.

This felt nice. Smooth. Warm.

He didn't think he would mind never letting go.

"Did you know..." she said suddenly, her head tipping back. He felt the weight of her skull pressing into him.

"Hm?" he hummed, his gaze trained upon her.

"Amethyst crystals are said to encourage you to dream. If you sleep with one near you or on you, you're supposed to have vivid dreams."

"Ah," he said. "Sounds like magic."

"Doesn't it?"

His fingers twitched again, yearning to reach up and touch the front of her neck. To sweep the braids to one side of her head so he could brush his fingertips along it and feel her shiver.

She may have been Tayshia, but that didn't mean he was broken. Tayshia was a girl. She was pressed up against him in warm, relaxing water. The cave around them was as gorgeous as every part of her face.

"Only one way to find out," he said. "You want to go see if we can take one out of the wall?"

"Isn't it technically illegal?" she asked.

"Once again—who cares?"

"Apparently, not you."

"You're so adorable when you learn."

Keeping his left hand on her waist, he moved behind her. He was careful as he moved towards a flat bit of rock that jutted out of the wall and the water. As he placed his hand flat upon it, his fingers dragged along her back. Then, his other hand was on the rock and he was using his arms to pull himself out of the water. His tattoo felt sore and he knew he probably shouldn't have gotten into the pool with it, but he didn't care.

"Okay, now come," he said.

Tayshia started making her way over, her hands clasped to her chest. A fear entered her eyes that he'd never seen before, not even during the times they hadn't gotten along in class. When her foot slipped, she managed to catch herself, but the look of terror that flashed across her face sparked an emotion within him.

He didn't know what to name it.

"Take my hand," Ash said, crouching down and reaching out to her.

She closed her eyes, not moving. "I don't like this. I'm freaking out."

"No, you're not."

"Yes, I am. I'm freaking out."

"Then don't move — just take both of my hands and I'll lift you out."

"Oh, yes," she said, sarcasm dripping from her quivering tone, "because you can lift my entire body out of the water by the hands."

Confusion roiled in his mind and then he shook his head. He snapped his fingers and used both of his hands to beckon her.

"Come on," he said. "Come here. I'll pull you out."

"No."

"Yes."

"Ash."

"Give me your fucking hands. For fuck's sake."

Her hands trembled in the air until he grabbed them tight. Their damp palms met, fingers wrapping around one another's.

A jolt ran through Ash's body. It reverberated up the length of his arms and down, where it coiled in the pit of his stomach. Heat spread across his cheeks like a flare from the sun in space. The feeling was unexplainable. Overwhelming.

Frightening.

Ash pulled, standing as he did so. She came up out of the water. They let go of their left hands. She wrapped her arm around his neck and he wrapped his around her waist. He felt her cheek pressing against his as he dragged her onto the rock with him. They stood there, dripping water down onto the cave floor and staring at one another.

Facing the wall, he felt around the amethysts until he discovered one that was loose. With a firm tug and leaning back, he was able to dislodge it. It was about three inches long, multi-faceted, and a dark shade of purple that reminded him of some of the flowers his father used to plant.

"This is so weird," he said.

"What is?"

"The fact that I was able to pull it out of the wall like that. I didn't think it would actually work."

"Really? Why?" she asked, sounding surprised.

"Amethyst doesn't crack." When she raised an eyebrow, he added, "Learned that one in geology."

"Maybe the amethysts in this cave do."

"Yeah, because these are *magic* amethysts." He rolled his eyes, his long fingers wrapping around the sides of the oblong shaped crystal. He pulled, twisted, tried to turn it.

And felt it shift.

"It's almost like..." Ash said quietly, frowning and twisting his wrists. "Almost like we could just — "

"Break it?"

Their gazes met.

Crack.

The amethyst broke into two shapeless pieces. Tayshia reached toward him, her fingers brushing against his as she took one half of the crystal from him. He found his gaze drawn to her face once again, to the way it looked as the eerie lights played off of it. He wished their fingers could brush again.

"It's the perfect size for a necklace," she said, smiling as she looked up at him. "Maybe we could — "

"Tayshia, what the Hell are you doing? Everyone's leaving."

Ash and Tayshia looked over, seeing Kieran leaning against an amethyst that was half his size. It jutted up out of the ground as though it were made to be a body rest. Kieran's hair was a mess and his eyes were unfocused. His drunkenness was apparent in the way he swayed even as he leaned against the rock.

The rage on his face sent ire of his own racing through Ash's mind.

"My bad," Tayshia complained. "Jeez. Why do you have to be so rude about it?"

"Just get back over here before I come over there and get — " Kieran's words were slurred. He dropped his head into his hand for a moment, the heel of his palm rubbing his eye. "Get you."

Tayshia and Ash got back into the water so they could inch their way around the edge and back over to the barriers. As Ash grabbed his weed and shoes, slipping them onto his feet, he realized that Kieran had already whisked Tayshia away.

Elijah stumbled over, grinning like a madman. "I saw you go in the water."

"I did." Ash tied his second shoe and then stood up straight.

"With Tayshia?"

"Yeah."

Elijah nodded, looking at him for a moment before he burst out laughing.

"I'm so drunk."

"Then let's get going." Ash held out his hand, even though it was still wet. In his other hand, he held his half of the crystal. The pad of his thumb stroked one of the faces of the jewel. "Give me your phone; I'll do the flashlight."

As the students began to file out, lurching forward like they were born in the cave, he found himself thinking the crystal felt nice. Smooth. Warm.

He might never put it down.

CHAPTER TWO

June 14th, 2017

She'd melted him like sunlight.

Ever since the night in the cave, Ash had gone from being frozen in the center of a block of ice to dissolving in an ocean of obsession that threatened to drown him.

He'd always been the guy who kept people at a safe distance, pushing them back every time they got too close. He swathed himself in snowflakes of distraction, patterns created by weed, girls, and tattoos that piled up around him and kept him in place while he shivered.

Anything to avoid feeling warm, even as his veins grew colder.

The echoes of a past where his family was happy, before his father fucked everything up. The prospect of a future where he did nothing except follow in his father's footsteps, with nothing to pull him back from the edge of that cliff. The fact that he didn't know how to process simple or complex emotions and instead, turned to lashing out at other people with his temper just to bear the brunt of it.

Ash preferred to freeze in place so he wouldn't have to face *any* of it.

Now, he felt like Tayshia Cole had wrapped her hands around his throat so she could hold him underwater and watch him die.

Never before had he possessed any desire to think about her beyond the amount of annoyance she caused. The detentions she landed him, or the bickering they did in the hallways. The occasional group projects where he specifically did less work just to get back at her. Until the cave, he hadn't had any reason to do anything other than dislike her.

When he got home the night of the party, he couldn't stop thinking about her. The things she'd said, the way she laughed. Her smile. The way she'd leaned into him, like she was comfortable letting him take control of the situation to keep her from going under.

He thought about Tayshia from the moment he woke up to the moment his head hit the pillows at night.

Sometimes, he picked the crystal up off of his bedside table and felt the smooth part. He wondered if she was feeling the same emptiness that he felt.

He didn't like picking it up and thinking about the fact that she might have thrown it away.

It felt like he existed shrouded in a foggy haze. Nothing brought him joy. The things that had once lifted his spirits and sent him soaring now chained him at the ankle and dragged him to the depths. He felt sick. Sick and wrong and empty. Like half of himself was missing.

Like she'd taken it.

And he was angry with her. Because before they'd gotten into those hot springs, everything was certain. Everything was in its place. He knew who he was, who he was going to be, and what it felt like to get into the water and swim.

Now, he was drowning.

His father, Gabriel didn't notice Ash's sudden plunge in mood. He never noticed anything but how much his pipe had left to smoke, and failure. Failure to sell enough in Crystal Springs. Failure to sell enough in Portland. Failure to sell enough, period.

Ash had been to Portland every day since graduation, working his ass off to sell as much as he could to make up for Gabriel's shortcomings, but if he came home without the arbitrary preconceived amount that his father had imagined in the span of *before I got high* and *after*, then Ash ended up getting his ass beat.

His mother did notice, however. Lizette noticed that Ash wasn't at home as much. He wasn't bringing Elijah around to play video games and hang out. When he was at home, Ash lay in bed, staring at the ceiling while lost in thought. He came down to eat, but he was mechanical and quiet.

It was difficult to interact with his parents at the dinner table when his father's veins were on fire, his mother was pretending she wasn't working her way through her third plate, and Ash was pretending his newest bruise didn't hurt.

"Are you gonna spend your *entire* birthday in your bed?" Lizette asked as she entered Ash's room for the third time that day. She set a can of his favorite soda on the top of his dresser, a smile spread across her face that brought light to her blue eyes. "Don't you want to come watch a movie with me? Or maybe we could take a walk together?"

It was nearly noon on Ash's nineteenth birthday and he still hadn't gotten out of his bed. He lay on his side, arms wrapped around his pillow with his hair in his eyes, staring. Staring at the air between his bed and the wall. Staring at the emptiness he felt inside.

"I'm not thirsty," he said.

"Thirsty? I asked you... Oh, right." She tapped her finger against the side of the soda can. "Well, it'll be here for you when you are."

"Okay," he mumbled.

"How's your tattoo healing?" she asked, coming to sit on the edge of his bed. He felt her touch upon his arm. "I never did tell you that I actually do love the gardenias. They're my —"

"Your favorite flower, I know." He looked up at her through his peripheral vision, too drained to lift his head. He had to go to Portland again later that night. "It's doing fine. Scabbing's completely gone and I didn't lose any pigmentation, so... It's all good."

"Oh, good." Lizette brushed back a strand of her shoulder-length brown hair, revealing her jaw. It looked like her lymph nodes were swollen, but Ash wasn't sure. "Is Elijah going to stop by today?"

"He was, but I don't know anymore. I don't think I have time."

His mother frowned. "Your father will be happy you've taken on that mindset."

Ash scoffed and rolled onto his back. He yawned and rubbed his eyes. "Man, I just feel so tired."

"Do you have a fever?" She placed her wrist against his forehead, something he would have batted her hand away for if he weren't feeling so empty. "You don't feel warm."

"I'm not sick," he said. "I'm just tired. I need a break."

"From working for Ricky?"

"From working for Dad!" he cried, giving a short, mirthless laugh. "I mean, this is fucking ridiculous. If it weren't for him, I wouldn't have to be picking up the slack."

"Well." Lizette gave him a stern look but said nothing about the curse word. "I wish I could help —"

"No." Ash sat up, raising his knees, resting his elbows on them, and holding his wrist. He shook his head. "Absolutely not, Mom.

Dad and I've got this."

His mother pursed her lips. "I'm just worried, is all. You're flying too close to the sun."

Ash shrugged, unable to think of anything encouraging to say that wouldn't be a lie. They *were* flying too close to the sun. His father was a drugged-out idiot. He kept skimming off the top, thinking Ricky wouldn't notice. He spent the earnings, too.

What would Ricky think if he came to their house and saw the brand new television his father had bought during an erratic high? The new couches? The new game console he'd left at the front of Ash's door that morning?

They'd be fucked.

He wasn't sure if it was the thoughts of Tayshia, the bizarre emptiness he felt, or the mistakes his father was making that caused his depression.

"Did you at least sleep well, lovie?" Lizette reached over and pushed his bangs back. They stuck up, the bleach-processed hair nearly always looking like he'd just rolled out of bed — especially when he *had* just rolled out of bed. "You've got the dark circles from Hell."

"I slept," he said, closing his eyes and leaning into her palm against his face. Behind his eyelids, he felt like all he could see were hazel eyes and black braids.

"Did you dream?"

"No," he said. "I never dream."

"You're lucky." She patted his cheek, her voice gentle. "Sometimes, all I have are nightmares."

Lizette's hand went back to her lap. She looked forward, her gaze falling blank upon his dresser. Her lymph nodes *were* swollen and she looked pale. Too pale.

Ash watched her, watched his mother continuing to fall apart before his eyes. Concern sunk into the sea of emptiness inside of him, filling it with something real but not tangible enough to keep him above the water's surface.

"Mom, did you eat today?"

"Of course." She looked at him, giving him the strained smile she always gave him when she lied. "Did you want to come downstairs and watch a movie with me after all?"

"Nah," he said with a sigh, scratching the back of his head. "I'm 'bout to lay back down, or something."

"Okay," she said, the light of her smile not quite reaching her eyes. "I'll come check on you in a bit. Until then, I'll be in the living room."

She reached over to squeeze his forearm, her knuckles brushing against his knee, and then she left the room. Ash noticed that she wore the same brown velour sweatsuit that she'd been wearing for the past three days.

It was his birthday. His mother had come into his room multiple times, hoping he'd be awake so she could spend time with him. His father had spent money they weren't supposed to spend on electronics and furniture, which probably caused her more stress than she needed to deal with because it certainly caused it for Ash.

Stress was the enemy. It was what would have her in the bathroom after meals or not eating at all. And if she was in the bathroom after her meals during the day, that meant she'd be in the kitchen all night and in the bathroom all over again. That meant that after he finished selling in Portland, Ash would be spending his night in the stairwell, or on the floor of his bedroom with his back against the door, waiting for her to stumble to bed so he could handle it before his father woke up.

If she wanted him to come watch a movie, he would do it.

After dressing in a pair of black joggers and black mesh shirt with a wide neckline, Ash looked at his bedside table. He didn't need the crystal to go downstairs, of course, but he liked to touch it. He liked to hold it and remember what it felt like before — when he was full and complete and oblivious.

But it wasn't there.

He got down on his hands and knees, searching the threadbare carpet to see if it had fallen in-between the tufts of fabric. Searched under his bed to see if it had rolled there, and behind the dresser to see if it had gotten tossed. Nothing.

Okay. That was weird. He didn't want to panic because it was only a dumb rock, but...

It wasn't *only* a dumb rock, was it?

It represented something to him. It meant something and had a purpose, he just didn't know what.

When Ash went downstairs and entered the kitchen, he felt surprised to see a cake with blue and pink frosting resting on the counter. He could see his mother sitting on the couch, staring at the black screen of the TV with the remote in her hand. She hadn't turned it on yet. The expression on her face was so forlorn that Ash's heart spasmed in his chest.

He hated seeing his mother so sad. He needed to pull his shit together, even if only for today.

"Hey, Mom!" he called from the kitchen. She looked at him and he grinned. "This cake for me?"

The desolation on her face split apart like rain clouds and sunlight glared through. She practically leapt to her feet, walking over to him.

"Yes, it is! The neighbor and I made it this morning while you were sleeping. It's red velvet cake, but with vanilla frosting in your favorite colors. Are you excited?"

"Oh, Hell yeah!" he said, enthusiasm pushing him to wrap one arm around her. His mother was so much shorter than him that he felt like he was hugging a child. He stuck his finger in the frosting, like he used to when he was a kid, and tried not to think about the fact that he felt too empty to taste anything. "It's good. So, what's for lunch?"

"Whatever you want." She wrapped her arms around his waist and pillowed her head against his chest. "I'm just happy you're going to spend time with me. How about roast beef sandwiches?"

"Sure," Ash said. He kissed the top of her head. "Don't forget to—"

"Extra cheese and light on the onions, I know. Go sit down at the table."

Ash walked towards the table, hearing the sounds of his mother gathering the ingredients from the refrigerator. He pulled a chair out.

"So, where's Dad?"

"He's at Ricky's, helping the guys pack for the week," Lizette said, and it was eerie how nonchalant she sounded. The soft sounds of her chopping vegetables for the sandwiches echoed in the small, old kitchen. "Ricky's been asking him for updates and—" She lowered her voice to a mutter. "—you know we don't have it."

"I'm guessing he thinks Ricky will be more lenient if he helps," Ash drawled, sinking into the chair and scooting down until his long legs stretched out.

"I'm guessing so."

They spent the next half-hour or so talking about Ash's plans for the Summer and for the pre-requisite program when the new school year began. His mother understood why he signed up to live in the apartment complex, but she was sad about it. Ash felt badly, too, because he knew he'd be leaving her alone with his father. But his father never hurt her — it was only Ash that he was physical with.

Ash could take better care of her if he were away from Gabriel, free to get a real job and bring in some clean money. He could help his mother out from afar so she never had to worry about what would happen when she ran out of food stamps each month.

When they were halfway through eating their sandwiches, Lizette looked up and over at the large window that the table was positioned against.

Once, it had been impossible to see their yard. There used to be flowers of all types and colors that would fill the space between the edges of the frame, giving them all something beautiful to look at while they ate.

Now, there was nothing. The window was clean, but the yard was barren. The grass had grown tall and there were weeds in the untilled soil.

"I can't wait for Winter for the roses to bloom," Lizette said, her tone wistful.

Ash slowed his chewing, his gaze averting to the left, into a living room filled with way too many new things, and a coffee table littered with drug paraphernalia. His father hadn't planted any flowers in two years. Still, his mother held out hope that he'd put down the pipe and pick up the seed packets again.

"I have something for you, Ash."

"Oh, yeah?" He ate his last bite. "Time for cake?"

"No, actually." She pulled her chair out and dusted crumbs off of her hands. When she smiled, her blue eyes sparkled. "It's a gift!"

His hands froze and his stomach lurched with panic.

"Wait, Mom. No. We don't have the money for that. The money in Dad's account is supposed to be for —"

"I know," she said, cutting him off with a pointed look. "This didn't cost me anything, lovie."

She continued to speak as she walked into the kitchen and over to the back door, her voice tinny as it wafted over to him.

"When I went over to Bertha's this morning, I remembered that she had jewelry-making supplies. I saw some of the things she made and I thought, *wow, those are really neat.* And then I remembered you had that amethyst."

Ash's brow furrowed as she walked back and set a tiny gift bag on the table next to his empty plate.

"She had to help me because it was my first time wire-wrapping, but now, you should be able to take it everywhere with you."

Ash reached inside the bag. His fingers came into contact with the familiar ridges of his crystal and he pulled it out. The top was wrapped in silver wire, attached to a black leather cord. His jaw dropped.

"I'm guessing you got it at the Caverns, huh?" she asked, looking excited. "I remember going up there with your dad when I was sixteen. Gosh, thinking back, it just cracks me up the things we got into. So, do you like it?"

He breathed an incredulous laugh. "Are you kidding? It's sick, Mom! I fuckin' love it. Seriously. It's sick."

"Well, it's for all your dreams," she said, fluttering her fingers with a dramatic flair. "I hope they come true. Amethyst enhances dreams, you know."

"So corny, and for what?" he joked. "Honestly, thank you."

Ash unraveled the cord from the slight tangle it had gotten itself into, and then pulled it on over his head. It was the perfect length for the crystal to brush against his sternum. He could tuck it behind the neckline of his shirts, or he could wear it out.

"I know it's not a fancy game system like what your father managed to get you—never mind the fact that I have no idea how he had the extra money for that when you guys have to pay Ricky at the end of the month—but I thought it would be something nice for you to have."

Ash stretched one arm up, beckoning his mother with his fingers. He used his other hand to lift the purple crystal up so he could look at the way the sunlight filtering in through the window reflected off of its jagged edges. She came to his side and bent down to hug him. He rubbed her upper back.

"Thanks, Mom," he said. "I really, really like it. This explains where it went, though. I thought I like, lost it somehow."

Lizette laughed and kissed him on the cheek. "Nope. I stole

it. I'm glad you like it."

"And don't worry about the stupid game system," Ash said, rolling his eyes. "I'll probably sell it if I have to."

"Let's hope you don't have to. Happy birthday, lovie." She squeezed his shoulder. "Cake now?"

"Hell yeah."

While she went to plate them up a slice of cake, Ash lifted the crystal again so he could study it. It looked different on a cord. More legit. Almost like it was something he'd intentionally bought.

Lizette gave him his cake and a fork, then took her seat again. The two of them tucked into the red velvet, eating and conversing. Ash talked about the necklace to her and the cavern, leaving out the parts about Tayshia just to keep the conversation from becoming about girls. Lizette loved prodding him about that and Ash didn't like her to know that he wasn't the type of guy to have girlfriends.

In fact, now that he thought about it, he'd never had a girlfriend other than Ji Hyun. Everyone else had felt so fleeting. Like someone to pass the time. Cold weather to help him stay frozen. Ji Hyun was different because they'd grown up together in Crystal Springs, had attended the same church during his parents' Christian phase, and had lost their virginity to one another.

He supposed that was why his mother wanted to know if he had a girlfriend all the time. She'd liked Ji Hyun and though they were still friends, Ji Hyun hardly ever came around.

Ash finished his cake right after his mother. The final bite was on its way to his mouth as she got up from the table and went to the bathroom. He set his fork down, feeling his good mood dissipating as quickly as morning fog during the rain.

Did she have to do it on his birthday?

The toilet flushed five minutes later and she came out of the downstairs bathroom. Her eyes were a bit glassy. She flashed him a quick smile as she grabbed her plate and went to grab another piece of cake. This one was much larger than the last. Each bite she took felt like she was eating another piece of his heart.

"Hey, Mom?"

Lizette looked up, sniffling. Her smile pulled at the corners of her eyes. "Yes, son?"

"I love you."

Her smile faltered. "I love you, too, Ash."

Ash sat in that chair while she proceeded to not only eat the large slice she'd taken, but the rest of the cake. He said nothing, knowing that once she got started, there'd be no stopping her. If he tried, she'd get emotional and cry. The last thing he wanted was for her to cry.

The fact that he was sitting here, watching her was the only thing that helped combat the shame she felt. Having him there was what he could do for her as a son, and it was enough.

When the cake was completely eaten, Lizette went to the bathroom a second time.

Ash placed his elbows on the table and dropped his head into his hands. He wished he could do more. He wanted to do more, but how could he? The fact that he knew but never said anything to her about it was the only thing holding them together. He was terrified that if he tried to stop her, then she'd pull away from him and wouldn't want to be his mom anymore.

He didn't want to be alone with his father.

After Lizette went over to Bertha's to return the dessert plate, Ash sprung into action. He knew he didn't have much time before his father wandered back through the door, and even less time before his mother came back home, but he was going to make an attempt to clean up anyway. Lizette never did it, and Ash wasn't sure if she noticed that he was the one doing it for her.

It may have been part of the web of feigned ignorance they'd woven around themselves.

The bathroom itself was clean, but the toilet was not. There were streaks of blue, pink, and red trailing down the underside of the bowl. Splatters of color had made it to the floor, the side of the counter, and the cream-colored shower curtain. He lifted the toilet seat and saw more flecks beneath it. Chunks were gathered inside the rim.

He opened the cupboard under the sink.

Ash was stoic and silent while he cleaned the toilet using a cloth, cleaner, and the brush. He scrubbed and he scrubbed and he scrubbed, even when the porcelain was glistening white. He scrubbed until sweat rolled down his temples and his hair was damp from it. Even then, he scrubbed some more.

Lizette had always been good at masking her emotions, but she'd never been good at hiding this. Gabriel didn't notice because he wasn't looking. But Ash?

Ash had known all along.

He'd known something was wrong since the time he woke up one night in middle school and found her eating a plate full of food at three in the morning. He'd known it when she was in and out of the bathroom multiple times during large meals, and in the bathroom after every small one. He'd known when he started noticing food going missing that was there the night before, and when he came home from school one day to find her crying over a bag of chips.

"It's just a snack, lovie," she'd said. Even back then, the sparkle had dulled in her eyes. "Go do your homework."

He hadn't gone to do his homework. Instead, he'd chosen to sit on the bottom of the stairs and listen while she opened plastic packages. Ash couldn't tell if it was the food that was making her sad, or if it was about so much more than food.

That was years ago.

Now, they had a silent routine. She ate. Ash cleaned up after her. Neither of them told Gabriel.

Later that night, after he got back from Portland and gave his father the money he'd made, he trudged up the stairs to his room. As much as he loved his mother, sitting in the armchair to watch TV with his parents didn't sound fun. Not with his father smoking for the duration.

"You better have liked that stupid thing!" his father called up after him, referencing the game console. "And you don't have to be a fucking dick, son. You can sit down here."

"I'd rather throw myself into the coast," Ash called back, "but thanks."

He was in his room with the door shut before he heard any part of his father's reaction to that.

Ash fell into bed, the exhaustion settling over him like a fleece blanket. He didn't bother to take off his clothes or his necklace, passing out within minutes.

That night, he dreamed of Tayshia.

CHAPTER THREE

June 22nd, 2017

Ash's father was high.

Gabriel drove like a maniac, his thin arms trembling as he handled the shift with one hand and the wheel with the other. His eyes were manic, wild as they darted about. The sound of his muttering, frenetic and paranoid filled the emptiness of the car, leaving Ash with nothing emotionally solid to grasp onto.

Where were they going? Why weren't they going to the dealer's house? The plan was to do all of the drops, collect everyone's payments, and then head to Ricky's place to pay him all of that week's earnings.

After Gabriel had not only smoked a large chunk of the product they'd been given to sell, but also spent the first few weeks' worth of earnings that month on whatever it was that was threading through his veins right then, Ash had been confident he'd get the money back together before today.

Clearly, that would not be the case.

Ash had one hand curved around the front of the seat by his thigh. His right elbow rested on the windowsill, and his forefingers and thumb were splayed out over his forehead, temple, and down the side of his cheek. He wanted to close his eyes, but the fear that he wouldn't see his own death coming kept them open.

There had been three near-accidents already, and Ash was sweltering inside the inferno of an anxiety attack. His father had mixed the dealer's product with Ash's weed and fried so hard that afternoon that he was gone. He was just fucking gone, and there was nothing Ash could hope to do.

At this point, he was waiting for the crash.

"Fucking idiots," he heard Gabriel snarling as he swerved

into the right lane, then dodged a suburban to swerve back into the left. "Fucking idiots, all of them. They don't know who the fuck I am. They don't know me, and they don't know how bad I could *fuck* them up."

"Dad," Ash said, forcing his tremulous voice to stay within a lower register. "You need to slow the car down."

"I don't know what we're gonna do, son," Gabriel said, his voice wracked with more emotion than Ash could handle at the moment. "I don't have it. I just don't have it."

"It's fine," Ash whispered, more to calm himself than for his father's sake. He heard horns honking at them, felt his heart rate spiking as the car sped up. "We can go to... We can go to the bank, or—"

Smack.

Pain, flaring along Ash's jaw and up into his eye. He saw stars.

Hands clutching his now-aching jaw, he hunched forward and tried to reign in the rage that had plagued him ever since his father lost control over their small family.

"What the *fuck*?!" Ash shouted, whirling on his father. "Dad! Jesus fucking Christ!"

"*Why are you so* fucking *stupid, boy?!*" Gabriel roared, his bloodshot eyes seeming to bulge out of his head. He turned fully away from the windshield, glaring at Ash as though he wanted to slit his throat. His black hair was starting to come out of its ponytail, which he'd scraped together at the base of his skull that morning. His stubble added to his overall feverish disposition.

He looked like a monster.

"There's no *fucking* money in the bank, you fucking idiot!" Gabriel continued to roar, taking his hand off of the stick shift and nearly stalling the car. Ash had to grab it and shift the gear before it did. "That's why I told you to go to Portland and try to sell there! You fucking—"

He cut himself off, biting his lip with a fury that looked soulless. Ash cowered against the car door, holding his left hand up in a defensive position.

"I did," he said, too terrified to look away from the road. "I went after graduation. Remember? I went to the—"

"No, you didn't!" Gabriel roared, his hand whipping out and grabbing the side of Ash's neck. He shook him with a violence, the movement and vehemence causing him to turn the wheel back and forth. The car went from left to right, and another person honked. "Because if you *had*, we wouldn't be in this *fucking* situation, you stupid piece of *shit!*"

"Nah, fuck that!" Ash shoved his father's hands off of him and pointed an angry finger in his direction. "I gave you five hundred dollars, Dad! I gave you five fucking hundred, and you spent it on—"

"No!" Gabriel yelled, shaking his head and turning so sharply that Ash fell against the door again. "No! You didn't give me all of it! You didn't—"

"Yes, I *fucking* did!" Ash's heart exploded in his chest, anxiety swirling together with ire, his hands splayed in the air by his head. "Are you fucking kidding me? Yes, I *did!* I gave you five hundred dollars right when I got back! And you fucking spent it on *PCP* and *crack* in *two days!*"

"No, you didn't. You gave me three. I remember. You gave me *three!*"

"It was *five* hundred dollar bills."

Gabriel said nothing, only choosing to shake his head repeatedly.

As the car went ripping down the next road, zipping around cars full of horrified and confused drivers, Ash's hand found the amethyst. He felt the smooth side of the crystal again and again, thumb passing back and forth over it. He wished he could just go back to that night. To that night with Tayshia in the hot springs. He would rather drown there than be in this car with his father.

He couldn't even call his mother. His father had taken his phone and thrown it out the window when he was going ninety down the freeway.

"It doesn't fucking matter anymore," Gabriel muttered. "Ricky's waiting. He is waiting for us to show up with two thousand dollars. We don't have it."

"How much do we have?" Ash asked.

Gabriel remained silent, shifting the gears and speeding up again.

"How much do we *have*, Dad?!"

"Not enough, Ash."

Ash scrubbed his face with his hands, feeling cramped. He was too tall for this car. This world was too small for him, this place where his father dragged Ash behind him by hooks pierced through his flesh. Where he ignored his screaming, ignored his agony, and kept walking.

He never should have started helping his father. The prospect of money for shit like tattoos and food and girls when he was sixteen had been too much to pass up. And now, here he was, riding the edge of death with Gabriel. Gabriel, who couldn't go one fucking day without shooting up and smoking like the waste of space he was. Gabriel, who couldn't go one fucking day without hitting Ash and calling him names.

Gabriel, who'd once spend his time planting roses for his wife that would bloom in the Winter, and gardenias that would litter the garden with white.

"We have to get some money," Gabriel said, and then he let out a sob. "We have to get some *fucking* money!"

Ash dropped his head into his hands, his panic threatening to send him into a tailspin. "Ricky's got guns, Dad. His men *literally* have guns."

"I know."

"He'll come to the house and kill mom, or me, or all of us!" Ash shouted. "How could you be such a fucking *idiot*?!"

He flinched when Gabriel raised his fist to him again. "I *know*, son! I know! And you know I'm trying."

Except that he wasn't trying. He hadn't tried in months. He'd lost everything. The only thing they had was the house, and that was because it had been in Ash's grandfather's will. Gabriel couldn't work because he was never *not* high. Ash hadn't had time to find a Summer job yet—not when he was driving the other car to the city all the time to fix his father's mistakes.

If Ash didn't sell enough, then how was he supposed to protect his mother from his father's selfishness?

"If Ricky finds out you smoked his shit..." Ash let out a groan and then buried his face in his hands again. "God *fucking* dammit, Dad! He's going to *kill* us. He's going to shoot us dead and *kill* us!"

Gabriel ran a red light. "He's not. We're gonna get that money. We're gonna have to... To... Fuck. *Fuck*."

Ash flinched when his father slammed his fist against his horn.

He didn't know what they were going to do. There were no options. None. Ricky was the one person in Crystal Springs who had complete control of everything coming in and out of town. If he didn't do it himself, he had plenty of people who would show up and handle their family for him.

They were *dead.*

"There."

"Huh?" Ash looked out his father's window. There was an ice cream shop there, a standalone building in with a small, full parking lot. The June sunlight glinted off of the shop windows as someone opened the door and entered it with their toddler. "It's an ice cream shop."

Gabriel swerved across the road, barreling through the oncoming traffic as he went hurtling into the parking lot. Ash's heart leapt in his chest, terror freezing his veins to ice, and he gripped the stability handle above his head. Gabriel yanked on the wheel, the back of the car whipping around and slamming into the bumper of someone's minivan. The crash caused Ash's body to jerk to the left, his elbow and bicep straining to keep himself upright.

"Out." Gabriel reached across Ash, breathing heavily as he opened the glove compartment. He reached inside and pulled his pistol from within. "Out of the car."

Wait.

Ash unbuckled his seatbelt with slow, cautious movements. His father glared at him as he ripped his own seatbelt out of the buckle. He opened the door, leaving the engine running.

"Dad?"

Gabriel said nothing. He got out of the car.

"Dad!"

His father clicked the safety off and cocked the gun.

"Get out of the car, Ash. Get out of the *fucking* car and do whatever I tell you to do."

Do what he told him to do?

His father was high. They were out of money. Ricky was waiting for them. Ricky would kill them if he found out that the money was gone *and* some of the product, too.

They'd just crashed into someone's bumper. Gabriel had a gun. He had a *gun.*

He wanted them to go into the ice cream parlor.

No.

"Dad, stop!" Ash cried, shoving his door open and

scrambling out of the car. He pulled up the back of his low-slung jeans as he went, wishing he'd worn something he could actually run in.

Because damn, did he want to run.

"Shut up," Gabriel snarled. He spun to face Ash, grabbing the front of his shirt and dragging him closer. "Do what the fuck I say, or else you're the one that's going to Ricky's. Do you want that, boy? Do you want to be the one who tells him that you don't have his money?"

Ash vibrated with the desire to leave. To convince him to do something different. To keel over and die right there.

He didn't want to do this. He didn't want to be involved in this.

He wished he could call his mother.

"Block the door," Gabriel said, pressing the barrel of the gun against the side of Ash's head. "Don't let anyone follow us in."

Ash's face contorted into an expression of pure hatred. He'd never hated his father more than he did at that moment. He'd never been in the position to see not a single speck of light in his father's soul. But here, right now, he saw none.

There was nothing in Gabriel's eyes. Nothing at all.

As his father turned around and wove his way between the cars, Ash looked down the highway. He saw the shopping center across the street. The cars zooming by. The blue sky, void of clouds with a sun beating down from high above. Everything was so peaceful. So normal. So nondescript.

He felt like he was trapped within a prison of his father's making.

"Ash," his father hissed from between two pickup trucks. "We're a *family*. We do this together, do you hear me? You're in this just as deep as I am."

"We don't need to do this," Ash said, tone pleading as he dragged his hands through his hair. "For real. This is fucked. We don't need to do this."

"Then what can we do?" Gabriel waved the gun in the air, the cars providing an eerily ordinary soundtrack for this horrifying moment. "What's the better option? Because this is *Ricky* we're talking about. You know what he's done. You know what he'll *do*. Do you want to see your mother die, son?!"

Ash was surprised he had the capacity to care when he was fucking high on PCP and crack.

"No," he said, biting the words out through clenched teeth.

41

"Then *let's*." Gabriel jabbed his chest with the gun and Ash nearly lost the contents of his stomach. "*Go*."

After a suspended moment spent holding each other's glares, Gabriel grabbed him around the back of the neck and dragged him towards the ice cream shop.

They neared the door, Ash lurking behind his father with sweating palms, a wildly-beating heart, and tears clawing at his eyes. A man was exiting, laughing as he told a joke to the woman beside him. When he nearly ran into Gabriel, the man's first reaction was to apologize.

Until his gaze fell to the gun.

"Cathy, get behind me." The man shoved the woman behind him, holding a hand up to ward Gabriel off. "Now, just hold on a second, man."

"Back inside." Gabriel's voice had hardened like diamond, but with none of the beauty. "Get back inside *now*."

The man nodded, he and the woman—who was already crying—moving backwards into the building.

Ash squeezed his eyes shut and turned his face away. It was almost too much to look at, watching his father be the one to do this horrible thing. He stood there for a couple of minutes, panicking and debating.

He could leave right now. He could leave his father to do this alone, leave all these people at Gabriel's mercy, and go home. He could tell his mother what happened. Maybe he could even convince her to pack up and leave. They could drive away from Crystal Springs without looking back.

But then Ash would have blood on his hands.

"Ash. *Now*."

"Fuck," Ash whispered, his voice breaking. "I don't want to do this. I don't want to—"

"*ASH!*"

He jolted, the sound of his father's tone frightening him into action, and he went inside.

The silence that had fallen over the entire shop was almost as horrifying as the nightmare itself. There were about fifteen people inside: a couple of families with small children, some younger girls from Christ Rising, the man with the woman named Cathy, and then two clerks behind the counter. Everyone was on the ground, hidden beneath tables. In the center of the room, on one lone table, were a pile of cell phones.

Gabriel brandished the gun at the clerks.

"I said give me all of the money you have in your *fucking* registers!"

The taller girl behind the counter cried, "W-We don't have c-cash here! We only—only have a c-card reader! I'm s-sorry, we just don't—"

"Shut up!" Gabriel whirled around, aiming the gun at each person in turn. He held the muzzle against his head, tapping his skull and gritting his teeth. "Fuck. Okay, just—everyone pull out your wallets. Come on. Let's go."

Ash stood in front of the door, his legs shaking and his hands unsure. He alternated between running his fingers through his hair and rubbing the line of his jaw. He couldn't look at anyone. Didn't want to.

He didn't want to remember any of this because they were *fucked*.

"Ash, get them," Gabriel spluttered, gesturing with the gun. Ash cringed. The people flinched. "Get the wallets! Get the fucking wallets!"

Ash hesitated.

Gabriel stomped over, shoving a table out of his way as he went.

If the door wasn't already behind him, then Ash would have backed up. He turned his face to the right, glaring at his father out of the corner of his eyes.

It felt like Gabriel didn't realize who he was. He wasn't aware that it was him. He was so lost to his high and his panic and his idea that doing this was the answer that he didn't realize he was holding a gun to his son's face.

"I don't want to have to ask you again," Gabriel breathed, his voice as sinister as shadows rolling across the moors. "*Do* what I say so we can *pay* Ricky and go the fuck *home*."

Ash cast his gaze downward, towards the tables and the floor.

Why didn't his father understand? They'd already gone too far. There *was* no going home. Even if they managed to get the money together to pay Ricky, would it matter?

Wait a minute.

There were two people underneath the far left table that he hadn't seen before. He couldn't see their faces, but something about the way they were sitting showed him that their muscles were tight. Sprung.

If Gabriel saw them, there would be problems.

"I'll do it," Ash said, shoving his father's hand away. His glare washed up and down Gabriel's frail body, watching the way the drugs running through his system—and ruining his life—made him tremble. "I'll do it, so just fucking move."

Gabriel did, and Ash went to the far right—to the table with the girls from his school. They stared at him in dumbstruck horror. They were probably thinking that he was exactly the person that everyone had always thought he was.

A fuck-up.

A failure.

A monster.

Ash collected the wallets, coin pouches, and purses of every man, woman, and child in the establishment. He hated the way it felt, looking into their eyes and seeing pure terror shining back up at him. The children were the worst. They didn't understand what was going on, or why the *bad man* was taking their allowances away. Their parents were trying to calm them through tears of their own, but it seemed that it was very clear that Gabriel was in an erratic, near-psychotic state of mind.

As he waited for the woman at the second-furthest table from the left to shakily pull her wallet out of her purse, Ash's gaze slid over. He could see that one of the people hidden beneath the furthest table was a girl. She was on the smaller side, with shorts and sneakers on—pink sneakers. Whoever was next to her was a burly man.

Ash's hands were clammy, slick with sweat. So slick that he dropped the fucking wallets. He hated the way it made his stomach churn.

What if his father forgot who he was and shot him?

As he crouched down to pick them up, Ash hung his head. He needed a second, just one fucking second. He let his expression crumble.

He wanted to cry.

"Ash."

The whispered voice sounded familiar.

His mind flashed back to the night before graduation.

The caverns. Crystals studding the walls. Sloshing water. His hands on her waist. Her body, leaning back against his own.

Tayshia knelt there beneath the table wearing a pair of denim shorts and a pink tank top. Her braids were gone, leaving her with the short Afro that he recognized her wearing a few times a year. Her facial expression was determined as she glowered at him.

Beside her was a big, burly man that Ash assumed to be her father. His head was shaved and he wore a simple pair of cargo shorts and a tee shirt. The expression painted upon the umber of his face matched her own.

Ash's heart dropped into the pits of Hell.

"Ash, what are you *doing*?" Tayshia whispered.

He stared at her. The amethyst around his neck felt heavy, like it weighed ten thousand pounds. He wanted to rip it off. It represented something else—some starry-covered universe that didn't belong to him. Not after this.

Why was she here?

Why did it have to be *her*?

"Stay here," he whispered back, his brows pulling together with desperation. "*Please.*"

Gabriel snapped his fingers. "Come on, Ash! What the fuck are you doing?! Bring me the wallets!"

Ash hurried to his feet and over to his father's side, dropping the wallets onto the table he stood next to.

Gabriel pointed to the pile with the gun. Sweat poured down the sides of his face, into his eyes where it clung to his lashes like raindrops. His eyes were woven crimson with the lasting effects of the drugs he'd taken an hour before.

"Wait. There's people over there."

Sinking, right to the bottom of Ash's chest.

"You forgot those two," Gabriel said, frantic gaze darting back and forth between Ash and the table. He aimed the gun directly for the peek of knees that showed. "Get them up. Get them—get them out. I want their wallets, too."

Ash didn't move.

Gabriel shoved the gun up against his son's temple until it hurt. *"Get over there before I shoot you!"*

Ash shuddered, fighting back tears.

He could remember a time when his father spent his days toiling in the garden, planting and growing the most beautiful flowers in the state. He remembered going to festivals with him as a child to showcase his famed roses and gardenias. Waking up on Christmas to bouquets that Gabriel had gathered just for Ash's mother. Hearing his parents' laughter through open windows in the Spring as they tilled the soil in the garden.

Sometimes, Ash dreamed of rolling hills covered in gardenias that he liked to think his father planted.

Everything was different now.

Ash's grandfather died and it broke him — took Gabriel and shattered him into thousands of pieces that never seemed to come together unless he was high. Ash had no idea when it started and he supposed it didn't matter. The first time Ash came home to see his mother crying at the kitchen table because the bank account was empty and the garden was seedless should have been the last.

Why was his father doing this to him? To all of these people? He didn't want anyone to get hurt. Not himself. Not the people in the restaurant. Not Tayshia.

Of all people, Tayshia deserved this the least.

Turning on his heel, Ash walked over to the table. He placed a shaking hand atop it and sunk down into another crouch. His eyes met Tayshia's, cerulean crashing against hazel in a silent argument. Because that was what they were good at, wasn't it? Arguing with each other. Not getting along. Despising one another for reasons unknown just because their personalities clashed.

"No," Tayshia said.

"You have to."

She narrowed her eyes. "No."

Ash frowned. Did she not grasp the gravity of the situation? Did she not understand that his father had a *gun*?

"Just give me your guys' money," he said, "and maybe he'll let you stay under here."

Tayshia didn't move. Beside her, the man he thought was her father wore a stern, calculating expression.

"Is your father intoxicated, son?" he said, his baritone oddly soothing in the tension of the moment.

Ash closed his eyes for a moment and then said, "PCP and — and cocaine."

"Crack?"

Ash nodded. It was so absurd, hearing the names of the drugs and having it not be in some *don't do drugs* ad. Absurd and sad.

It didn't matter how soothing this man's voice was. It didn't matter how calming or assuaging or settling it was. Ash's family was broken. After this, it was destroyed. Eradicated like a black hole had ripped it into shreds and devoured it.

"Ash, what's taking so long?!" Gabriel roared, causing the children across the room to start screaming and crying anew. "Hurry the fuck *up*!"

"Leave my daughter alone," Mr. Cole said to Ash, his voice still calm as he reached into the pocket on the side of his shorts leg. He withdrew his wallet with a slow hand. "Leave her be and take my wallet. It's better that you just do what he wants you to do."

"Okay." Ash accepted the wallet, looking at Tayshia one last time. "But you have to stand up."

Tayshia opened her mouth, clearly about ready to protest, but her father covered her shoulder with his hand. He gave Ash an encouraging smile.

"We're standing now, all right? Together, with you."

After a few seconds, they all three stood at the same time. Tayshia's father wore a facial expression that was as tranquil as one of the hot springs in the caverns on the mountain. He looked like he knew what to do, and that made Ash feel better about the fact that he was scared.

He started over to his father, casting a glance in the direction of the cowering, terrified hostages. Then, his father stopped him in his tracks with an angry look.

"What are you doing?" Gabriel growled. "Get her wallet, too."

"She doesn't have one," Ash said, his free hand clenched into a fist at his side.

"What're you *talking* about? You haven't even checked her!"

"She doesn't *have* one."

Gabriel's eyes flashed like lightning. He stormed towards him.

Ash didn't think—he didn't think because he couldn't. He reacted. Spinning, he sidestepped and moved in front of Tayshia. There was a table between them but it didn't matter. He just knew that he couldn't let his father think she was accessible. He knew there were other people in the shop—other people who also didn't deserve to be shot.

But they weren't her.

His father nearly slammed into him, causing Ash to stumble back against the table. He reached behind him to grab the edge and steady himself. The hardness of the barrel pressed into the center of his chest as Gabriel held his gaze in silent threat.

They were the same height, so Ash was less intimidated by him than he was by the pistol itself. He knew he had to be careful. As long as he was trying, it might be enough.

"Not her," Ash said, his tone low.

"I don't have time for this shit, boy." Gabriel slammed the gun into the side of Ash's head, holding it there until Ash turned his face away. "You turn around and search her. *Now*. Search her, or I'm gonna shoot her in the face."

"She doesn't have a fucking wallet! Let's just take the ones we have and go, okay? Let's just grab the shit, go to Ricky's, and then go *home*!"

Gabriel's face contorted with anguish. He smacked the gun against his own forehead multiple times in quick succession. He held a fist to the other side of his head and began to pace.

"No. No, no, no. You don't get it, Ash. You don't *get it*. If we don't have enough, we're going somewhere else to get more. Get her fucking money so we can *go*!"

What?

"Dad." Ash felt nausea rolling through his stomach. "We can't do this again. We need to go home."

"We *have* to! Why don't you understand... No. You know what? *No*. I'm done with this."

He caught Ash by surprise, his hand whipping forward and to the side. The pistol connected with the side of Ash's skull, the loud *crack* seeming to echo around the room. Blinding pain careened through his head, rendering him speechless. He nearly fell over another table as he clutched his hand over his throbbing temple.

Gabriel moved past him. Ash heard Tayshia scream, heard feet shuffling, and then he whirled around. A gasp of horror left his lips as he watched the events play out in slow motion.

Tayshia scrambled back towards the wall, the anger that had been displayed on her face when looking at Ash fading to become fear. She cried out for her father, who moved toward her. He reached for his daughter. The moment he did, Gabriel jolted as though the movement were too sudden.

He pulled the trigger.

BANG.

Mr. Cole hit the ground.

Tayshia screamed and fell to her knees beside her father, who lay prone on the floor beside one of the tables. A small hole in his chest leaked blood, the stain spreading outwards from the wound, crimson soaking fabric.

This was all Ash's fault. If he would have fought harder to grab the wheel from his father, or if he would have refused to come with him, maybe they wouldn't be here right now. What could he have done differently? What choices could he have made to fix this? How could he fix it now? *Could* he fix it?

Thoughts whirled in his mind, racing one another to be the one that made the most sense. And all the while, he watched his father staggering around in a panic and Tayshia covering Mr. Cole's wound with her hands to try and stop the bleeding.

Ash felt as frozen as a star.

"Help me!"

He blinked himself out of his reverie. Tayshia was looking at him, her eyes pleading even as the tears filled them. She was trying not to cry.

"Ash, you have to *help* me! Please. *Please* call the ambulance!"

"Don't do it," Gabriel said, his voice slurred. "No. No, you can't. Don't do it, or I'm—I can't let—You can't—*Fucking* Hell!"

Ash's shoulders jumped when his father whirled to face a table and kicked the chair so hard that it clattered to the floor. Whimpers arose from the hostages.

"*Please,*" Tayshia whined.

He couldn't take it. Couldn't take hearing Tayshia beg like that. It made him feel sick to his stomach. Ash didn't want to be this person, but there was nothing he could do. No way to turn back the hands of the clock.

Mr. Cole was on the ground, bleeding, gasping for air. His eyelids were fluttering. Children were crying. Gabriel was probably going to pull the trigger again. Everything felt so out of control.

Tayshia uttered his name again, leaning over her father as she pressed down on the wound as hard as she could.

"I'll do anything." Her gaze held steady even as her voice shook. "I'll do anything if you just *help* us!"

Ash's heart pulled in his chest, tearing in half.

With those words, she had broken him down and remade him in the image of a disaster.

Behind him, he heard the click of the gun. His father had cocked it once again, readying himself. Preparing.

"Please, Ash," Tayshia said. "Help him. He's my *dad*."

He wanted to help. He did.

But how?

His father had a fucking gun. He'd already *shot* someone—*her* father. He couldn't do anything without risking *himself* getting shot. And maybe that made him a coward. Maybe it did. But he was just a fucking kid. He'd *just* turned nineteen. Ash was terrified.

So he just stood there.

A clatter.

Ash and his father looked behind them.

The man who they'd run into at the door. He stood at the table of cell phones. He'd dropped one.

"I-I already c-called," he stammered, his hands up by his face.

Ash felt the blood draining from his face.

"You absolute fuck." Gabriel pointed the gun at the man. "You *motherfucker*."

"They're on their way," the man replied, his voice tremulous. "They said there was a cop coming into this area."

"They're *what*?!" Gabriel brandished the gun again, causing several screams to ring out. "Oh, *fuck* no! Fuck, fuck, fuck! Ash—Ash, get the—no. No, there's no time. We'll have to go out the back. The back. It's our only way out. We have to—we have to figure it out."

Ash felt like he was sinking into the ground, deep down into the Earth where he hoped he would suffocate. He didn't deserve to breathe the air after this.

Then came the sirens.

Someone spoke on an intercom or a megaphone—some sort of speaker—and warned Gabriel to put the gun down. He had completely lost it, muttering things to himself that sounded hallucinatory. He was sweating even more, stumbling around and knocking into chairs.

"Dad, come on," Ash begged, his hand curved around the back of his own neck. "It's over. We just gotta take the loss and say it's over. Drop the gun."

"No, it's not—your mother—Ricky—" Gabriel looked at him, but he didn't seem to know who or what he was looking at. His father had lost his senses.

"Dad!" Ash cried, his voice cracking. *"Drop the gun!"*

He did.

The moment it hit the ground, the cops swarmed the shop. Ash heard more sirens sounding in the distance. Red and blue lights flickered faintly across the walls, the sunlight warring with them. He was shoved to his knees from behind, a hand pressing on the back of his head to keep him hunched.

Ash watched the pool of blood spreading from Mr. Cole's body, creeping towards him like it wanted to touch the skin of the man who caused it to pour.

He was dragged to his feet, hauled backwards, and steered towards the door. The police officers were reading his and Gabriel's rights with gruff voices. The children were sobbing. Tayshia's father's eyes were closed, and her hands continued to press on his chest while the paramedics rushed toward them. Tears streaked through the make-up on her face.

Shoved into the back of a police car, Ash still wished he could call his mother.

CHAPTER FOUR

June 30ᵗʰ, 2017

"Mr. Robards, can you tell me what was going through your mind when you saw that your father had a gun?"

Ash shifted in his seat on the witness stand, the chain links on his handcuffs sounding loud in the full courtroom. His palms were slick with sweat, which he continued to rub on the grey legs of the pants the county jail had clothed him in. His blond hair fell into his eyes, damp, but he was unable to find the courage to lift his hands and push it back. His pale white skin possessed bruises between the tattoos that he had on his arms. The rose tattoos on the backs of his hands looked darker from the contusions a fight in the cafeteria had landed him.

His temper had followed him, even to jail.

There were so many people here, watching him with hateful expressions on their faces. People he'd known since he was little, growing up in Crystal Springs, and people who'd heard all about the shooting and wanted to watch him get nailed. Teachers from Christ Rising and teachers from the public schools he'd gone to up until ninth grade. People from their old church. People from his own neighborhood.

The Cole family was not present.

And he did feel bad. He *did*. Ash hadn't wanted to be a part of that. He hadn't wanted to terrify all those people, to hear those children crying, to watch Tayshia's father collapse with blood leaking out of his chest. Seeing the red streaking over Tayshia's fingers as she tried to save her father's life. As she begged Ash to help.

But he was terrified.

The judge was a redheaded man named Judge Steven, and the bailiff who stood in front of Ash's spot had a nametag that read

Evans. There was a court reporter — a woman with glasses and brown hair — and the jury spots were empty.

He was *so* fucking lucky this was a bench trial.

The district attorney, Mr. Richardson, was perched upon the side of his table, one foot on the ground and his hands folded in his lap. His facial expression was patient as he waited for Ash to collect his thoughts and answer the question.

"I was —" Ash stopped to swallow, his dry throat sticking together inside of itself. "I was thinking that he was high, and that he was making a mistake. I knew what he was doing was wrong, and —"

"But you went inside anyway?"

Ash paused, his anger already flaring. He hated being interrupted and he'd seen plenty of law-based TV shows. He knew what the lawyer was trying to do.

"My father had a gun," he said slowly, wrapping decorum tightly around the throat of his building ire. "He had a gun, so I didn't have a choice. He threatened me."

"But you did have a choice," Mr. Richardson said, his gaze locking onto Ash's. "Didn't you?"

Ash said nothing.

"Because," the lawyer went on, "earlier this week, we heard from witnesses at the scene who stated that when your father entered the shop, you were not with him until about two or three minutes later. So, you had a few minutes to think about it, right?"

Ash shifted again. There was no point in lying. He was going to jail no matter what.

"Yes."

"Okay." Mr. Richardson raised his grey eyebrows. "During those three minutes, you didn't stop and think that maybe you should go for help?"

"I mean, I —" Ash cut himself off. "I *did*, but things were difficult."

"Things were difficult."

"Yeah."

"Care to explain?"

Ash said, "My father and I sold drugs for this guy named Ricky. We'd been doing it since I was sixteen — so for about three years. He started before, I mean, but then I joined in."

"And what did you sell?"

"PCP and cocaine. Crack, to be specific." Ash reached up to rub his nose.

"And that made things difficult...?" Mr. Richardson laughed. "I'm sorry. I'm just not following here. Why don't you start from the top?"

Ash heaved a sigh.

"After I turned sixteen, I was wanting to make some money. I could have got a real job, but my dad was already selling and he told me he could give me a lot of money if I did it with him. So, I did. We were supposed to pay Ricky every month, but my dad's been skimming off the top for a while now. My mom—" Ash looked out across the courtroom, to where his mother sat. Lizette was beside the elderly neighbor, Bertha, and they were clutching hands. "My mom's dad died when I was in middle school and then my dad's dad died sometime after. We had some money from that and my dad just... Drained it buying drugs. When he started selling, it was so he could get more."

"All right," Mr. Richardson said, beginning to pace. "So, how does this connect to the events that took place on June 22nd?"

"My dad was high. He fried before we left for the day. We were supposed to go do one last drop before we went to Ricky's to pay him. My dad had spent a huge chunk of that month's earnings on a TV, a game console, and some other shi—stuff. And I had to sell extra to make it all back. I—"

"And where did you go to sell that?"

"Portland," Ash said, grimacing. "I sell on the streets around Alberta."

"Okay. Continue."

Ash sighed again. This time, he did run his fingers through his hair, though it was awkward with the handcuffs.

"I gave my dad like..." He pushed against his cheek with his tongue and cast his gaze upward in thought. "I think it was like two grand or something before it all happened. I worked like, every night since I graduated to make that money. And I guess he spent it."

Mr. Richardson steepled his fingers and nodded. "Okay. I see. So, your dad was high the day of the incident. This was while he was driving?"

"Yeah," Ash replied. "He was like, swerving back and forth, and hitting me, just going ape. He tried saying I didn't pay him. I was like, that's cap. I literally gave him five hundred dollars the night before, and money every night before that. It was just nuts."

"Cap?"

"A lie."

Mr. Richardson nodded slowly. "So, he was driving erratically. That's what you're saying."

"Yes."

"How did you come to be at the ice cream shop?"

"He picked it out randomly, swerved across the lanes, and hit someone's car. Then, he basically told me to do whatever he said and he pulled a gun out of the glove compartment. I tried to convince him it was a bad idea, that we didn't have to do it, but he was gone. He was just gone."

"Gone?"

"Fried." Ash's eyebrows rose. "It's when you do PCP and crack at the same time. It makes him crazy. He like, hits me and shit. Oh, shit! My bad! For real, my bad."

Judge Steven scowled, but said nothing.

"Why don't you just tell us your perception of the incident from the moment you got out of the car, until the moment the police arrived," Mr. Richardson said, returning to perch on the table again.

Ash straightened his back.

"I tried to convince my dad multiple times not to do it. He threatened me, and then he reminded me that Ricky would hurt my mom if we didn't get the money that we needed. He went inside and I hesitated because I really didn't want to do it. I knew it was wrong. And I just—I just remember looking out at all the cars and thinking, *fuck. This is my life. I feel trapped.*" He hung his head. "Sorry. I just keep messing up."

"Just... Keep going," Judge Steven said. "Try to watch your language."

Ash went on, "I went inside because I was scared of what would happen to my mother if we didn't get the money. I was scared. When we got in there, obviously my dad was waving the gun around and demanding money from the clerks, but apparently, they only had a card reader and a tablet. So, he decided to take everyone's wallets. He had me get them all, and then I put them on a table."

"Then what happened?" Mr. Richardson asked, his brows pulling together in deep thought.

"I dropped one of the wallets and I..." Ash trailed off, his heart clenching at the memory of seeing Tayshia and her father kneeling beneath the table. He knew her father had survived, however it was still painful to think about. "I saw a girl from my school there with a guy who turned out to be her dad. I guess."

Mr. Richardson said nothing, so Ash continued.

"She asked me what I was doing, her dad asked me what my dad was on, and I told him. Then, I tried to pretend they weren't there."

"Why would you do that when you hadn't done that for anyone else?"

"Because I knew her," Ash said, shrugging his shoulders. Not for the first time, his neck felt weak and empty without the crystal around it. The county jail had it now, along with the rest of his things that he'd been arrested in. "I dunno. I just—felt responsible."

"Did you for some reason not care about anyone else in there? The women, the children...?"

"Nah, that wasn't it," Ash mumbled, lowering his gaze. "I just didn't want her to get hurt."

"Hm."

"Anyway, things escalated and my dad saw them. He made them stand up. I tried to tell my dad that she didn't have a wallet, but—"

"Why?"

A bit caught off guard at being interrupted again, Ash stammered, "I-I was trying to protect her... I think."

"Ah, I see." The lawyer tilted his head to the side. "Explain the shooting to us."

"Well, a lot of it was in slow motion for me because I was scared and in shock, but... Essentially, Tayshia's dad like, moved toward her, or whatever. My dad pulled the trigger. He..." He stopped to swallow again, feeling his throat ache. "He shot Mr. Cole in the chest. And he went down. Mr. Cole went down, I mean."

The courtroom was so silent that Ash felt like he was ensconced in a sphere devoid of sound.

"Tayshia looked at me... And she asked me to help. She begged me." Ash hung his head, shame pulling his chin to his chest. "But I was just too scared. I didn't do anything."

Silence continued to breed, broken only by someone coughing in the audience. Ash felt ashamed. More than ashamed. Hearing himself say it, replaying the memory in his mind as he did, he could see how badly he'd fucked up.

But he wasn't the one who pulled the trigger.

"Mr. Robards," Mr. Richardson said, "please state for the judge and the court, of course, what you are here being tried for."

Ash frowned, irritated. He felt guilty, but he was *not* the one who pulled the trigger.

"For holding up a fucking ice cream shop."

"Mr. Robards. For the last time." Judge Steven sighed. "Watch your language in my courtroom, or I'll hold you in contempt."

"Sorry," Ash drawled, leaning back in his seat. "You want the truth? All right. Yeah, I'm here because I'm ratting my father out. I'm ratting my father out so the police can nail Ricky. I'm here because I fu—messed up. And I don't want my entire life ruined because of this. Because of him."

"And so you've agreed to testify at his trial in exchange for your testimony. Is that correct?"

"Yeah."

"So... You had the opportunity to turn around and walk away, but you... You went inside." Mr. Richardson began to pace. "You could have gone for help. You could have flagged down another motorist. I mean, Mr. Robards, this is... You have to know how this looks."

"I do know how it looks. And I know what I did was wrong," Ash said. "But what if I hadn't gone in, and my dad shot everyone? He was high."

"Yes, that explains what happened when you went inside. But that doesn't explain why you didn't flag someone down for help." Mr. Richardson's voice grew edged with passion. "You went inside because you decided that your life was more important than everyone else's. You were worried about Ricky. You were worried about the money. You were worried about your family. And you made the decision to walk inside that ice cream shop and participate in a crime.

"Because in spite of what you've agreed to do to help prosecute your father, you still took part in something terrible." He shook his head. "Something horrific. You helped your father put those people through a nightmare. You may not have been the one to shoot Mr. Cole, but you were present and did not do anything to help. You, Mr. Robards, walked into that shop with the knowledge that your father might use the gun to hurt someone, and because of that—because of your choices—you are a culprit in this crime."

Ash felt each of his words like a pickaxe to the ice around his heart.

Mr. Richardson was right.

He'd had a choice, and he'd made the wrong one. He'd had a chance to get help and he hadn't. Selfishness had taken over, spurring him to make a bad decision. One that would affect him for the rest of his life. One that would affect everyone else's lives. Mr. Cole's and Tayshia's especially.

Mr. Richardson turned to face the courtroom, clasping his hands behind his back.

"Mr. Robards, did you walk into the ice cream shop knowing that your father would shoot if no one gave him any money?"

Ash's brows pulled together. "What?"

The lawyer turned around to face him and strolled closer.

"We've learned from you that your father was high. You knew he was high when you got into the car. You knew he had spent the money. Yes, you stated you gave him your earnings for the week—however, you also said that he admitted in the car to having spent it. You knew he was erratic because of the way he was driving. He threatened you multiple times outside of the shop. He went inside without you. You had two or three minutes where you stood outside and contemplated your next move.

"Therefore, it's understandable and logical to conclude that when you walked into that ice cream shop, you *knew* your father would shoot someone, and you didn't *care*. When you made the choice to walk inside, you accepted the inevitability that *someone would get hurt*. And you didn't care. *That* shows intent. *That* shows that though this was not premeditated, you are still *guilty*."

Why was he yelling?

"Nah," Ash said, feeling his anger rising. His moved his arms enough to wave his cuffed hands in dismissive motions. "Nah, that's outta pocket. Because my dad's never tried to shoot anyone before. I had no idea he had a fuc—a gun, all right? I was freaked out and I didn't know what to do. Just because I walked inside, doesn't mean I *wanted* anyone to get hurt. I just wanted us to get the money and *go*."

Mr. Richardson crossed his arms. "You just wanted to get the money and go. No matter what the cost."

"No," Ash said slowly. "I understood the cost. I didn't want the cost. I didn't want *any* cost. I just did what I was told in the hopes that we could go *without* hurting anyone."

"One witness stated that Tayshia Cole looked up at you and specifically stated..." He scrambled back to his papers, which were spread out along his table. He read from one. "'*I'll do anything. I'll do anything if you just help us. Please, Ash. Help him.*'" Mr. Richardson slapped the paper down again and spoke each word like a separate, livid sentence. "*He's. My. Dad.*"

Ash flinched, turning his face outward, towards the courtroom windows. He could still hear her pleading. It made him feel sick.

"So, Mr. Robards, if you could stand there and watch someone bleed out," Mr. Richardson snapped as he approached the witness stand, "then it stands to reason that you could walk into that ice cream shop and not give a *damn* what happened to anyone in there. Doesn't it?"

Ash glared down at him, their faces only a couple of yards away. There was a glint to Mr. Richardson's brown eyes, like a fading star big enough to become a black hole.

"Doesn't it, Mr. Robards?"

Ash glanced past him, to his court-appointed lawyer.

She gave him the tiniest shake of her head.

He was fucked.

Ash kept his mouth shut and was dismissed back to his place beside his lawyer.

Judge Steven sighed once again, as though the entire trial were a bore, and then called a thirty minute recess so he could contemplate. It was a bench trial, so the conviction and sentencing would be decided by him. After he disappeared into the back, Ash's mother leaned forward in her seat to embrace him. He turned so she could.

Mr. Richardson locked eyes with Ash, but his facial expression was unreadable. This was just business for him.

As Ash's lawyer explained the ins and outs of what was going on, where they'd gone right, where they'd gone wrong, and what was likely to happen, Ash found his mind wandering. His mother wouldn't stop asking questions, alternating between hugging him around the shoulders and holding one hand against his face. Bertha wore a sympathetic look that never once faltered.

Everything Mr. Richardson had said was true. Ash had really, *really* messed up. He should have flagged a car down. He should have worked harder to help save everyone. He should have done the right thing.

Instead, he'd made the wrong choice.

Ash didn't want to go to prison. It terrified him. It was cold and lonely. In the county jail, his roommate was barely out of high school and cried himself to sleep every night. Ash had been in three fights already with boys who were older than him, and there was a group of men in the yard who kept trying to pick one with him, too.

If he had to go to *prison*?

He didn't think he would make it.

His hands shook as his mother, Bertha, and the lawyer discussed his fate in frantic tones. Lizette was convinced the judge would find it in his heart to give Ash a chance. The lawyer wasn't confident that they'd avoided jail time because the witness' statements at the last trial part had painted him as a willing accomplice. Bertha was sure that he was going to be sent to jail, but that it wasn't going to be long.

No one mentioned his father.

The entire time they were in discussion, Ash couldn't help but stare back at the audience. At the angry glares and vehemence he saw on everyone's faces. He'd never been in a position where he was hated by so many people. If Mr. Cole hadn't survived, he was sure the entire town would want his blood.

They already wanted his father's.

"All rise," the bailiff announced.

Ash stood, his legs trembling with a ferocity that nearly had him sinking back into his chair. His throat continued to ache as though someone had struck it. He wanted to cry but he didn't want to look like he only cared that he'd gotten caught. He truly was remorseful, he just didn't know the best way to show it.

"Mr. Robards," Judge Steven said, peering over the rims of his glasses, "would you like to make a statement?"

Ash gulped and looked up at the judge. He hadn't realized he'd have to make one. There were a lot of things he wanted to say, but none of them were enough. None of them would ever be enough to fix what he'd done and the part that he'd played.

He truly felt like a monster.

"Yeah, I... I'm sorry. I mean, I'd like to say that I'm sorry. For everything. I should have... I should have tried harder. I should have done more. I don't..." He hung his head, his hands clammy and heart racing. He felt like such a piece of shit. "I don't think there's anything I can do to make up for it except get what I deserve. And I'd like to apologize to the families I—that I hurt. And that my father hurt. Especially the Coles. I wish I could go back and make the right choice that day so that Mr. Cole wouldn't get hurt. So... Yeah. I'm just sorry."

Judge Steven pursed his lips and scrutinized Ash for a long, drawn-out moment. Then, he began to speak.

"Well, Mr. Robards, you've certainly allowed your father to pull you into a predicament here. You committed a crime. You aided and abetted him in committing it. And someone got hurt. It's very fortunate that Mr. Cole lived because if he hadn't, circumstances would have been very different for you. You demonstrated that to some extent, there was intent to commit robbery when you entered the ice cream shop. You willingly assisted your father to that end.

"Still, you have demonstrated that you are remorseful and that you understand what you've done wrong. You have made it very clear that you knew what was going on was illegal. The witnesses did state that they heard you repeatedly attempting to talk your father out of his actions. That means something. I think that you're a kid who made some bad choices. But it's your parents' job to take care of you and ensure you're on the right path.

"The Cole family—as well as all of the families of the victims involved in this incident—have made it very clear that they do not want you to go to prison, nor do they want to press charges against you. It is clear that you were manipulated by your father in many ways to not only participate in this crime, but to be involved in the others before. These charges are being carried out by the prosecution and to that end, I hereby sentence you to eleven months in the county jail, to begin immediately. I..."

His voice faded out as water rushed past Ash's ears.

What?

They don't want to press charges?

He couldn't believe it.

How? Why? Why didn't these people want him to suffer?

Judge Steven continued to speak, reading off the full verdict, but Ash only heard the parts that mattered.

Eleven months in the county jail. Three years of probation. Restitution to be paid to the victims and the business.

Ash's knees buckled. His ears rang. He felt fear warring with relief in his mind, telling him how fucking fortunate he was to not be getting worse. He deserved worse — he knew he did — but this felt like a lifeline in the ocean he'd been drowning in for weeks.

"All right. Mr. Robards, you'll be notified when it's time for your father's trial, and then you'll be called for testimony. Court is adjourned."

The moment Judge Steven slammed his gavel down, Ash heard his mother let out a keening wail.

Ash's eyes stung. He needed to keep it together. He had to. Under no circumstances could he fall apart at any time. Especially not in front of his mother. She needed him to be the strong one because his father wasn't. Lizette needed Ash to be the man of the family and keep everything together.

Lizette threw her arms around his shoulders, because she was much too short to get them around his neck. She sobbed into his chest, her entire body wracked with emotion. Ash knew that she wasn't only losing her husband, but her son, too, and all she had to look forward to was an empty house. She hadn't worked in years and had no skills and no resume. Her father's money was gone, drained by Gabriel and his drugs.

Who would take care of her? Who would watch over her while she was filling herself up and destroying herself just to feel empty again? What if she died, and there was no one to find her?

I'm a bad son. A failure. A monster.

Overcome, Ash dropped his head into the crook of his mother's neck and shoulder, unable to hold her due to the handcuffs. His heart cracked in his chest, the pieces shattering with his anguish.

"I'm so sorry, Mom," he said, his muffled voice breaking. "I'm so fucking sorry."

She held him tighter, sobbing so hard that her words didn't sound like English. And as the cops grabbed his arms, gently trying to pry Ash away from her, Lizette had to be held up by Bertha. Her face looked crestfallen. Desolate. Her eyes swam with tears, which streamed down her face as she and Ash held their gazes as long as they could.

As they neared the door that would take him away to the next eleven months of his life, Lizette gave a great, heaving gasp.

Her hands clutched at the center of her chest. Another gasp. Her eyes widened.

Ash frowned, confused.

What was happening?

"Wait a minute," he said, looking back at her and struggling against the officers' holds. "Wait. that's my—*Mom! Mom! What the fuck?! Mom, no! Momma!*"

Lizette had collapsed.

Bertha screamed.

The last thing Ash saw as they hauled him through the door at the back of the courtroom was a crowd of people swarming the place where his mother had gone down.

☼☼☼

July 3rd, 2017

Ash ducked out of the way of another punch, his lungs spasming.

He was getting tired.

"You fucking teenage piece of shit," snarled the man as he grabbed the front of Ash's grey shirt and shook him. This was the first time he had ever been in the presence of a man that was as tall as him. At close range, he stood no chance. "I'll fucking rip your insides out and feed them to you."

Ash had one moment to blink before the prisoner slammed his large fist into his right eye, which was still ringed in a dark, tender bruise from Ash's last fight. He barely managed to stifle a groan as the man slammed him up against the wall. The back of his head cracked against the stone. He saw stars.

They were outside in the yard for recreation and it wasn't even lunchtime yet.

The man began beating Ash about the head, the full force of his knuckles pounding into already-bruised parts of his skull. Ash had done well in every fight before this one, but this was it. He hadn't heard any news about his mom in three days. He'd been in Hell ever since—emotional and physical.

This was his limit.

"Hey!" shouted a correctional officer, waving a baton as he dashed over. "Hey, knock it off! Knock it *off*!"

Ash stumbled back against the wall in a daze, his vision blurred. He could see the other prisoners watching with disinterest. They'd been ignoring the spat, which was over what area of the yard Ash had been standing in when he finally skulked out of the corner to use the water fountain.

Blood leaked from his nose, over his top lip, and into his mouth. And then he fainted.

☼☼☼

When Ash woke, he was in the infirmary.

His head ached, throbbing with lasting pain. It had to be a concussion. The faint taste of metal lingered in the recesses of his mouth. His face felt swollen. In the mirror to the left of the bed, he could see that it was.

He looked and felt like shit.

Ash had officially been in the county jail for eleven days, but it had only been three days since his trial concluded. In that time, he'd been in at least four fights. Something about his attitude pissed everyone off. He couldn't find welcome with anyone, not even his soft-hearted cellmate, who'd managed to find a group to hang around within days.

This wasn't his first time in the infirmary, either. He had a feeling by the end of his sentence, he and the nurses would know each other's damn social security numbers.

But Ash knew he had to start trying to let things go. His body was falling apart. He couldn't keep going through this, fighting day in and day out. It was destroying him.

Maybe he'd try to befriend Diego, the guy who did the tattoos in the North end of the yard.

The door opened and a corrections officer that Ash hadn't learned the name of yet poked his bald, brown head in.

"You got a visitor," he said, voice gruff. "Can you walk?"

"Yeah," Ash said, his voice hoarse from disuse. He tossed the blanket aside and swung his legs around. His head spun. "I just need a second. Shit."

The officer watched him, waiting while he slipped his feet into his shoes.

Ash took slow, measured steps. The fight he'd had before last had given him a sprained right ankle and as long as he didn't put too much weight on it, he was able to walk without a limp.

"Not settling in well, are you?" the officer said with a small grin. His keys jangled as he plodded along.

Ash was used to the morbid humor of the officers by now. He ran his fingers through his hair and shrugged.

"Not really."

"Ah, well." The officer patted Ash's shoulder, causing him to wince as he touched the tender contusion there. "You'll do all right eventually. Kent told me you been through it since you got here. Somethin' like eight fights? Nine? Damn."

"I have a temper," Ash muttered.

"Well, a temper ain't gone serve you for your sentence, son." The officer laughed. "Best advice I can give is to make friends with the right people, keep your head down when seniority's involved, and stay away from the bald white ones."

It took a second, but then Ash was laughing.

"Yeah, all right," he said, voice still a bit scratchy. "I'll keep that in mind."

"How long you in for?"

"Eleven months."

"Oh, that's not too bad. You'll be fine, kid. It's not like this is prison."

Yeah, thank fuck.

When they reached the visitor's area, the officer unlocked the door and then led Ash into a room with windows and phones. In the third window from the left, Ash saw that someone was there. His heart leapt with the first feeling of joy he'd had in days.

It was Elijah.

"You got fifteen minutes, all right?" the officer said, and then he positioned himself by the door with his hands on his belt.

Ash sat down in the chair and picked up the phone.

"Elijah," he said, the relief pulling a sigh out of him. "I can't fucking tell you how good it is to see you."

"You look like ass," Elijah said, grinning at him. His eyes seemed guarded, and he wore a blue tee shirt. "How is it like... Like, *going* in here? Like, is it crazy, or do you have friends? Is it like extreme high school? I mean..."

"It's a trip, man," Ash said on an exhalation of breath. He slid down in his seat. "I don't get along with *none* of these bitches."

Elijah let out a laugh but something felt off about it. Hollow. Like he was entertaining pleasantries before getting to the beginning of the meal.

What were they going to be eating?

"I can see that, dude, because what the actual fuck is going on with your *face*? You look terrible."

"Facts." Ash flashed him half of a smile. It hurt, stretching parts of his cheeks that were freshly-bruised. "I got my ass beat, I guess."

"Clearly."

Ash huffed and then tipped his head back. He rubbed the back of his neck with one hand, gritting his teeth against the ache. "But bruh, for real. It feels *good* to hear your voice. I've been dying in here, waiting to hear what's going on out there. Is my —"

"Everyone's good right now," Elijah said. "Ji Hyun gave me some money to give you for your commi-whatever. And then Andre wanted me to sneak you in some —" He pinched his forefinger and thumb together, holding them to his lips with a pointed look in his eyes. " — but you know how dumb he can be. As if they'd let me sneak that shit in."

"Wait a minute." Ash pulled a face. "Money?"

"Yeah, she gave me like, fifty bucks. Can you just tell her I brought it when she calls? She was freaking out."

"All right, bet," Ash said, distracted. "But why would Ji Hyun need to fill my commissary? Why didn't you just ask my mom? She should have at least a little money."

Elijah stared at him. He opened his mouth, a sound escaping his lips as words died there. When he averted his eyes to the side, Ash felt his stomach churning.

Something was wrong.

"So, what brings you here? Just visiting?"

"No, uh—well, I mean, yes." Elijah's eyelids fluttered as he waved a hand. "I'm here to visit, but I'm also here to... To talk to you."

"Talk to me about what, man?"

"Fuck." Elijah's head fell back. He stared hard at the ceiling, and Ash knew then that something was *really* wrong.

"Talk to me about *what*?"

"I'm sorry."

Ash desperately wished he could freeze again. He was tired of feeling. He was tired of drowning in the remnants of when he used to feel nothing. He wanted to go back to a time when the roses and gardenias filled the frost-stained window in the kitchen, and his mother and father looked at one another because they loved each other. Back to when his father didn't look to drugs, and his mother didn't look to emptiness.

"No," Ash said, shaking his head. "Don't play with me right now, Elijah."

"She —" Elijah's voice broke and he turned his face away again to let out a quiet sob. "Ash, I'm —"

"Shut your mouth," Ash said, his eyes starting to fill with tears. His heart was tearing, small shreds beginning to dissolve within him. "Don't. *Don't* say it."

"Ash."

"Don't you *fucking* say it." Ash squeezed his eyes shut and pulled the phone away. He placed the earpiece on his forehead, his right fist against his temple. Glaring at Elijah with the agony he felt burning in his eyes, his anguish started to suffocate him. He couldn't breathe. "Don't you fucking say it, Elijah."

"I'm so sorry, Ash, but she's gone."

CHAPTER FIVE

May 30th, 2018

Jail was as shitty as the movies made it out to be.

Eleven months passed by at a crawl so agonizing that Ash thought he might die in there. Sure, it was dramatic to think that way, but everything Ash did was dramatic. He saw the serious, deeper undercurrents that ran beneath the surface of the way everyone lived their lives. After everything that had happened with his father, he saw pointlessness in pleasantries and knew that there was no amount of treading water that could keep him from drowning.

Because his mother was dead and it was all his fault.

He'd spent so many nights in his cell, tears leaking out of the corners of his eyes as he beat himself up inside. His father was a piece of shit, but Bertha could have helped. Bertha could have done something to save her if Ash would have just *told* her — or anyone else, even Elijah — that his mother was sick.

Ash could still remember the day he'd gotten the news. Could still remember the way his heart had torn itself to shreds with every word that came out of Elijah's mouth. Could still remember slamming the phone down on the tabletop, telling Elijah to *fuck off*, and asking the officer to take him back.

Lizette had experienced a heart attack, right there in the courtroom. She'd collapsed into unconsciousness and the paramedics had been able to resuscitate her long enough to get her onto the gurney. But her heart was weak and she flatlined several times.

She'd died before the ambulance made it to the hospital.

"Why didn't you come tell me right when it fucking happened?" Ash had snarled through the window at Elijah, tears trickling down his cheeks as his rage overpowered his despair. *"Why would you let me*

have hope?"

"Because things were already so hard for you! I didn't want you to have something else to worry about! I was helping my mom and your neighbor take care of everything."

"For three days?" He'd slammed his palm flat against the bulletproof glass, earning himself a scolding word from the officer who'd walked him there. "Three days go by, and you can't even stop to fucking call?"

"I was busy handling your mom's fucking funeral, Ash!" Elijah had yelled back.

Ash had stared at him in horror, his eyelids fluttering. When he'd spoken, his voice cracking on a slight whine.

"What? You already held her funeral?"

"No. We couldn't afford it and you guys don't have any family."

"We have family friends. The neighbor — Bertha. Or the neighbors on the other side, the Sunamuras. Didn't you ask them?"

"No! We just did what the coroners said. We couldn't afford a funeral, so we had to go with the less expensive option. Ash, this came out of my mom's pocket and you know how hard shit is for us."

Ash had closed his eyes against the pain. "You had her cremated?"

"I'm so sorry, man. We just went by what the coroners were suggesting." Elijah's voice had faltered. "You're in jail. It's not like you could make the arrangements from here."

Ash had been unable to look at him for a second longer after that. Elijah was one of his best friends and had been since they were kids, but this was too much. He'd gone too far.

He hadn't accepted any phone calls from him until Christmas.

The days hadn't blurred together as fast as he'd hoped. Between trying to keep up on his schoolwork, fending off the inmates who didn't like him, and managing the jobs the warden assigned, his days were long and full.

He'd managed to make friends with one person in the yard — the guy who did everyone's tattoos, Diego. He was a tattoo artist who'd gotten into a bad bar fight and was serving out the remainder of his sentence. Once he had befriended Diego, the amount of fights Ash got into tapered off until the energy in the jail shifted.

The more Ash hung around Diego, the more people started to give him a chance. And since Diego did everyone's tattoos — including some of the more lenient officers — he did Ash's, too. He just charged everyone else for them.

Ash had never had the highest pain tolerance, but the longer he sat under the needle, the more he found he liked it. Perhaps it was the vibration. Perhaps it was the pain itself. Perhaps tattoos were the only way he felt like he had control over his life.

He wanted more.

Ash had started his sentence with less than ten tattoos. Now everything, from his upper body to his neck to his chest, to his abdomen to his back, to his arms to the backs of both hands, were all covered in whatever Diego wanted. As long as Ash let him have creative freedom, he didn't charge him anything. Ash got to keep his commissary, and Diego got to flex his artistic abilities.

Jail was shitty, but at least he'd gotten a Hell of a lot of free tattoos.

When he stepped off of the curb that hot May day in 2018, into the parking lot of the jail, his best friends were there waiting for him.

The first person he saw was Andre Gonzales, one of his best friends. Ji Hyun was bouncing on her heels, holding Andre's hand until the very last minute. Elijah was leaning against the side of Andre's car with his arms crossed and a grin on his face.

When Ji Hyun saw Ash, she burst out into happy tears and took off towards him. He felt what was left of his heart bursting with joy in his chest, causing him to bend at the knees so he could catch her around the waist and lift her into the air.

He spun her, marveling at how good it felt to be in someone's arms again.

The next thing he knew, Elijah and Andre joined into the hug, and then they were all talking at once. Everyone missed him. There was a welcome home party at Andre's apartment that night. They couldn't believe how many tattoos Ash had now. Ji Hyun complained about how long his black roots were getting at the crown of his head. The teachers couldn't stop remarking how peaceful classes and the hallways were without him wandering the halls. Ji Hyun, Andre, and Elijah were all happy that he was back.

And they were taking him to his mother's grave.

☼☼☼

"You like, nervous and shit?" Andre asked as the group traipsed across the lush, green grass of the immaculately-tended church graveyard. The sunlight made the lustrous gold of his skin seem to glow. It glinted on the heights of his sharp cheekbones. His curly hair was tucked beneath his backward snapback hat, a couple tufts peeking out.

Ji Hyun and Elijah were walking ahead of them, leading the way. Andre and Ash had fallen behind, talking amongst themselves in quiet voices. Andre had a blunt in his right hand, the smoke reaching lazy tendrils towards the clear sky.

"Nah," Ash said. He wore the same skinny jeans with the rips in the knees and the V-neck that he'd been arrested in. His crystal once again hung around his neck, its weight familiar in a comforting way. His hair was so grown-out by now that it hung shaggy around his chin and his skin was glad to finally be kissed by the sun. "I've been waiting for this day, you know? I never got to say good-bye."

Andre placed a hand on his shoulder as he took a drag off of the blunt. His brows pulled together beneath his hat as he looked over at Ash. "I'm so sorry, bro. You never should have had to know what it feels like."

Ash looked at him. "How'd you get past it?"

"I didn't." Andre let out a laugh the seemed as mirthless as it was telling. "You never will. But you'll get to a point where it's bearable."

"Yo, can I get some of that?" Ash asked as they crested the top of a hill between a row of headstones. "I haven't had any in so long."

"For sure, for sure."

Ash accepted the blunt from him and took a drag, feeling the burn as it swelled in his lungs. The effect was instantaneous. Calm, settling over him and into the depths of his bones until it turned him weightless. He felt like he floated down to the bottom of that hill, the same way he'd been floating through life ever since he lost his mother.

"Here it is," Ji Hyun announced as Ash and Andre approached. She slipped her arms around Andre's waist, giving Ash a sad look. "It's right over there. It's exactly the one you told us to get."

"White marble, favorite Bible verse engraved, and gardenias every two weeks," Elijah added.

Ash nodded, gazing forward.

His mother's grave lay almost within a plot of its own. The other graves were spread apart from it. Much like she had in life, it existed separate from everyone else's. In its own world. The headstone looked gorgeous, having been paid for by the life insurance money her death had brought him. But Ash knew.

No amount of money would ever bring her back. He'd rather be destitute with his mother at his side than flush with cash without her.

He sat down in the grass, hugged his knees to his chest, and started planning how to get his shit together again.

Ash was on probation for the next three years. He had plenty of money thanks to his mother's life insurance but would need to get an accountant to help him arrange to pay his fines. He had plans to get a job of some sort so he could have something to do when he wasn't in school, given that Christ Rising had allowed him to remain a student as long as he did his assignments in jail and mailed them to his teachers.

The house was essentially his. It was paid for, having been given to their family in the will of his grandparents and even though it was technically in his father's name, it was Ash's. He knew everything was still there, painted prone on a canvas of the past. Stepping into it would be like diving into the oldest, darkest parts of the ocean. He might never come back up.

He wasn't sure he could do it.

As he gazed upon his mother's grave, he felt relieved. At least he was free of a cell. He was home.

The bars that caged him in were a different kind now.

☼☼☼

September 1st, 2018

Ash stood in the center of his new living room, hands on his hips as he glanced around at the new furniture he'd purchased.

He hadn't been able to go back home. He hadn't wanted to, and he wasn't sure he would for a long time. Letting everything continue to collect dust was preferable to walking through that door and seeing everything frozen in time like he wished he could be.

He'd chosen to live with Andre until it was time to move into the school-owned apartment complex. They'd saved his application from the previous year and were carrying it over to the current year, so until move-in day on September 1st, Ash crashed on Andre's couch. He bought a suitcase and new clothes at the mall so he would have something to live out of, and spent his time getting any financial things that needed to be dealt with handled.

Ash had maintained fairly good grades while in jail. He wasn't worried about settling into his classes, or understanding the course material of the pre-requisites. He'd never liked homework but that didn't mean he was unintelligent. He was just worried about the way the students were going to treat him now that he was a known felon.

Who would his roommate be?

The beige-and-brown complex was situated at the foot of the mountain road leading up to the school. For the students of the program who didn't have cars, there was a shuttle bus that took them on the twenty-minute drive up. It was a large complex and thus, the apartments were large, too.

When he'd moved into the two-bedroom apartment a few days before the end of August, he'd realized that furniture was *kinda* important.

He'd called Andre and Elijah up, and the three of them had taken Andre's truck out to Portland. They went to the furniture superstore so he could furnish the house. He'd chosen all black, grey, and purple, complete with a black suede sectional, galaxy-inspired art, a black area rug to go over the pale carpet, and modern floor lamps that made him think of space.

Ash figured the guy he'd be rooming with would be okay with it. The letter from the school had informed him that his roommate had checked off the box under *not bringing furniture*.

Now that everything had been dropped off and his friends were gone, Ash stood in the living room ensuring everything was arranged the way he wanted it. The deliverymen from the superstore had placed the dishes, cookware, and silverware on the counters, so that was next on his list. The roommate could be there soon and he might want to eat. It was after six, so it was a plausible conclusion to come to.

Ash's bank account wasn't hurting, but he definitely wouldn't be doing this again. Everything he bought, he planned on taking with him to wherever he lived next. Whether he went to a university after the program or not. The roommate was required to pay their half of the rent and utilities, however they could just consider the furniture as a temporary gift.

Changing the song on his phone, which was hooked up to the speaker he'd bought, the sounds of deathcore music began to play over the speakers. The heavy guitars, slamming screams, and pounding drums filled the apartment. He headbanged as he opened the box containing the different-sized plates he'd picked out.

It felt good to hear music again. He and Andre had spent the entire Summer getting blazed and planning on going to shows but never actually getting out of the house to do it. The second he could go to a show again, Ash was going to.

He loved shows. The rush of energy in the room as everyone jumped up and down. The feeling of hands shoving him to the left and the right in the pit, people taking out the aggression that the bullshit in their lives caused. The music playing so loud that he couldn't hear himself think, let alone hear himself screaming the words at the top of his lungs.

Rocking out in his kitchen would never compare.

Suddenly, the front door swung open.

"Maybe she's not here—oh! There's music playing."

It was a girl's voice. Ash didn't recognize it but something about it inspired nostalgia. It was high-pitched, not nasally, almost melodic.

A girl with jet-black hair that fell in waves to her elbows entered the room, her blue-eyed gaze piercing across the living room and into the kitchen. Her brow furrowed in confusion, her purse swinging off of one arm and keys jangling in her hand. She wore a striped bodycon dress with short sleeves and her lips were shiny with gloss. Her heart-shaped face was pale and freckled.

He recognized her.

Standing in his living room was Quinn Baker, a girl who had gone to Christ Rising with him since ninth grade. She looked stunned to see him and she glanced around, obviously looking for something as she stepped out of the way of someone entering after her. That someone was taller than her, balancing a box in her arms, and in the middle of speaking in a strained voice.

"Can you check if she's picked a bedroom yet? I need to figure out which one is mine. I'm finna put this shit down before I die."

Ash nearly dropped the stack of black porcelain plates he held in his hands.

Now *that* voice he recognized. It was a voice that he hadn't heard in eleven months, but that he couldn't stop dreaming about since he'd gotten out of jail. Because the moment he got his crystal back was the moment the dreams started up again.

Tayshia.

The two girls stood there, staring at each other and then at him in turn.

"Uh... Ashley?" Quinn said with a grimace.

"*Ashley*?!" Tayshia pulled a face that lingered somewhere between shock and revulsion. "Your name is *Ashley*?!"

Ash felt what little color he possessed draining from his pale face. "Well, fuck," he said.

CHAPTER SIX

Ashley was his legal name.

The name he'd hated since birth. The name that he'd complained about being given for years and years and years. The name that had gotten him bullied mercilessly in elementary school before he started to grow so tall that everyone was scared of him.

It was why he had a fucking nickname.

"There must have been a mix-up," said Quinn. "Maybe the person reading the applications assumed...?"

"Oh, Hell nah." Tayshia shook her head, still holding the box. Her kinky curls, which fell out of the top of her head like a waterfall to her shoulders, fanned out around her head when she shook it. "Absolutely not. *Absolutely* not."

"Well, we can just go talk to them," Quinn said, breathing an awkward laugh. "I'm sure they can get you into a new apartment, I mean—it's a Christian school. And this complex is *not* co-ed."

Tayshia set the box onto the ground, standing up with a hand over her chest as she caught her breath. Her hazel eyes cut through to the core of him. Within them, Ash saw all the things he knew he deserved.

Mistrust.

Fear.

Hatred.

"I'll go down to the leasing office right now," she said. "There's no way they're allowing this."

Ash said nothing, watching her walk out the door, leaving he and Quinn alone. They stood there in silence for a moment before Ash resumed putting the dishes away. Tayshia could move if she wanted—he wasn't going anywhere. He'd signed the lease.

"This is so weird," Quinn said. "I mean, it's not like we know each other, but it's like, really weird."

Ash bit his lip. He didn't know what to say to that. He'd known that he was bound to encounter negativity—it would be naïve for him to think otherwise. He and his father had held an ice cream parlor full of women and children at gunpoint. There was a slim-to-none chance that anyone in school was going to welcome him with open arms, religious and forgiving or not.

"Except that it's like, horrifying," Quinn said.

Ash raised one eyebrow.

"Not that you're like... A horrifying person, or anything." She laughed again, pulling all of her hair to one side of her head and relaxing one hip. Her dress was extremely tight. "But it's like, a horrifying situation. I mean, for Tayshia. Not for me." More laughter. "I'm sure you're like, super nice and everything."

Ash grabbed three large, stacked pots with one hand, his gaze remaining trained on her as he opened the cupboard beside the oven and slid them inside.

She tittered, clearly flustered.

"But like, she's kinda freaked out by you. You know what I mean?" Quinn's gaze flickered up and down the parts of him that she could see. "Which she has like, every right to be, or whatever. Because you know you..." She grimaced again. "You know?"

Ash narrowed his eyes. "I what?"

"You like..." Another grimace, and she took her left hand—which didn't have her purse and keys—and made a gun with her fingers. "You *know*?"

Ash placed his hands on the counter, leaning over it and hanging his head for a second. Something about Quinn's personality had rubbed him the wrong way long ago, in spite of the fact that she was a smoke show. But right here—right now—she was pissing him off.

"I'm not scared of you," Quinn went on, rolling her eyes. "I'm sure you're like, super nice and super, you know—whatever. But Tayshia like, she had these nightmares for a while that she'd like, text me about and it was really hard. Like, it was *really* hard for a while there. Which is understandable, because... Well, you know."

Ash gritted his teeth. Quinn paced towards the couch, taking in the sight of all the furniture.

"I'm glad you're out, though." Her tone was sickly-sweet. "I mean, you were in *prison*. That's super, super... Well, it's not *cool*. But it's something. Something to tell people, that's for sure. Did you get into like, fights and stuff?"

Ash just stared at the counter.

"I mean, if Tayshia can suck it up and stay, it might still be cool. You guys could like, make up and be friends. She needs to relax. She's been so uptight since her trip to Paris this Summer. Seriously, she's so — you know."

You know, you know, you know.

Of course he knew. He didn't need a fucking reminder.

"Yo, can you like, shut the fuck up?" he said, lifting his head to glare at her. "I don't give a fuck what you think or what your friend is doing."

Quinn's head pulled back on her shoulders. The keys jangled as she crossed her arms over her chest, pursed her glossy lips, and lifted her chin. Her expression turned cold and judgmental.

"I'm surprised they let someone like you have his own place. Don't they have to check your record?"

"Okay," Ash said, standing up tall. "I don't know who the fuck you think you are, but this is my fucking house. And you're not gonna talk to me like that. If you have opinions, you can take them *outside.*"

"You're lucky I'm not in the program," she said. "Because I can tell we would *not* get along."

"Good, because I already can't wait until you leave." He gave her a false twist upward of the lips and then went back to putting the new dishes away.

The front door swung open again.

Tayshia stormed inside, a sour expression on her face. She marched up to the box of her things she'd left, seemingly unaware of the negative atmosphere in the apartment. As she lifted it up, she cast Ash a scathing glance.

"They said since we signed the lease, we'd have to pay the early termination fee to break it."

"For real?" he asked, eyebrows up.

She nodded, frowning. Then, she looked at Quinn. "Can you help me get the rest of my stuff out of your car?"

"Yes," Quinn said, sounding relieved. She dropped the keys onto the counter, glowering at Ash, and then she left.

Alone, Tayshia and Ash stared at one another. Tayshia's gaze washed over his body — his neck, his arms coming out of the sleeves of his short-sleeved grey button-up, his hands. He knew what she was looking at.

Ash had gotten a few *more* tattoos that Summer.

Diego was out of jail and working out of Portland, so driving to see him was no big deal. Especially with the use of Gabriel's second car, which had still been sitting in the driveway the one time Ash went by his family home.

He hadn't gone inside, of course, choosing instead to send Elijah in to grab the keys from his bedroom.

Diego had insisted on adding more to the dragon on his back, as well as finishing up his right arm to fill in any empty space on his sleeve. He'd also added a bit to Ash's chest piece and added some color to the roses and chains tattooed around his neck.

After that, Ash had stopped spending so much money. He'd gotten 100,000 dollars from the life insurance, and he knew better than to be the type of person who blew it all on stupid shit when he had the rest of his life ahead of him and no idea what he wanted to do for a career.

Tayshia cleared her throat.

"They told me that even though the school owns the apartment complex, they still have to follow the law when it comes to leasing," she said, voice monotone. "We signed a one year lease, so we have to stay for the entire duration."

Ash tilted his head to the side. "How much is the fee?"

"It's literally over two thousand dollars," she said. "But I think it goes down every month."

He knew he could afford that. With how much money he had right now, it was akin to spare change. But something inside of him didn't want to pay the fee on principle. While he felt guilty for participating in the situation with his father and the ice cream shop, he didn't feel like he should have to pay a fee just because *she* wanted to leave.

"You got two thousand dollars?" he asked.

"Obviously not."

"I thought your parents were rich."

"Not anymore." She turned, shifting the box to a better position in her arms. "Which room is mine?"

Ash watched her, not saying anything.

"Which room is *mine*?" she asked again, raising her voice in annoyance.

"The smaller one," he said. He'd picked the master because he was an asshole, but now he felt like he deserved it. "Why?"

"Why what?"

"Why aren't they rich anymore?"

She gave him a disgusted look. "Because my dad got shot and was in the hospital for two months. That's why. I'm lucky they saved my college fund. Otherwise, I wouldn't be here."

Tayshia disappeared into the hall, leaving him alone with the music and his guilt. He felt his stomach churning with remorse and embarrassment.

As she walked back out, Tayshia turned to face him. He saw that she wore an oversized white sweater with a wide neckline that made her tawny skin look rich in color, and black leggings that caused her legs to look long and lean. Before he had a chance to find it odd that she was wearing a sweater at the end of the Summer, his gaze fell upon something he recognized.

Her half of the amethyst.

It was hanging on a silver chain from a tiny hole that he assumed was drilled into it. Yes, it could have been any crystal, but he felt it. He just knew it was the same one from that night in the cavern. His own crystal hung around his neck on the black leather cord, hidden beneath his shirt with the rock warm against the bare skin of his chest.

He wondered if she dreamed, too.

After he'd gotten out of jail, he'd gotten so drunk at the party Andre threw him that he'd passed out fully-clothed. He hadn't taken his necklace off and he had dreamed. He'd dreamed of Tayshia, just like he had the night of his birthday. He knew it was ridiculous — that there was no such thing as magic or legends — but he did know that the dreams had stopped when he was arrested. The first night after he'd been released, he dreamed of her again.

And he dreamed of her every night that he wore the necklace after that.

The dreams were so vivid that he often woke on Andre's couch, gasping for air. They were always arbitrary, smidgeons and flashes of memories from a life that belonged to her. Drops of her spirit from a distance splattered across the canvas of his mind. He saw them like a movie.

Tayshia talking with her friends. Tayshia with her family. Tayshia with Kieran.

He wasn't sure if they were dreams or memories.

Ash had gone days with only a few hours of sleep that even weed couldn't rectify. Days without any answers.

And here she was, standing before him with the crystal hanging around her neck.

Why would she keep it?

"We can make this work." Tayshia said. "We'll just have to set rules and stick to them."

"Oh, yeah?" The silverware was loud, clattering as he sorted it into the plastic divider he'd bought.

"Yes. There's nothing we can do, so we may as well take the L and make the best of it."

"Bet," he muttered. "As long as you keep your fucking friend away from me, then we're good."

"Quinn?" Tayshia looked puzzled. "But—"

Quinn came back inside, carrying a box. Tayshia took it from her so she could go back out and grab more. She didn't come back out of her room, so Ash assumed she was unpacking. Everyone fell into quiet concentration, working on their own tasks.

It took the girls fifteen minutes to get all five boxes and the one large suitcase that Tayshia had brought into the house. When they were done, it was time for Quinn to go.

"My parents are coming up on my birthday to bring my furniture," Tayshia said to Quinn at the door. "Can you come up with them?"

"I'm not sure if I like, can," Quinn said. "Because I might have a lot of homework or like, projects. I mean, it's university, so..."

"No, I get it," Tayshia said. They started walking towards the door. "Are you sure you have to go right now, though?"

"Yeah, I have to get on the road. It takes two-and-a-half hours to get back to Medford," Quinn said. She gave Ash a curl of her lips that felt as fake as plastic, and then she pulled Tayshia into a hug. "Plus, school starts for me next week and I wanna spend as much time with my family as I can before I have to like, drive back and forth to Ashland every day. Ew, right?"

"Ew." Tayshia hugged her back. "Well, if you change your mind, girl, let me know. We can do a sleepover."

They said their goodbyes. Every second felt like Ash was walking to the guillotine. The front door clicked shut and then Tayshia turned around.

"Rules?"

"What?" he said, in the process of putting the last of the dishes away.

"For the apartment. Do you have any rules?"

Ash was silent for a moment. He'd never had control over anything in his life like this. His father had always been the one in control of everything in the house. With his mother, her issues with food had controlled them both. In jail, Ash hadn't had control over anything at all. Now, Tayshia was giving him a modicum of agency that was new to him.

"I guess... Just pay bills on time and keep shit clean," he said, crossing his arms and leaning his hips back against the counter. He studied her through the pieces of hair that kept falling into his eyes. "Can you do that?"

She blinked as though taken aback, her brow still furrowed as she nodded.

"Verbal confirmation would be grand," he said, wrapping his words in sarcasm.

"Okay. Damn. My parents are paying for the bills here," she said, appearing annoyed. "From my college money. And yes, I can keep shit clean."

Now that he was looking at her — *really* looking at her — Ash could see that she had changed quite a bit in the year since he'd seen her. She didn't carry herself the same. Where once there had been a flame of ferocity in her disposition, now there only existed a hollow anger. There was an emptiness in her eyes, something there that he couldn't explain. Something that he could only describe as what he thought depression might look like.

He felt the guilt once again weaving its way through him like poison in his veins. Quinn had said Tayshia had nightmares after the ice cream shop. Could it be that she was still affected by it? By that fear — the fear of seeing her father's blood spreading on the floor as she pressed on the wound? Of knowing she held her father's life in her hands while he, Ash just watched?

Why did it feel like it was something worse?

"I guess my rules for you would be... No parties. No drugs. Don't drink. Typical stuff."

"Aw," he drawled without mirth. "That's all the fun stuff."

"You're not twenty-one. You can't drink."

"I've been drinking since I was in middle school. I'd say that means I can. You just don't want me to."

"How old are you?!" She looked irritated.

"Twenty," he said, "but I literally will do whatever the fuck I want. I cannot stress that enough to you."

"Clearly," she spat out. "Whatever. You've said your rules, and I've said mine. It's up to you whether you follow them."

"Same to you."

She turned to go, then stopped. When she looked back at him, her lips downturned and eyes glittering, he thought she might truly hate him.

"If you don't get on my bad side, Ash, I won't get on yours. The only way this is going to work for this lease is if you recognize and understand that we don't have to be anything—enemies or friends. You're nothing to me and as long as you don't piss me off, I won't become something to you. Do you understand?"

She stomped off to her bedroom. He heard the door slam shut moments later.

Ash sighed. Things didn't have to be this complicated. He had the money to easily pay the early termination fee and get her out of the lease.

He just didn't think he wanted to.

☼☼☼

In his room, Ash still had some things to arrange.

The clothes he'd collected while living with Andre were piled on the floor and needed to be hung up. He'd bought hangers earlier that day, too, so he had plenty in the closet to be able to do it.

As he worked on hanging his jackets up, he glanced over at the dresser. He'd had his mail forwarded to Andre's house and hadn't had the chance to open that day's mail. There were spam envelopes, ads for grocery stores, and one letter.

From his father.

Gabriel had been sending letters from prison to Ash at the county jail once a week since Lizette died. Ash had refused to read them, finding that it was easier to blame the person who had failed him than it was to blame himself for making poor choices. Because if he blamed himself, then that would mean facing the fact that he was a bad person. Bad people didn't deserve good things.

But his father?

His father had made it clear who he was from the moment he first got high. From the moment he first raised his fist against Ash. From the moment he grabbed that gun out of the glove compartment, Gabriel had been honest about who he was.

He had failed at the one job that should have come the easiest to him: being a *father*. Gabriel had turned Ash into a haunted shadow of his once outgoing self, causing him to find solace in things that made him forget the world around him. Gabriel's neglect had given Lizette the perfect environment within which her problems could fester.

Now that he knew better, Ash just wanted to finish school and get on with his life.

He knew there were going to be people at Christ Rising who expected or hoped for some form of apology from him, whether on his own behalf or Gabriel's. But he felt like there was no point in apologizing when what he'd done was unforgivable. Not when Mr. Cole's shooting could be blamed on him. Not when he'd taken part in collecting those wallets and terrorizing those people.

And then there was Tayshia. Tayshia, the person he'd probably hurt more than anyone else.

He couldn't even say her name aloud.

Ash wasn't going to read his father's letter. He never read any of them. He had just stashed them underneath his pillow in his cell and brought them all to Andre's with him. Now, they were stuffed in a small wooden jewelry box that Andre's mother had left behind before her death. He'd given it to Ash as a form of letting go, but Ash had accepted it knowing how important it was to him. And inside of it, he'd put all of his father's unread, unopened letters.

He couldn't look at the envelope anymore.

After hanging the leather jacket in his hands up, he snatched the stained envelope up and stuffed it into the wooden chest with all of the others.

CHAPTER SEVEN

September 2017

They'd been in school for two weeks and so far, they had been coexisting on ice that was thin.

It turned out that Ash was excellent at following rules: he'd kept his weed smoking to the balcony, he only drank on the weekends with his friends, and he never invited anyone over. He hardly spoke to Tayshia, but he could tell she was surprised that he was actually sticking to the agreement.

Which sort-of sucked since he hadn't slept with anyone in over eleven months.

It wasn't like he could just have a date over to Andre's *couch*. Andre had Ji Hyun over, but it was *his* apartment. Ash had bought a new phone and downloaded all of the dating apps, but he hadn't actually made any accounts besides one yet. He'd talked to one girl for a hot minute but then realized it might be awkward to have her over with Tayshia there, so he'd unmatched her before the number exchange.

Tayshia, on the other hand, was horrible at following rules.

Ash had bought a TV when he went to the furniture store, so every day, she could be found sitting on the floor between the couch and coffee table with her classwork on the glass top and food in her mouth. She left her dishes everywhere.

Every-fucking-where.

She left them on the coffee table, put them on the kitchen counters, and let them pile up in the sink. She ate constantly, cooking things and leaving a mess behind. And each time Ash cleaned the kitchen until it was spotless, she never said thank you.

The only thing that kept him sticking to the rules was his guilt over what happened to her father.

She was weird, too. She would be in the bathroom for thirty or forty minutes with the fan on the entire time. He didn't want to judge anyone's bathroom activities, but like... Did she pop laxatives like addies every day, or...?

It was annoying. Everything she did was annoying.

At school, they had two classes together: Myths & Legends and Intro to Psychology. Ji Hyun was in both of them, too, so Ash always had someone to sit next to, but it was clear by the energy from the other students that he was not someone they were fond of.

In the hallways of the school, it was the same. Whether he was walking past the high school or the pre-requisite program students, he endured silence and glares. Even the kids he'd hung out with before graduation looked at him with wariness, in spite of the fact that most of them had been at his welcome home party.

It felt like he was surrounded in a thin glass case and the people around him were carrying rocks, waiting for the moment to strike. Any day, he knew someone would grow tired of waiting and the glass would shatter.

"How do you feel about that?"

Ash looked down at Elijah, blinking off the shroud of his thoughts. His cheeks grew hot as he realized he'd been staring out across the cafeteria at Tayshia. They were on their lunch break, waiting for their next class to begin. Tayshia was at a table near the wall, while Ash and Elijah were near the large glass windows opposite her.

"What did you say?" Ash set his fork down on his empty paper plate, the colorful tattoos on his arm coming into view as he did so. "Also, we need to go."

"I said I'm going to kill you." Elijah grinned. "How do you feel about that?"

"I feel that that would not be ideal." Ash grabbed the strap of his black backpack and stood up. "I may have to kill you in return. It's only fair."

"Facts." Elijah hopped to his feet and his grin turned wolflike. "But that would imply that you have the power to come back after death. You can't do that—this isn't a video game."

"I can do whatever I want," Ash said, gathering up his plate and the plastic fork so he could throw them away. "I have the power to do things you can't even imagine."

Elijah narrowed his eyes and then pointed at him. "No. Nope. You can't *do* that. I'm laying you out with my fist, or a game controller. Whichever feels more satisfying."

"Why not both?" Ash said with a smirk. "You can come over after school and game if you want. Only thing I ask is that the fist is CGI. We can play a fighting game first."

Elijah's face lit up. "Both. I like both."

As they walked toward the door, Ash glanced over at Tayshia again.

She sat alone. She had categorized the different components of her chicken salad on her plate by color. As odd as he found it, it wasn't the first time he'd seen her do strange things with her food.

He watched her often when he went to the cafeteria for breakfast or lunch. At home, he'd seen her spend an hour making one meal just to scarf it down and spend a second hour making another one. He'd also seen her organize the refrigerator by color after she bought her groceries.

Tayshia was fucking *weird*.

Ash didn't mean to, need to, or want to stare at her when he was trying to put her behind him. When he was trying to forget about the fact that everything was shitty and *had* been shitty since the ice cream incident. Though the despondency his guilt caused had never gone away, it was bearable now. The staring just seemed to happen from time to time. Usually at mealtimes, and usually because she was doing something strange.

Part of his reason for staring was because she still wore the necklace.

He wondered if her dreams were as vivid as his.

Ash noticed that he was being stared at as they walked out of the cafeteria. He was used to it with how many tattoos he had now. They were random but they told a story. One that only Ash knew the plot of. A plot that he would never be able to explain.

The school didn't seem to care that he or any of the other of-age students had tattoos. They only cared about grades. So, the teachers didn't do much more than ask questions or ask to see the ones on his arms. But he could see it in their eyes — they were wary of him, too.

The tattoos that seemed to land him the most stares were the ones that crawled along his neck, wrapping around the front of it like a collar. When he hadn't been able to stop thinking about how desperate Tayshia's pleas for help for her father had been, he had

Diego tattoo roses wrapped in chains across the base of his throat. They stretched above his already-tattooed collarbones, choking him.

So, he wasn't surprised that everyone was staring at him now.

He probably looked like a felon.

☼☼☼

On the night of August 17th, Ash had endured a nightmare.

He couldn't explain it. It was dark—just inky blackness in his mind. He didn't know what he'd seen or what had happened because it was so dark and so confusing, but he knew that it was her that he heard screaming. He heard her voice saying the same three words that had destroyed him at the ice cream shop.

I'll do anything.

He'd woken in a cold sweat on Andre's couch, stumbling into the kitchen to guzzle an entire glass of water in the darkness. Feeling dazed, he'd occupied himself wondering if maybe he'd just smoked too much weed before he fell asleep, only to remember that he'd fallen asleep after taking one dab. That definitely wouldn't cause a full-blown hallucination.

The nightmare was just that—a nightmare.

It was the only nightmare he'd had since putting the crystal back around his neck, and he didn't think he'd ever get an explanation for it. It unsettled him.

She unsettled him.

"You're so lucky," Elijah whined on the present day as they climbed into Ash's car. He looked down to buckle his seatbelt, a lock of his wavy hair falling forward into his eyes.

"Why?" Ash asked, one hand on the back of Elijah's seat as he turned around to look out the back windshield while pulling out of his parking spot at the school.

"Because you get your own apartment—*with a kitchen, Ash!* Do *not* rob me of my envy!" Elijah held up a dramatic finger when Ash started to speak. "I'm still at home with my mom and we have a damn roommate. And you know that bitch is in the kitchen twenty-four-seven."

Ash rolled his eyes. "No one is trying to *rob* you. You're welcome to cook shit in my kitchen."

"Didn't you say Tayshia's always there, though? How does she feel about guests using her appliances? Can I keep leftovers in your fridge? Any leftovers I put in mine just get eaten, and my mom always takes her side."

"She's around."

They turned up Elijah's music on the aux cord as they drove down the mountain road, passing the school shuttle bus on its way up. The band playing was one that had released a new album while Ash was in jail, so he was hyped to hear it blasting out of his car stereo. They rolled the windows down, lit a joint, and bumped the speakers as loud as they could stand.

There was something deeply freeing about being able to just drive down the road with the windows down, blasting deathcore. He'd only been in jail for eleven months, but sometimes when he was lying in his cell at night, nursing wounds from fights that day, he felt like he would never be free again.

He'd taken a lot of things for granted.

When they got back to the apartment, they were both shocked to see that the kitchen was a disaster. There were dirty pans on the stove, containers that had been used to prepare ingredients scattered all over the counters, and dishes stacked in the sink that nearly reached the faucet. The smell of multiple types of cooked food mingling together gave Ash an almost instantaneous headache.

Of all things Ash would have thought about Tayshia Cole, he would not have thought she was *this* messy.

His gaze swept to the right, into the living room. There were dishes and cups all over the coffee table. If he counted, he was sure he'd discover that she'd used every single dish he'd bought.

"Whoa," Elijah said, eyes widening as he looked at all of the nonsense Tayshia had left everywhere. "It looks like the kitchen blew up in here. It reminds me of — "

"Hell?"

"Not particularly, but..." Elijah snorted with laughter. "I mean, what sort-of Hell do you think they're sending us to? If there's food, sign me the fuck up."

Ash dropped his backpack onto the dining room table, casting a distasteful glance into the living room. Among the dishes on the coffee table was an open textbook with a notebook placed haphazardly across it. The TV was on. The bathroom door in the hallway was closed.

"Well, you're wrong about one thing," he bit out through clenched teeth. "This already *is* Hell."

Elijah looked around and crossed his arms over his chest. "I

would have thought Tayshia was the type to be like, *clean*. This is...
Well, it's kinda—"

"Out of *fucking* pocket."

Ash stormed over to the coffee table and started cleaning up. He
slammed Tayshia's textbook shut with the notebook inside it, then
gathered up all of her dishes and set them on the counter by the
kitchen sink. His forehead ached from how hard he was frowning.

Ash had lost count of how many times he'd told her in a calm
tone to clean up after herself, and he was about ready to stop using a
calm tone. He was starting to want to raise his voice.

The last time he raised his voice to another person, it was to a guy
he fought in jail.

"I don't think I've ever seen you look so pressed," Elijah said,
sounding amused.

"I'm going to lose my shit," Ash growled from the sink, "if she
doesn't knock it off."

Ash turned away from the messy sink, facing Elijah. He looked
disturbed.

"What?"

"It's weird," Elijah said.

"What's weird?"

"You." Elijah's eyes narrowed into slits.

"How am *I* weird?"

"No, *you're* not weird. You're *being* weird. There's a difference."

"No, there's not."

"Oh yes, there is."

"How am I *weird*?" Ash was *very* close to yelling.

"You're being so calm about this. You spent the past four years
treating her like trash. Like, you didn't even treat her like the trash *in*
the can." Elijah lifted his hands and moved them about, pantomiming
the shape of a trash can. "You treated her like the can the trash goes
into, and then you threw your trash into her for four years. Why
aren't you like, flipping out and screaming? Bro, it's *weird*."

Ash felt his guilt rising up.

He hadn't bullied her or anything, but he hadn't been nice to her.
She hadn't been very nice to him, either. In ninth grade, the first time
they'd met had been because she stumbled upon him and a few of
the other scholarship kids smoking weed behind the school. He'd
cussed at her and called her a cunt and while it wasn't his crowning

achievement in life, it hadn't stopped her from calling him a waste of space.

Ash had learned in jail when it was important to reign in his temper and when it was important that he let it out. Tayshia was messy — exorbitantly so — but he didn't want the exhaustion that came after him blowing up. Especially if it wouldn't solve anything.

The clock would have to continue to tick for now.

"It's not weird," he said, turning back to the sink so he could start organizing the dishes for cleaning when he had the energy. Lord knew Tayshia wasn't going to do it.

"Yeah, it's a little weird."

"Just drop it," Ash snapped, waving a tattooed hand in a dismissive motion. "The last thing I need is to start yelling and get the cops called on me."

"For real," Elijah said, walking up to the bar and leaning over it, watching Ash organizing dishes. "They'd probably arrest you for breathing at this point."

Ash smirked and moved to retort, but the door to the bathroom opened suddenly, drawing the boys' attention.

Tayshia stepped out of the hallway wearing a pair of leggings and a sweater, like she always wore. Her curls were pulled up into a knot at the top of her head, a few coiling pieces hanging down around her face to frame it.

She looked surprised to see Elijah standing there. It was only the second time that he'd been in the apartment, and she never had anyone over, so seeing other people inside of it was jarring.

Ash wasn't surprised to see her, as she usually made it home before he did because her last class ended twenty minutes before his did, and she got rides home from friends. However, when Ash saw her in the halls at the school, she wasn't quite as social as she'd been the years before.

It seemed like she was a completely different person.

She always had seemed like she had a lot of friends, so he surmised that either she was a private person now, or she'd never really been friends with any of those people. Even though most of their graduating class had gone on to universities instead of staying on for the program, he distinctly remembered her having friends in all grades. But he never saw them with her anymore. As for Kieran, Ash had seen him around, but they didn't have any classes together. According to Tayshia's audible phone conversations at night, she and

Kieran were still together.

"You just gonna stand there staring, or you gonna be polite?" Ash arched one eyebrow and gestured to Elijah with mock-theatrics.

"Dude, it's fine," Elijah said. "We're cool."

"Cool?"

"Yeah. We're friends."

"Then why is she just standing there?" Ash asked, frowning.

"Because I can stand wherever the fuck I want." Tayshia raised her eyebrows. "And I was just surprised to see you still had friends."

Her words smashed into him like rocks and he fought the urge to flinch. Something about her insults hit harder than they should have. Like she could burn him with her voice.

Ash supposed he deserved that, after everything he'd done. He and Tayshia didn't speak, so it wasn't like he'd ever had the chance to sit her down and *talk* about the past. He knew he'd done bad things. He'd made mistakes, and he'd served time to pay for them. He was *still* paying for them in installments for restitution.

But he wasn't a monster.

"Yes," he snapped, glaring at her, "I know it's hard to believe. But yeah. I have friends."

Tayshia merely gave him a once-over with her gaze, then walked into the living room. She walked over to the coffee table, bending over to grab her textbook. In the awkwardness of the silence, Ash could sense that she was disgruntled by the fact that he'd cleaned.

He looked over at Elijah, seeing that he was grimacing.

"Yes, Elijah, it's always this awkward."

"Uhh... No, I... That's not..." Elijah's eyes widened as he looked back and forth between Tayshia and Ash.

She stood there, hugging her textbook and notebook against her chest as she stared directly into Elijah's eyes. She was shorter than both boys, coming only to about Ash's shoulders, but with the way she carried herself, she seemed taller than both of them.

"It *is* awkward," she said.

Elijah winced. "Yeah. A little."

It wouldn't be so awkward if Tayshia wasn't such a bitch half the time. She said things so bluntly. Ash had always been the bluntest of his group of friends. He always felt the urge to say what he really thought, lest anyone form preconceived notions about him and use them against him.

He wasn't used to someone else being just like him.

Tayshia gave Elijah a bit of a smile, then headed for the hallway.

"I'm sure you've noticed the mess," Ash said, tone icy as he spoke to her. His words stopped her dead in her tracks. "Gonna leave it for me to clean up, as usual?"

"Gonna smoke weed on the balcony like I can't smell it whenever you do?" she retorted. "*As usual?*"

"In the bathroom for forty-five minutes?" Ash's voice held a note of challenge as he viewed her. "*As usual?*"

"Interested in my bathroom activities, Ash?" She raised the gentle arch of one eyebrow. "I didn't think you were one of *those* guys."

Ash ran a hand through his hair in agitation as he once again considered raising his voice. "How would you know what sort of guys there are? I highly doubt you've interacted with any guy other than Kieran. And that's not a compliment."

Her eyes flashed. "I don't need *interactions* to know what different types of guys there are."

"Where'd you learn about them?" Ash smirked. "The Bible?"

"Just because we go to a Christian school doesn't mean we're all religious," she shot back. "And even if I was, I wouldn't need the Bible to tell me that you're a bad guy."

Elijah ran his hands through his hair, appearing anxious. "Guys..."

Ash walked out of the kitchen. He towered over Tayshia, causing her to have to crane her neck. Her glare faltered, but she kept her back straight.

"What are you gonna do?" she challenged. "Hit me?"

Okay, now he was mad.

Gabriel had beaten his ass for years. The fact that Tayshia thought *that* low of him made him sick to his stomach. Did she really hate him that much? He wasn't sure which bothered him more. Her insinuation that he would hit her or being considered *anything* like his father.

Both fucking sucked.

"Why don't you keep leaving your shit all over the apartment?" he said, his voice starting to rise. "Then you can find out how bad a guy I can be."

Her eyes were alight with indignation. "No matter how many interactions I may or may not have had, they're not your fucking business, Ash."

"Oh. She says fuck now." He sneered. "Not so much of a good girl anymore, are you?"

"She bites, too," she snarled. "And if you don't stop running your mouth, you'll find out."

Ash crossed his arms, breathing a laugh as he took the final step toward her. He dragged her gaze up her body in a scrutinizing way and then locked eyes with her.

"If you don't start cleaning up your shit..." he said, his voice a slow hiss. "... I'll show *you* what I learned in jail."

The flames died out within her eyes. She took a couple of steps back and for the first time, she looked genuinely nervous. Uncomfortable.

Afraid.

"Ohhh, dear." Elijah scrubbed his face with his hands and pulled the largest grimace Ash had ever seen him pull. "Why don't we all just... Just chill, all right?"

Tayshia lowered her eyes for a moment, a strange expression that looked like a mix between puzzlement and languor crossing her face, and then she blinked.

Ash let out his breath and then cleared his throat. He opened his mouth to speak, but it felt like the walls of the room were closing in on him.

He wasn't like his father. He didn't want to be, but she was driving him fucking *nuts*. With the books on the floor and the dishes and the bathroom trips and the attitude, it was just...

Frustrating.

"You cleaned," Tayshia finally said in a tight voice, just when Ash thought he was going to pass out from how thick the air was in the room. She scanned the area, glare roving the floors and the couch as if seeing them for the first time. "So I'm not sure why if you're so upset by me leaving messes, you keep cleaning them up. If you'd just left today's mess there, I would've gotten around to it."

"It was disgusting."

"Everything was exactly where I left it."

"It was a *mess*," Ash repeated in a slow, incredulous tone.

Elijah held up his forefingers. "An *organized* mess."

Tayshia and Ash both stared at him. Ash wanted to shave all of the hair off of Elijah's head, but Tayshia laughed. She actually laughed and Ash couldn't help it.

He stared.

She had a ridiculously nice set of teeth. Had they always been that white?

Tayshia moved past him, into the kitchen. "Even took my dishes, too, didn't you?"

"Right." Ash scowled. "That."

"Yes. That." She pursed her lips and furrowed her brow, twisting her mouth as though she were lost in thought.

"'That?' What is 'that?'" Elijah looked confused.

"The princess doesn't like her dishes being touched, moved, cleaned, or otherwise acknowledged," Ash said in a saccharine-sweet voice, his upper lip curling.

"Queen," Tayshia said, lips still pursed. There was so much attitude in her face that it grated on Ash's nerves. "Don't do me like that."

"Why?" Elijah asked, scratching the back of his head. "The dishes, I mean."

Ash turned to Tayshia. "Yes, Your Majesty. *Why?*"

As usual, he saw her gaze dip down to the tattoos on his neck and collarbones, and the ones on the part of his chest that disappeared into the neckline of his shirt. He wondered if she knew what guilt the ones on his neck represented.

She glared at him for a moment before she turned her nose up into the air. Holding her textbook and notebook against her body with one arm, she gestured to the sink with a flourishing wave of her hand.

"I just don't like my dishes being touched when I haven't finished my food."

"The dishes were *empty*," Ash spluttered.

Tayshia whirled on him. "*They were still mine!*"

"*Yours?* You wanna get technical?! Fine, let's get technical. Everything in this place is mine. The couches, TV, dishes, the shit in the bathroom. I'm the one who bought all of it!"

"Yeah, and where'd you get the money? You ain't even got a job, bro! Did you steal it?"

He breathed another mirthless laugh. "Oh, you fucking bi—"

"In all fairness... !" Elijah clapped his hands once and rubbed them together. "They *were* empty. They looked empty."

"Unless you like licking the bowls? Because you can pull them right back out of the sink and do that if you want," Ash said in a sarcastic tone. "And for the record, I'm not a fucking creep. It's one thing to be a felon, but it's a completely different thing to literally *listen* to someone while they're in the bathroom. Which is what you were insinuating."

She scoffed. "I was just—"

"Running your mouth," he snapped. "So, if you're finished standing around and causing drama, can you go? I have to clean the kitchen."

Tayshia scowled. Without another word, she stalked off. Her bedroom door slammed shut.

Elijah let out an audible sigh.

"Jesus fucking Christ, that was... That was a thing."

Ash went back to the sink to start cleaning, not replying. This wasn't the first time he'd had a negative interaction with Tayshia, and he was sure it wouldn't be the last.

In fact, if she kept leaving her mess all over the apartment, he was sure of it.

CHAPTER EIGHT

Ash realized now that he really could have gone to someone for help that day, instead of making the decision to walk into that ice cream shop.

If he would have made a different choice, it might have changed his entire future. His mother might still be alive if he hadn't been sentenced. If she had no reason to get upset, then nothing would have caused the heart attack.

His father might still have been addicted to drugs or dealing, but Ash didn't give a flying fuck what happened to his father. It was Gabriel's fault that his mother was gone. It was Gabriel that Ash wished was dead.

Ash set his spoon down, staring at the bowl of cereal in front of him. He took slow, deep breaths. He needed to stay calm. Under no circumstances was he going to allow himself to have a fucking meltdown in the cafeteria before class. Not over his poor choices.

He had made those choices himself. He needed to live with them.

Ash resumed eating. He glanced around at all of the students, his gaze landing on the table where Tayshia sat. For the first time in a while, Ash saw that Kieran was sitting there with her. His eyes still crinkled at the edges when he smiled and the perpetual dark circles were there beneath them, but his hair was a bit longer. It curled around his ears, sandy and brown.

Kieran had his hands all over Tayshia, as though she were the type of girl to enjoy that sort of thing. He was saying something to her over and over, continuously trying to kiss the side of her throat. It was clear that she didn't like it because her shoulder kept rising.

Why did Kieran look so *angry*? God, what was he gonna do? Kiss her against her will?

Ash would fuck his shit up if he tried that, and he didn't care if he and Tayshia could barely stand each other. Any guy who had the balls to touch a woman without her consent was a man who deserved to have his ass kicked. In Ash's opinion, a man like that was worth going to prison for.

Men like that were the sort of men who were tough until they were standing in front of another man—then they were weak.

Not that he *cared* about Tayshia like that. At least, not beyond the general regard for her well-being as a human being who didn't deserve to be treated poorly. It wasn't like he *liked* her, or anything. He didn't need to like someone to want to make sure they were treated well.

But if he really sat there and looked at her, he could see that she *was* pretty. It would be stupid of him to act like she was ugly when she really *wasn't*. She had one of those faces—the kind that seemed to look presentable whether she wore make-up or not. Her brows were feathery, sitting proportionate to her eyes. Eyes which were fringed with long lashes that always curled up just so.

And her hair was always so interesting, changing every few weeks to some new style. It was in curls now, but he was sure it would be something else soon. Braids, waves that cascaded, straight, completely different colors, in twists... It was cultural and it was just interesting to see.

She had a mysterious, almost sultry look to her. Her lips were full—the type that might look swollen after kissing them. Sometimes, Ash wanted to slide his fingers along her jaw, take her chin in his hand, and see if her lips really did swell up.

Ash stood up, grabbing his backpack so he could head to his first class of the day—Math 120. He needed to get out of the cafeteria before he got caught staring at her like some creep.

He had a decently full class schedule to finish up his transfer degree in the program. After Math, he had Intro to Psych. Then, after lunch, he had a free period, a Literature class called Myths & Legends, and then a bit later, a Geography class. It was a full load, but he had nothing else to do. He'd spend Winter term with a lighter one if he needed to.

Later, in Intro to Psych, Ash took his usual seat beside Ji Hyun, who barely looked up from inspecting her nail polish as he did so.

"Ash," she greeted in a haughty tone. "You're looking moody."

"Ji Hyun. You have a bitchy air about you."

She scoffed and rolled her head to glare at him. Her oval face was done-up perfectly, framed by her long jet-black waves. She gave him a once-over. "Still dressing like a 2011 Scene kid, I see."

"Don't be shitty, Ji Hyun." He smoothed out the front of his zip-up hoodie, which was black with a white zipper and white drawstrings. He also wore skinny jeans with a dark wash and a brown belt. "The day I stop dressing like I'm going to Warped Tour is the day I die."

Ji Hyun's sour expression cracked open like an egg, revealing a sunny-side up disposition. She grinned and leaned forward to press a kiss to his cheek, squeezing his jaw between her fingers. "I know. I'm just hoping if I pressure you enough, you'll stop."

Ash rolled his eyes.

"Good God." Ji Hyun shook her head. "Your roots are *killing* me."

"Enjoy death."

"Whatever. So, open your ears up," Ji Hyun said as the classroom slowly filled around them. "You're *not* going to believe the gossip I just heard in my last class."

Ash reached into his backpack to pull out his notes from the teacher, Mrs. Morrows' continuing series on mental disorders, and a mechanical pencil. He sunk down in his seat, stretching his legs out.

"Well? Don't just stare at me." He raised his eyebrows at his notebook as though it looked stupid. "Lay the nonsense on me."

Ji Hyun clucked her tongue against her teeth but chose not to scold him as she folded her arms on the table and leaned towards him.

"I have it on good authority that one Kieran O'Connell was seen *canoodling* in a room at the football team's party last weekend with one Quinn Baker. And they may or may not have had clothes on."

"What?"

Ji Hyun's rouged cheeks reddened further with excitement and her eyebrows shot up. "Oh, yes. And not only — listen — not *only* is Quinn his girlfriend's best friend, but she's got —" She mouthed her next word, "*tits* the size of boulders. I mean, listen, Ash. Look."

Ash's eyes darted downward. Ji Hyun was holding her hands spread-eagle over her chest. His gaze lifted back to hers. She wore an almost comically-surprised expression on her face. Ash arched one brow.

Ji Hyun nodded. "Uh, *yeah*."

Ash swiveled his head back to the front, where he could see Tayshia sitting at a table near the front of the room. She was in the process of writing furiously in a notebook, and she sat with her whole body in the chair — one arm wrapped around her knees, which were pulled to her chest. He couldn't help but remember how uncomfortable she'd seemed with Kieran in the cafeteria at breakfast.

Was it because she knew?

Ji Hyun's voice came into Ash's ear. "D'you think Miss Perfect knows her boyfriend is making out at parties with her busty broad of a best friend?" She then said in a high-pitched, exaggerated voice, "*I don't thiiiink so.*"

Ash eyed Tayshia a second longer. He remembered the day she'd moved in, when she'd asked Quinn to stay and she'd said she couldn't. Had she been in a hurry because she was heading over to wherever Kieran lived? Would she show up for Tayshia's birthday and leave in a rush again?

"I'm concerned," he said.

"Why? About *her*?"

"About my apartment. Do you know what kind of messes she's going to leave when she finds out her boyfriend is a whore?"

When he looked at his friend, he saw she looked grossed out.

"Is she really that messy?" she asked with a grimace. "I didn't think she was the type. I mean, *I'm* the type. You should see mine and Andre's apartment. But she's always been such a..."

"Goody two-shoes?"

Ji Hyun nodded.

"She likes her things to be left exactly in their place," Ash said in a light tone as he pulled his hood up onto the back of his head. "And typically, that place is wherever she decides to leave them."

"Really? That's so weird. She doesn't just like, put them away?"

"Nah, and she's so weird. Like, she's always in the bathroom."

"In the bathroom?" Ji Hyun appeared confused. "That's really weird. Like, multiple times, or just once a day?"

"No. I'm talking multiple times a day. We only have one bathroom and I have to use the fucking public one at the leasing office all the time because she's *always* in there. For over thirty minutes at a time. It's ridiculous."

Ji Hyun studied him for a second, opening her mouth to speak. Then, she shook her head and turned to her notebook. Suspicion filled him.

"Do you have like, a guess as to *why*?" he asked.

"No," she said, shaking her head. "Probably just girl stuff. I wouldn't worry about it—I'd worry more about her being messy. Messy roommates are horrible."

Just then, Mrs. Morrows bustled into the classroom with her blonde hair pulled back into a ponytail, almond-shaped glasses on, and a pinstriped pantsuit on. She had a coffee cup in one hand and a donut in the other. She launched into class before she'd even made it to her desk to set the food and drink down. Once she had, she went to the podium and continued to speak.

"Today, class, I want to continue our study of mental disorders," she said. "If you'll turn to the chapter in your books, we can just jump right back in. Does someone want to pick up reading aloud where we left off? Ah, yes—Melissa, go ahead."

As Melissa, a girl Ash had only ever had one class with in tenth grade spoke, Ash inevitably found his mind wandering back to Ji Hyun's information. While he was not Tayshia's friend by any stretch of the imagination, he had a feeling it would suck to find out your boyfriend was a cheater.

To be even more frank, the guy was a complete idiot. Ash had had plenty of classes with him where he struggled with understanding the simplest things. All he cared about was partying, girls, and football. There had to be something wrong with him to be sleeping with his girlfriend's best friend.

Come to think of it, Tayshia didn't really spend much time with Kieran. She never brought him back to the apartment, she had a full class schedule, and she never really went anywhere on the weekends. Tayshia spent most of her time sitting on the floor of the living room, eating and watching TV while doing her studies. Sometimes, she was playing a handheld game console on the couch or scrolling through her phone.

She either had no time to fuck her idiot of a boyfriend or no desire to, and that could be the reason why he was sleeping around.

But that reason seemed so *thin*. Thin, and juvenile.

They were all adults now. Was sex so important to Kieran that he'd actually *cheat* on Tayshia, the girl he'd been dating since day one of ninth grade? Hell, they seemed to have been dating for a century. He couldn't possibly be that immature.

There had to be another reason why he would step out on her.

Ash snuck another glance up in Tayshia's direction. She was hunched over her knees, taking notes that would likely make Mrs.

Morrows ask her to teach the class.

Fuck, she was living rent-free in his mind, wasn't she?

"All right, class, let's move on to what's probably one of the most important subjects we'll talk about during this portion of the term. Eating disorders," Mrs. Morrows said twenty minutes into class. "If you'll turn the page, you'll see that there's only a small section in the book dedicated to this particular subset of mental disorders, and I think that's a crime. So, we're going to spend the next few days in class on them, and then I'm going to have you write an essay."

Ash shifted in his seat, trying not to think about his mother.

This was going to suck.

Tayshia's hand shot up and she spoke without waiting to be called on. "Mrs. Morrows, is this portion of the term skippable?"

Mrs. Morrows frowned. "Of course not, Tayshia. This is probably the most important section of the term."

"Oh, okay," she said, and then she rested her chin in her hand.

"Are you worried about triggering content?" Mrs. Morrows asked, crossing her arms over her chest and leaning against the podium.

"No," Tayshia said quickly. "That's not it. I'm just uncomfortable with the subject matter, especially because most studies available don't include statistics on Black women with disorders. Since I'm a Black woman, I'd just prefer to learn the most unbiased information that I can."

Mrs. Morrows tilted her head in thought. "Thank you for telling me that. I don't want anyone to feel uncomfortable in my class at all — and that goes for all of the rest of you, too. How about we start with the textbook today? And then tonight, I can do some research and see if I can come up with some diverse peer-reviewed studies. And you're welcome to bring in some of your own, of course."

"What exactly will we be covering in this section?"

"What do you mean, Tayshia?" Mrs. Morrows peered at her over her glasses.

"Like, which disorders?"

"Well, there's quite a few, but namely Anorexia, Bulimia, and Binge Eating Disorder. In your essays, you'll have the chance to research the others. Now, class, we —"

"Wait," Tayshia said, raising her hand for a moment again. "We won't be putting focus on weight, will we? Because there's been a *lot* of studies done that prove that anyone can have a disorder, regardless of their weight. I just want to make sure none of the curriculum will be weight-focused. I think that's something I'd consider triggering."

Mrs. Morrows blinked. "We won't be focusing on weight, numbers, or BMIs, no."

"And we won't be talking about thinspo, will we?"

Mrs. Morrows looked perturbed. Several students whispered *what's thinspo?* to one another. When Ash looked at Ji Hyun, he saw that she'd pulled a face of puzzlement.

Damn, Tayshia was thorough. She always had been, but this was so extra. Why didn't she just wait and find out like the rest of the class? Plus, it sounded like she knew everything she needed to know already.

Ash himself wasn't too ecstatic about this section of class because of his mother, but he wasn't going to make a big deal out of it. He'd skip the assignments if he had to. The points couldn't be that big of a deal in the overall grade.

Mrs. Morrows said, "Er, no. We won't be discussing the culture around eating disorders. Just the medical facts and the way it affects the brain as it pertains to psychology."

Sometimes, Ash wondered if Tayshia really understood how bizarre she was.

At the end of the period, he finished jotting down his notes and then began putting his things back into his bag.

There was a bit of a fiasco at the door as Tayshia pushed her way through the crowd, and then her footsteps could be heard receding down the hallway at a rapid pace. Ji Hyun scoffed but said nothing as she waited by the desk's edge for Ash to follow.

"I don't know about you," she said as they trudged down the hallway, "but I don't think she's a slick as she thinks she is."

Ash moved aside as a group of younger students came barreling by, laughing and screaming like children. He watched them, wondering if he'd been that annoying in high school.

The only downside of attending the pre-requisite program was having to be subjected to immaturity.

"What's there to be slick about?" Ash asked, running his fingers backward through his hair. He pushed his hood off with the movement.

"I told you — it's just girl stuff." She pursed her lips. "If you don't already know, then you won't get it."

"Uh... Okay," he said. "So, anyway—who told you about Kieran and Quinn?"

"Andre did, actually," she said as they walked. "He saw them when he was using the bathroom during class. They were underneath the staircase on the other side of the school from here. In the west wing."

"Shit."

"Shit is right. I don't understand what's wrong with her—why doesn't she just dump him? She can't really be so oblivious that she doesn't know he's cheating. He's so stupid."

"Says the girl who got back together with Kyle last year after he cheated on you."

Ji Hyun elbowed him. "Stop. I'm pretty. I can get away with being stupid. At least I'm with Andre now."

"And I'm not pretty?" Ash countered with a lopsided grin as he looked down at her.

"Of course you are. You've got good hair—it does that swooshy thing when you push it back. You've got a jawline that could cut diamonds. And your tattoos make you look dangerous, but in the sort of way that's intimidating and not frightening. Your eyes are unsettling, though. I've never liked blue eyes."

"Rude."

"So, what are you going to do about Tayshia being messy?"

"Nothing," he said. "I can't force her to clean, and she won't do it. I just do it myself."

"God, it's not like you're hooking up with her. You can put your foot down, you know."

"I'm not hooking with anyone," he said with a breathy laugh. "But if I was, I'd still be able to tell them to clean up their shit."

They exited through some doors that led to another hallway. This one was emptier than the last because it didn't have lockers in it. Instead, there were classroom doors and religious paintings lining the walls.

Ash could feel Ji Hyun's gaze upon him, searching and accusatory.

"You're not hooking up with Tayshia, are you?"

When he glanced down at her again, his gaze felt cold.

"Of course not. Isn't that what I already said?"

Ji Hyun tossed her hair. "You're so defensive about it. I really hope you're not. Do you know how messed up that would be? No offense, but with her dad and everything... Not a good idea."

"You're so loyal. It's a good look for you."

She scowled. "I *am* loyal. I'm here, still friends with you, aren't I? But I'm not going to sugarcoat it for you, Ash. You and your dad held people at gunpoint and stole their wallets. Her dad got shot. If you're trying to hook up with her, or if you've already hooked up with her, that's—"

"Can you not and say you did?" he snapped, grinding his teeth. "I'm not fucking Tayshia, and that's the end of it."

Ji Hyun responded with a huff.

CHAPTER NINE

Things settled into a routine.

Ash went to class, spent his free time with Elijah, and cleaned up after Tayshia in the apartment as needed. He felt exhausted by it, so he didn't have the energy to heckle her for leaving her things everywhere. If he did, every day would be a fight. It was best to just let her be a tornado and then clean when she went to the bathroom. If he did that, she only had time to make one more mess before she went to the bathroom again.

What the fuck was she *doing* in there?

On the morning of the third Thursday in September, she took one hour in the bathroom and he nearly came close to picking a fight with her. Not only did she take an hour, but she made an extravagant breakfast of eggs, French toast, and bacon, completely trashing the kitchen in the process. When Ash stumbled half-asleep into the kitchen and saw it, he thought he might actually take his own life.

She seemed to sense his poor disposition, because when she left the hallway headed for the front door, it was in a rush.

"Hey," he said angrily as she bustled towards the front door in her typical leggings and oversized sweater.

Tayshia stopped with her hand on the doorknob, taking in the sight of him at the sink. He was shirtless, wearing only a pair of grey joggers, and his tattoos were on full display. She didn't seem to know which one to look at.

"Can you try not to make a Disneyland buffet in the morning, please?" he said, his words coming out strained and irritated. "I'm gonna be late for class."

"Or, you could just leave it," she said, giving him a strange look. "Not everything has to be cleaned all the time."

He stared at her.

"I'm literally ascending right now," he said in a flat voice. "I am ascending. Why would you insist we set rules the day we moved in, and then proceed to follow none of them?"

She frowned. "It's not like I'm doing it on purpose. I'm trying."

Ash didn't understand that. He did not understand how cleaning was something that had to be attempted.

"Well, try *harder*," he said through his teeth. "I shouldn't be standing here, cleaning up your fucking mess in the morning when I have—" He glanced at the microwave clock. "—legit twenty minutes to get ready."

"*Sorry*," she said, sounding annoyed. "My parents used to make me clean as a punishment, so I hate doing it. But I *am* trying."

Ash gestured to the complete disaster that was the kitchen. "Doesn't really look like it."

"Can't you just for *once* leave it for me to do later?" She heaved a sigh, adjusting the strap of her messenger bag on her shoulder. "I don't understand why this is such a big deal. It's not hurting you."

"It's a matter of respect."

"Oh. You wanna talk respect." Tayshia raised her eyebrows. "Where was the respect when my dad got shot?"

Ash looked at her, suddenly noticing that her hairstyle had changed. She had long burgundy waves that rippled down to her lower back now, with wispy bangs that fell across her forehead. It warmed up her already terracotta skin tone and brought all the attention to her eyes. Her eyes, which blazed with the flames of preemptive triumph.

Fuck.

"That's what I thought," she said, opening the front door. "You can either leave it for me to clean up later, or you can just suck it up."

The front door slammed shut.

Ash tipped his head back and cursed under his breath. His anger expanded in his chest, warring with his ever-present guilt. He wished he'd made better choices. He hated the fact that the consequences were following him, even after jail. Why couldn't there be a better way for him to navigate living with her?

What, did she want an apology? Did she want him to get down on his fucking knees and beg for her forgiveness? Or did she just want him to clean up after her because she believed he owed her more than that?

Didn't she understand he'd give anything to go back to that day and do everything differently? At least then his mom might still be alive.

It took *all* of his inner strength to resist the urge to break a plate against the wall.

☼☼☼

Ash stared at the text on his phone.

Hey, kid. I honestly struggled with sending this because I wasn't sure if I should. You down to talk? – Ryo.

At the front of the classroom, Mr. Rothger droned on about something number-related that had been melting Ash's brain for the past three days. The classroom was full, most of the students sitting towards the front of the room. No one sat to either side of Ash at his table.

He wasn't surprised. Most of these kids were either religious nuts or the type of Christians who pretended to be Godly when really they weren't. They were and always had been terrified of him. There was only one other friend he had in the class but that kid was so zooted that he paid attention to nothing but the window.

And now, Ash had a text message from someone he hadn't heard from in over a year: his father's best friend and their neighbor, Ryosuke Sunamura.

He closed out of the texting app and went to his social media, scrolling through his newsfeed in his lap until his vision blurred.

How was he supposed to just pick up the phone and talk to someone from his past like that? He'd ignored his father's letters. He'd ignored all of Bertha's attempts to contact him.

Why didn't the universe understand that he wanted nothing to do with a life that existed when his mother was alive? He didn't need the reminder.

"Mr. Robards."

Ryo wasn't a bad guy—he never had been. He and his husband, Steven had been like second parents to Ash when his father started doing drugs. They'd met because Steven loved seeing the flowers Gabriel planted from his kitchen window, and both couples had hit it off. They didn't have any kids, so they loved having Ash over to visit when he was in elementary school.

Because their families were so close, Ash went over there whenever he needed a break from his dad. There were multiple times when he was fifteen that the Sunamuras wanted to call the CPS, but Ash would beg and beg and beg until they relented. As Ash started to get involved in his father's business, their families started to drift.

By the time he was arrested, none of the Robards had spoken to the Sunamuras since Christmas of 2016.

And now he just wanted to *talk*?

Talking to Ryo would just bring up emotions that Ash had been working hard to staunch. It would just remind him of the fact that his mother was dead.

"Ash."

He jolted and looked up.

Mr. Rothger stood there, his salt-and-pepper hair falling forward over his shoulder as he bent toward him. Everyone in the class had turned to stare at Ash, and he could feel their eyes lingering on the tattoos on his exposed arms and hands.

"Yeah?" Ash said.

"I'm unsure if you're aware," Mr. Rothger said, "but this is class. Weird, huh?"

"Sorry," he muttered, turning his phone over so the screen was flat on his thigh and his hand held it in place. He rested his elbow on the table and his chin in his hand. When Mr. Rothger hadn't moved, Ash barely managed to stop himself from snapping into a rage. "It's okay. You can continue."

"Who'd have thought? I couldn't continue my own class without Ash Robards' permission."

Mr. Rothger returned to the front of the room and resumed his lecture.

Ash spent the rest of the period and all of lunch in a stormy, brooding mood. He held his brows low on his forehead, his stomach too upset to eat much of anything hearty. He ate soup, forcing himself not to look at the table Tayshia and Kieran sat at, lest she catch him.

But he did glance at her once.

She was tucking into her meal with great zeal, her mouth stuffed to the brim as Kieran talked to someone from the football team over the top of her head. She didn't seem to be contributing to the conversation, and Ash was surprised to see that her food was not separated. It was piled somewhat high on her plate, a convoluted mess of colors that blended together.

Weird.

Ash saw Elijah heading over, so he nodded to him. As his gaze made its way back down to his food, he caught sight of Tayshia hurrying her way out of the cafeteria. She disappeared out the doors without glancing behind her, her hair flying out in a curtain of waves.

Ash looked at Kieran, seeing that he was still talking to his teammate, and he wondered if he felt guilty.

Andre wasn't the type to tell a lie. He was a complete stoner, but he wasn't a liar. Ash believed that if he'd seen Quinn with Kieran at a party, that meant that it was true.

Was Tayshia really *that* oblivious?

Ash sighed and shook his head.

"What?" Elijah asked as he slid into the table across from him. He'd gotten a burger that day, just like he had every day for lunch since the dawn of his time at Christ Rising. It was his favorite meal.

"What do you mean, what?"

"You're sighing and moping," Elijah replied, pulling the top bun off so that he could squirt ketchup from packets onto the meat and cheese. "What happened?"

"Nothing, just having a shitty day," Ash said.

"Aw," Elijah said, biting into his burger. "Sucks."

"Yeah."

"Well... Wanna talk about it?"

"No," he said.

Elijah eyed him. "Kinda seems like you might wanna talk about it."

"Mm..." Ash looked thoughtful for a second, then scooped up another spoonful of his soup. "Nope. Not me."

"Right."

What would make Kieran cheat on Tayshia, and why? Was she fucking her boyfriend, or wasn't she? If she was, was he still cheating on her in spite of it? If she wasn't sleeping with him and it meant enough to him to seek it elsewhere, how long before he grew tired of waiting?

How long before Kieran simply left?

Ash was no friend to Tayshia, but there was no doubt in his mind that they had a connection. It had something to do with those damn crystals. If it wasn't all in his head, then the dreams — and the nightmare he'd had that Summer — were real.

Jesus, fuck.

Ash was losing his mind. Thinking about her. Dreaming about her. Analyzing her relationship.

He was about to cancel himself. He didn't care about Tayshia's relationship with her pet white boy, and he didn't care about Tayshia.

Fuck them both.

✿✿✿

The last time Ash saw his father, it was in the courtroom.

Gabriel looked like a mess, of course. He had been held in a different facility than Ash and after the trial, he was transferred to the state penitentiary. It was clear that he wasn't doing well and was still in the process of withdrawals. He could barely look anyone in the eyes, let alone a lawyer or judge. Let alone his *son*. All he did was scratch, breathe, and look around wildly.

At the time, Ash hadn't been doing much better.

He'd gotten into a fight with two guys that morning, so when he was brought to the courtroom to give his testimony, Ash's face was swollen and bruised. He was depressed after Elijah's visit and felt like he was looking down the barrel of a shotgun. Knowing that he still had over ten months left in his sentence had been overwhelming.

But he'd done his job. He'd testified against his father.

He told them everything—from the drugs, to the dealing, to a play-by-play of the events that had taken place at the ice cream shop. His father's lawyer had tried to take an angle that depicted Ash as emotional because of his mother's death, but it hadn't worked. Ash was not the type to cry unless he hit a breaking point and he certainly didn't cry in front of people. He had remained strong and firm in his testimony, and it had gotten his father convicted.

Gabriel landed charges for distribution, possession, intent to sell, and attempted murder. He was charged for assault and armed robbery, too.

He'd be gone for a long, long time.

When Ash got home from school that day, Tayshia had already gotten the mail. She was in the living room on the floor with her handheld game console balanced on her knees, a hoodie on with the hood up, and a pizza pocket in one hand. She ate while using the fingers of her free hand to press buttons.

The kitchen was still not clean.

Ash glanced to the left and saw that the mail was sitting on the table. The newest letter from his father sat right on top of the pile, distracting him enough to sap his irritation.

Taking the letter to his room, he looked down at the envelope. There it was—the spidery scrawl with the long loops and short tails, spelling out his name. Since Ash had changed his address with the post office so that his mail could be forwarded, it still had his old address at the jail.

After he put it into the chest with the rest of them, he kicked his shoes off into the corner and went out to the kitchen to start cleaning. Tayshia obviously wasn't going to do it.

With a sigh, he pushed the sleeves of his purple crewneck up to his elbows and got started.

"Um... Just letting you know, my birthday is tomorrow."

Ash glanced up ten minutes into doing the dishes. Tayshia stood there in the entrance to the kitchen, her pizza pocket gone and her console in her other hand. He saw now that she wore a pair of slippers and leggings with her hoodie.

He slowly placed a plate in the dishwasher, saying nothing.

Tayshia said, "Quinn said she's gonna come sleepover tomorrow because she has to study this weekend."

Ash fought the urge to side-eye her. She clearly had no idea who her *best friend* was. If she did, she wouldn't be inviting her over.

"All right, bet," he said, turning back to the sink.

"I mean, is it okay?"

He pulled a face where she couldn't see, his arms plunged into hot, soapy water. "Why would I need it to be okay?"

"Well, you was talkin' about respect and shit this morning," she said quietly. "So, it would be disrespectful of me to have my friend over without asking."

He rolled his head back and gave her a deadpan expression. "Yet you can't extend that same respect to me when it comes to cleaning...? I mean, today I made it pretty fucking clear that it would have been nice if you cleaned up this *one* time."

"Why? You're doing it."

She turned and walked back to the living room.

Ash had never felt such a vehement, blazing hot anger in his entire life. He slammed the dish in his hand into the sink, causing it to send water sloshing onto the counter. He took a vicious towel to his hands and forearms to dry them, and then he left the kitchen.

"Deadass, I'm really about to lose my shit," he said, voice loud as he looked at her. "Who the fuck do you think you are?"

Tayshia stared up at him in shock. She was on the floor again, the console in both hands. Her thumbs paused in their tapping and the music from the game played like a morbid 8-bit soundtrack to their Hellish roommate situation.

"Excuse me?" She breathed an incredulous laugh. "I know you're not talking to me like that."

"I have asked you ten *thousand* times to clean up after yourself!" he said, gesturing to the kitchen. "It's disgusting. You are disgusting. You leave your fucking dishes covered in food *everywhere* and I'm so sick of it!"

"No, because I *know* you're not talking to me like that!" she yelled, tossing the console onto the couch behind her and standing up. "I'm not disgusting just because I don't pick my dishes up!"

"*Fuck!*" He scrubbed his face with his hands, growling in his frustration and rage. "If you don't start cleaning up after yourself, I'll go down to the leasing office and pay the stupid fee to break the lease. Then, you can get your own place and you can trash it all you want. But this is *my* shit. *I* bought this stuff and I'd like it to be taken care of, *please.*"

"Yeah, because you have two thousand some-odd dollars lying around," she spat out bitterly, crossing her arms over her chest.

He raised his eyebrows. This was the last time he was gonna let her words hit into him like physical blows. Yes, he'd made bad choices. Yes, he probably did owe Tayshia some form of apology. And yes, he definitely owed her father one.

But did he deserve to be taken advantage of?

"In case you forgot, my mom is dead," he spat, his glare cutting across the distance towards her. "So yeah, I do have money lying around. Just a little under one hundred thousand dollars."

She blanched, sinking down onto the couch. "Oh."

With a scowl, Ash went back into the kitchen. His temperature was running high, his ire bringing sweat to prickle along the back of his neck. He reached over his head to grab the back of his crewneck, yanking it off and tossing it onto the dining room table. He felt his hair sticking up in multiple directions, but he paid it no mind as he fixed his tee shirt.

As he grabbed a dirty dish from the counter and plunged it beneath the surface of the hot water, taking a sponge to it, she came to stand beside him. She stood with the counter to her left and him to her right, her arm brushing his.

He stiffened.

"*What?*"

She glared up at him. "I'm coming to help, jeez! Why do you have to be so rude?!"

"I don't want your help."

"Kinda sounded like you did when you were out there screaming at me."

"Except that I wasn't screaming."

"Except that you were."

"Yeah, well fuck you." Ash's words came out as a snarl. "How 'bout that?"

Their eyes met, two separate flames of anger meeting to form an inferno.

"Why make such a big deal, yelling at me and acting pressed if you're just gonna act like a jerk when I'm here, actually doing it?!" she said, shouting. "You can't tell me to clean, then get pissed when I do!"

"Because you're only in here *because* I yelled at you, headass!" he shouted back. "You're not in here, trying to help because you actually want to. Even if you helped me now, you'd just go right back to being a fucking pig tomorrow!"

"I can't *stand* you!" she cried, shoving against his arm. "I'm not a pig! Who *says* that? God, you're so fucking rude!"

"And *I* can't stand *you*."

He shoved her back with one wet, soapy hand and she nearly careened to the left.

The moment his hand brushed against her hair, she smacked it away with a loud noise. Her voice when she spoke was threatening, the tone low.

"Do *not* touch my weave."

He scoffed. "Just get the fuck out."

"Do you want me to clean, or not?!"

"I want you to clean but right now, I want you to get the fuck out of my God damn face!" he shouted. He couldn't remember ever feeling this angry. He felt like he was dangling at the end of a frayed, burning rope. If she didn't knock it off, the rope was going to break and drop him into a vast coulee of fury.

"*Then stop yelling at me!*" Tayshia shoved him again, this time harder than the last.

He lost it.

"Are you fucking kidding me? No, for real—are you *fucking* kidding me right now?! You yelled at me first, all because I'm asking you to pull your fucking weight around here, and now you push me?

This apartment is *both* of ours. We *agreed* to keep shit clean!"

"It's not about the cleaning, all right?!" she said, one hand curved around the edge of the counter behind her and the other pointing a finger up at him. Her hood fell off from her having to crane her neck to look up at him.

"Then, what is it? Huh?" He turned to face her. She moved away, her lower back hitting the edge of the counter as he took a step toward her. "What is it? You trying to prove something to yourself? Is that it?"

"Stop," she said, her voice faltering. Her hand came up, pressing flat against his chest to stop him.

"Don't *touch* me!" he snapped, grabbing her wrist to pull it away.

She jumped, her eyes widening in fright, and she yanked back on her arm. Catching him by surprise, he stumbled forward, his hand slamming against the counter beside hers.

Trapping her.

"What is it you need to prove?" he asked, both of them breathless from the argument. It was late in the afternoon and the placement of their apartment in the complex awarded them only a little light. The kitchen had one window. Sunlit shadows flickered across her face. "You want to prove I'm a bad guy so you can feel better about doing whatever you want?"

"No," she said, her voice falling into a whisper. "I don't need to prove it to know it. And I do whatever I want, whenever I want."

"I guess that means if you don't want to clean, you're not going to."

"Did you want me to get on my knees and apologize to you for it, King Ashley?" she said, her tone snide.

Ash almost laughed, his hands back in the water again. "If you're gonna get down on your knees for me, it's not gonna be to apologize."

The silence stretched between them, so taut that Ash felt like he couldn't breathe. It was too far. He'd said something completely out of pocket. Honestly, this entire situation was the *epitome* of going too far.

And then Tayshia snapped.

She whirled on him, her hands balled into fists as she beat them against his arms and chest. She looked beside herself with a combination of terror and anger that went beyond a boiling point.

This was deeper than a fight over the dishes.

Ash's mind went blank. He saw red, painted across his field of vision like it were trying to color him with rage. His father had laid hands on him more times than he could count. He wasn't about to stand here and let Tayshia do it, too.

They fought, hands slapping against forearms, fending one another off, until Ash got fed up with her antics. He managed to grab both of her wrists and slam her back against the counter, their bodies flush against one another's. She writhed in his grip, twisting her hands and baring her teeth up at him. It was like she'd gone feral.

"What the fuck is wrong with you?!" he yelled, his hair shrouding his eyes from the struggle. "Are you high?!"

"Don't touch me! Let me go! Let *go* of me!" She was screaming, shrieking like a banshee and red in the face.

What the Hell was wrong with her?

Somehow, his confusion caused him to loosen his hold. She got her right hand free and then, before he could blink, she'd slapped him. Smacked him right across the face like she weren't the one who needed to be restrained. Her hair was in her face, her cheeks flushed and lips parted as she gasped for air. She looked terrified.

But *slapping* him?

Absolutely fucking not.

Ash's hand slammed up, gripping the lower half of her face. His fingers spanned from cheek to cheek, pressing inward as he forced her to look at him. He wasn't thinking. He was only reacting.

"Don't fucking hit me, little girl," he breathed out, his gaze scanning her terrified eyes. "I am *not* the one."

Something inside her eyes changed, shifting like the tides of the ocean, and her hands came up to curl around his fingers on either side, trying to pry his hand away.

"Let me go," she said, her voice small and strained. She looked like she was about to start crying. "I'm sorry. I'll clean. Just please let me go."

Shit.

Ash let go of her, his wet hand shaking as he pushed it through his hair. He moved away from her and she dashed out of the kitchen without saying anything else. He heard her bedroom door slam shut moments later, leaving him alone in the kitchen.

He faced the sink, leaning over it with his hands on the counter. He took deep breaths, struggling to calm himself down.

It was so stupid. An argument over the dishes had just become a domestic dispute. Tayshia had managed to pull emotions out of him that he hadn't felt before. Anger that was blinding. A complete lack of control.

And a really bizarre urge to kiss her.

CHAPTER TEN

The next day—September the 22nd—Ash made it to one class before he went home.

He felt sick to his stomach after what had happened yesterday. It wasn't just Tayshia that had acted out—he had, too. They'd both crossed a line that never should have been crossed with one another. There was no way to talk about it, either, because not only was he embarrassed, but Quinn was supposed to be driving in that day. He doubted Tayshia had any desire to talk about the fact that they'd fought the day before her birthday.

As he drove down the mountain, he thought about getting her something.

It would be an apology gift more so than a birthday gift. Yes, she'd freaked out on him and started throwing blows, but when he thought about it, it was his fault.

Because he *had* freaked her out. While he was cleaning the kitchen, he'd gone over the events that had taken place in his mind and realized that she'd had a meltdown *because* she was scared. He'd scared her. And she clearly was the sort to lash out with anger when afraid.

Just like him.

So, yeah. He felt like he needed to apologize. They were just dirty dishes. Dirty dishes did not warrant a full-blown screaming match. And it was her birthday today. Thus, a gift.

He didn't really know what she was interested in. She was always wearing hoodies or sweaters, and he never saw her wearing any jewelry except for the crystal.

Which was strange.

Ash knew why he wore his. It tied him to his mother and to a time before everything was shitty. It represented something that ran deeper than nostalgia.

What did it mean for her?

Ash went to the store, standing in front of one of the gift card towers for so long that he wasn't sure what he was looking at anymore. He knew she liked food because she was always cooking and eating, but what restaurants did she like? Were restaurant gift cards good birthday presents? And even if they were, would she *accept* a gift from him?

It wasn't like he was friends with her.

He'd finally reached up to grab one when an elderly woman stopped beside him with her cart. She peered at him for a long moment, until he looked down at her in confusion.

The woman was glaring at him.

"You should be ashamed of yourself," she'd spat, her pearls seeming comically nineties against the backdrop of her paisley shirt. *"You should have left when you were released. This town would like to heal from the damage you and your father caused. Not have to look at it all... Covered in tattoos while they're grocery shopping."*

He left without buying Tayshia anything.

When he got home, there were still four or five hours left in the school day, so he had the apartment to himself. He blasted his music and laid on the couch, staring at the ceiling and contemplating leaving town. It wasn't like there was anything here for him, besides his friends. But his friends were all going away for college at the end of the school year, anyway. The pre-requisite program was meant to take the place of community or junior college—it had an ending, and then everything would change.

When they all left, what would be here for him?

There was always the Sunamuras.

Ash hadn't texted Ryo back yet. He wasn't ready. Maybe he would be someday but right now? Especially after what that woman had said to him in the store?

If he tried to reconnect with them, what if they felt the same way?

All the questions rolling around in his head sent him drifting off to sleep, right there on the couch.

✡✡✡

"Kieran, chill. What I'm wearing is fine."

"Tayshia, are you stupid? No, really—are you *stupid*? It's shorter than a pair of *shorts*! Drop literally *anything*, and you'll be showing everyone your ass cheeks!"

"Oh, God. Whatever. The hem is at my *fingertips*. It's not shorter than the dresses that everyone else at school wears, and I'm not gonna let you just... Like, assassinate my character to make the way I look easier for you to handle. It's *just* a *dress*!"

"Just a dress? *Just a dress*? A dress that *invites*, Tayshia. Your chest is—and your *legs*."

"Yes, Kieran. I have legs. I have legs, an ass, and tits, and I've even got a vagina. Shocking, I know. You're unbelievable. *Absolutely unbe*—"

"So you're going out like that? You're just gonna... Walk around like some slut again? Then you wouldn't mind if I treated you exactly the way you're wanting to be treated. Since that's how you're insisting on dressing."

"Can we just not fight? Please? Quinn is literally almost here and it's my birthday. My roommate is right down the hall."

"Oh, your roommate? Your roommate, huh? Yeah, and I bet you'd fuck him, too."

Ash heard the angry voices coming from the hallway, digging holes into his sleep and rousing him from a deathlike slumber. It took him a moment to realize that the voices he was hearing belonged to Tayshia and Kieran.

He remained in his position, stretched out along the length of the long side of the sectional with his ankles crossed and his phone on his chest. He didn't know what was going on, but what he knew for certain was that Tayshia was so far from being a slut that if he woke up one day to find out she was, he might just think he was living in an alternate dimension.

When he heard a gasp, an *ugh* of frustration, and then the sounds of a bit of a struggle, it chased the last vestiges of Ash's sleep away.

Ash was not Tayshia's friend, but none of those sounds were acceptable.

"Get your hands off of me!" Tayshia sounded white-hot with rage. "*Kieran, don't touch me!*"

"Why? You're fine with letting everyone look at you, but you can't even let your boyfriend touch you?" Kieran scowled with mirthless amusement. "Well, that's unsurprising."

"What the Hell is your problem, Kieran? Stop it!"

Ash stood, holding back a waking yawn and combing his fingers through sleep-ruffled hair. He walked across the living room, around the short side of the couch, and looked down the hall.

The completely mismatched, unfortunate couple stood in front of Tayshia's bedroom door, Kieran towering over the smaller girl with his hands in the air between them. Tayshia had both of her hands wrapped around his wrists, and she was clenching her teeth as she pushed against them. Her arms shook and his didn't, so it was clear that she was fighting to keep him from touching her. She looked angrier than Ash had ever seen her.

Upon seeing the way her arms were about to give out, Ash was certain that he was angrier than she was.

Kieran scoffed. His back was to Ash, and neither he nor Tayshia had realized he was at the mouth of the hallway.

"I'm starting to get frustrated, Tay," Kieran said. "You keep saying over and over again that you're not ready and that you just need time, but it's been *weeks* since Paris. It's been weeks of excuses and deflection, and it doesn't make any *sense*. You're my *girlfriend*, and I think we've waited long enough, don't you?"

Tayshia looked offended, and then her eyes slid past her boyfriend's upper arm. Ash, who had drifted closer to stare without shame, caught her gaze.

He arched one eyebrow as if to say, *Do you know what you're doing?*

She immediately shut her mouth. Upon the faltering of her strength, Ash saw Kieran surging forward to kiss her on the mouth. A muffled cry rang out.

"It's not so bad, Tayshia, see?" Kieran said between kisses to her jaw and neck. "If you'd just relax, then everything... Would be... Fine."

Tayshia's eyes widened as Kieran pushed her against her bedroom door hard enough to rattle the wood on its hinges. Her hands came up to flail a bit before slapping against his chest as her gaze traveled a frantic path between the two men.

Well, Ash was going back to jail.

Kieran groaned in frustration, hands held against Tayshia's pinned shoulders as he tilted his head back.

"Tayshia, this is fucking – "

The waters of ire churning inside of Ash rose, snapping to attention. Within moments, he was standing behind Kieran with his hand tangled in the brown hair on the top of his thrown-back head. Ash glowered down into his eyes, blazing blue meeting astonished brown.

"This is fucking *what?*" he snarled. "Care to finish your sentence in front of the whole class?"

Kieran looked disoriented, as if he couldn't understand where he was, and then his face twisted with rage. He reached up and clawed at Ash's hold on him. Ash let him go but grabbed the shoulder of his jersey and yanked him backward, away from Tayshia. In one smooth movement, Ash turned his back to Tayshia, stepping halfway in front of her.

"What the fuck is wrong with you?!" Kieran cried.

"She's a woman, fuckface," Ash said, "and while I know that's something that probably makes no sense to you, when she says she doesn't want to fuck you, it means she doesn't want to fuck you."

Kieran stood up to his full height, the two men at eye level, and hissed, "Mind your own business, you tattooed freak. The fact that you're sharing an apartment with my girlfriend is shitty enough. I don't want to actually have to speak to you."

"What a coincidence. I didn't want to have to speak to you, either. Yet here we are."

Kieran's upper lip curled and he lowered his voice. "You don't know how fucking *lucky* you are."

"Okay, come on, you guys," Tayshia said. "This is so extra."

Tayshia moved forward, but Ash threw his arm out to the side to stop her. She gave him an incredulous look, no doubt as confused as he was to his anger, but he knew better. He would be able to handle this nonsense better than she could.

"Tell me, Kieran," Ash taunted in a menacing tone. "Do I need to speak to you, or can you behave?"

"Ash, for real! This is stupid!" Tayshia cried.

Ash's outstretched hand twitched in a firm, final movement to silence her. He watched as Kieran flexed his fists. His body tensed. He didn't want to fight him but if he had to, he would. It wasn't like Kieran didn't deserve it after all the assholery he and his football teammates had put the scholarship kids through over the years.

That was the downside of being on probation. If Ash got into a fight, even to defend someone, all it would take was one word to his probation officer to tear what little opportunity for a future he had apart.

"You're a piece of shit, Ash," Kieran growled, but his hands remained at his sides. "What my girlfriend and I do is *our* business—"

123

"In the middle of our tiny, shared apartment?" Ash snorted. "I was napping right there, in the open. I *heard* you."

Kieran bared his teeth, taking a step into Ash's personal space. "Soon, you can go right back to napping, can't you? When I knock you out the way I've been wanting to for *years!*"

Ash smirked and held Kieran's gaze.

"That makes two of us."

"Both of you!" Tayshia cried, trying to push Ash's arm out of her way. "Stop it! You're acting like *children*."

Ash ignored her, curling his arm back to move her behind him. He was acting on pure instinct at this point, and instinct told him that in five seconds, he was going to throw away his entire future to punch Kieran O'Connell in the face.

"Or maybe I should give you a taste of your own medicine," Kieran went on to say. "Maybe I hold a gun on *you* and remind you the reason why your dad is rotting in a cell."

Ash's ire was blinding, interrupted only by the fact that Tayshia was trying to go around him again. If this bitch didn't knock it the fuck off... He repeated his earlier movement, holding his arm outward to block her path.

He almost felt bad for her. She had no idea about her little boyfriend's sordid activities with her best friend. Ash had no intentions of using that information until it was absolutely necessary, but right now he felt *sorely* tempted.

If it weren't for the fact that this asshole needed a lesson about consent, he might have said fuck it and blurted it out.

Instead, Ash said, "You literally know fuck-all about me. But in a few moments? You're going to know all that you need to. If a girl doesn't want you, then you step back. You don't force yourself on her in the hallway."

"I wasn't forcing her to do anything!"

"No means no. Did they forget to teach that to you at church, or do you just ignore it to get what you want?"

Kieran whipped his fist back, but Tayshia wasn't having any of it. She ducked underneath Ash's arm and stood in the middle of them both.

"Knock it the Hell off!" she said through her teeth, snapping her fingers in a slashing motion across the air. "Right now! This is beyond outta control."

"What, are you on *his* side?" Kieran scowled with disgust.

"Tayshia, I'm not some felon. I'm not going to force you to do anything you don't want to do."

Ash let out an incredulous laugh, but Tayshia spoke before he could. Her words were clipped in tone.

"Boy, you just did, and it's *not* okay. But I am not discussing this with you until we're in private. I want you to wait outside for me."

Kieran opened his mouth to reply, but a knock at the front door had them all looking back down the hallway.

"It's probably Quinn," Tayshia muttered, pushing past Kieran to go answer it. She opened the front door, putting on a fake chipper voice when she greeted her friend. "Hey, girl. Took you long enough!"

"Happy birthday, girlie!" Quinn threw her arms around Tayshia, shaking her from side-to-side with excitement.

"Thanks," Tayshia said. "Come in and set your stuff down so we can go eat."

"He's not like, *here*, is he?" Quinn practically crept inside, carrying a pink tote bag along with her purse. She grimaced when her eyes met Ash's, then frowned when she saw Kieran standing in front of him. "Oh. Hey, guys."

Ash raised one eyebrow. Was her awkwardness from speaking because she hadn't realized he was there, or because she was looking into the eyes of Kieran, the guy she was cheating with?

"What's like, going on?" Quinn asked, following Tayshia down the hall. "Why are you guys standing in front of her door? That's sus."

"We were having a discussion," Kieran said with a tight smile.

"Yeah, and the discussion is over," Tayshia said, moving in-between the boys again. She looked up at Ash with a pointed look. "Can you move so she can put her stuff in there?"

Ash opened his mouth, but Kieran cut in.

"Oh, so you can be all nice to *him,* but when you talk to me, you act like a complete bitch?" Kieran appeared revolted. "What, did *he* tell you it was okay to dress like a slut? Is *he* the one you're spreading your legs for, if it isn't me? You like criminals covered in ink? You might as well start sending letters to prisoners. Better yet — why don't you just write to his dad?!"

"*Kieran!*" both Tayshia and Quinn cried at the same time.

"I'm going back to jail," Ash said, laughing in incredulity as he dragged his hands down his face. "I am *going* back to *jail* if you don't get him the fuck out of my face."

"Oh, shut your dramatic ass up, Ash." Tayshia said. Then, she turned to Kieran. "I don't know what's going on with you, but you are a literal nightmare lately."

"I don't know what's going on with *you!*" Kieran threw his hands up into the air, all but shouting down into her face as though Ash weren't even there.

"This is so toxic." Quinn crossed her arms over her chest, leaned against the wall, and popped her gum. "You guys shouldn't be together if you can't treat each other right."

Ash wanted to roll his eyes. She *would* say that. Anything to free him up for her and absolve herself of the guilt.

"There's nothing going on with me," Tayshia said, her brow furrowed. "You're the one who's always angry with me, Kieran. You're the one who's always acting like you're three steps away from punching me in the face."

"Maybe that's because you piss me off!" Kieran snapped. "Ever since this Summer, you've acted like a complete prude."

This Summer?

What happened between them this Summer?

Tayshia paled. "Kieran, this isn't something we should talk about in front of people."

"Why, because you don't want everyone to know that you're like, the *worst* girlfriend on the planet?"

"No!"

"Wait a minute." Kieran peered at her. "Are you cheating on me?"

Ash almost dissolved into laughter when he saw Quinn's eyebrows shoot up. The *delusion*.

"Are you for real?" Tayshia asked, her hands on her hips. Her hair rippled red down her back. "Are you fucking *serious*?"

"The only reason why you could be so *against* sleeping with me is because you're hooking up with someone else like a *fucking whore!*"

She stumbled back, flinching under the loud onslaught of Kieran's words. When her back hit Ash's chest, his hands came up to grip her shoulders on instinct.

The tension in the air.

The slight tremble he felt in her body.

The fact that a man was raising his voice to a woman with

126

shoulders that were small enough to break with the right pressure.

The guilt at the fact that Ash had yelled at her just the day before.

"Get the fuck out of our apartment," he said, lowering his chin and giving Kieran a dark, stormy look. It was a look that he felt searing to the core of his bones. "Right now."

"Our?" Kieran stepped closer, until Ash felt Tayshia leaning back into him to keep distance. "*Our?*"

"*Mine.*" Ash's fingers flexed against Tayshia's shoulders. "Get the fuck out of *my* apartment, before I lay your ass out."

The silence was thick, broken only by Tayshia's anxious breathing. Kieran inhaled. Ash prepared himself for a fistfight right there in the hall.

Quinn scowled, shattering the tension.

"Just go outside, Kieran."

His mouth opened and closed in protest. "But—I—"

"*Go* outside!" Quinn fixed him with a reprimanding look. "Wait for me and Tay downstairs."

Kieran sneered one final time at Ash, his face flushed with anger, and then he stormed out. He exchanged glances with Quinn that probably meant nothing to Tayshia. Glances that Ash could decipher from a mile away.

When the front door shook the wall, Ash turned Tayshia to face him. He dropped one hand to his side and used the other to comb his hair back again.

"Are you losing your mind, or is it only me that you stand up to? You *let* him talk to you like that?"

Her face was calm. "Don't talk to me about losing my mind when you lose your shit over dirty dishes."

"Oh, that's hilarious, coming from the girl who can't stand when I touch those dishes."

"It's neither my fault nor my problem that you have a problem with my relationship. Nor is it my problem that you don't understand that sometimes, homes get a little dirty. Now, thank you for—"

"Don't," he said with a disgusted look. "Don't do that."

"Don't what?"

"Don't thank me. Handle your business."

"*Handle* my business?" She glanced behind her at Quinn, who just shrugged and looked away. Tayshia tsked and faced Ash again.

"Handle my business. Okay."

"It looks like you've got two choices," Ash said. "You either break it off, or you fuck him. And since you don't want to do the latter, it should be crystal clear."

"It's not *your* business."

"You *made* it my business when you carried on your throw-down in the hallway."

Her eyes flashed with fury. "Then if we're sharing business, would you care to tell me why you're always staring at me in the cafeteria?"

Ash wanted to laugh and scream at the same time. She was like a damn firecracker. Before Kieran, she'd been like a mouse beside a lion. But here Ash was and she was a lioness transformed, with a mane of flames and words that cut like claws.

He tilted his head to the side and scrutinized her, crossing his arms.

"Why *aren't* you sleeping with him?" he asked.

"I told you, it's not your business."

She started past him, towards her bedroom door, but he moved in front of the doorknob. Ash unfolded one arm and held up a hand to the front of her shoulder before recrossing his arms. Behind Tayshia, Quinn watched the entire conversation with a wide-eyed, interested expression.

"Why haven't you slept with him? He's your boyfriend, your *man*. You guys have been together for like, four years. You must love him or have some sort of attraction to him. So, why not sleep with him?" Ash decided to push the boundary, uncaring of the fact that Quinn was there. "Aren't you worried he might find what he's looking for in some other girl?"

At his words, Quinn coughed and shifted her weight from one foot to the other.

Tayshia averted her gaze for a moment before it snapped back upward. "I *said* it's not your fucking business, Ash. And fine, I won't thank you for what you did. I guess I was asking for it. Must be the dress."

He hadn't even thought to look at the catalyst to this whole situation. Arms still crossed, Ash's gaze swept down the length of her body.

Holy fuck.

Tayshia wore a thigh-length black dress with long sleeves, a cinched waist, and a floaty, short skirt. It had a plunging neckline that went to her sternum and silver detailing woven around the hem. Her legs were clad in sheer black tights and her feet in a pair of black combat boots. Her make-up was done, complete with false lashes and her lips stained red. Around her neck hung the silver chain that connected to her half of the amethyst. The crystal stood out glittering and purple against the backdrop of black fabric.

He'd never really looked at her body before, and now that he was, he could feel something turning in his abdomen. She was tall, her shoulders narrow and her neck long and lithe. Her cheekbones were round and her chin sharp, her nose wide and straight. She had one of the most expressive faces he'd ever encountered; the emotions she felt flickered across it like candlelight.

In the back of his mind, something nagged at him. Something that shook and trembled, warning him that somehow and in some way, it was dangerous to be this close to her. To be talking to her like this. It was a tension that was as terrifying as it was enticing.

It was like she was a drug that he'd been denying himself access to for years and now, it was right in front of him.

Ash leaned forward a bit, his lips twisting into a smirk. He spoke in a murmur.

"Kieran's an idiot. If you were my date, and you were wearing that dress? I'd be spending my evening eye-fucking you—not berating you like I'm blaming you for being hot."

Her eyes searched his and then, she moved back. Quinn was still leaning against the wall, looking on as though they were a daytime soap opera.

"It's not your business," Tayshia repeated, the words coming out slow and sure.

"What the Hell is wrong with you?" Ash said. "Why are you letting some guy walk all over you when you literally come for me every chance you get?"

"It's not," she hissed, eyes bright, "your *business*. Quinn, leave your stuff here in the hall and let's go to dinner."

Quinn dropped her bag to the floor, her lips pursed in a *this is so awkward* expression as she turned and started for the front door. Tayshia went after her, but Ash moved as fast as he could to block her way.

"Will you wait?" he said, irritated. "For fuck's sake. Quit trying to leave. I'm *talking* to you."

She stared up at him, a crack showing in her armor—the armor he could now see wrapped around her. Her mouth opened as she searched for words. The tension increased, to the point where he almost wanted to be the first one to look away. Then, she faltered and lowered her eyes for a moment. She stared at his neck tattoos, gaze tracing the outlines, and then finally she looked past him at her friend and the door.

"I need to go," she said quietly. Defeated. "I... I hope you have a good night."

Ash spun to face her as she walked past him. "Where?"

"What do you mean *where*?"

"I mean, where are you going? Which restaurant?"

Quinn gave him a weird look. "Why, are you trying to come, too?"

Tayshia whirled around. "We're walking down the street to go to dinner. What do you care?"

"What?" Alarm bells rang in his head. He walked out into the living room. "*Why*?"

"Because it's my birthday and it was already my plans. Quinn is here specifically to go to dinner. Kieran's waiting." She eyed him with suspicion. "Why do you care?"

"Bro. He just assaulted you in the hallway, and you want to go to dinner with him."

"Yeah, but like... Why do you *care*, though?" Quinn asked, interjecting. "Because like—I mean, yeah."

Ash straightened his back. "I don't."

Tayshia stared at him for a second longer before she turned to go. Quinn opened the door, letting warm, early Fall air in.

Ash's thoughts raced against one another. He didn't know why he was so invested in this situation, but when he thought about who he was now compared to who he was before jail, he knew that he couldn't let the past get in the way of him making sure she wasn't attacked by her boyfriend again.

Could he really just sit in the apartment eating microwave meals or some equally lame shit, knowing that Kieran was so entitled that he'd assault her in the hallway while Ash was *asleep* on the *couch*?

"Well, which restaurant is it?" he repeated.

Quinn and Tayshia exchanged bewildered glances.

"Gianni's Diner," Tayshia said. "Again—*why*?"

"One second," he muttered, walking around the couch. He retrieved his phone, typing in the passcode and pulling open the texting app to formulate his lie.

"What are you doing?"

"Elijah's gonna come through. He and I were already going to the store tonight. Maybe we'll come in to eat."

"*With us?*" Tayshia spluttered. "Kieran wouldn't like that, Ash!"

"Do I," he said as he typed a hasty message to Elijah to come over, "look like a guy who cares what Kieran likes?"

Quinn cleared her throat, hiding a short laugh.

"You can't come to the restaurant with us," Tayshia said. "You literally cannot."

"Yes, I can," he said, his gaze snapping up to meet hers after he sent the message. "I can do whatever the fuck I want."

Her head pulled back. "Well... Yes. Obviously you can *go* to the same restaurant. But you can't come sit at our *table*."

"Why not?"

"Because you can't."

"Why not?" The phone buzzed. Elijah had replied.

"Ash. You can't invite yourself to *my* birthday dinner."

"Oh, *my* God," Quinn said, popping her gum, raising her eyebrows, and twisting her lips to the side. She tucked her hair behind one ear.

"All right, fine," he said, seeing that Elijah was on his way. "But we can walk with you. We're going in the same direction, aren't we?"

"What?"

"Wait here." Ash turned and walked towards his room to grab his wallet.

"No! I—"

"I said *wait*."

He left her there. As he was pulling on a black hooded sweatshirt with a deathcore band splashed across the front, his phone buzzed again. Elijah was already pulling into the parking lot of the complex. His mother's house was only two streets away, so Ash wasn't surprised he'd arrived so quickly.

When Ash came back out, Quinn and Tayshia both looked like they'd just eaten sour grapes.

"I've never felt more unwanted," Ash said.

"You're not serious, are you?" Quinn said. "Are you actually like, serious? You're coming with us."

"Yeah," Ash said as he slipped his wallet into the back pocket of his skinny jeans. He looked down at them while he adjusted his hood.

"On the *entire* walk?" Tayshia asked.

"Yes, on the *entire* walk."

"Ew," Quinn said.

Ash narrowed his eyes at them both.

"Is the public street off limits to me? Am I not *allowed* to walk on it when you're there? Do you *own* the street? Can I not—"

"What are you trying to pull?" Tayshia's teeth were clenched.

"I was already going," he lied with effortless skill. He then moved towards the door and shot the girls an impatient look. "Come. I don't have all night."

"But—" Tayshia looked like she was high as a kite, she was *that* dumbstruck. "But we're going with Kieran."

"And now I'm no longer allowed to walk down the street if your dick-for-brains boyfriend happens to be on it at the same time?"

"That's not what I..." Tayshia trailed off. She looked to Quinn, who gave her a shrug. "All right. Fine. You can walk with us. But you better not pop off on him. Just keep your hands to yourself. When we get there, then you and your friend need to go off to do whatever felonious things you have planned to do."

Ash stood aside as the girls walked past him. His keys jangled as he used them to lock the front door. He heard Elijah's and Kieran's voices echoing up the outdoor stairwell.

"Verbal confirmation, bitch," Tayshia snapped.

As Quinn headed down the stairs to get to Mr. Secret McBoyfriendson before his actual girlfriend did, Ash leaned over Tayshia's shoulder from behind. He bit his lip through a grin and raised his eyebrows. Tayshia stopped dead in her tracks, looking up at him as he spoke in a quiet voice.

"Don't pop off, hands to myself, felonious things. Got it."

CHAPTER
ELEVEN

"What the Hell is *he* doing here?"

"I'm coming with you," Ash said. "Although, Tayshia here has explained to me that I'm not allowed to go if you're going. Imagine my surprise, because I could swear Crystal Springs was a town that was open to everyone. Even felons."

"Oh, for God's sake." Tayshia scowled and pushed past the both of them, leaving Quinn behind beside Kieran.

"That's not what I said. Let's just go."

Kieran stood rooted to his spot. Ash gave him a lingering stare before he followed Tayshia, a slight spring to his step. When both Kieran and Quinn failed to come, Tayshia whirled around, her face shadowed with anger.

"Kieran! Quinn! Come *now*, or I'll go to this stupid dinner by myself!"

After an exchange of disgruntled glances, the two surged ahead, leaving Ash behind with Elijah.

"So... What is this?" Elijah murmured as they headed across the apartment complex's parking lot, weaving through cars.

"Damage control," Ash muttered.

"And who did the damage? You or him?"

"We both did."

Elijah started to say something, but as they stepped onto the sidewalk, Tayshia's voice came floating back towards them.

"Knock it off, Kieran. He's literally just walking down the street."

"What, he can't walk *before* we do? Or after? Tayshia, I don't want anyone to see us and think we're actually friends with the guy who —"

"*Just — !*" Tayshia angrily pinched her fingers together and pulled them across the air in front of her lips. "Zip it."

"It's a little sus, though," Quinn added. "I thought you guys like, hated each other?"

Tayshia made a little noise of exasperation and then threw her hands up into the air. "I give up. It's my birthday and you guys are ganging up on me. I'm sick of all this negativity. It's stressful. So, you guys can either cry about it, or go back to your cars and drive off. Otherwise, I'm hungry and want to go to Gianni's to get my damn pasta."

Ash held in a spurt of incredulous laughter. It was rather nice having the front row seat to someone else's dismantling at the words of Tayshia Cole, rather than his own. He'd known she was snarky, but he supposed he'd never noticed due to always being on the brunt end of it.

"No one is *ganging up* on you," Quinn said. "Don't be dramatic and play the victim all the time."

"I hope you know you're buying me whatever I want," Elijah said to Ash, pulling his attention away as they all traipsed down the quiet street. They passed buildings that were no longer in business, factories, and random shops that had been there for years. "You got that cash-cash, so I wanna see you pay up. You pulled me off of streaming tonight."

"Your stream will be fine," Ash said, rolling his eyes.

"Um, no. Every minute I spend *not* streaming is another minute of money lost. The only reason why I'm *not* on scholarship is because of it."

"Whatever. But yeah, I'll buy you food, man. But pretend you actually want to be here—my lie was shit, but it still needs to hold."

"It'll be so, so, so difficult," Elijah said with a grimace.

Ash rolled his eyes and slung his arm around Elijah's neck for a moment, pulling him along with the group. As they neared the other three, Tayshia turned. She smiled up at Elijah, who was about three or four inches shorter than Ash.

"Hey, Elijah," Tayshia said. "What's up?"

"Hey, Tayshia," he said with a grin. "Happy birthday. Hi, Quinn."

Quinn turned to give Elijah a quick smile, then faced the front again. Ash didn't know if Elijah noticed the bitchiness, but Ash sure did. He fought the urge to sneer.

Who was she to act rude to his friend when she was fucking Tayshia's boyfriend?

"I was gonna get you a present," Elijah said, "but you know, poverty. So, are we all eating at the same booth?"

"*No!*" Kieran shouted, his voice ringing in the air, which felt thick with the humidity of impending rain. "I'd rather be dead than share a table with him."

Elijah grimaced, but Ash's reply came lightning-fast.

"It's probably for the best," he said. "I don't feel like paying for all of the meals."

"How do you have any fucking money?" Kieran cried. "How does he have any money?!"

Ash walked ahead of them, stifling laughter against his knuckles as he heard the consternation behind him. Poking fun at Kieran was too easy. He didn't care if it was juvenile—he was so reactionary.

"So, Ash, I gotta tell you this *really* crazy thing that happened today in my literature class."

Elijah jogged forward, turning to walk backwards ahead of Ash and waving his hands about as he spoke. His face appeared animated, with his sparse eyebrows wiggling and his brown eyes widening with every inflection of his tone. He kept looking behind him, making sure he wasn't going to trip over anything.

Tayshia fell in-step beside Ash, her eyes fixed ahead of her. Ash didn't care where Kieran was, but he assumed he was plodding along behind them with his tree trunk legs and boulder feet, Quinn at his side.

Ash arched an eyebrow.

"You need my permission to speak, or...?"

"Oh, right, yeah. No. Okay, so first like, it was Miss Iqbal and she was..." He blinked and shook his head out. "Wait, no. Let me start over. Okay, okay, okay. So, you know how I have Myths & Legends first period? You guys have it for an afternoon class, right?"

Following Elijah's stories had always been like trying to hold onto an eel with oily hands.

"*Right?*"

"Yes," Ash and Tayshia said simultaneously.

"Right, so, Miss Iqbal was showing us this fairytale about this guy who was trying to trick a fey into letting him go. Cuz like, he got trapped by one." Elijah appeared excited. "And so I was like, but what if you didn't want the fey to let you go? Like, what if it was like, a really hot faerie with like—" He gestured to the top of his head. "—Really nice hair, you know? And—"

Tayshia snorted. "That wasn't even the point of the fairytale. The point was cultural. Back in the time it was written, the people were actually scared of faeries. So, it was like, a warning for children. Like a, *stay away from the hills* type story."

"Well, like," Elijah said in an awkward tone, still walking backward, "it was just a fairytale for kids. It wasn't serious. I'm just talking like... Like out of my ass. I'm not trying to debate fairytale logic. I don't think the fairytale was that deep. I'm trying to tell you guys what happened today."

"Are you kidding me?" she said to Elijah, a bit breathless as she walked.

"Wha—how? How would I be kidding?"

"It *is* that deep. Fairytales are important literature because they show us what was going in the world culturally back then. Things that you can find in history books. That's why Miss Iqbal wanted us to analyze the story. It's not..."

Ash tuned her out, looking back over his shoulder. Kieran stomped a few yards back, muttering to Quinn under his breath. Ash then turned back to look at Tayshia, cutting her off.

"Look, we know you've got a hard-on for academia, but can't you just let it go? This is annoying. It's just a book, and neither of us care."

"I don't have a *hard-on* for anything!" Tayshia hissed, her fists clenching. "Just because I *care* about my classes doesn't mean I have some sort of... Weird obsession. Unlike the two of you, I *read*, and—"

"*What?*" Ash gave a loud gasp, his head snapping down to look at her in horror. "You *read*?!"

Elijah burst out laughing, and Tayshia raised her hand as if she were going to smack Ash's arm. She stopped herself, but still glared at him.

"Holy shit, Ash." Elijah said, holding his stomach and slowing down his pace on the pavement. "Stop. I'm dying."

Suddenly, Kieran called Tayshia's name. She whirled around, her hand flying up and nearly slamming into Ash's face. He barely pulled his head out of the way in time, his hand snapping up to wrap around her wrist. Ash looked down, noticing that there were some darker brownish marks on the knuckles of her forefingers that looked somewhat singular and out of place. Like they didn't belong there, or like someone had painted them onto her.

"Can you watch it?" he said in a low tone.

She stared at him like a deer in headlights.

"Let go of my hand."

Ash did, and then Quinn and Kieran stopped beside them. Quinn watched with the same curious expression she'd had on her face in the apartment.

"Sorry to interrupt your friendship circle," she said. "What were you guys talking about?"

Elijah said, "We—"

"Does it matter?" Kieran snapped, glaring up at Ash. "There's no reason why you should be walking alone with guys who aren't your boyfriend, Tayshia."

God fucking *damn*. Ash wanted to blurt out the truth about him and Quinn *so* bad, but he couldn't. It would ruin Tayshia's birthday and while they didn't get along, he wasn't cruel.

"She can walk where she wants," Ash drawled. "Fuck's sake."

"So, walk."

Kieran wrapped his hand around Tayshia's wrist, dragging her. She yelped, her feet stumbling as she pitched forward, and then she fell onto her knees. Her wrist wrenched out of his grasp as gravity tugged her downward. He gave her a wry look.

"Get up off the ground," he said. "You should be more careful."

Elijah and Ash both moved forward toward her at the same time, but Ash got there first. He leaned down and took her by the elbows, hauling her to her feet.

"Thank you," she said. "Er—well, you said not to thank you. But I don't really care, so thank you."

He was silent.

Across his mind's field of vision, he saw her the way he saw her in his dreams: smiling bright and merry through a haze of shadows. Then, the image shifted and he saw darkness, hearing her screams echoing in his skull. August 17th—the nightmare. The one where he saw nothing but heard everything.

He wished he knew what it meant.

Ash let go of her arms as though she'd burned him, and then he sent a dark look Kieran's way. Quinn stood behind him, still popping her gum.

"Do you make it a point to treat your girlfriend like shit, or is that just your personality, dickwad?" Ash snarled.

"What's it to you?" Kieran shot back. "Because we can talk about it, if that's what you want."

"It was an accident," Tayshia said, dusting dirt off of the runs in her tights. Her face looked somewhat crestfallen.

It pissed Ash off.

"An accident." Elijah said the word as if he were tasting it.

Ash turned and resumed walking down the street. He didn't know what the Hell he was doing. He wasn't Tayshia's friend, and he wasn't about to get sent to prison for defending her against her pet bulldog. She saved her dad's life by holding her hand over his gunshot wound.

She could take care of herself.

The group reached the halfway mark and turned the corner. Ash could see dark grey clouds rolling towards them across the Oregon sky, passing over the mountain their school was hidden upon. It would be the first rain of the Fall.

Ahead of them, the shopping centers were just beyond eyesight. They had about a mile to go before they reached the one that had Gianni's. Elijah and Ash would have to cross the street to get to the store they were headed to.

"How often do you think those *accidents* happen?" Elijah asked in a mutter.

"Who knows?" Ash rubbed his nose with the back of his tattooed hand, his eyes scanning the street. There weren't many cars out that evening. "I'm not exactly keeping tabs on her."

He shot a quick glance backward, seeing Kieran with his gaze on the ground as he walked. Quinn was beside him, her mouth moving as she said something. Tayshia had strayed to the back, her arms wrapped around herself with an expression of distaste on her face. He let his eyes linger for a moment.

"It's so bizarre," Elijah went on to say. "They're not as in *love* as everyone thinks they are. He's a jerk, isn't he?"

"Yeah." Ash turned back around to face the front. "He's always been, though."

"Does she know he's... You know...?"

"He's what?"

"You *know*. With Quinn?"

Ash side-eyed him, wondering if Elijah knew because of Ji Hyun and Andre, or because Kieran was an idiot. "If you knew who she was, why did you need to be introduced?"

"Because I didn't *know* her. I just knew what she looked like from before graduation. So, does she know?"

"Nah," Ash said. "I doubt it."

"Maybe we should like, tell her? Or something?"

Ash was silent, contemplating the purpose and the benefits. Telling her wouldn't erase their past, nor would it resolve the problems of their living situation. Telling her would gain him nothing because he had no personal stake in the matter.

And it would obliterate her birthday.

"Not our place," Ash said. "And I don't care."

"Yeah, yeah. You're right, you're..." Elijah trailed off, crossing his arms. "Ash, what if he like, hits her?"

Ash felt an uncomfortable chill run down his spine.

"What do you suggest?" he said. "Knock him out, tie him up, and shank him? I mean, come on."

"No, no, no!" Elijah waved his hands and then smacked Ash's arm. "Bro, no. I'm only saying that we—you're serious? No. We can't—no."

"There's not anything we *can* do, dude. In case you forgot, we aren't their friends."

"Hey. Tayshia's a friend to me. And Kieran's so..." He lowered his voice. "Suspect."

"Can you honestly say that if I tried anything with Kieran, I wouldn't get arrested? I was facing time in prison for what I—" He turned the conversation a bit. "Bottom line is that there's no point in interfering. I doubt Tayshia would stay with a guy that's beating on her."

"What if *I* care?" Elijah gave him a pleading look. "Come on! Just walk beside her and ask her. I'll distract the other two."

"Me? And you can't talk to her because... Why?"

"Do *you* want to distract him? I thought you were worried about *jail*?"

Ash paused, narrowing his eyes at his friend. He would prefer not having to spend time talking to Kieran, and he rather liked *not* being behind bars.

"Fine."

"Fine?"

"*Fine.*"

Elijah turned around and threw his hands up. "Kieran! Quinn! You guys up to talk superhero movies? Who's your favorite?"

He slung his arms around their necks and tugged them further down the sidewalk.

Ash stopped, looking behind him to see Tayshia still lagging behind. She plodded along like a toddler in too-big of shoes, her hair fluttering behind her. The early evening sunlight glinted off of the wavy burgundy strands, and her lips were parted, the tip of her tongue sticking out of the side of her mouth with exertion as she panted for breath. She looked up as she neared him. He saw her face take on her usual stoicism when she laid eyes on him.

"Ashley," she greeted, like they hadn't already walked three-quarters of the way to the restaurant together.

"Cease calling me by my government name if you don't want to be cancelled," he replied, falling in-step with her. He held up a hand. "Also, you walk slow."

"No, I don't." She was trying to control her breathing, like the walk was really taking it out of her. "You're simply too tall."

"Or maybe you're too short."

She huffed. "Why are you walking beside me? Why are you even walking *with* us?"

"I told you, I was already going to—"

"Cut the shit. I'm not stupid."

"Maybe I was just bored."

"Or maybe you're just being sus," she countered. "You're either trying to hide something, or cause drama."

Ash let out a laugh, watching the others conversing ahead of them. "I can assure you, I'm always trying to cause drama."

"So, you're *not* trying to hide something?"

"Nope." He rubbed the back of his neck with one hand. "What are you going to do? Beat me again?"

The silence was oppressive, broken by the slow pounding of their feet on the ground.

"I didn't *beat* you," she said in a haughty tone.

"Your hands were in fists like it was a tantrum, little girl."

She didn't speak and when Ash glanced down at her, he saw that her cheeks were as red as blood.

"And if the silence is an answer," Ash drawled, "then my next question would be why?"

"Tell me, O tall, white King. Why would I *beat* you?" Her tone was sardonic but her eyes were downcast. "It was a meltdown, but it was not a beating."

"I think you hit me because you wanted to," he said, leaning

140

down to lower his voice as they walked. "Because you're Tayshia Cole, and you're used to doing whatever you want."

"I'm not..." Her voice faltered. Ash saw her fidgeting with her fingernails. His gaze fell upon the brownish marks again. He wondered why they were only on those three fingers, and if they were a birthmark of some sort. "I'm not a violent person, but you were in my space and I thought you were going to... I just freaked out. So, I hit you. I didn't beat you, but I *did* want to do what I did. I was scared, Ash. You were screaming at me. It was an accident."

"An accident." He stretched out the syllables.

"Yes. An accident."

"Sort-of like how your boyfriend dragging you around was an accident." He gestured to the torn knees of her nylons. "Your tights are ruined, by the way."

"Ash, can you just fuck off?"

He felt her words like a lashing to the ears.

Tayshia's gaze slid off to the side. She focused on the cars on the road as though she were anxious. The expression was so out of place on her face that he felt his anger drain a bit.

"Right," he said. "Well, don't expect me to help you when he inevitably shows you how fucked up he is."

"I didn't ask for your help. I didn't ask for *anyone's* help, and I certainly don't need it."

"Oh, *clearly.*" A sour taste lingered in his mouth. "Your relationship is about as messy as the way you treat our fucking house, so I'm wholly unsurprised."

"How would you know me well enough to be surprised or unsurprised?!"

They were nearing the entrance to the shopping center. Elijah seemed to have led the others into it, so Ash and Tayshia were now alone.

"Oh, I know you," he said to Tayshia, stopping with his hands slipping into his pockets. Several strands of his blond hair fell forward but he didn't bother to push them back. "The person you show everyone outside of our apartment isn't the person you really are. The books and the studying and the attitude is all just a disguise you wear to cover up that your life is as much of a mess as everyone else's."

She faced him, hands balled into fists at her sides. "You think my life's a mess just because I leave a few dishes around?"

"I think your life's a mess because you spend so much time trying to prove to everyone that you've got everything all figured out. You're Tayshia Cole, the good little girl who brings home straight-A's, dates the football player, and follows all the rules." He sneered. "But it's all a lie. A façade. You spend hours in the bathroom doing God-knows-what. You scream at me for cleaning your dishes — dishes that you'd be perfectly happy leaving around for days if it meant that you had control over what happened to them. You literally take none of my shit and call me out for everything. You're Tayshia fucking Cole, but I just watched your boyfriend pull you so hard that you fell over, and you said it was an accident. I know you, and you're a pretty good actress."

Her eyes caught fire and blazed up at him.

"Miss me with that bullshit," she said. "You say all that to me as if you don't have your own share of problems. You're not qualified to judge me."

"Oh, really? And how's that?"

"You use sarcasm to cover up the fact that you're still just as much of a coward as you always were. You pick fights with me because I'm a girl, and because it makes you feel like a bigger person. You never liked me when we were younger because I represent the type of girl who you could never get — a girl who's not a complete disaster. And the reason why you're a bad guy is because your dad succeeded at it first."

"Have you lost your fucking mind?" Ash loomed over her. "If you're talking about my family, I'd like to ask you to shut the fuck up. You don't know anything about my dad, and you don't know anything about who I am."

"What?" Her face twisted with rage. "You think I forgot what it feels like to have *your* dad's gun in my face? *My* dad's blood on my hands? The only reason why you think you know me is because it makes you feel better about the fact that no matter how hard you try, you'll never make amends for your stupidity. For standing there and doing *nothing* while your dad committed a crime."

Ash was angry.

Very angry.

"Shut up."

"No," Tayshia said, jabbing her finger into the center of his chest. "It was *your* dad who did it. *Your* dad who almost killed mine." She jabbed his chest twice more. "And you just—you just *stood there* and watched while I *begged* you for help! You just—"

Ash snatched her hand away from him and yanked, pulling her forward until she was pressed against him. He glared down into her face.

"I said... *Shut up*," he breathed, so angry that he shook. He gripped her hand tight. Her skin felt cold beneath his own. The crystal around his neck hung heavy. "Shut your fucking mouth."

"Or else what?" she hissed. "You'll hit me?"

"No. But maybe we can go tell Kieran his suspicions were true. Maybe we go tell him you and I *are* sleeping together."

"We're not."

"He doesn't need to know that."

She tried to yank her hand back. "You wouldn't. You—"

"Things are different now," he said in a dark tone, gripping her hand enough to make her lips part in a wince. "I may have been a coward back then, but I'm not anymore. But you? You're so scared of your own boyfriend that you can't seem to grasp the fact that he's not the one you should be scared of."

The fire in her eyes dimmed to embers.

Okay, that was too much. Too far. He didn't want to threaten her. He would never hurt her, and he didn't know why he'd wanted her to think he would.

What the Hell was wrong with him?

"Fuck," he said, loosening his hold. "I'm... I didn't—"

"Move away from me," she whispered. "Now."

He did.

"I know he's not the one I should be scared of," she said, her hazel eyes seeming glassy in the sunlight. "Believe me. I know."

She shoved past him and ran the rest of the way into the shopping center. Ash watched her go, feeling the heaviness of his guilt pulling on his heart.

He wasn't the person he used to be. Before the ice cream shop. Before his mother's death. The person he was when he slid into the hot springs in the caverns on graduation night and held her so she wouldn't go under. The person he was when they both agreed to try and be friends.

Ash was angry because she was right.

CHAPTER TWELVE

Elijah met Ash on the sidewalk.

"Where were you?" he asked. His hands were in his pockets and a puzzled expression was on his face. "Tayshia came tearing through here, and I was like, *whoa, where the heck are you going?* And she was like, *not* interested in talking to me. Did something happen?"

Yes, Ash thought. *She absolutely murdered me with her words, so I lashed out and hit her harder.*

"No," he said. "You ready to eat?"

"Can we go to the store first? I should really get her a gift."

"Fine," Ash muttered, pushing his hair back.

They headed down towards the crosswalk. Elijah chattered his ear off while they walked, ranting about how mind-melting it was trying to talk to Kieran. Ash tuned him out, his thoughts speaking to him too loudly for him to be able to focus.

Ash was a coward and he always had been. Before jail, he possessed only a strange double-sided need to mess around with his friends and take care of his mother. He shoplifted, sold drugs for his father, and went to parties. He slept with girls, smoked weed, got drunk, and got tattoos from artists who were too unethical to check his age.

He lived recklessly.

Now, he was angry all the time and didn't really know what he cared about. His mother was gone. His father may as well have been dead because he was dead to him. He had his friends, yeah, but it wasn't the same.

He felt like he had nothing left to care about.

The worst thing of it all was that Tayshia knew him based upon his poor actions, and there was nothing he could do to reverse that. Every day, he regretted walking into that shop behind his father. He regretted it with every ounce of blood in his body. There were so many things that could have happened differently and it hurt to think about them all.

There was one thing she was wrong about, though.

He didn't pick on Tayshia because she was a girl. He picked on her because it was easy, and because she infuriated him. He picked on her because she always rose to the challenge.

It was as simple as starting an argument.

And he liked it.

Ash and Elijah entered the grocery store across the street, walking towards the candy aisle. The fluorescent lights wore on Ash's nerves—he'd never been a fan of grocery store lighting. He glanced around at the aisles, seeing quite a bit less customers for a Friday night than he would have expected. Which was relieving, given the encounter he'd had with the elderly woman. In the candy aisle, he stood and watched as Elijah scrutinized the various colored sweets.

"So, what was all that about?" Elijah asked as he rubbed his chin and read candy labels.

"What was all what?" Ash turned, pretending to read the greeting cards.

"The walk down the street."

Ash shrugged. "I just felt like it."

"Dude." Elijah picked up a candy bar and read the label on the back. "There's no way you just felt like taking a walk with Tayshia. You guys despise each other."

"It amuses me."

"Whatever." Elijah glanced back at him. "How did it go?"

"How did what go?"

"The distraction of Kieran O'Connell. Did you ask her?"

"Ask her what?"

Elijah gave him a strange look. "Ash, the whole purpose of the distraction was to find out if he was like, you know, *hurting* her."

Embarrassment caused Ash's heart to falter. He'd gotten so wrapped up in his own frustrations that he'd forgotten to ask.

In the silence, Elijah studied him and then said, "Do you *like* her?"

"No," Ash said, his eyes flicking to meet his friend's with cold regard. "Don't be stupid."

Elijah's eyebrows rose as he gathered up a few chocolate bars. "So, we won't talk about it. We'll just ignore it."

"Ignore what?"

"The fact that you like her."

Ash's hand tingled. He almost reached out to smack the back of Elijah's head.

"I do not like her," he said through clenched teeth. "I can barely tolerate seeing her function on the same plane of existence as me."

"You don't like her, but you care about the fact that her boyfriend is a complete asshole?"

Ash felt like someone was both sewing his mouth shut and trying to force words out at the same time. He exhaled through his nose, struggling to contain his frustration at the situation. He didn't know why he'd inserted himself into things with her.

He wasn't sure if he regretted it or not.

"Kieran *is* a complete asshole," Ash muttered. He touched the packaging of some other type of candy. He wasn't much of a sugar person. The last time he'd had sweets was the blue-and-pink cake on his nineteenth birthday. "But I don't care about the fact that he's her boyfriend."

Elijah added some more chocolates to his armful of candy. "But you had me pretend that we were already coming here tonight, so we could walk with them, because you don't care. Right."

Ash rolled his eyes and said nothing, waiting while Elijah selected more candy and a birthday card from the card wall behind them. He grabbed a gift bag and tissue paper, and then they went to stand in line. There was only one lane open so although the store wasn't very full, the line dragged a bit.

"I think I should tell her."

Ash's thoughts dissipated and his attention focused on Elijah. "Tell who what?"

"Tayshia." Elijah shifted his selections in his arms to make it easier to carry them. "About Kieran and Quinn."

"Who exactly did you hear about it from? Ji Hyun?"

Elijah shook his head. "No, I saw them. It was at the mall last weekend. They were at the food court, holding hands across the table while they ate. Who did you hear it from?"

"Ji," Ash said. "She saw them. You're sure it was Quinn?"

"Yeah, I remember seeing those girls joined at the hip practically from Freshman year. Plus, I told you—Tayshia and I are friends."

Ash side-eyed him. "Since *when?*"

"Since the school year while you were gone. Why does it matter? I can't be friends with people just because you don't like them?"

"It's not that. It's just weird."

The line moved. Elijah placed his things on the belt, grinning up at Ash.

"It's not. You just don't want me to be friends with her."

Ash sneered but remained quiet. He watched the cashier interact with Elijah, his thoughts wandering.

The fact that Kieran was getting his rocks off with Tayshia's best fucking friend was hilarious. Had Kieran gone completely *nuts*, or was he living in the clouds above a delusional football field of grandeur? Did he find some sort of rush from playing both sides of the field? He was no linebacker, and he was a shit quarterback. Even worse as a wide receiver.

When would he fumble the ball and lose the game?

"Don't tell her," Ash said when they walked away from the register.

"What?" Elijah frowned and shook his head in defiance. "No. *No.* We can't just sit on that information. We —"

"Elijah," Ash said in warning. "All it's going to do is cause problems. Just stay out of it."

"Since when do you care about anyone's problems other than your own?" Elijah spat, his words bitter.

Ash stared at him in shock, his pace slowing to a halt as Elijah exited the store through the automatic doors. What the Hell was up his ass? He bit his lower lip, trying to make sense of his swirling emotions. Grief and confusion stuck out the most of all.

He knew he was selfish. It was his selfishness that had landed him in jail, and his selfishness that had caused him to keep his mother's secret. Perhaps if he'd been less selfish with her, he'd at least have been able to fix her.

After a moment, he exited into the coolness of the evening. Elijah was there, standing on the curb with a contrite expression on his face. As Ash started to pass him, to step down from the curb, Elijah placed a hand on his chest to stop him.

"It's okay if you care what happens to her," he said in a quiet voice. "It's okay to care, even if it's out of guilt."

Ash narrowed his eyes. "I *don't* care about her."

"Shit, Ash. You're such a nightmare sometimes. Here."

Ash watched as Elijah reached into his shopping bag and pulled something out. He held it out to Ash, whose hand turned palm-up to receive it on instinct. It was one of the candy bars he'd bought for Tayshia.

"What's this for?"

"For Tayshia, Mr. I-don't-care." Elijah grinned. "If there's one thing I know, it's the sentimental side of women. Whether you guys get along or not, it's her birthday and everyone likes presents."

Ash held the candy bar awkwardly in his hand. He didn't want to *give* anything to Tayshia, lest she think it was him trying to tell her he wanted to befriend her. Or worse: think he was acting guilty.

Plus, giving her *one* cheap candy bar for her *twentieth* birthday? How cringe.

"Women deserve to be treated like they matter, Ash," Elijah said. "They deserve nice things."

Pulling his hood up onto the back of his head, he turned to cross the parking lot.

Ash stared at the candy bar, chocolate wrapped in a bright orange wrapper with punchy letters spelling out the title. It was a candy bar and it was cringe and he wasn't going to give it to her.

But he would give her something else.

It didn't matter if they hated each other. It didn't matter if they didn't get along. He couldn't imagine any woman deserving anything less than something nice.

"Here," he said after catching up to Elijah. "I'm gonna get her something else later."

"Fine, but I'm holding you to it." Elijah dropped the candy back into the bag. Then, he gave him a serious look, one that Ash rarely saw on his face. "Tayshia deserves nice things from someone who cares what happens to her. She doesn't deserve to be pulled so hard that she falls down."

✧✧✧

They decided to go to Gianni's.

The restaurant was toasty and warm when they walked inside, and the smell of food already had Ash's stomach rumbling. He cast a casual glance around, seeing the booths mostly occupied. He recognized a few girls from Christ Rising eating and giggling in the corner, and some people he'd gone to church with years ago. The latter looked in his direction, their wary gazes trained upon him.

He was used to this treatment.

The restaurant was open seating, so they picked a booth and took their seats across from one another. Ash pushed his hood off as he sat

148

down. A waitress appeared and they ordered drinks from her.

Ash peered past Elijah's head. Right across the room from them, he spotted them.

Tayshia and Kieran sat on opposite sides of their table from each other, with Quinn beside Tayshia on the inside. Kieran was tucking into his food with zeal, and Tayshia was leaning forward over her plate with her elbows on the table, picking at a burger without talking. Quinn's mouth was moving so much that she looked to have not stopped talking long enough to eat much yet.

What an unfortunate group.

"You are *so* buying me whatever I want."

Ash tore his gaze away from the other booth and then looked at Elijah. "You got to buy Tayshia a present, so this trip was mutually beneficial. I rescind."

"Okay, stingy. Then you can buy it for me because we're friends and you love me."

"Bold insinuation." Ash leaned forward with his elbows on the table, covering the knuckles of his right hand with the palm of his left. His lips curved up into a smirk.

"You love me, and you know it," Elijah said. "Come on, dude. I don't get paid until the day after tomorrow. And *you* pulled me from streaming tonight, so fuck you and buy me food."

"Fuck it. Fine. But you've gotta tell me who you're seeing."

Elijah shot him a look. "I'm not seeing anyone."

The waitress brought them their drinks and menus, and Ash took a sip from the glass. The water felt icy against the walls of his throat. In a way, the cold soothed his anxiety with a shock.

"You must be." he said. "You've been way too interested in whatever flame you think I'm holding for her, which means you either like *her*, or you're seeing someone and want me to start seeing someone, too. So, if you're not talking, I'm not paying."

"So who's paying then?" Elijah pulled a disgruntled face after he sipped some of his water. "Yuck, I hate this. Boring a-f. Water tastes like nothing."

"If you want it to be me, then tell me who you're trying to keep me from finding out about. And if you hate it, then why did you order it?"

"Nobody." Elijah gave him a Cheshire grin. "I just wanted to be like you, big brother."

"Bruh, shut up."

Ash picked up his menu and Elijah followed suit. As they perused the options, he looked up and across the room at Tayshia again. She was walking toward the bathroom, and her plate was now empty. He was surprised that she had gone from a full plate of food to an empty one in less than five minutes. He almost regretted not seeing her chomping down on it.

Kieran's plate was empty as well, and Quinn was finally eating. Kieran was the one whose mouth was moving. And right beneath the table, he could see Quinn's foot sliding up the length of Kieran's calf. As if on cue, Kieran leaned forward to fold his arms on the table, sending her a look that only promised debauchery.

Ash snorted. Tayshia could return from the bathroom at any moment, and her boyfriend was ogling the girl he was fucking on the side *openly* at their dinner table? And Quinn, playing footsie with him? They were so *idiotic.*

Tayshia could do better than both of them.

Elijah began chattering on about the different food choices, how he'd tried them all, and his favorite things about each one. Then, while Ash was still watching them, Kieran turned his head and looked around. His gaze settled on Ash's.

A silent tension grew.

Arching one eyebrow, Ash sent a pointed look towards the bathroom hallway, where Tayshia had disappeared.

Kieran smirked.

Ah.

So he knew what he was doing. He knew he was committing the worst betrayal, and he didn't care. Kieran cared so little for Tayshia's feelings that he was content toeing the line, flirting with another girl while his girlfriend was in the bathroom.

Was it because he loved the feeling of getting away with it? Or was it because he thought he was so much better than Tayshia that she deserved to be lied to?

Something about that bothered Ash. With her obsession with following the rules and getting good grades, her inability to clean up after herself, and her argumentative personality, Tayshia was infuriating. But she was someone who seemed to have her shit together—she seemed to have a plan for the future. She was strong. Ash had known that from the moment he saw her press her hands flat over her father's fucking *bullet* hole.

He didn't know what type of guy she deserved, but it certainly wasn't a cheating asshole like Kieran.

"I'm getting another damn burger," Elijah scowled, slamming his menu down. The sound jolted Ash, drawing his gaze. "I have eaten one burger a day for the past three hundred years, and I will eat them for three hundred years more. Call me predictable."

"Yeah?" Ash folded his menu shut. "I'll get one, too."

"I'm so sick of the food at school," Elijah grumbled. "I mean, their burgers are *good*, but they're not like, a *restaurant burger*."

Once their food had been ordered, Ash settled back into his seat with his hands relaxed in his lap. Elijah began to rant about Myths & Legends again, finishing the tale he'd been trying to tell on the walk.

Ash's gaze lifted when Tayshia came back from the bathroom. She had a bit of a dreamy expression on her face and she'd taken her lipstick off. Her skirt waved about her thighs, adding to her altogether lofty disposition.

Suddenly, she held the heel of her palm against the left side of her forehead. She took another couple of steps and then —

Bam!

Elijah and Ash both watched as she ran into a table, causing its legs to scrape against the floor. Staggering forward with a loud gasp that could be heard across the dining area, she clutched a hand to her thigh. She winced, limping back to the table. Quinn said something to her and Kieran just looked mildly annoyed.

"I don't know what she sees in him," Elijah muttered, appearing revolted. "She almost just ate shit and he's just like, *whatever, no big deal*. Such a piece of trash. Tell me, Ash. Why do men?"

They conversed for a while, each of them sharing their past negative experiences with Kieran. He was a popular guy at school, but not with any of the scholarship kids. He was boring, rude, and conceited.

The waitress appeared, carrying their plates. She set them down, refilled their water glasses, and then was gone.

"Bro, why are you so obsessed with her, though?" Ash said, picking up his burger and taking a bite. "Do *you* like her, or something? Is that why you're not seeing anyone?"

"What? *What*?" A large amount of tomatoes and ketchup fell from Elijah's burger as he glared at him. "No. *No*! Stop."

Ash laughed, watching as Elijah picked up his napkin to clean up the mess. He glanced over at Tayshia's booth as a waiter walked over to it, setting an ice cream sundae the size of his hand in front of her. She tucked into it, her leg shaking under the table as though she'd rather be anywhere but there. Kieran shifted in his seat in impatience, drumming his fingers on top of the table. He was looking at Quinn.

"Tell me what the Hell is going on," Elijah said.

"What?"

"This whole situation is like, so, so, so bizarre. You've done nothing but complain about Tayshia since she moved in, and now we're walking down the street together so you can watch her on her date with Kieran? There's an obvious dynamic, or whatever. So, what happened?"

Ash opened his mouth to speak, hesitating.

Behind Elijah, Tayshia raised her hand to signal the waiter, pointing at the menu and ordering something else. She smiled up at him and when she lowered her eyes, they caught Ash's and held. She was still smiling. His heart skipped a beat.

She'd hadn't smiled at him since graduation night.

When he looked at Elijah again, his friend had his arms crossed over his chest.

"Okay, Ash," he said. "You're telling me what happened. Like, now. Right now."

Ash took another bite of his food, focused on his fries as he searched his mind for an answer to give him. He didn't want to just *tell* him that he'd been dreaming about Tayshia, nor did he want to tell him about the huge fight they'd had in the kitchen the day before.

He didn't know why the dreams were happening, however he did know why they'd fought. And he felt uncomfortable with Elijah knowing both situations.

"Nothing happened."

Elijah held his burger with both hands. "You're lying."

"I'm not lying."

"Yep. You're lying."

"I'm *not* lying."

"You're lying, Ash, but I'll let it slide. For now. But next time you need me to go with you to cover for you?" Elijah pointed at him with one finger, still holding his burger. "It's gonna cost you."

"Oh, yeah? It's gonna cost me?" Ash wanted to steer the conversation away from Tayshia. "Yeah, all right. I'm guessing it's gonna cost me this time, too. Anything to get me to pay."

"Yup."

They finished their meals in relative silence, Ash unable to stop himself from glancing at Tayshia's table. Again. She was already almost done with her sundae, which was a miracle, since Ash still had half of his burger left. He couldn't believe she'd ordered food three times already.

Later, as Ash was taking his card out to pay for their meals, the waitress waiting patiently by the table, Tayshia, Quinn, and Kieran got up to leave. They headed towards the booth Ash and Elijah were at. Before they passed it, Tayshia stopped. She held up a finger as she walked toward the bathroom again.

"I'll just use the bathroom real quick," she called. "Before we go back."

Kieran sent her a sour look, where she couldn't see. "All right, but hurry. I need to get back home. We'll wait outside."

"Yeah, we'll be out there," Quinn said. She and Kieran exchanged glances.

"Okay!" Tayshia replied, then she once again disappeared into the hallway.

They left the restaurant, Kieran holding the door open for Quinn. She walked by him, his hand brushing her lower back.

Ash nearly burst out laughing.

That was *brave*.

He and Elijah got up, leaving into the night. It was dark now, the heavy, oppressive humidity weighing him down. The smell of rain was everywhere, but the shadowed skies had yet to open up. Only the moon peeking through some of the clouds provided illumination where the streetlights wouldn't be able to reach.

They started down the sidewalk, towards the street so they could try to make it home before the rain. As they neared the end of the shopping center, Ash heard Kieran's voice.

"Hurry. You need to hurry, Quinn."

"I *am*," came Quinn's snappy response. "*You're* the one who needs to be quick."

"We should just leave her."

"Like, to walk by herself? I mean, we can."

Ash stopped, causing Elijah to stumble against his back.

He glanced behind himself and held up a finger for silence to Elijah, whose face took on that rare serious expression. Together, the

153

two of them crept down the sidewalk in front of a shop with its lights turned off due to early closure. Ash kept back behind the corner with his arm holding Elijah at bay. Together, they poked their heads around enough to see.

There was Kieran, his back to the stone wall. Quinn was kissing him with all the fervor of a girl trying to hook up, her hands working with frantic speed at his zipper. Kieran's hands were roaming all over her body, squeezing and groping as he kissed her back.

Tayshia was in the bathroom inside and Kieran was outside, making out with her best friend.

Ash pitied her. The situation was so messed up, he wasn't even sure how to process it.

Happy fucking birthday to Tayshia.

Quinn pulled back.

"Okay, let's do it," she said, breathless.

"What?"

"Leave her."

Kieran kissed her again, the two of them breathing heavily through their noses. "Are you sure? Won't it seem suspicious?"

"I'll text her. It'll be fine."

She grabbed Kieran by the hand, and they took off. When she turned to grin at him over her shoulder, her teeth seemed to glint under the moonlight.

And then they were gone.

"What the fuck?" Ash said as he looked down at Elijah with wide, troubled eyes.

"That's it." Elijah's face had darkened. "I'm telling her."

Ash felt unease twisting its way through his abdomen. The fear of something that didn't quite make sense to him. He wasn't sure if he felt so guilty for how he'd watched her father bleed, or if he really did care about her.

What if it was both?

"You're *not* telling her, Elijah."

"Ash, it would hurt her not to know."

"It's going to hurt her worse *to* know," Ash said in a low tone. "Let her live in bliss."

"I *need* to—"

"No."

"But we can't just—"

"No." Ash shook his head. "Listen to me, Elijah. *No.*"

154

"But *why?*"

Ash's mouth remained shut. He started the walk home and Elijah followed. The rain was coming, the scent so prevalent in the air that there was the possibility they wouldn't make it home before it began.

Elijah was angry, but Ash didn't care. This time, Ash was the one who was right. If Tayshia found out that Kieran was this careless with her heart, she'd be devastated. Ash had caused her enough pain. He didn't want to cause her more by being the one to break the news.

As they made their way underneath the streetlights, almost to the corner that would put them on the street the complex was on, Elijah finally cracked.

"You're so fucking infuriating, Ash."

Ash bristled but didn't turn around. "Oh, yeah?"

"Yeah, and I know why you don't want me to tell her."

"*Do* read my mind, man."

"You just don't want me to tell her because you're afraid of what will happen when she's looking for someone to pick up the pieces," Elijah said as they walked. "You're afraid that she'll come looking for you, and then you won't be able to stop yourself from doing what you do with every girl. Sweeping them off their feet and then shoving them to the ground. You're afraid you'll be worse than Kieran. You're afraid to be worse than your father."

Ash seethed. Elijah continued.

"You act like you're not a bad person. You act like you don't even feel remorse. Like you're proud to have gone to jail, and like everyone should just forgive you because it was your dad's fault. But you walked into that shop. You told me you had a fucking chance to get help and then you didn't. You told me you watched her dad almost die. So why the fuck would you be anything less than a bad person for that?"

Rage ripped through Ash like a forest fire. He whipped around, gripped the fabric of Elijah's sweatshirt, and pulled him threateningly close. The plastic bag that had Tayshia's candy in it rustled.

Ash understood that this was Elijah—that he was his best friend—but the storm inside of him had filled him to the brim. It was telling him that everything was going to fall apart.

And he was *livid.*

"Shut up," he snarled. "Shut the fuck up, Elijah. You don't know *anything.* You don't know a *damn* thing about me."

Elijah glared back at him in stony silence, his eyes full of unshed, angry tears.

Ash backed away, turning to continue on, but Elijah ran ahead of him and whirled to face him, holding his forefinger up.

"Tell me the truth then. Why are you so invested in Tayshia and Kieran? Why do you care how she finds out?"

Ash gritted his teeth. "I *don't.*"

"You *do,* or else you would let me tell her!"

"Why do you want to know?! Why can't you just—" Ash scowled, his lungs squeezing. "Just leave it alone?"

"Because I'm tired of you acting like you don't feel anything!"

Ash slid the fingers of one hand into his hair as though he had a headache. He didn't want to think about anything. He didn't want to have to face the fact that he'd shut himself down against anything and everything since the day that Elijah had given him the despairing news about his mother.

Panic exploded within him.

"Because I feel *guilty,* all right? I feel fucking guilty for what happened with her dad. I feel bad for just standing there. Because she wouldn't *be* with that fucker if it weren't for *me* making her think she was worthless. If I..." He trailed off, overcome as he remembered their hope for friendship when they took that crystal out of the wall. "She's with him because I made all the wrong choices. I don't know why I feel that way. I just know that I fucking do."

"So, what? You're saying she would..." Elijah's brow furrowed. "She would be with *you?*"

Ash's hand snapped up to finger the leather cord around his neck. He felt the crystal's jagged edges brushing his bare skin. The dreams he'd been having felt like a pathway back to the caverns.

And now everything was fucked.

Elijah's facial expression softened.

"Ash, you can't possibly be the reason why Kieran treats her like shit. It's *his* fault. *He's* the one who's hurting her. It's not your fault."

"It *is* my fault!" Ash shouted. "Maybe not directly, but my actions that day in the shop were my own. If I hadn't—maybe if things had been different—"

Elijah cut him off. "If you live that way, you'll never be satisfied. We all wish things would have been different. Everyone wishes they could go back and do things a different way when they make a mistake."

"It's *not* the same." Ash hissed out his words, his eyes flashing with caged ire. "My mistakes terrorized people. My mistakes got someone *shot*."

"You're right about that—your mistakes hurt people," Elijah said, sounding desperate. "But we still need to tell her."

"It's not our business that Kieran's cheating on her," Ash said, running another furious hand through his tousled hair. He glared through Elijah, rather than at him. "But I plan to make it my business what happens after she does find out." Elijah's lips parted to speak, but his eyes widened at a point somewhere behind Ash's shoulder.

Fuck.

"Kieran and Quinn left."

Tayshia stood behind them on the sidewalk, a few yards back, bathed in the warm glow of a streetlight. The corners of her lips turned downward as her brows met. There were tears on her cheeks, but they didn't look fresh.

"They left me here, so I just started walking, hoping—hoping I would catch up to you guys, and..."

She looked devastated, like her entire world was crumbling out from beneath her feet. Her feet, which she swayed upon as though the revelation of the betrayal was enough to topple her. Her voice came out as a whisper that seemed loud against the backdrop of the humid, precipitation-thick air.

"He's cheating on me?"

CHAPTER THIRTEEN

The rain began to fall.

The droplets were light—the sort that Ash couldn't feel unless he brushed them with his fingertips. The sort that rolled like tears down his cheeks. All around them, turning the sidewalk from light grey to dark, staining the street shiny and black. Though it was dark outside, the reflection of the moon against the wet pavement caused the sky to look like it was glowing. It felt like a different world, one made of starlight.

Tayshia stood before them like a small animal illuminated by the streetlight. She looked like herself yet somehow, she looked like a person who couldn't claim her own name. A person who couldn't be the same girl that had screamed and fought with him in the kitchen last night.

The way she wrung her hands, the pigeon-toed way she stood, the way her feathered brows came together on her forehead to map out her anxiety.

It was out of character.

"Is Kieran cheating on me?" she asked again, her voice strong and sure in spite of her stance.

Elijah and Ash exchanged glances, the former giving Ash a look that told him it didn't matter what he wanted. She already knew and if she didn't, she was hurt anyway.

Ash pulled his hood on and threw his hands up in resignation, shaking his head.

"Yes. Kieran is... Yeah. He is," Elijah said.

A blank look materialized on Tayshia's face and she frowned, casting her gaze downward. She wrung her hands again, fingers twisting around her wrists and the backs of her palms. The silence felt as thick as the humidity.

"With—with who? Do you know?"

Ash turned his face away. He wasn't going to say anything. It wasn't his business and he hadn't wanted to get involved. Somehow, he'd tricked himself into thinking he wanted to and now—standing here, watching her sway like a confused willow branch as she tried to make sense of everything—he felt trapped.

"Does it matter?" Elijah said. "All that matters is it's true. And—and if you don't believe us, well... Ask Ji Hyun."

"Ji Hyun?" She sounded crestfallen.

"Yeah. Kieran's not exactly—"

"Subtle," Ash muttered.

"Yeah." Elijah sighed. "Look, if you want me to talk to him, then I will. I've got no problem—" Ash shot him a sharp, curious look but he continued, "—talking to him for you. You don't even have to say another word to him if you don't want to. I can—"

"I think she knows how to handle her business, Elijah," Ash said, keeping his gaze trained upon his friend. "It's not like it's ours, is it?"

A tense charge ramped up between them, like a swirling electrical storm, but Tayshia didn't seem to notice it.

"When did this happen?" she asked.

"Does it matter?" Ash said. "Kieran's straight trash. Throw him away and get with someone else. Be glad you never gave him what he wanted."

At this, both Tayshia and Elijah's gazes found him, and he realized he may have said too much.

Because how would he know that unless he'd been watching her, obsessing over her and analyzing her life?

Tayshia hung her head.

"Yes, I—I guess I should just... Text him and end it," she said in a soft voice. "That way, I don't have to speak to him again."

"Good idea," Elijah said. "I know you guys have been together since like, the dawn of time... But I'm sorry."

Tayshia nodded in a numb way. A far cry from the girl who had single-handedly kept her father from dying with his blood all over her hands, the Tayshia that stood before them looked lost. Like she didn't quite know what to do next. Ash watched her for a moment, watched her metaphorically folding in on herself, and he found it disturbing.

She was hurt. It was understandable that she'd want to fall apart. Why in front of them?

In front of *him*?

He thought back to the first day they'd moved in together. Where was *that* girl? The feisty girl who marched down to the leasing office to immediately try and get away from him? The girl who had said, *"If you don't get on my bad side, Ash, I won't get on yours. The only way this is going to work for this lease is if you recognize and understand that we don't have to be anything — enemies or friends. You're nothing to me and as long as you don't piss me off, I won't become something to you."*

This girl was the one he'd heard screaming in the nightmare.

"Let's go home," Ash said. "We shouldn't stand out here in the rain."

Elijah nodded. "If it rains any harder, we'll all be soaked. We'll walk you back. Oh, and here."

He handed Tayshia the plastic bag.

"I was gonna actually put the candy *into* the gift bag and sign the card, but you look like you could use some cheering up right now. Happy birthday."

Tayshia took it and looked inside. Her lips curled up. "Wow, Elijah. Thank you so much. That was really nice of you."

She stretched an arm upward and rose onto the tips of her toes to hug him. The way Elijah wrapped his arms around her in a full-body hug irked Ash for some reason. He wasn't sure if it was just because he still didn't know how Elijah and Tayshia had become friends.

The boys turned and started off through the rain. Ash wondered what was going through Elijah's mind, and what his intentions were. Did he like Tayshia? Was this cheating fiasco some sort of *opportunity* for him?

Something similar to discomfort twisted in the pit of his stomach, swirling like the drowning waters that plagued his mind.

The thought of Elijah and Tayshia together was just as awful as the sight of her with Kieran. Elijah was his best friend, but for Tayshia? He was just... Wrong. Tayshia would run him ragged. He wouldn't be able to keep up.

Damn.

Why did it bother him so much?

"I wanted to be good enough."

Ash and Elijah's footsteps slowed to a stop. Heart pounding, Ash was the first to turn back around.

Tayshia still stood bathed in the glow of the streetlight, the lantern washing her in an orangish glow faded by the grey haze of the rain. She'd only made it three steps, it seemed, before she'd stopped. They were all yards apart, but close enough to hear each other.

"What?" Elijah said with a nervous laugh. "What are you talking about, Tayshia?"

"I've always wanted to be good enough for everyone." She frowned, staring at the wet pavement beneath her. Beside them, cars zoomed by, louder as they neared and quieter as they passed. "I've never wanted to be the best—I've always just wanted to be enough for everyone. But it always seems like no matter what I do—what I learn, who I fight, who I love—it's not going to be enough. Sometimes, I wonder if I'm the one who's out of place in my own story. I wonder if I'm the side character in a narrative that belongs to someone else."

Elijah took a step toward her, but Ash's arm shot out to stop him. He did, but not without some resistance.

Tayshia lifted her gaze from the ground. Ash's stomach did another turn.

Her eyes were full of tears. He could see them shimmering in the streetlight.

"I knew Kieran and I weren't going to end up together. I knew it wasn't possible for us to work after Paris—after I was—" She let out a dejected sigh and looked down again. "I knew it wasn't a good match. But our families were so sure. I kept trying to make it work but it was like trying to hold fire in my hands. I'm not smart all the time. In fact, sometimes I wonder if I'm really that smart at all."

"That's the stupidest thing I've ever heard," Ash said, gazing at her through the rainfall. It was starting to pour, droplets clinging to his lashes and streaming down his face. "Maybe you're right."

"Dude," Elijah growled in warning. "Come on."

Ash started to reply, but a sound escaping Tayshia's lips wrestled the words into nothingness. Panic rose inside of him.

"I just get tired sometimes," she said, her voice cracking. "And then I want to cry."

"So, cry," Ash said, because it was all he could think to say. He took his hand away from Elijah's chest, satisfied that his friend understood his silent wish, and then he put it back into his pocket. "And we'll stand here with you while you do."

Tayshia looked up at him, her lower lip and chin quivering. The tears in her eyes shone like the crystals around their necks. They overflowed, slipping down her cheeks one-by-one to join the sky's.

"Yeah," Elijah said, adding the words with a smile. "Go ahead, and—and we'll be right here with you."

"Okay."

And then she began to weep.

Together, they stood in the rain as Tayshia let her emotions flow free. She held the hem of the front of her dress, twisting the fabric in a stressed manner as she indulged in quiet sobs. Her wet hair fell forward to curtain the sides of her face, shrouding it from view, and her shoulders shook from more than just the cold temperature.

Elijah turned his head away, likely out of respect, but Ash found that no matter how much he knew he should... He couldn't look away. Something inside of him told him that to look away from her was to leave her in loneliness. They weren't friends but after everything he'd put her through, the least he could do was stand here with her.

It was almost terrifying. It felt false. Like a surreal, lifelike version of one of his dreams. Except in his dreams of her, he wasn't there. He was just watching her life from afar like a movie.

But now, he was here.

He was here and for some reason, he felt like he could imagine himself crossing the distance to her. He could *see* himself wrapping his arms around her. Which was strange, given that the only woman he'd ever embraced simply for the sake of comfort was his mother.

So, he watched her cry because it was all he could do. If Ash was good at something, it was giving what he could.

That was usually enough.

☼☼☼

It took them a while to get home.

Ash had given Tayshia his hoodie to wear, since Elijah wasn't wearing one. It dwarfed her frame, the sleeves nearly covering her fingers. Ash didn't know how to explain why he liked the sight of it. It wasn't that he thought it was attractive.

He just liked it.

"Are you going to be all right?" Elijah asked from Tayshia's right side, his voice sounding odd and muted.

They'd just finished crossing the parking lot and were now standing on the sidewalk in front of Elijah's car — the only new thing he owned. Elijah was on Tayshia's right and Ash was on her left. It felt like they were emerging from a bubble of time that existed separate from the rest of the world.

"Of course," Tayshia said. "I think I had a feeling all along that something was going on. I guess I just didn't want to believe it could be true."

Ash was unsurprised. To everyone at Christ Rising, it seemed like anyone who acted like a *good Christian* was perfection incarnate—including Kieran and Tayshia. They were angels with halos of gold who carried no sins on their backs.

Though Ash himself wasn't religious, he knew everyone had sins. It stood to reason Kieran would have some, too.

"I think we all like to believe the best of our friends," Elijah said, his gaze meeting Ash's over the top of Tayshia's head. "But sometimes, we're wrong about them."

Ash tried not to grind his teeth together.

Elijah was his best friend, but the fact remained that they'd just had a fight that showed that Elijah didn't think Ash was the best person. He knew that Elijah thought the worst of him, in spite of taking care of everything that needed to be taken care of when it came to Lizette's death.

What if there was something else going on?

"Apparently," Tayshia said in response to Elijah's words. "I knew I was wrong, though. I knew it from the beginning. I just ignored it."

Ash knew what that was like—ignoring the worst so he could hope for the best. Pretending that his father was the right one to follow. Pretending he was a good man and someone to look up to.

"So, what are you gonna do?" Elijah asked.

Tayshia looked pensive for a moment, her hands in her pockets, too. "I'm not going to give him a second chance, if that's what you mean. I'm going to end things between us."

"It's for the best," Elijah said, grimacing. "And like I said, I *can* talk to him for you."

Ash wanted to tell him to quit acting like such a simp but he kept his mouth sewn shut.

"There's no reason to talk to him," Tayshia said, pulling Ash's attention. Her tone had drifted back to its normal territory—clipped and almost haughty. "I'll text him. And since he's pathetic, he'll probably never speak to me again. I can handle that. In any case, it's not your responsibility. He's my—he *was* my boyfriend."

"Okay," Elijah said, "but if you need me, let me know."

At this, Ash wanted to sneer. He forced himself not to care, until feigned indifference smoothed his face blank.

Elijah was getting on his nerves.

"Thank you, Elijah." Tayshia turned to him and held her arms out, giving Elijah another embrace in spite of the rain. The top of her head, still covered by the hood, tucked beneath his chin. She closed her eyes and exhaled in a way that showed she wasn't as all right as she was trying to sound. "You're a good friend."

Ash's fingers flexed at his sides.

"Of course, Tayshia." Elijah hugged her back, a smile pulling up the corners of his lips. "And Kieran's a dick. He's literally gotta be an idiot to let a girl like you go."

"Oh," Tayshia said, sounding a bit embarrassed as she stepped out of the circle of Elijah's arms. "Well, he's not a *complete* idiot. I don't know if I could let the years we've spent together as friends like, *fade* or anything. I mean, we've been friends since our families met at church. But it's clear that we aren't meant to be in a relationship. I wasn't what he wanted and that's... Okay."

Ash stared at her in incredulity. So forgiving, even when she was insecure. And insecurity didn't seem like the sort of dress she liked to put on. It was so out of place on her person that he didn't recognize her.

Not that he knew her well enough to know if there was anything to recognize.

And how the fuck could anyone not want her? He thought. *She's so...* What?

She was so... What?

He averted his eyes, feeling a bit off-center.

"I hope you'll rethink that," Elijah said, as if reading his mind. "He doesn't deserve you as a friend, let alone a girlfriend."

"I don't think I will." She offered him a small smile. "But I can see why you think I should."

After saying their goodbyes, Elijah went to his car and opened the door. Ash and Tayshia headed for the stairs.

"Do me a favor, Tayshia?"

Tayshia turned completely around.

"Yes, Elijah?"

"Promise me you'll really think about it before you make your decision about keeping a friendship with Kieran," he said, his expression concerned and pleading. "Just promise me you'll think about it."

Tayshia gave him a short nod and then set off up the stairs.

The boys looked at each another one final time. Ash found that he wasn't quite sure what his friend was thinking, beyond not wanting Tayshia to find out Kieran had cheated with Quinn. His expression was unreadable. However, after the small argument they'd had, Ash didn't want to be able to read it.

He was already tired of hearing what Elijah really thought about him.

"Night, man," Elijah said.

"Yeah."

☼☼☼

The apartment was dark.

The only source of light came from the window in the kitchen, and one of the lights adorning the side of the apartment complex's outdoor walls. The rain had increased to a torrent, the clouds blocking the moon. The glass panes overlooked the backside of the complex, which sat atop a grassy hill leading down to a golf course next door.

Inside, it was quiet as Tayshia took Ash's damp hoodie off of her and dropped it onto the floor in a sodding heap. If it weren't for the fact that he felt bad for her, he might have reprimanded her for it.

Because what was the point of dropping it onto the floor when she could walk down the hall to the washer?

Ash sighed, standing in the opening of the hallway. Tayshia stood near the front door, looking at him. The darkness and quiet felt oppressive.

"I know you said not to," she said in a soft voice, "but I'm going to thank you."

Ash shrugged one shoulder, forgetting that she probably couldn't see it.

"I don't like to... Show that side of myself," she said. "Especially because I'm supposed to be a strong woman."

"Supposed to be?" Ash lifted one eyebrow. "No one's supposed to be anything other than themselves. I played that game for *way* too long. All it got me was a trial and jailtime, a dad in prison, and a dead mom. Don't get caught in that trap."

He turned to go, knowing that the only thing keeping the grief at bay from his own harsh words was his own distaste for himself.

A *clink* behind him caught him off guard, stopping him before he could go far. He turned right as the dining room light was clicked on.

Tayshia was at the dining room table beside the kitchen bar, lifting two small plates and a bowl off of it. For some reason, she looked frailer than usual in her sad dress with the hoodie off — like crying had taken all of the air out of her and shrunk her down. Like she was someone who needed to be carried.

He didn't like it.

"Oh, I didn't see those," he said of the dishes.

"I'll clean them," she said, the words tumbling out in a quick rush. "I'm sorry. I left them here earlier."

Ash watched her carry them to the sink. He stood there for a moment, thinking about how he really wanted to change out of the rain-soaked clothing he wore, but something nagged at him to go to her.

Walking down the hall towards the kitchen, he entered it right as she turned the water on. She pushed the plug into the drain and began to fill the sink with dish soap and hot water.

He wasn't sure which was more surprising: her washing dishes, or her washing them by hand.

Ash snuck up behind her, reaching around her for the dish in her hand, the warm water spilling over his fingers as he did so. She jolted, moving back on reflex only to be trapped against his chest with her damp hair brushing against his equally-damp shirt. She went still.

Normally, he would kill to make her to do the dishes for once, but not today.

"What are you — "

He cut her off. "Don't worry about it this time."

She ducked underneath his arm and stood to the side of him, looking up at him with her mouth agape. "But you *hate* — "

"I *said*," he held her gaze, tilting his chin down, "don't worry about it."

He washed the plate with the sponge and liquid soap, ignoring the slimy feeling and grime that he was sure would stain his fingernails. Maybe he was being dramatic, but yeah — he did hate washing dishes. Which was why he hated that she left them all over the common room. But if there was one thing he'd learned from watching his mother, it was that when people were sad because of the way others treated them, they didn't deserve to stress.

"You don't have to do that," Tayshia said.

"To do what?" He set the plate on the dish rack and reached for the second plate.

She wrapped her hand over his fully to intercept him, fingers and thumb hooking around the sides of the back. The moment she did, their wet skin touching, he felt his stomach lurch. Tayshia frowned, looking at their hands.

Ash didn't know what it was, but it felt like a hurricane had whipped up from the depths of his psyche to pummel him from all sides. It was different than anything he'd felt before now — different than the dreams, the weakness, the waters. It was too much.

His gaze snapped to hers.

"Drop my fucking hand."

She held tighter and glared up at him, eyes piercing.

"You don't have to tip-toe around me and treat me like glass just because I cried in front of you. It wasn't an invitation. It was a—"

"A gift?" He clenched his teeth, gripping the plate with his other hand so tight that it hurt his knuckles. His stomach was spinning and swirling, urging him to do something, *anything* to relieve the ache inside of his heart. He didn't know what it was or why it was happening.

Why wasn't he pulling his *own* hand away?

"A gift." She scoffed. "There's no part of me that's a reward, especially not my tears."

"Then what were you thanking Elijah for? His presence?"

"Yes. And yours. I know kindness is a foreign concept to you, Ash, but when you do something kind, people typically like to thank you for it."

"Ah, yes. I'd almost forgotten about your superiority complex. I thought it was because you were a good girl, but now I know it's just you."

He saw her gaze fall to his neck, traveling down along his arms, and then snapping back up.

"And I almost forgot who *you* really are. Tell me... If you fail a drug test, do you go back to jail, boo?"

Her taunting lanced through him, right to his core.

"There she is," he snarled, turning his hand in her own, sliding it up, and wrapping his fingers around her wrist. She let out a cry as he yanked on it, bringing her up against his side. The side of her head brushed against his chest, she was that short. "The hissing, spitting cat I know so well."

The hurricane ebbed a fraction.

"What's that supposed to mean?" she snapped. "I can't cry because it doesn't fit the good girl narrative? It doesn't remind you of the cold, icy bitch you hate so much? Afraid it'll make you feel something like compassion for me?"

"You can cry. Just don't thank me for standing and watching you do it. I don't need the charity of your gratitude for doing what the fuck I want."

She reached for his right hand with her left, lacing her fingers with his. It boxed her in-between his arms again. As much as he knew it was because she was challenging him, arguing and bickering because she was offended and angry — he liked it. He liked the feeling of her hand in his own.

He wanted to know what it felt like to hold it all the time.

"Why? Do you like it, or something?" she said, tone snide. "Do you like watching me cry?"

Ash let go of her wrist. Before he could stop himself, he leaned forward, curled his dripping fingers around her chin, and tilted her face up to look into his eyes.

"I don't like watching you cry, Tayshia. I like watching you fall apart. And I like watching you fall apart because it means you're just like the rest of us. You're not perfect. Just because Kieran couldn't accept your imperfections doesn't mean that no one else will. It doesn't matter if you weren't good enough for him. There's other people who are fine with you just the way you are. Stop trying to fucking hold it together and be perfect all the time. You certainly don't need to do it for me."

Without warning, her face crumpled like a stack of cards.

She burst out into tears. Sobbing, right there at the kitchen sink with the water running, their fingers intertwined, and his hand on her chin.

It didn't feel uncomfortable.

There was something familiar in the scent that hovered around her hair. He could smell the floral fragrance of her perfume just as well as he could smell the Fall in the drying raindrops on her damp hair. The weight of her pressing into him felt as welcoming as he imagined it would feel to embrace his mother.

He wished he could do that just one more time.

"See?" he murmured, his hands releasing her. With some hesitation, he wrapped his arms around her shoulders, one elbow bending so he could cup the back of her head. It felt right. He didn't know why. It just did. "Cry. Just don't lose yourself to how bad it hurts."

"I'm sorry," she said between sobs, her tears soaking a shirt that was already damp. "I'm so sorry."

"Hush," he said. "Do what I tell you, and cry."

Her weeping paused, the sound suspended in the air as she took a gasping breath. Then, the silence burst and she fell into her emotions again. Ash wrapped his arms more tightly around her, holding her upright. The feeling of her against him was nothing compared to the way the sobs were wrenching their way out of her gut.

It reminded him of the day he'd lost his mom and how hard he'd cried in his cell that night.

Ash clenched his teeth and turned his face up to the ceiling for a second. He fought his own emotions, feeling overwhelmed and despaired.

This wasn't like hugging his mom at all.

Tayshia cried until the water ran cold, and then she jumped away from him. He lifted his arm so she could move back a few steps.

"I'm sorry," she said, frantic as she scrubbed at her face. "I'm literally so gross for that. So embarrassing."

He could still see her cheeks tracked with moisture, but he didn't tell her that. He simply returned to washing the plate.

She went on, "Thank you for being there for me, and you're right. I won't let it eat me up, and I'll handle my business better. You and Elijah are both good friends."

Ash looked at her in surprise, a lock of his hair falling forward that he couldn't touch due to his wet hands. Of all the things he was to her, he didn't think she considered him a friend. All they ever did was fight.

Tayshia Cole and Ash Robards, friends?

He didn't know how he felt about that.

"Good night, Ash," she said.

"Yeah."

Ash finished the last couple of dishes, washed his hands, and then dried them. After that, he pulled out his phone. There were still two hours left in the day — two hours that it was still her birthday. He could let Kieran be the lowlight and Elijah be the highlight of her twentieth birthday.

Or he could do better than both of them.

Ash passed the bathroom on the way, seeing the light filtering out from beneath it. Good. She wouldn't notice him leaving. He grabbed hoodie, pulled a denim jacket on over it, pushed his hair back with his fingers, and put a maroon beanie on the back of his head.

Grabbing his car keys, Ash headed out the door, locking it behind him so Tayshia would be safe.

☼☼☼

He returned with a glittering purple gift bag.

There had only been one store open this late. While there, he'd been one of the few people in the store, so he hadn't encountered the problem he had with the elderly woman like he had before. It was a breeze to wander the aisles and throw whatever he wanted into the basket.

He wasn't the best at gifts but he figured he did all right.

Inside the gift bag, Ash had gotten her some headphones on the expensive side, a nice box of chocolates from the candy section, a pair of silver hoop earrings, and an oversized knit sweater with a hood that he thought looked cool. Since she liked sweaters so much, he had a feeling she'd like it.

And it was better than Elijah's gift.

Right as he entered the hallway, the bathroom door swung open. Tayshia walked out, eyes puffy and reddened nose sniffling. She reached to turn off the light, then gasped when she saw Ash standing there.

He hid the bag behind his back.

"Did you leave?" she asked.

"Yeah," he said. "You good?"

"I'm fine. Was Quinn's stuff out there?"

"No, I didn't see it. Did you—"

"I texted her and told her I knew, and to come get it. Then, I put it on the mat outside the front door. I guess she came by."

She still had her dress on, but she'd removed her torn nylons and her legs were bare. She'd pulled her hair back into two buns at the side of her head, right above each ear. Her bangs were choppy across her forehead, framing her face. Her face, with tawny brown skin that looked as soft as gardenia petals, and lips that were pouty and full.

Damn, he thought, nearly losing his train of thought. *She looks* —

"What did you need?" she asked, hazel eyes wide.

— cute as fuck.

"Tell me, did Kieran get you a birthday present?" he asked.

She opened her mouth, averted her eyes in thought, and then frowned. "Not that I can remember. I think he bought me dinner a few years ago. But that was because our parents insisted. Why?"

Ash held the gift out to her.

Appearing shocked, Tayshia took it from him, their fingers brushing in the process. An answering whip of feeling lashed through his abdomen. He'd learned something about her tonight.

Her hands were soft.

"What's this for?" she asked, looking inside of the large bag.

"Women deserve nice things," he said, echoing Elijah in spite of his earlier irritation with him. "Remember that when you're texting them, trying to keep the friendships."

She gave him one last look, this time with a hint of an excited smile, and then she sank to a crouch on the floor in the light the bathroom gave off. Ash crossed his arms over his chest and shouldered the wall, feeling a bit of satisfaction as he watched her tearing the tissue paper out. She withdrew the earrings first, pursing her lips as she looked up at him.

"Why hoops?"

"Because I like them," he said, smirking. "Problem?"

She blinked. "Oh. All right."

Next, she pulled out the sweater. Holding it up, he saw her eyes widening.

"Oh, shit—this is *cute*! How did you know my size?"

"I don't. But you always wear oversized ones, so I went with a bigger one."

Her smile faltered a bit as she looked at the size tag, but then it was back. "Thanks. You know my style, it looks like."

"Mm."

He watched her pull out the headphones and give him a stunned expression. "You did not."

"I did."

"These are—"

"And?" He was trying not to let his smirk turn into a grin.

"Ash, these are *hella* fucking expensive."

"You're welcome."

She eyed him warily, looking him up and down, and then reached into the bag one final time. She pulled the chocolates out, reading the company name on the front. Her facial expression was unreadable as she turned it over and read the nutrition label, then turned it back over again.

"This is my favorite chocolate brand," she said, her voice faint. "Thank you."

"It was a guess," Ash said, and then he pushed away from the wall. "Happy birthday."

Without further conversation, he went to his bedroom.

A lot had happened today. A lot that didn't make sense. The encounter with Kieran in the hallway, the argument and conversations with Elijah, and the strange intimacy of standing with Tayshia while she cried. Twice. It was all strange and weird and bizarre and just...

Why did he feel so exhausted?

Later, as his head relaxed into the softness of his pillows, he realized what he'd seen there in her eyes as she gazed upon the chocolates.

Terror.

CHAPTER
FOURTEEN

Saturday dawned to a torrential downpour.

If he weren't from Oregon, Ash would have called it a monsoon. He was used to it, though. The Northern half of the state felt like it rained more than the sun rose in the Fall. It was almost comforting to wake to grey lighting instead of blue, to hear the gentle thrumming of the raindrops slamming against the roof without cessation.

Ash woke on the couch. He'd stayed up all night playing the video game he was currently making his way through and had smoked so much weed that he'd fallen asleep with the pause screen still on. It wasn't a difficult game, but he was trying to get to a point where he unlocked a secret boss, and he'd been working on it since living at Andre's. It was Saturday, so he was about to jump right back into it.

He trudged down the hallway, seeing to his luck that Tayshia wasn't awake yet. That meant the bathroom was unoccupied. Before the fates decided to wake her up, he locked himself inside and turned on the shower.

Hell yeah.

As he stood beneath the hot water, feeling the heat seeping into his muscles and soaking his hair, he found his mind wandering.

He'd dreamed of her the night before. It was odd, like watching a broken, half-burnt recording of yesterday's events. Flashes of her morning, flickers of her night. A vivid series of images of her crying while he put his arm around her. It was strange. All of her dreams had been like that, like linked memories, chained together by the day's events.

If they were memories, then what had happened to her on August 17th?

Gazing down at his hands, he turned them over, watching the water roll across the roses spanning the backs. It seemed like so long ago that he'd gotten them tattooed. Like a completely different lifetime—a different version of himself. A person who existed without the weight of grief and guilt.

He wished he could go back to when he felt free.

The chains tattooed on his neck, woven around the blooming red roses felt like they were real. Like they were wrapping tighter and tighter by the day. One day, he would suffocate by his own doing.

Hopefully his father suffocated first.

After he got out of the shower, his hair hung in messy, wet strands all over his head. Ash felt the ends tickling his chin, pieces of wet bleached hair falling into his eyes. He wrapped a towel around his waist. Torso bare and hand holding the towel closed, he left the bathroom.

God, he hoped he could unlock this boss or he was gonna rage-quit his entire life.

As he turned to walked towards his room, he nearly ran face-first into Tayshia. When she screamed, his heart leapt into his throat.

"Jesus, *fuck!*" he exclaimed, his hand snapping up to grip her elbow on reflex. "You scared me."

There was a panicked expression in her eyes as she first let her gaze dance all over his upper body, like she didn't know where to look first. Then, she looked up at him. Her hands were up by her face, almost as though she were anticipating having to defend herself. She took a shaky, hitched breath.

"Let go of me," she said. "Please."

Ash frowned and released her arm. "I'm not gonna *hurt* you. What the fuck?"

Her brow furrowed as well, and then she crossed her arms over her chest. Thoughts flickered across her face, silent and mysterious.

"I'm sorry," she said. "I just got freaked out."

He raised an eyebrow. "From running into your roommate in the hallway? Which is literally inevitable, by the way."

Tayshia's cheeks flushed and she glared at him. "Okay, rude in the morning. Bye."

He stepped aside as she brushed past. The bathroom door slammed shut. Shaking his head, he went to his bedroom to finish dressing, wondering why her gaze had felt so warm.

Ash pulled a white tee shirt on over his head and then dragged a pair of black skinny jeans with horizontal zippers adorning the front up his legs. He left his hair alone, walking back out to the living room. He turned on the console and TV, sat down on the couch amongst his pillows and blankets, and picked up the controller.

It was time to fuck shit up.

Two hours later, Ash was about ready to fuck the TV up.

"*Fuck!*" he snarled as his character died.

Again.

This was ridiculous. It was like the entire thing was rigged. He was at level ninety-nine. He had every keychain for his blade. He had his stats maxed out. His items were fully stocked. His magic was at its highest level. All of his abilities were set. The boss should *not* have been that difficult. He opened up the menu, scanning his information to see if there was something else he could do.

"You sound like you're going to break the controller in half."

Ash tore his angry gaze away from his stats screen, seeing Tayshia plopping down on the far end of the sectional. She was fully dressed, wearing her usual leggings and sweater. She had no make-up on, her skin seeming lustrous with some sort of skincare product. Her weave was in twin tail braids today, with her bangs out to stretch across her forehead. In her hands, she held a quart of strawberry yogurt and a silver spoon.

"I'm going to," he said, his voice a bit hoarse. Before this last go-through—while she was still in the bathroom—he'd filled his pipe and smoked it. Weed always made him sound scratchy. "I'm about to lose my shit."

Tayshia pulled her knees to her chest and began to eat.

"Why does his sword look like a giant key?" she asked around a spoonful of yogurt.

He paused the game and stared at her. She shifted, appearing to be in some modicum of discomfort.

"What?"

He said nothing, his upper lip curling as though she'd just sprouted three heads.

"*Bro!*" she yelled, gesturing with the spoon. "What is your *problem? What?*"

"You did not just say those words to me."

"What did I do?!"

"No. Nope. You did not just say those fucking words to me." He tried to hide his desire to laugh by tilting his head back to look at the ceiling. "I always see you playing your thing—how do you not know what game this is?"

She shrugged, eating another bite of her yogurt.

"You can't be serious."

"I like the ones with animals and pocky monsters," she said in a bit of a whiny tone. "What's so bad about that?"

"*Pocky monsters*? Why are you calling it that? That's so cringe."

"Because. It sounds cute." She took another bite.

Their eyes met and for a moment, their lips twitched upward like mirror images. Then, as fast as the moment had come, it was shattered. Tayshia got up from the couch. Ash heard the trash can lid a second or two later.

"Wow, you ate that whole tub fast," he said.

"I was hungry," was all she said before went to the bathroom.

The game still paused, Ash scooted forward until he was sitting up, on the edge of the couch cushion. He pulled the blue glass pipe and his lighter from behind the pillow beside him. There was a little weed left in the bowl so he brought it to his lips, lit it, and inhaled. It burned, almost itchy as it traveled down his throat and expanded in his lungs.

By the time Tayshia returned, Ash had smoked a second bowl and was sufficiently high. A pleasant buzzing had settled over his body, like a thick fleece blanket. His head felt full of cotton and a light mirth hovered around his lips in the form of a permanent, faint smirk. His eyes half-shut, he resumed the game and triggered the boss' cutscene again.

Tayshia sat down on the couch and watched. She let out an occasional sniffle, drawing Ash's curious gaze for a brief second. He couldn't look at her long, though—this was the most damage he'd managed to inflict on the boss before the countdown clock ran out. His thumbs flew with speed that was record-breaking. He hadn't even sat back on the couch—he was still perched on the edge of the cushion, his back straight and the veins on his forearms protruding through his tattoos as his thumbs worked.

He was determined.

Tayshia suddenly said, "Is that... Donald—"

"Yes," he sat, rolling his eyes as he cut her off.

"And Goo—"

"Obviously."

She watched in silence for a while before she spoke again.

"The coat on the guy you're battling reminds me of a cow," she said, and then she burst into a fit of giggles.

When she didn't stop giggling, he said, "And what's so funny now?"

"I'm just thinking," she said, her head falling back against the couch as her laughter intensified. She held a hand over her eyes. "Those memes from the internet. It's cracking me up."

Ash ran his teeth along his tongue to hide his smile.

"Why aren't any of your attacks landing?"

"He did like, this magic thing to take away the main character's heart. He doesn't have anything you can like, hit, so you have to use magic and whatnot. You—*oh,* fucking fuck me." His stomach dropped as he narrowly escaped death. He healed his character, then jumped back into the fray.

"These button-mashing games are so hard," Tayshia said. "I never was good at console games. Handhelds for me."

"Hey, well," he said. "At least you game. Not many girls do."

"And I'm not like *other* girls," she said in a mocking tone.

He glanced at her, and it was inevitable. Like a tidal wave crashing over them.

They both started laughing.

"I'm just playing," she said, watching the screen again. "I do like video games, but I'm not like, a *gamer.* I play them, but that doesn't mean I'm good at them."

"I cannot say the same," Ash said, distracted as the countdown clock on the screen dropped lower.

"I think I play more for the escape," she said, sounding thoughtful. "The colors and the music, and feeling like I'm in a completely different world with manageable problems. Problems that I can handle."

The furious speed with which he was clicking the buttons provided a weird soundtrack to an equally bizarre moment. A moment during which he was having a real, actual conversation with Tayshia Cole. Much like that night long ago in the hot springs.

"I play games for the same reason—because I like knowing there's an answer or a place to go. Like, an end goal. But this game series in particular is my favorite."

"How come?"

He glanced at her, their eyes meeting. He saw caution there within her. Then, right as he turned his face to look at the screen again, he saw her gaze dropping to look at his forearms and his fingers on the controller. But before he could think anything of it, the boss got the jump on him and he had to focus on beating him back.

He knew this was strange. They'd had a huge fight on Thursday, then another fight on her birthday and the subsequent breakdown in the kitchen. Now, she was watching him play video games. They were getting along.

When would the dream shatter?

"Because it deals with things like bad and good—darkness and light. And it shows that no one is ever completely existing on one side of the line. The best people can still have darkness inside of them, and that's what makes them human."

She nodded. "And even the worst people still have potential to be good."

"Yeah." Their eyes met again. For some reason, Ash's heart skipped a beat. He continued to press the X button, moving the analog stick to make sure he was still in the battle. "Exactly."

"Sounds religious," she said.

He gave her a crooked grin. "Everything's religious when it feels good."

"Well." She blushed and looked away. "Don't tell my parents that."

After a moment, Ash said, "Sounds like you're not Christ Rising's resident Good Girl anymore."

"I'm not religious anymore," she said, shrugging. "I don't think I ever really was. Universe is too big. We probably came from like, aliens and shit."

"Amen to that."

Suddenly, Tayshia glanced down at her phone. "Oh, they're almost here."

"Who?" Ash asked, eyes trained on the TV. The boss was almost dead. His heart was pounding—he might actually beat him this time. He might actually—

"My parents."

On the screen, Ash's character let out a groan, the screen fading to black as he died.

"What?"

"My parents are coming because it was my birthday," she said. "They texted and said they're coming off the freeway now."

179

Ash felt the panic creeping into his heart, sending it into a frenzied pattern of wild beats. The thought of Tayshia's parents entering the apartment, her father's eyes meeting his...

The guilt was too much, unbearable in its immensity. He didn't bother resetting the cutscene.

"Do they know you accidentally got housed with me?" he asked, trying to keep himself calm. "Like, do they know I'm here?"

"No," she said, standing up from the couch and stretching. "I told them I had a roommate, but not that it was a man, or that it was you. I figured when they got here and saw the way we live, they'd be more likely to be okay with it."

"Are you fucking kidding me right now?" Ash's panic started to mingle with a rising anger. "Why would you think it was a good idea to bring them *here*?"

Tayshia frowned. "Because it's my home. It's where I live. They're my parents. Of course they'd want to see what it looks like."

"I highly doubt they want to see *me* inside of it. Are you *nuts*?"

She threw her hands up. "They're not staying the night, Ash! They're just coming for a day trip. It's not a big deal."

"Not a big *deal*? Do you *hear* yourself?"

"Yes, I do!" she cried. "I don't see why I should have to keep my parents out of my home, though!"

"*Bro!*" he shouted, eyes wide. "My dad *shot* your dad! Why would you think he would want to be within *any* vicinity where I am present?"

"My parents are Christians, Ash. They've already forgiven you."

"Fuck!" Ash's rage spiked and he jumped to his feet. Whirling around, he hurled the controller at the wall, where it crashed to the floor. He glared at her, barely able to think past the terror swirling through his sensibilities. "Because that makes it *so* much better!"

Tayshia's facial expression was calm.

"Do not scream at me."

Ash's anger faltered. He blinked, a bit taken aback at the quiet, seething fury burning in her eyes.

"I don't care how angry you feel," she said, voice soft as she held up a warning finger, "but I am not the one."

"Oh, but it's okay for you to attack me in the kitchen like you did Thursday?"

"I apologized."

"Still doesn't erase that it happened."

"No, you're right. But I felt trapped. You had me in a corner."

Defensive, he cried, "And your first reaction was to act like I was going to hurt you?!"

"Did you or did you not go to jail?" When he averted his eyes, she took a step closer to him, the coffee table the only thing between them. *"Did you or did you not go to jail, Ash?!"*

He turned his face away.

This was it. The real-world consequences of his actions. He may have only been sentenced to eleven months, but the punishment would last a lot longer. He'd failed to think about any of that before he'd entered that ice cream shop. Whether he and Tayshia were friends, or hated each other, or got along, or didn't, all that mattered was his past.

She was scared of him.

"Look, I'd prefer it if your parents didn't come up here. Just meet them outside or something." He moved around the table, ignoring her wary expression and the way she stepped to the side, though he was nowhere near her. "It's just as much my place as it is yours. We both pay half the rent. We should respect one another."

"Oh, like you respect me?"

His head snapped toward her as he rounded the back of the couch. "What are you talking about?"

She crossed her arms, her eyebrows rising. "The joint or pipe or whatever it is you got hidden out here. You think I don't know what weed smells like?"

Ash scoffed. "We agreed to follow each other's rules on day one. I said keep shit clean, and you immediately did the opposite. I'd say me being able to smoke is a fair trade."

"Ash, they are my *parents*!" she said, clapping her hands to emphasize her words. "I can't just tell them to stay outside!"

"You can, and you will," he said, storming into the kitchen to grab a soda from the fridge. The *pop* of the lid was loud. "We're both on the lease, so we need to respect that."

"Ash —"

"I said no." He tipped the soda down his throat, feeling the crispness as he gazed across the room at her. "This is my house, too. And I have the right to say who gets to come inside. Unless you want to force me...?"

Her brows twitched together. "No. No, I don't want to force you

181

to do anything."

"Good. Then you can meet them outside."

"Ash, they're bringing my furniture."

"Cry about it," he said.

Ash returned to the living room, retrieved his discarded controller, and perched on the edge of the couch cushion again. He set the soda can on the coffee table and then triggered the boss' cutscene again. His gaze remained trained upon the TV screen.

Tayshia's phone buzzed. Without another word, she stomped down the hallway. He heard her keys jangling and then moments later, she was out the door.

Relief flooded his veins like blood.

He didn't want to see Mr. Cole. He didn't want to look him in the eyes and have to explain to him why he'd just stood and watched him bleed. Didn't want to have to apologize when he wasn't ready.

Didn't want to have to face his sins.

CHAPTER FIFTEEN

Ash didn't beat the boss until three hours later.

Right as he did, he felt the pride tearing through him, eradicating his earlier bad mood. He jumped to his feet, his arms outstretched above his head in a silent cheer. As the end-of-boss-battle cutscene played, he did a small dance of joy.

"Fuck *yes*!" he hissed, pumping his right fist in triumph, the left still holding the controller. "Fuck yes, fuck yes, fuck *yes*!"

He went to the kitchen to retrieve his third soda for the day, then went back to the living room to smoke another bowl in celebration. He played music on his phone—the band Thy Art is Murder, to be exact—and then prepared to start the New Game Plus version of his game.

He heard the keys in the front door, and then it swung open. He didn't bother halting his process, holding the pipe to his lips with one hand and the lighter to the bowl with the other. He clicked the button on the lighter, bringing life to the flame.

Tayshia walked in with the hood on her hoodie pulled up and the front pieces of her hair and bangs damp from the rain. Ash caught a glimpse of the stone walkway outside, seeing the furniture stacked upon it. There was a small lavender end table with a couple of drawers, a large lavender dresser, a simple white desk, a folded metal bed frame with wheels, and a mattress.

"You need help?" he said begrudgingly, pausing his game.

"No." She glared at him. "My mom and I got this all to the outside, and I can get it all in my room. Thanks, though."

"Couldn't your dad..." Ash trailed off, the guilt suffocating his words.

He had a feeling people with year-old chest wounds probably couldn't do much heavy lifting.

As Tayshia carried the small end table into her room, Ash sighed. He wasn't *that* much of an asshole. He set the controller down and went outside to grab her bed frame. She stood to the side of hallway as he did, frowning.

When he entered her room, he grimaced. Whereas his room was fully decorated complete with band posters on the walls, hers was sparse and bare. Her walls were empty and the only thing she seemed to own was a sleeping bag and the boxes she'd brought on day one. It was clear that she was living out of them.

He set the bed frame down against her wall. She could do those parts by herself.

Coming back out, he saw her still standing there. The look on her face was easy to read.

"Let's go," he said. "I can't lift the big shit by myself."

"Okay," she mumbled.

Together, they worked to carry everything inside. The mattress was the most difficult due to its size, but the dresser and desk were fairly easy. Once it was all inside, he left her to it so he could go back out and finish watching the ending cutscenes of the game.

After a little while, Tayshia walked back out to lock the front door.

"Hey," he said through the exhalation of marijuana smoke, looking her up and down as she threw the latch. "I beat that boss."

"Oh, cool," she said, her voice soft. She didn't seem perturbed by the smoking, which was odd after all the fighting. "How long did it take?"

"Uh, three hours. I literally just beat him before you walked in."

"Nice."

Tayshia stopped at the mouth of the hallway right as Ash set the pipe down on the table and picked the controller back up.

"We gotta talk," she said.

"Huh?" He looked at her, the sounds and music of the opening cutscenes to the game played, warring with the music from his phone. "About... Before? Or—"

"No, I need to tell you something." She turned to face him, fidgeting with her fingers. "My parents and I fought."

"Okay," he said slowly, holding the controller with both hands while placing his elbows on his thighs.

Tayshia looked at him and then looked away. "They cut me off."

Ash immediately paused his music, grabbed the remote, and muted the TV.

"What? Why?"

"Because I had to tell them the truth. Well, part of it. I had to tell them why they couldn't come up."

"You *had* to?"

"I don't like lying," she said, shrugging. The keys jangled again as she turned them over in her hands. She then reached up to push her hood back, revealing her hair. She'd pulled it into a tail at the base of her scalp, the crimson strands seeming lifeless and damp from the rain outside. "I told them I accidentally got placed with a boy."

"Did you tell them it was me?"

"No. I—well, I think that even if they forgave you, they wouldn't be okay with me living with you. So, you were right."

Ash raised one hand to rub at his chin, fingers sliding along the stubble on his jaw. "Sorry."

"It's not your fault," she said. "And my parents understand that it was a mix-up. They offered to pay the ETF fee."

"And what did you say?"

"I told them no."

Their eyes met. Ash gave her a confused look. He knew he could have paid the fee, but he'd decided not to on principle. She'd been given the chance to get the money another way. She hated him.

Why wouldn't she take the opportunity?

"Why?" he asked.

"Because I don't want to move," she mumbled, looking down. "I feel... Safe here. I don't know."

Hold up.

She felt *safe* living with him, but not on Thursday when she went ballistic in the kitchen? He wanted to call her out on it but the longer he stared at the dejected way her shoulders slumped, the harder it was to feel irritated by her.

Had him allowing her the freedom to cry somehow changed things for her?

"So, what do you wanna do?" he asked.

"I'm gonna have to get a job. They told me that as long as I choose to live with a boy, then they can't support my living expenses. They'll pay for my tuition to the school, but not my rent and phone bill."

"What are you gonna do about the rent then?"

She shrugged, looking as though she were seconds away from despair.

"Well, it's Saturday," Ash said, wheels in his mind turning like the cogs in a machine. "You want me to take you to pick up applications?"

She grimaced. "Is that okay? I don't want to do it online because if I do, I'll just get overlooked. Rent is due in like two weeks, so..."

Ash didn't know how to tell her that there was no way in Hell she'd have the rent in two weeks with a new job. Not with how long the interview, hiring, and orientation processes took. Even if she landed a job that night, she wouldn't get her first paycheck for an entire month unless she was lucky enough to get a job that paid weekly instead of bi-weekly.

He was high, they'd had a fight, and he could pay for the entire rent if he wanted to. Driving her around all day wasn't exactly something that sounded like it was going to remain amicable and polite.

But he'd do it.

"Shit, yeah," he said, sighing as he set the controller on the coffee table. He stood up and walked to the console, pressing the button on the front to turn it off. "Let's go, I guess."

"Okay, thanks," she said, her lips curling into a meek smile.

They both went to their rooms. When Ash got to his, he pulled on one of his jackets. It was dark grey denim that looked sleeveless, but the sleeves and hood were made like that of a sweatshirt. Then, he shoved is feet into his shoes. After grabbing his wallet and keys, he pulled the hood up onto the back of his head and went back out to the living area to wait.

Tayshia walked out of the hallway. Ash, who was leaning back against the kitchen bar with his arms crossed, looked up.

Damn.

She'd changed into a pink-and-lavender plaid miniskirt with pleats, a long-sleeved black shirt, and opaque black tights. Over the outfit, she had donned a black velvet coat with an A-line dress shape and a hood with black fur on it. Her hair was no longer in the ponytail—now it hung loose down her back. There were pink pearl bobby pins adorning her hair near her temple and though she wore no make-up, her lip balm stained the brown of her lips rose-pink and some sort of equally-rose blush had been puffed onto the apples of her cheeks, contrasting prettily with the tawniness of her skin.

Around her neck, the crystal hung from its silver chain like it belonged there. He resisted the urge to reach beneath the neckline of his white tee and touch his own.

Damn.

Ash wasn't blind.

"Ready to go?" she asked.

"Uh... Yeah," he said, clearing his throat.

He stood up straight, towering over her with the strangest urge to wrap his arms around her that he'd ever had. He could still remember what it felt like to put his arm around her while she cried, and what it felt like to stand in the hot springs with her while the stars shone above them.

She gave him one last unreadable look, and then she pulled her hood up. He followed her out the door.

☼☼☼

They headed to some shopping centers first.

Ash would park at one end of the lot and wait in his car while Tayshia braved the rain to go to each store. She'd fill out the applications in the car, then run back in to drop them off. They didn't talk much, except for her to give him a run-down on who was hiring and who wasn't. By the third shopping center, she seemed to be in less of a forlorn mood.

While he waited, he'd close his eyes and listen to the rain as it drummed a grey song into his head. He nearly dozed off several times. After they finished with the major shopping centers, they headed to the mall. It would be their last stop before heading home — it was almost seven at night.

They headed into the mall, which was so crowded that it was hard to make their way through. Ash wasn't surprised. It was always this full on Saturdays, as it was the only mall for miles without driving the hour journey on the freeway to Portland. People from other towns near Crystal Springs came to this mall to do their shopping. It had a lot of stores and was two stories high, so he had a feeling Tayshia would have some luck in here.

Ash liked shopping but didn't feel like it at the moment, so he sat down on a bench while Tayshia walked down one side of the top floor. He watched the people walk by, pretending not to notice the ones who gave him nasty looks.

He was so beyond used to it that it was annoying.

Tayshia came back and sat beside him, using her leg to fill out her applications. She seemed to be in a good mood.

"Hey, what does it mean if it says this?" she asked. "I keep seeing it, but I've never had a job before, so I don't know what it means."

Job hunting wasn't exactly his forte. He'd had a fast food job up until his father *employed* him, for lack of a better word. After he started getting paid from that, it felt pointless to clock in and fry burgers all day when he was making twice as much with his dad. All they had to do was sell the stuff and pay Ricky, and then Ricky paid them. Things didn't start to go awry until the drugs took over and Gabriel started skimming off the top.

"Lemme see," he murmured, his left arm stretching along the back of the bench they sat upon. He leaned over her, taking the application from her. Her acrylic nail—almond-shaped and painted a sparkling lavender—pointed to the section in question. "Oh, this is no big deal. They just want to know if you have any special skills aside from prior work experience."

"Like if I can type fast or something?"

"Mm-hm," he hummed. Her handwriting was a lot messier than he would have expected from her. Kinda like the way she treated the kitchen.

Her perfume smelled good. Like a fragrant combination of flowers and sugar that was a heady as it was sweet.

"What sort of prior skills would I need to work retail?"

"I don't think it's a necessity. I think they just wanna know if you do. Maybe they'd look for experience working with people, familiarity with a register and handling money or like, experience in sales?"

"Oh."

"Yeah."

She looked up at the same time that he did, their faces mere inches apart. Her saw her cheeks flush redder than the rouge she'd spread across them. His heart skipped a beat for the second time that day as his gaze fell to her lips. Her tongue darted out to wet them and his eyes tracked the movement.

Holy fuck, Tayshia was cute.

"Well, I'd—I'd better go turn these in," she said, her voice coming out as a cracked whisper. She stood up so fast that he had to jerk his head back to keep from getting his nose broken by her skull.

"I'll be here," he said.

"Uh—okay. Yes. I'll be... Okay, bye."

She turned and walked away, melting into the crowd.

Ash ran a hand down his face, taking a ragged breath. He

couldn't remember the last time he felt that intense of an urge to kiss someone.

It was *Tayshia*, for fuck's sake.

Ten minutes later, Tayshia came rushing back over. The look on her face set an alarm bell ringing in his mind. His hands rested on his knees as he leaned forward and looked up at her. She couldn't seem to meet his gaze for longer than a second.

"Did something happen?" he asked.

"Uh, it—" She closed her eyes and shook her head, waving a dismissive hand. "It was bad. Just—it was bad. It was really bad."

"What do you mean?"

"I sounded stupid and people were looking at me and just—I don't know. It was really, really bad."

Ash frowned. That didn't sound right. When they were in their high school years, Tayshia was always the first person to volunteer to present projects and give speeches. She wasn't someone who he could see failing an interview. That didn't make any sense to him.

"Can we go?" Her voice broke, sounding high-pitched. Her gaze darted about the crowded walkway. "Please?"

Ash stood up, tugging on his hood to make sure it was still on. "Okay, but what happened?"

"Nothing. Let's go."

She turned and started walking. Ash followed her clear until they were headed for the doors out to the parking lot. Her head was down and she was wringing her hands in front of her.

He stopped, grabbing her arm and spinning her around. She looked up at him with wide eyes as he held tight, refusing to let her go. People milled about around them, some of them students from the public school that looked at the two of them like physical anomalies because they went to a different school than them. Some of the people walking by were older adults who seemed to recognize Ash and they gave him a wide berth as they passed. But Ash didn't care.

Something was wrong.

"I asked you what happened."

"Nothing." She tried to pull herself away.

"Did someone say something to you?"

"Yes, okay?"

She tried to pull herself away, but Ash tightened his hold on her arm. He arched one eyebrow in impatience.

"It was a guy at one of the clothing stores," she said quickly. "He was fine when he gave me the application, but when I came back to give him the filled-out one, he looked annoyed. I gave it to him and then I started to leave, but he called me back and said he wanted to interview me right there."

"What did he say?"

"It was just a weird interview, all right?" Tayshia said in a low voice, looking mortified. "He kept asking me if I had any felonies, if I'd ever shoplifted before, and how many times I'd been fired."

Ash's jaw nearly dropped, shock and revulsion rocketing through his body. He wasn't blind and he wasn't an idiot. He knew why the interviewer had treated her like that, why he'd interviewed her on the spot.

This was a mountain town in Oregon, after all.

Ash nodded slowly, rubbing a hand along his jaw. He glanced back over his shoulder, towards the crowd as it moved to the left and right past them. He and Tayshia weren't friends, but Ash wasn't okay with mistreatment.

Besides, Ash was someone who couldn't get a job easily. He was someone who *did* have a felony. Therefore, he had nothing to lose if he beat the shit out of a guy in the mall.

He started walking back inside.

"Ash, no! What the Hell is wrong with you?" Tayshia grabbed the back of his jacket, yanking to stop him. "It's not like it's abnormal!"

"It's *wrong*," he growled.

"I know that!" she snapped. "But I don't need you to save me. Jesus Christ. Let's just go. I wouldn't want to work in a place like that anyway."

Ash scoffed at her sarcasm. His anger felt hot and virulent inside of him, causing his hands to flex into and out of fists. He knew that it wasn't his place to save her or anyone else from anything, but after the way he'd really screwed up with his mom and the way he'd fucked up when Tayshia's dad was bleeding on the ground, he couldn't imagine *not* doing something about it.

He wanted to see how disrespectful the guy could be towards Tayshia if he were standing behind her, covered in tattoos and taller than a fucking tree. He knew he looked scary. He knew he terrified the more simple-minded people in town.

Maybe he could have terrified the guy into apologizing.

As they rode through the busy, suburban streets of Crystal Springs, Ash found himself unable to calm down. He drove with one hand on the wheel and the other threading through his bleached hair over and over. He was so agitated that he forgot to turn the music on.

"Can you stop?" Tayshia said into the silence. "Every time a white person finds out how shit really is, they gotta act all new and extra. You been knew it's like this—don't act like it's an anomaly."

"So it's a bad thing that I think prejudicial treatment is wrong?"

"No. It's a bad thing to act like a white savior for a Black woman who didn't ask you to save her."

"Forgive me for caring how people get treated," he said, the sarcasm turning his tone nasty. The clicking of the blinker annoyed him. He was glad when the light turned green and he was able to turn. "And forgive me for wanting to handle that shit correctly."

"*Correctly*?" She side-eyed him. "Let me guess—you got into fights in jail?"

He said nothing, glaring out his window.

"It's not really something your anger can fix, Ash," she said, elbow on the windowsill and her cheek resting against her knuckles. "I'm Black. This stuff happens to me. It's my life. I'm used to it."

"No one should have to get used to that." He shook his head. "It bothers me."

"Welcome to America."

"So what am I supposed to do, huh? What the fuck am I supposed to do?"

"Be a good person. Don't be a racist. If you see something, speak up. But don't insert yourself where you don't belong."

"What's the difference between me beating the living shit out of the guy, and speaking up when I see something?"

"You weren't there. You didn't see it, so marching in there to get yourself thrown back in jail is ridiculous. It's enough for me personally to know that if something *did* happen in front of you, you'd handle it. But you have to understand something. We literally live in a system that actively works to oppress the people who exist further away from whiteness. The closer to whiteness you are, the better your privilege. For you to act like this is the first time you've heard of racism and that you're so infuriated by it that you're gonna—gonna just *risk it all* for a girl you despise...? It's frustrating.

191

It's *beyond* frustrating. I don't need pity, sympathy, and a knight. I need you to listen, learn, and reject the privilege you have *before* you start throwing punches in the God damn hillbilly mall, bro."

Her words caused a heavy blanket of something so familiar that it was uncomfortable. Hearing that it was *enough for her* and that she knew he'd *handle it* on the same day that he'd heard her say she felt *safe with him*?

His fingers itched. For some reason, he wanted to reach for her hand.

"What do you care, anyway?" she said, sounding bitter. "You don't even like me."

"I don't have to be overly fond of you to want to make sure you're treated right. It's not like your worth devaluates just because someone can't get along with you."

"Huh." She tsked. "My worth."

"Yeah." He glanced at her, one hand on the bottom of the wheel and the other resting in his lap. "Your worth."

She looked up at him, searching his eyes until she scowled. "Watch the road, or you'll get us killed."

The silence only lasted a few moments before Ash spoke again.

"So, why exactly did your parents and you get into a fight?"

She let out a heavy sigh.

"They're angry with me. Well, mostly my mom is. She thinks Kieran is the husband God picked out for me. She thinks I must have done something to make him want to cheat. And she thinks I should pray about it and take him back."

Ash's upper lip curled. "No."

"I know. That's what I said to her. But she's a religious fanatic and delusional. She told me his family is still coming to our house for Christmas."

"What the fuck?"

"Yeah, and I said that was nuts. But my Dad agreed with her—they think he's my person."

"Wow."

"Exactly. And I think they think Quinn has a demon, or something—they think she seduced him."

"She probably does have a demon," Ash muttered, turning the wheel with the heel of his palm. "That bitch gets on my nerves."

"Ash."

He shrugged. "Sorry, not sorry. She's a cu—"

"*Don't...* Think about it."

Ash couldn't help but smirk.

✧✧✧

Ash dropped his keys on the counter as he clicked the lightswitch on.

"I have to be honest with you," Tayshia said once the kitchen light flooded the space with warm light. "I don't know if I can do that again. That was so stressful. What if everyone thinks that way? What if I get no callbacks? What if —"

"Okay, okay," he said, holding up a hand to quiet her. Then, he placed his hands flat on the counter, leaning over it. "Just chill."

"What do I do, Ash?"

He hung his head, his hair falling forward into his eyes. "I'll... Take care of it."

"Wait... What?"

He turned his head toward her but didn't lift his gaze from the counter. "I'll take care of it. For a while."

"You... You mean the *rent*? The entire rent?" She sounded stunned. "Ash, that's — *How*?"

"I'm good on the money front," he said, his heart clenching as the faint image of Lizette smiling faded across his mind's field of vision. "So don't worry about it. Just focus on school. But you have to *promise* you're gonna look for a job when you feel like you can handle it."

Ash knew he was acting crazy. It was completely out of pocket for him to pay the entire rent for her when they were *barely* getting along today.

He walked over to the refrigerator and pulled some leftovers out. As he plated them up, he noticed Tayshia watching him. He turned to her.

"Did you want some?"

"No, I already ate," she said.

He gave her a strange look. "When? We've been out for hours."

"I mean with my — with my parents."

"That was forever ago," He stuck the plate into the microwave.

"It was a buffet," she said, her words tumbling out in a rush. "Really, I'm not hungry like, at *all*."

"All right," he said with a shrug.

She stood awkwardly by the bar, still wearing her coat — as though this weren't her home. Like she was just visiting. Like the

193

second he offered to pay for everything, she'd signed the lease over to him. In a sense, she had. If he was going to pay the rent and all the bills, then in everything but legality, this place was his.

He saw her bite her lower lip, so he looked away. If she was a girl he'd picked up from a dating app, he'd already have her on the couch for doing that. He'd have her on the couch underneath him, writhing against his body as his hands —

But she wasn't. She was Tayshia Cole. Even if he could stand her personality, he didn't deserve her after what his father had done. After what *he* had done.

Was she the hook-up type of girl, anyway? She didn't seem like it. Clearly, she and Kieran hadn't been seeing eye-to-eye on that front. Ash and Tayshia fought like feral cats, so the last thing she'd want to do was hook-up with him.

Not that he wanted to hook-up with Tayshia. Because that would be crazy. It wouldn't be something that happened or existed in this realm.

Almost like a dream.

The microwave hummed as the food spun. Ash leaned against the counter again, right beside the stove. He pulled his phone out, not sure why Tayshia was standing there and not going to her room.

"What is that?" she asked.

He looked up from his phone. "What's what?"

"The cord around your neck. I always see it, but you never have it out."

Oh.

Right. That.

Slowly, without averting his eyes from her own, he withdrew the crystal from where it lay hidden. Tayshia's lips parted, surprise widening her eyes as the kitchen light glinted off of the amethyst's many jagged faces. Her hand rosed to wrap around her half of the crystal, clutching it tight.

"You still have it?" she whispered.

He nodded. "And you still have yours."

This time, when their gazes met, it felt like they were looking at one another through the crystals. Viewing each other through multifaceted layers, seeing the gems that lay hidden inside. For the first time, instead of the mistrustful distaste he usually saw there, he saw someone else entirely. He saw a girl he was getting to know. Someone with feelings and emotions that went beyond hatred.

Someone he'd considered risking going back to jail for.

Just then, the microwave beeped, breaking the spell into thousands of pieces. Tayshia looked away as he turned to retrieve his food. The silence felt oppressive as he did so, especially when he pulled the silverware drawer open and grabbed a fork.

"Good night," he murmured, the plate heavy in his hand as he walked past her and went into his bedroom.

CHAPTER SIXTEEN

Ash couldn't sleep.

His mind was too full, too heavy with thoughts. They fluttered around his mind like butterflies, trapped and frantic. His worries about the fact that he hadn't texted Ryo back. His lingering grief over his mother. His argument with Elijah. The fact that he *wasn't* arguing with Tayshia.

The intense, stomach-clenching yearning he had to taste her lips once, just to see what it was like.

He tossed and turned for a while, unable to lower his energy enough to get to sleep. He felt bone-tired, exhausted from the day's events. No matter how hard he tried, it was like his slumber was being held behind a barrier of agitation.

Maybe if he went out to watch TV, he could fall asleep on the couch.

Clad in joggers yet shirtless, he gathered up his fleece blanket and left his room.

As soon as he opened his bedroom door, he saw the telltale flickering shadows that the television cast. The volume was down low, but he could hear the distinct sounds of an *anime* of some sort. He made his way down the hallway and out to the living room. Startled, he stopped in his tracks.

Tayshia lay on the long end of the couch, which was against the wall. She was using his pillow—which he'd left there earlier—and her legs were curled up underneath the hem of her hoodie. She wore her fuzzy socks again and her weave was tucked up into a satin bonnet.

"Damn," he said. "You can't sleep, either?"

She jolted, lifting her head. Her eyes were half-open. She looked tired.

"Sorry, do you want your pillow?" she said. "Did you want the couch, too? I can go to—"

"Nah, it's cool," he said, cutting her off.

He lay down on the short end of the sectional, resting his head back against the couch pillows that adorned the cornered center. It elevated him a bit to where if he rolled his head to the right, he could look at her.

"Why couldn't you sleep?" Tayshia asked.

"I'm like—I feel strung out," he said. "I dunno. You?"

"Same."

"You could always smoke a bowl with me," he said, sitting up and swiveling so he was facing the coffee table. He stood and leaned over, grabbing his pipe and lighter from the side of the table that was nearest her. "It'll put you right to sleep."

"Hah. Funny." She rolled her eyes, not lifting her head from his pillow.

He smirked as he sat down on the edge of the couch, holding the pipe to his lips. It would be exactly what he needed to cross the border of waking. There was plenty left for him to get decently high—which was good because he didn't have much left.

Ash clicked the lighter on and looked over at her.

She was staring at him.

Curiosity twisted its lazy way through his gut as he inhaled. He didn't look away from her, wondering what she was thinking of him as he sucked in as much smoke as he could and held it in his chest. His lungs spasmed for air.

When he blew the smoke out, he tilted his chin up so he could exhale it above.

And she watched him.

They watched the *anime* she had on for a short time—one with flying robots and a girl with pale green hair—and then Ash felt himself starting to drift.

He remembered reading somewhere that people couldn't sleep when they felt unsafe. That something in their brains made it difficult to wind down when they felt like they were in some sort of danger. Their adrenaline would just keep rising, higher and higher, keeping them awake until they felt invincible.

Ash didn't feel invincible around Tayshia.

"Do you sleep with it on?" she asked, her voice tiny.

"What?"

"The crystal. Do you sleep with it on?"

"Mm-hm," he said, his eyelids fluttering shut. He'd felt so awake in his room, but something about being in the living room with the cool, blue light of the TV and Tayshia opposite him made him feel so comfortable that he was falling asleep. "Do you?"

"Every night."

Ash wanted to look at her, but he was too exhausted.

"How did you get it made into a necklace?" he asked.

"My mom helped me. We took it to a jeweler."

He almost laughed. "You would, with your rich ass."

"Shut up," she said, and he could hear the smile in her voice. "Tch. Not no *more*."

His mirth disappeared.

How could he have forgotten? It was Ash's father that had put Mr. Cole in the hospital. It was Ash's fault that he hadn't tried harder to stop Gabriel, or to help stop Mr. Cole's bleeding.

"What about you?" Tayshia asked.

Ash felt his throat aching, his body sinking into the couch. He remembered that day—his nineteenth birthday. The cake, frosted baby blue and cotton candy pink. His mother, eating the entire thing.

The way she couldn't stop herself from getting rid of it, even on his birthday.

"My mom made it for me for my birthday," he whispered, the pain lowering his voice. "She like, went to our neighbor's and baked me this cake. The neighbor helped her make the crystal into a necklace because she—well, she saw me holding it all the time. And then she gave it to me."

As soon as he finished, he felt embarrassment flooding his body in a rush of heat. He hadn't meant to open up that much—didn't want to, either. But it felt like a bridge had been washed out by the rain, or like the wood of the gate blocking his memories had rotted.

Tayshia was quiet for a moment before she spoke in a soft tone.

"Ash, that's really sweet."

"Yeah," he said, his voice hoarse from the weed.

"Hey, Ash?"

"Yeah?"

"I'm really sorry about your mom," she said, and he could hear her voice shaking as though the words were difficult for her to utter. "It was all over the news. Do you know what happened?"

Yes.

"No," he lied. "I had to find out in jail."

"Ash," she said, her voice a sympathetic whine. "That's awful."

He closed his eyes, curled on his side beneath his blanket. Barely awake, he mumbled, "They confiscated all my shit when I was in, but I put the necklace back on the second I got out. And then I dreamed of you."

"You did?"

He didn't answer. He'd dozed off.

☼☼☼

At some point, Ash jolted awake.

The channel they'd been watching was playing infomercials, the blue flicker gentle. Tayshia was moving around the coffee table, stumbling sleepily toward the TV. Ash sat up.

"Sorry," she whispered, sounding like she'd just woken up, too.

She looked at him while she pressed the button to turn the television off, plunging them into pitch-black darkness. The only light came from the tiny green letters on the microwave and the larger ones that blinked on the stove. One read two-o-clock. The other flashed twelve-o-clock because they'd never set it up.

"I can't see a fucking thing," he said, laughing to himself.

"Here," she said, and then he felt her hand brushing along his jawline by accident. The surprise of it raised pebbles on his arms and across his shoulders. "Take my hand."

Ash did, wrapping his fingers around her own. Through the fog of sleep, he focused on how it felt, smooth and soft. It fit perfectly within his own. Tayshia pulled him to his feet and even though he couldn't see, he felt the heat of her body near him within inches.

Her hand slipped away.

Ash followed her, his eyes adjusting enough to see her outline like a haloed shadow. His slumber had hovered between light and deep, his body tired even though his mind was not. It had caused him to doze on the couch in a painful way that kept him from fully succumbing.

He was *tired*.

Tayshia slowed in the center of the hallway, forcing him to have to stop to keep himself from running into her.

He felt his heart pounding again, beating another tattoo into his chest. Sucking in his breath, he held it as he saw her silhouette turning to face him in the dark. He couldn't tell if she was looking at him or not.

What was she doing?

"Why did you keep the crystal?" Tayshia asked, her voice a small, quiet whisper. "Why did you keep that memory of me?"

Ash heard her words, heard the way her voice trembled. She was scared to ask him, but the importance of the question had urged her onward. The heaviness of it awarded him the ability to keep his eyelids open.

"Because it represents something to me," he said. "Why did you keep yours?"

"Kieran was so... So *mean* to me all the time. He made it seem like something was wrong with me every chance I got. In the cavern, you just treated me like a normal person — not some fucked-up excuse for a human being. You made me feel like I wasn't full of darkness and sin."

"*Kieran* is a fucking hypocrite," Ash said. "The last thing you are is bad."

"And that day in the cave, even though we were just breaking the rules and getting into the hot springs..." Her voice got quieter. "... It felt like I was normal. I'm just so, so tired of feeling like everything about me is *wrong*."

Ash could see a bit better now. She was facing away from him, her back only an inch away from his chest.

"The crystal means something to you, too," he replied. "Doesn't it?"

She turned to face him, and he saw her eyes like shadows in the dark.

"Do you feel bad? About what you did?"

It took him a moment to catch up, his mind still hazy with his sleepiness, but when the realization snapped together in his mind, his back straightened.

"Yeah," he said, his voice still a bit scratchy. "Of course."

"So do I."

He opened his mouth to speak, but the words died in his throat when he felt her hand pressing flat to the center of his chest. Heat spread across his bare skin, traveling outward to wrap him in a sudden desire that he hadn't realized he felt for her. A desire that felt as enticing as it was forbidden.

Like her.

"You do?" he choked out.

"Yes," she whispered. "I feel bad for blaming it all on you. I know it was your dad. I know that—that he was the one with the gun. I knew you were scared but I was trying to act tough. I was trying to act like a good person—the one who did the right thing. Like it was really that black-and-white. But then today, you said there's always light in the darkness, and that there's always darkness in the light. And it showed me that if I'm not perfect, then neither are you. I don't think it's fair for me to think you're a bad person for not being able to help my dad when you were just—"

No.

He didn't want to hear this. He couldn't.

It *was* his fault. The ice cream shop. The drugs. His father's abuse. His mother.

His *mother*.

Ash's anxiety, fear, and self-hatred swirled together, gathering towards him and lending him control. He moved toward her, letting his body do the thinking for him as he drowned in his own desperation for silence.

"Stop," he said, his words hoarse and choked as he cut her off.

"What?"

He snapped, grabbing her arm and turning her so fast that she gasped. Her back hit the wall right as his forearm did, framing her head he grabbed her chin from the front. His fingers pressed into the fleshy parts of her cheeks, right beneath her cheekbones, curling inward. Like he wanted to shut her up.

Like he wanted to hurt her.

That scared him.

"I said stop," Ash said, unable to decipher whether his grief was anger, or if his ire was pain. "Don't talk about things you don't understand."

Tayshia stared at him, unable to speak around the press of his palm over her lips. Lips that felt soft as satin upon his skin. Her eyes were wide in the darkness, the whites seeming grey.

He loosened his hold on her jaw. She released a shaky breath and he felt it, damp as it brushed against him.

And then she spoke, her voice naught but a whisper of air.

"Does it make you hate yourself less when I tell you that you're not bad?"

Something twisted in his stomach. On reflex, he jerked forward, his body pressing flush to hers.

"It makes me want to do things to you," he hissed through his teeth, unable to tear his glare off of the way her lips had parted. The way they seemed to call to him, plush and plump.

"What does it make you want to do to me?"

Why was she doing this to him?

Why was she saying these things?

"It makes me want to use you." He sucked in his breath, feeling every nerve ending in his body sparking with the energy of holding himself back from what he really wanted to do. "It makes me want to prove to you how bad I can be."

He felt her moving upward, pushing onto the tips of her toes to get closer. Her gazed darted up and down his face, settling on his eyes.

"So use me, Ash."

Ash swallowed. Hard. So hard that his throat throbbed in pain.

His fingers twitched against the wall and then moved to her bonnet. Slowly, he pulled it off. It was dark but his eyes were adjusted, so he was able to watch her hair tumble in waves to her elbows. His fingers sifted through it, feeling the tracks of her braids and the netting above them.

And then he clenched his hand into a fist and dragged her head so far back that she was looking straight up.

Trailing his other hand downward, he felt her half of the crystal between his fingertips. It was smooth in different places, but the jagged pieces were the same. Two pieces of the same whole, forever apart yet fitting together perfectly.

If they wanted them to.

He exhaled in defeat, his eyes half-shut.

"Just... Come here."

The span of two breaths passed and then his head snapped forward.

Ash captured Tayshia's lips mid-gasp, his head tilted to the side as he pushed all of his lust and need and loneliness into the press of his mouth against hers. He wanted her to know everything that was wrong with him without him ever having to say it aloud.

He was the son of the guy who shot someone she loved. The guy who yelled at her over stupid things. The felon. And he was going to rip out whatever silly fantasy of him she had in her head and fill the emptiness she'd torn into him with the triumph of her ecstasy.

He was going to consume her.

To kiss her until she remembered why she hated him.

But then she kissed him back.

It was only for a moment. One brief moment where her fingers were against his face and neck and she was on the tips of her toes. Where the angle of her head made it difficult for her to breathe, but she used it to fuel the way her tongue caressed his. Inside, he felt every part of his body swelling and singing and burning.

Tayshia tasted like starlight, present and significant enough to be beautiful.

Unattainable.

She turned her face a bit, as much as she could with his fingers clenched in her hair. He heard her take a ragged breath. His lips descended upon her bared throat, teeth nipping and tongue laving against a pulse that fluttered with the wild beating of her heart. Her hips twitched between his and the wall, and the feeling of it sent all the blood in his head rushing South. He grabbed her around the backs of her thighs and lifted her up.

And then he heard it.

A moan.

It was small, but he heard it. It lit him aflame.

"I'm sorry." Tayshia sounded nervous. Her hands gripped his shoulders like she didn't know where else to put them, her rapid panting as he kissed down the line of her throat mingling with the darkness in the hallway. "I-I didn't m-mean to."

"No. No, come here," he murmured, letting go of her hair so he could put his hands exactly where he wanted them. He squeezed the sides of her neck, enough to make her breath hitch. Her eyes were closed — as though she'd just tasted the sweetest fruit in Eden. "I like it."

"You do?" she breathed, their lips brushing once again.

"Yeah. I do."

Ash pulled her forward by the throat and kissed her again, tongue wet and searching — taking everything she had and pulling it into himself to fill that emptiness. That emptiness that *she* had carved.

He wanted her.

He wanted to hear her whine for him, begging him to keep going until she came. He wanted her to wear the rose tattoo on the back of his hand like a necklace. He wanted to squeeze so he could watch the thorns pierce her flesh.

He wanted to fuck her.

The realization brought him up for air, lifting his head so he could heave for it, his chest expanding and contracting. He needed to stop, or she needed to ask him to. One more wrong move. One more wrong choice, and there'd be no going back.

Something nagged at the back of his head, feeling as wrong as if the sun were out at night.

Was this because she'd just broken up with Kieran?

But he didn't like that. As deprived as he was from women since jail, what if she just wanted to feel some semblance of normalcy that Kieran wouldn't allow her to have?

What if she was a virgin?

His hands loosened their hold on her.

"Wait! No, please—please," she whispered, sounding desperate as she tightened her thighs around his hips. "I want this. I do."

"I don't believe you."

Her eyelids snapped open. She appeared confused, like she thought he was joking.

"I *do* want this." Her words halted, tripping over themselves. "I *do*."

"Fine. Then I'm going to pull you open and fuck you against the wall," he hissed into her ear because he didn't believe her, his hands sliding to grip the swell of her rear. He kneaded his fingers, spreading her apart in a way that had his mind reeling with a need that he forced himself to fight. "Would you like that?"

She didn't speak.

Still holding her, he dragged his hips against hers, hard, firm, and in the spot that he knew every woman wanted touched when they consented. Her mouth fell open in the dark and this time, she sighed. He did it again—for reasons that were as selfish as they were exploratory—and then he did it a third time. He felt a moan growing in his chest, but he held it in.

"Okay!" she cried. "Okay, okay, okay. Please put me down. Put me down!"

Stone-faced, he did as she asked. When her knees buckled and her hands went to his shoulders to keep herself upright, he glared down at her.

"Rebounds when you're a virgin aren't typically advised."

She was silent. So silent that he could hear his heart beating. Her fingers twitched on his skin, drumming as she searched his eyes.

And then she walked into his bedroom.

Ash stood there, his heart continuing to race.

What was he supposed to do?

Yeah, she was his roommate. Yeah, it was probably a bad idea, especially given that this lease had only begun two fucking weeks ago. Yeah, he wasn't sure how he felt about her.

But he'd hooked up with girls within less than fifteen minutes of knowing them. And he was no stranger to sex. It didn't have to be complicated. He didn't have to care.

She'd repeatedly said she wanted to. She'd just walked into his room. He hadn't fucked anyone in over a year.

Ash ran his fingers through his hair, decisions flickering through his mind.

It could be that simple.

It could be just a hook-up.

"Shit," he muttered under his breath, walking backward toward his room. "Shit, shit, shit."

☼☼☼

Tayshia was already sitting in the center of his full-sized bed, nestled amongst his black-and-grey comforter and pillows.

She tucked a wavy lock of hair behind her ear and cast him a wary glance. He came to stand next to the bed, arms crossed over his bare chest.

"Are you a virgin?" he asked.

"No," she said, tone flat.

"And what is your goal?"

"To forget."

He frowned. "So, a rebound."

"Does it matter? A rebound is only bad if you want to date me." Her tone was snarky. "Do you want to date me, Ash Robards?"

"No."

"Then why are you complaining?" She scooted down until she lay flat, her hair fanning out across the pillows. "It's just a—a hook-up, or whatever."

"Or whatever?"

"Yes. I mean—yeah."

Ash crawled over her body, still wearing his joggers as he knelt between her legs. His hands reached for the hem of her hoodie, but she stopped him. There was a fearful look in her eyes.

"I need to—I mean, I wanna leave it on while you—while we—"

Ash's stomach curled at the thought of fucking her in nothing but her hoodie while her nails scratched his chest tattoos. It didn't take any convincing. He moved forward to settle atop her body and kissed her, drawing her into a smoldering whirlwind of lips and tongue. His hands reached down and pressed against her inner thighs, spreading them apart. The moment his fingers touched her skin, she jumped.

"Do what you were doing before," she said quickly, her gaze trained on the ceiling. She was shaking.

"What?" he murmured, pressing a kiss to the inside of her knee as he hitched her thigh to his hip. "What do you want me to do?"

"What y-you did on the—against the wall," she said. "Do that again."

"Why?"

She hesitated and then whispered, "Because it felt good."

His hand ran soothing lines up and down her right thigh, his other hand pressing flat to the mattress. He looked down at her face, his gaze as intense as the desire coursing through his body.

"And you like when it feels good?"

She nodded, eyes trained on his lips.

There was no protest from her when he leaned forward and rocked his hips against her core. No protest when his lips met hers again. No protest when he wrapped an arm around her waist and pulled her spine into a deeper arch so that the downward tilt of her hips would put her exactly where she needed to be.

Her eyelids fluttered.

"There?" he asked.

"Y-Yes."

"You're so sweet," he breathed out, because he knew she was the exact opposite. He was unable to stop the feeling that jolted up his spine when he felt her hips grinding back.

"I'm n-not." Her back arched and she let out a long, low moan. "You don't have to—to say that."

"You are," he whispered, tasting the spot beneath her ear. His fingers stroked her thigh. "You're sweet and soft. So fucking soft. Your skin's like satin."

"Don't say that."

Ash raised his eyebrow, not stopping the pace of his hips. He wanted to be inside of her so badly, but there was something about this that he liked. Something about the ice around her melting beneath him as he rendered her to nothing.

What would happen if he touched her?

This was so juvenile yet she seemed so into it. Like it was the only time she'd ever felt this good. In the dim, opalescent moonlight that fell across the bed from his window, he could see her brows pulling together, her mouth falling open.

There was something there—something in her face. Like she wasn't looking at him, but instead looking *to* him. Like she needed him to confirm that she was making the right choice.

A warm feeling washed over his body, one that he'd rarely felt before. It was almost protective in the way it urged his body to press closer to hers. He no longer wanted to hurt her, or use her, or do anything except make her feel good.

It was just a hook-up but that didn't mean it needed to be quick.

Tayshia trembled like she was nervous, but her eyes shone like she was scared.

"Tell me what you want me to do," he breathed, his lips brushing the shell of her ear. "I'll make it good for you. I promise."

She covered her face with her hands, her thigh muscles quivering.

"Come on," he said. "Tell me."

Tayshia took a tremulous breath and then said, "I want you to—to go harder. But don't pull away when you do it. Just—"

Ash's fingers dug into her thigh. He moved his hips in hard, grinding motions. Her eyes rolled as she sighed. He found himself aching. He couldn't take his eyes off of her face.

"You like that?" he said, the ghost of a smirk hovering about his lips. "Tell me if it hurts."

Tayshia nodded, the concentration on her face apparent as he resumed what he'd been doing to her in the hall. With how wide he was holding her legs open and how firmly he rolled his hips against her, he could feel her body getting limper beneath him. It wouldn't be enough for him, but it seemed like it was for her.

As her concentration began to fade and turn into something euphoric, he found that he wasn't sure he was right about himself.

Maybe he did care.

"You want me to play with your clit?" Ash murmured, his voice rumbling in his chest. He tried not to purr when she placed a hand on the right side of his chest and lightly scratched her nails downward—as if testing out how it felt. "Huh? Do you want me to play with it?"

"I don't know," she said. "I think so."

He looked at her for a moment, trying to reconcile the fact that she was so unsure with the fact that she wasn't a virgin.

Was Kieran *that* bad?

"Has anyone ever made you...?"

"No," she said, her tone a bit icy. "And what? What about it?"

"Not even yourself?"

She pulled a sour face and said mockingly, "*Masturbation is a sin, Ash.*"

"So, do you want me to touch you or not?"

Tayshia swallowed, studying him.

"Yes," she said. "But just on the outside. Not under my underwear."

Okay, so she obviously wanted to go slow. He could handle that. His fingers slipped between them and found the apex of her core outside of her panties with practiced speed.

"Here?"

Her response was to whimper and nod as he held her left thigh open and moved his fingers in a way that used her arousal and dragged the fabric against her, creating friction. He dropped his lips to the side of her neck as he did, leaving light kisses that made her shiver each time. Her body was rigid. She let out the air in her chest and instead of a breath, it sounded like a sob.

It was simple enough to figure out the way her body worked. She was like a book, pages open to him and turning easily with each pass of his fingers across her. He had always been able to read her, and she was good.

She was so good.

"Such a sweet girl," he cooed into her ear, ignoring the way her whining stuttered. "Come for me now. It's okay. Come for me. Tell me when you do."

"Now," she said, her voice strained and head thrown back. "Like, *now* now. Right now, right there, right there, right —"

With one more slow circle of his fingertips against the fabric, against soft, tender flesh, she shattered like glass against the floor. She came with a violent shudder that ripped through her body and left her choking for breath. He touched her gently through it, his hand holding her pelvis down.

She was so fucking gorgeous.

Why had he never noticed before?

"W-Wait—I don't think I can again. Ash. I'm too s-sensitive. Ash, *please.*"

Her panties were completely soaked. It was easy to use all four of his fingers to drag them along her core, as gentle as though the touch were barely there. Her back arched upward when his fingers curled and pressed inward.

"Shh," he murmured, keeping his fingers gentle as he continued to touch her. "Be sweet. You can take it, can't you? Can't you?"

She whimpered and then said, "I can take it."

"Good girl."

Her legs fell open wider.

Fuck.

She was like an ice princess whenever he looked at her, her tawny brown skin always appearing as soft as a blanket of snow, with her heart draped in sheets of frostiness that only seemed to melt when she wanted it to. Back there against the wall, with his hand around her throat and his tongue inside of her mouth, it felt like she was melting because she was letting him pour heat into her.

Why did she always have to say the things that made him feel the coldest?

His eyes caught sight of the silver chain around her neck. He felt his own crystal swinging away from his bare chest.

He should have tossed it.

Ash regretted not getting rid of it, and her with it. He regretted not shedding his skin, cleaning her out, and donning the person he used to be before jail. But the moment their lips had first touched, it was like the water filling his mind—the ocean that had been drowning him slowly since they pulled that amethyst out of the cavern wall—churned with the beginnings of a tidal wave.

One of her hands slid from his chest to the flexing muscles of his abdomen. He saw her head roll to the side, her teeth sinking into her lower lip to stifle the sounds of her cries. She watched his forearm as it moved up with the massage of his fingers against her. He heard her begging him, heard her saying *please, Ash, gentler please,* but never once did she tell him to stop. Never once did she say no.

Why did he feel so guilty?

"Ash?" Her voice shook like she was about to cry. "*Ash!*"

"Hm?"

"I'm gonna—" Her eyes opened wide and she gasped. "—again."

"I know," he said softly. "God, I wanna fuck you *so* bad."

Tayshia's breathing caught. "You do?"

"Yeah. Of course." He almost laughed. "Why does that shock you?"

"I don't know if I'd feel very good."

Ash leaned down to kiss her. Then, he angled his hand until just two of his fingertips were on her, pressing tight circles. The fabric was so slick that it slid against her like she really was made of satin.

"You'll feel so, so good on me," he groaned, sucking her earlobe into his mouth, making her shudder. "You will, and then I'll fuck you until you come all over me."

He sped up his pace. She practically screamed.

"That's it," he breathed out in a growl. "You can *fucking* do it. Come on. Give me one more. Give me one *fucking* more."

Her fingernails dug into his chest until he feared she might break the skin.

When she came, sobbing with her head turned to the pillows and her entire body convulsing, he saw tears in her eyes. Panic bloomed like gardenias in his chest. Had he misunderstood her consent?

"I wanna stop," she whispered. "I need to stop."

Ash moved away from her faster than he could blink. All the blood in his body rushed back to where it was supposed to go, fear pushing the adrenaline.

"Did I hurt you?" he asked, keeping his distance and pushing his hair out of his eyes. "I'm—"

"No, you didn't," she said and her voice sounded choked. "I'm just overwhelmed. I'm overwhelmed, and I don't think this sort of thing is for me. I mean, I just got cheated on, my boyfriend and I broke up, and I'm gain—I'm just not doing well, and this was a little intense for me."

"Which part? The things I said? Or the hooking up?" *Or could it be the fact that you just had post-nut clarity, and realized you still hated me?*

"All of it."

She said nothing more and left the room.

As his bedroom door slammed shut, Ash came to another realization about Tayshia Cole.

Tayshia was the brightest ray of light in the room because she

211

costumed herself to be. She'd always painted a smile onto a sunlit face every morning, and from the moment he saw her in their shared apartment each morning to the moment she closed her bedroom door at night, she wore that smile like a suit of armor. A suit of armor weakened by the frost that had begun to gather in the grooves, collecting bit-by-bit as it froze her.

And he could tell—she *wanted* to freeze. She wanted to freeze because then she wouldn't have to think about being the person everyone expected her to be. If she were frozen, then everything could come to a complete halt, and she wouldn't have to be terrified anymore.

She was sitting out in the middle of a snow-covered field, shivering because she thought no one was watching.

CHAPTER SEVENTEEN

Tayshia was so weird.

"25... 26... 27... 28..."

In the morning, when Ash finally stumbled out into the hall to use the bathroom, he could hear her in the living room. The sounds of her exerted pants reached his ears in the dimness of the hallway.

What the fuck was she *doing*?

"32... 33... 34... 35..."

He peered around the edge of the hall, into the living room.

Tayshia's back was to him. She was clad in naught but a navy blue camisole with thin straps and a pair of grey cotton shorts that were shorter than any he'd ever seen her wear before. She was exercising, alternating between running in place and dropping down to one knee. Her red waves bounced free and dripped with sweat.

"44... 45... 46... 47..."

Was this what she did in the mornings before he woke? Or at night? He knew it wasn't nighttime so was she just unaware of the time? Did she think he was gonna sleep through class, or something?

Did she not care if he saw?

Pushing his fingers into his messy sleep-hair, he stifled a yawn and watched her until she collapsed onto the floor. It wasn't until she was choking and gasping for air on her hands and knees, still unaware of his presence, that he realized she'd counted to one hundred.

How was it that she could make it to one hundred knee-drops or whatever they were, but she couldn't walk through Gianni's without running into a table?

She lifted her head and glanced over.

Ash blanched, backing away as quick as he could. Somehow, he felt he wasn't meant to see what he'd seen, so he hurried to the bathroom and closed the door. By the time he finished showering for the day, she was back in her bedroom.

The previous day—Sunday—had passed much less eventfully than Saturday had. Ash had left around noon to go get his hair done, and he hadn't seen or heard Tayshia leave her room once.

He wasn't surprised. After their hook-up and the way she'd panicked at the end, he wasn't expecting her to want to talk to him. Not only had they both been dumb enough to break the one rule to house-sharing by hooking up, but it was just plain awkward. She hadn't even specified that she wanted to have sex and he'd acted like they were going to.

Thank God they hadn't. He didn't think that was a good idea.

Elijah had texted once and Ash had replied, but he didn't text again. There was clearly tension between them. Ash wasn't sure what to make of it, so he figured he'd just leave it alone.

Some things just needed time.

The hair stylist had done a good job on his hair. She'd given it a trim and style, followed by bleaching it one more time and toning it on top to a pale golden-blond. It was now short around the back and sides of his head, with the top being choppy, layered, and long. It was cut so that it would fall forward to brush his cheekbones unless he put his fingers through it, in which case it would stick up all over the place like a character in one of Ash's Japanese video games. They'd also dyed the short parts light brown, giving him a unique two-color style.

Having two-colored hair was as edgy as he could get at this point, so he fucked with it.

When he got home from the hair appointment, Tayshia was in the kitchen. She complimented his hair in a mumble, her cheeks reddening, and then she disappeared into her room again.

He supposed that meant that she fucked with it, too.

Ash spent most of his time in his dorm room studying. He was supposed to turn in his grades to his probation officer that week and there was a quiz in one of his classes on Monday morning. The only times Ash left his bedroom for the rest of that day were to make food in the kitchen.

Tayshia didn't leave her room until he was back inside of his.

Now, it was Monday, and he'd just seen her exercising in the sitting room. Did he think it was weird? Obviously. Was he starting to think she was more than a little bizarre? Yeah.

Did he mind seeing her in those shorts?

No comment.

☼☼☼

Thursday rolled around sooner than Ash expected.

After a busy week with school and seeing his probation officer to turn in his grades and get drug tested, he left school with a spring to his step after his final class of the day. He was excited to get a text from Andre asking him if he wanted to chill at his house.

Ji Hyun and I got shrooms and she's gonna make shroom brownies with them. Andre had texted. *You guys down to try tonight?*

Wtf are shroom brownies? Ash had replied as he drove with one hand down the mountain highway. *Bitch, I am on probation.*

Then don't do them, Andre replied. *Just come chill and we'll do them. Ji Hyun wants you to invite Tayshia, too.*

It's a Thursday.

And? Bruh.

Fine. Whatever, Ash typed. *Bring the weed.*

Bet.

Well, that settled that. Ash just had to ask Tayshia if she wanted to go. He wasn't sure she'd want to since they'd hooked up and things were so awkward between them, but perhaps a new friendship with Ji Hyun would be enough to sway her.

He sent her a text as he drove, figuring it would be better if he did it that way than asking her in person where she could freak out. He thought it best not to tell her there would be shrooms. Somehow, he didn't think she'd come if he did.

She replied right as he was pulling into the parking lot.

Yeah, sure. I'll go. What time?

For some reason, Ash's heart skipped a beat.

He replied and then went upstairs to go into the apartment and get her.

When she came out of the hallway, her crimson weave was pulled up into two buns at the top of her head, her bangs wispy across her forehead with two longer pieces framing her cheeks. She also wore the hooded black knit that Ash had gotten her for her birthday — the sleeves were too long and the hem tightened under her rear.

She looked so adorable that Ash had to turn the TV on so he wouldn't stare. They watched a show for a bit until Ash was ready to go.

215

The car ride was exactly as awkward and silent as Ash expected it to be.

When they got to Andre's apartment, Ji Hyun was getting off of the couch to go into the kitchen and start baking. She greeted Tayshia with enthusiasm, hugging her and falling into quick conversation with her. Andre and Ash slid their palms together to greet one another, and then went into the living room.

Tayshia sat down on the very end of the brown suede couch and pulled her knees to her chest, which left Ash two cushions or the loveseat to choose from. He chose to sit on the loveseat, leaning forward with his elbows on his thighs like he always did when he smoked. He was content to busy himself with Andre's piece, holding it with one hand to his mouth while he lit the bowl and inhaled.

Andre plopped down beside Ash and grinned at Tayshia. "You gonna get in on this?"

"She doesn't smoke," Ash said, his voice strained as he held marijuana smoke in his lungs. He coughed as he breathed it out, already feeling the heavy calm of the high. He shot Andre a pointed look. "She doesn't do anything."

"Shit, okay." Andre nodded slowly, a knowing look in his eyes. "All right. Got it. That's cool."

"Yeah, sorry," Tayshia said. "I'm just here to chill."

"Ah, okay," Andre said, and then he held the piece to his mouth. The lighter clicked.

Ji Hyun bustled about the kitchen, singing to herself as she baked. Ash decided to head in there to talk to her. As he walked, he heard Andre start talking to Tayshia, trying to get to know her.

The second Ash entered the small kitchen, Ji Hyun was giving him the side-eye.

"You and Elijah are in a fight," she said.

"Well, fuck," he said.

"Well, fuck is right. So, what did you do? Get lost in her cunt one cold night?"

"Ji Hyun," Ash snarled below his breath, his gaze heated as it fell upon his friend before being cast surreptitiously over his shoulder. "If you don't shut your *fucking* mouth—"

"You'll what? Make me cry so you can stand there with me in the *rain*?"

"Bitch," he spat. "You're such a bitch."

Ji Hyun smirked as she held the mixing bowl with one arm and used her other hand to stir the brownie batter.

"At least I'm predictable," she said. "You, on the other hand, have surprised me. So which of you is it that has the bigger crush on her? You or Elijah?"

"*Shut the fuck up!*" Ash hissed, struggling to control the volume of his voice. "Ji Hyun. Seriously."

"Don't tell me to shut up—"

"I *will* tell you to shut up! I *will* tell you to—"

They went back and forth, hissing likes snakes at one another. Finally, they stopped when Andre and Tayshia laughed at something together.

"There's no reason to fight about it," Ji Hyun said. "I'm only teasing you. It's not a big deal if you like her."

"Unless you're telling me it's a big deal to Elijah."

Ji Hyun set the white bowl on the counter. Then, she started chopping and crushing the mushrooms on a small cutting board beside it.

"He hasn't made it clear, but it seems like he does. He's just giving me those vibes."

"Well," Ash said, crossing his arms and leaning back against the counter, "he's literally been exactly as annoying as I'd expect him to be if he did. Maybe he does."

"Maybe he does."

Ash didn't know how he felt about that. Elijah didn't have a claim to her and neither did Ash. But Ash had hooked up with her.

What did that mean for he and Elijah's friendship?

Once Ji Hyun had gotten the brownies into the oven, she cleaned up and called for Tayshia. There was some sort of make-up she wanted to show her. Ash turned and leaned down to Ji Hyun's ear.

"Don't tell her there's shrooms in those brownies."

"Damn, she doesn't do them?" Ji Hyun asked, tossing her long, black hair back. "Okay, I won't say anything."

Tayshia walked into the kitchen, so Ash left. Walking back to the living room, he sat down on the far end of the couch, close to the side of the loveseat Andre was now sitting on. Andre passed the piece over to Ash so he could smoke again.

"Time to spill."

Ash blew smoke outward. "Spill... What?"

"About you and Tayshia." He grinned, all teeth and mischief.

"You're fucking her?"

Great.

Of *course* Ji Hyun would tell Ash about Elijah's suspicions. She probably told him everything. Ash needed to nip it in the bud now, before it became a real problem.

"Will you—" Ash lowered his voice to a hiss. "Shut up. Don't say that so loudly."

"You like her, or something? Come on—don't hold out on me."

"No. God, no," Ash whispered. "Ji Hyun misunderstood."

Andre searched his eyes in the way that Ash hated. The kind of way that made him feel like he was in front of Judge Steven again.

"Well, do you wanna maybe explore it a little bit?" Andre said. "I mean, come on. Tayshia's got a little something there. Don't pretend you don't like, *look* at her."

It didn't matter. He didn't like Tayshia, and the thought was absurd. You didn't have to like someone to hook up with them. He'd gotten involved with the Kieran situation out of respect. He'd given her a shoulder to lean on while she wept because he wasn't heartless. He'd been having dreams about her, sure, but that didn't necessarily mean he *liked* her.

Even if four-and-a-half months of nightly dreams was a long time to have someone floating in his head.

"Do you really think I'd want to?" he whispered, leaning closer. "With *Tayshia Cole*?"

"I mean..." Andre's gaze washed over his face. "I mean, it's just fucking, right? Not like you'd have to marry her. Bruh, why would Ji Hyun misunderstand Elijah telling her you liked Tayshia?"

The girls' voices and laughter could be heard coming from the bathroom down the hall. The sweet aroma of the brownies was starting to fill the apartment. Ash sighed.

So it was Elijah who was causing these problems.

"Because he lied. That's why."

Andre set the bong on the coffee table. "Because he—"

"Yeah, he lied."

Andre's facial expression went deadpan. "He lied."

"Yeah," Ash said, nodding as though he were stupid. "He lied. He's a stupid fuck and is just trying to cause drama."

"Why? Because he—does he *like* her?"

"Yeah. I think."

"But why would he *lie* about you liking Tayshia?"

"Bro, how am I supposed to know? Elijah's an asshole, apparently."

Andre's eyes narrowed a fraction, but his smile never faltered. "Yeah, but like... Why, though? Why would he think that unless he had a reason to? Just tell the truth. Are you guys like, cool or good, or...?"

Sweat prickled on the back of Ash's neck. The awkwardness of the moment made it hard to breathe, driving the temperature in the room up to the ceiling. Under no circumstances could Andre, Ji Hyun, or Elijah find out that he'd hooked up with her. If they did, there'd be a whole situation.

Or maybe the weed was just making him paranoid.

"I mean, she wants to be friends," he said.

Andre continued to scrutinize him. "Well... Is that what you want?"

"I don't know why you care." Ash rubbed his palms against his knees, and Andre watched him do so.

"Why do *you*?" Andre countered.

"Why do *you*?"

"I dunno." Andre's lips twitched up. "Is Tayshia fuckable?"

"Who am I to decide who's fuckable and who's not?"

"Depends. Would you fuck the unfuckable? That'll answer my question."

"Would *you*?"

"This isn't about me," Andre said with another smirk.

"This is — "

"Ayy!" Andre turned his head to look at the hallway. "There's my girl."

Tayshia and Ji Hyun came traipsing back out into the living room, chattering amiably about something they'd seen online. Ji Hyun came to sit beside Andre on the loveseat while she waited the last ten minutes on the brownies. Tayshia crossed the living room, her eyes meeting Ash's as she went.

Ji Hyun had done her make-up for fun. Her cheeks were rosy, there was razor-sharp winged eyeliner on her catlike eyes, and she was wearing a pair of fluffy false lashes.

This was getting ridiculous. Every time he thought he'd come to the conclusion that he didn't like her, she found some way to look hot as Hell. He was about to sue.

"Your little hair buns are cute, Tayshia," Andre said, exchanging glances with Ash.

"Uh... Thank you, Andre."

"I think Ash likes them, too. Don't you, man?"

Without thinking, Ash reached for the piece and pretended to accidentally knock it over. The sight of it toppling to the side had Andre's annoying grin dissipating as fast as melting snowflakes. Ash stifled a laugh as Andre practically dived to save it, managing to just in time.

With a smirk, he turned his gaze on Tayshia's. He could have imagined it, but the look in her eyes seemed a bit expectant. Like she was hoping he really did find them cute.

Did he like them?

"How cute are they, Ash?" Ji Hyun said, her tone pointed.

"Very," Ash said.

Tayshia smiled, a quick twitch of her lips, and then the oven beeping stole everyone's attention away. Ji Hyun got up to go pull the brownies out. Andre glared at Ash, still nursing his bong as though it had actually fallen.

Ash got up to go to the bathroom. He was only gone for a few minutes. When he returned, the lights were out, Ji Hyun had brought the brownies out on a plate, and Andre was selecting a horror movie from a streaming app on his TV.

And Tayshia was already eating a brownie.

Ash, Andre, and Ji Hyun exchanged glances. Ji Hyun and Andre were each eating one, too. Ash didn't have one due to his probation, but he knew it was going to be quite interesting watching the way Tayshia reacted. Andre and Ji Hyun were usually chill when they did shrooms, but Tayshia might be an entirely different story.

"Hey, that necklace is sick," Andre said after he turned the television volume down a notch. "Where'd you get it?"

"It's from the caverns," Tayshia answered. "Ash has one, too."

Ash went rigid. She was lucky there was an entire cushion between them, and he was lucky it was dark. It hid his flushed cheeks.

"Oh, word? That's cute," Andre joked. He sounded like the weed high had already gotten to him. "You guys got friendship necklaces."

"Get the fuck outta here," Ash said, his voice hoarse from the smoking. He rested his elbow on the arm of the couch, sinking down and stretching his legs out. He was so high that all he wanted to do was sit there. His eyes were half-lidded.

They all watched the movie for a bit. About twenty minutes in, Ji Hyun was already asleep, curled up with her head on the loveseat arm. Tayshia had finished picking at her first brownie. She was working on her second.

"She fell asleep fast," Ash said. "Ji Hyun did."

"She is *zooted*." Andre burst out laughing. "She's so fuckin' high, dude. So am I."

"Same." Ash couldn't help but grin.

"But not the same as me."

"Shut *up*."

Ash glanced over at Tayshia, the light from the TV flickering across her face. She didn't seem to notice anything. She was only interested in the movie and her third brownie.

"Okay, okay. I can't," Ash said, laughing. "Tayshia, put it down."

"What?" she said, licking brownie off of the side of one thumb.

"Those are literally shroom brownies."

"What?"

"Yeah. They are literally brownies with shrooms in them."

"And you let me eat two of them?!"

"Yeah. So you might wanna put the third one down."

"Ash!" She dropped the partially eaten brownie back onto the plate with the others. "What the fuck?!"

Andre giggled and it cracked Ash up so much he started laughing. Ji Hyun continued to sleep.

"Am I gonna be okay?" Tayshia sounded terrified.

"No, it's fine," Ash said through his laughter. "Seriously. You're gonna be fine."

"Guys, come on." Her voice was shaky. She sounded like she was about to start crying. "Am I gonna die? I don't know anything about this stuff. I'm freaking out."

"Oh, my God, no. I'm telling you, it's *fine*."

"Did I overdose?!" Tayshia whined. "Why do you guys find that funny?!"

Ash and Andre were falling about in peals of more uncontrollable laughter. Andre was laughing so hard that he was kicking his leg and clutching his stomach. Ash covered his face with one hand and allowed himself to laugh until his own stomach hurt. He couldn't breathe. His laughter had transcended to the silent kind.

Tayshia got up and ran to the bathroom. When the door slammed shut, Ash started to calm down.

But the moment Andre made eye contact with him, they were laughing again. It took them ten minutes to calm down and by then, Ash was too high and exhausted to do much more than sit and stare at the television.

Time wore on. Tayshia was still in the bathroom. Andre didn't seem to notice or care. Eventually, he stood up and announced that he was going to bed. He picked Ji Hyun up and carried her to the room. The bedroom door shut minutes later, leaving Ash alone in the living room.

He supposed he should feel guilty. Tayshia had seemed genuinely afraid. But Ash knew it was no big deal. It was *just* shrooms. They really weren't a big deal and if she had a bad trip, he'd just say whatever he needed to say to keep her calm.

After a full thirty minutes in the bathroom, Tayshia came back out into the darkness of the living room. She'd pulled her sleeves down over her fingers and had her arms hugged around her body. She returned to her seat on the couch, falling into it as though she were exhausted. She rested her head against the back of the couch and closed her eyes. With those false lashes on, she looked like Sleeping Beauty but with hair buns.

"You good?" Ash asked.

"Yeah," she said, her voice a hoarse croak.

"Uh, you sound like shit."

She answered after a delay, her eyes remaining closed. "I threw them up."

"You did? Damn. That's fucked," Ash said, giving her a surprised look. "That's definitely a way to keep yourself from getting too high."

"I didn't want to be high at all," she said, her tone clipped. "And I'm kinda pissed off."

"Well, do you wanna call my probation officer, or...?"

"Um, you have no right to be a jerk," she shot back from her end of the couch. "You knew there were drugs in those, and you let me eat them anyway. So, fuck you."

"Are you feeling the effects, or—"

"I got it all up, thanks."

Ash didn't say anything after that. He just closed his eyes and listened to the movie play until he passed out.

✧✧✧

Ash woke in the darkness, another movie playing.

Groggy and eyes heavy with sleepiness, he sat up and looked to his left. Tayshia was asleep, curled up on the end of the couch just like Ji Hyun had been earlier. She was visibly shivering.

Ash stood up and stretched, heading to the bathroom. He didn't turn the light on so his eyes could get used to the darkness. When he was done, he walked back out to the hallway closet. He gathered the large, thick fleece comforter that he'd used as a blanket the entire time he'd crashed on Andre's couch that Summer.

When he got back, Tayshia was awake. She had used her hands to lift herself up on her side, her legs still curled beneath her.

"Are we staying the night?" she asked.

"Mm-hm," he said, getting back onto the couch. "That okay?"

"I guess. It's just cold."

"Nah, for real, though," he whispered, holding back a yawn. "This blanket is the best shit. It's warm as fuck. Come here."

"Huh?" She sounded confused.

Ash scowled, too tired to go back and forth with her. It was freezing cold and he was tired. She couldn't sleep cramped on the loveseat, could she?

He sat up and grabbed her by the elbows, dragging her forward. She let out a soft cry as she fell on top of him, her legs splitting to accommodate him between them. Her head pillowed on his chest as he pulled the blanket over them both and laid down.

"Wait, I—"

"Chill," he said, folding his arms behind his head and closing his eyes. "I'm tired. Just sleep."

They laid in the silence for a while before she began to speak.

"I'm sorry about... Last time," she said.

Ash cracked one eye open. He knew what she was talking about. "Okay."

"I know, I'm such a freak. You're probably so embarrassed to have like, done anything with me. It's just humiliating."

Ash reacted on instinct. He took one hand and placed it on her back. He began to caress it, up and down in soothing motions.

"Nah, you're good," he yawned. "It's not for everyone. If you didn't like it, you didn't like it."

"That's not—that wasn't—" Her fingers twisted in the fabric of his shirt. "That wasn't the problem."

"Oh." His heart stilled. "Then what was the problem?"

"I got overwhelmed. It was too bright. I don't know."

"It was too bright? Huh?"

"Well, because of the—the window. The moon, you know."

He couldn't stop the quiet, scratchy laugh that left his lips, his hand stroking up her spine again. "The moon. Okay."

"It's dark right now."

Ash's hand froze. What was she saying? Was she saying that she wanted to hook up again?

"We're on the couch in another person's like, *house*. I mean, if you got overwhelmed last time, won't it just overwhelm you again?"

"I don't care. Do you?"

"Nah," he said.

"Do you want to try again?" she said, her voice tiny. Her head felt heavy on his chest. "Because we can try again, if you—if you want."

"I'm down," he said, trying to sound nonchalant even though he was becoming painfully aware of every curve on her fucking body. "What do wanna do?"

"Do you want me to kiss you?"

"Do *you* wanna kiss me?"

Keeping the blanket on with her hands on his chest, Tayshia pushed herself up onto her knees. Slow and steady, she lowered her head until he felt her breath, hot against his lips. His arm remaining bent behind his head, Ash took his other hand off of her back and moved it to the side of her neck. His fingers felt the tickle of her weave hair as he pulled her the last millimeter forward so their mouths could touch.

Their kiss was every bit as slow as their last ones hadn't been, but the fire it stoked inside of Ash's loins was an inferno.

The movements of their bodies and tongues were sensual as Tayshia fell into the kiss, collapsing atop him with a quiet sigh into his mouth. She rolled her hips, slowly rocking them against his, and he couldn't stop the gasp that escaped him. A feeling he recognized coiled tight in his belly and he found himself rocking his hips up to meet hers.

The sounds of the movie were quiet in the background, hardly a nuisance to what was going on underneath the blanket.

Ash's hands went to her hips, where he gripped them tight, using them as anchors to help him move her more firmly against him where he'd grown hard. Their lips broke apart for a moment in the dark, both of them letting out ragged breaths. Her fingers sought the hem of his shirt, slipping beneath it to feel his bare skin, playing against his ribcage.

She pushed his shirt up until his chest was exposed, her head disappearing beneath the blanket. His eyelids fluttered when he felt her dropping kisses to his sternum. His muscles flexed. Both of his hands went to the back of her head, beneath her hair buns.

And then her lips closed over his left nipple.

No one had ever done that before. It was so sensitive that he had to clench his teeth to stop himself from crying out. It sent a lightning bolt of desire slamming right between his thighs.

He was going to have a difficult time holding back if she kept doing that.

Before he could lose control, he pushed her back a little.

"Holy shit," he said. "That's intense."

"I'm sorry," she whispered. "I'm sorry."

Ash didn't know what she was sorry for. He just knew it felt good and he didn't care about anything else. He was too tired to care about anything else.

"You'll be all right," he said, distracted by the feeling of her heat pressed up against his jeans as she began again to grind on him. They were straining. He wanted to unbutton them or unzip them. Something. Anything. "*Fuck.* You're all right."

"I shouldn't be — I just — " Tayshia ground downward, backward and forward, then down again. Her words choked off into a stifled moan. Then she squeaked out, "I'm so sorry... I just want it."

His entire body reacted to that.

"I got you," Ash groaned, and then his nose brushed against hers. His long fingers slid to her thighs. He pulled her hard against him, grinding up into her from below. It was so warm underneath the blanket, almost too warm. "Fuck. I'll give it to you. Yeah, like that. Mm-hm. Like that."

"I want — "

"What do you want? You wanna come while you're on top of me?" His teeth closed around her earlobe. She buried her face in his throat when his hands slipped between their hips and gripped her between her thighs, massaging and squeezing. He heard her whimper. "Yeah, you wanna come, don't you?"

The reply she gave was a strangled *yes.*

Ash kissed her neck, tasting her pulse like he had the last time. He found the spot beneath her ear that had seemed to feel good for her, his chest warming when it caused her hips to jolt. He moved his hand upward and slipped it beneath the waistband of her leggings, making sure to stay above her panties so she didn't get overwhelmed.

She was wet for him.

"Stay quiet," he breathed when he began to press gentle circles into the apex of her core. "Good girl, like that. Stay quiet for me."

Tayshia cried out. His teeth grazed her neck.

"I'm sorry," she squeaked again. "I'm s-sorry. I'm—I'm sorry. I'm—*oh*—sorry."

She kept saying it, lost in pleasure as Ash held her hip with one hand and touched her with the other. He could feel her body growing rigid the closer to her undoing he brought her, and he found himself wanting to get lost in it, too.

God, she was so fucking hot. The sounds she made were un-fucking-real.

"I-I—"

"Tell me," he moaned softly, his stomach coiled so tight that it hurt. "Come on."

"I'm g-gonna—" Her breath caught and then she whined again. "Ash, it feels so good. I'm so sorry."

"I know it does."

She ground her hips harder, in circles again his fingertips. "I'm sorry, I just—*please.*"

"You're sorry?" he said, and he began to move his hand faster. "Show me how sorry you are. Come on my fingers. That's it."

Tayshia's hips rolled to meet the cadence of his hand, and then with a sudden convulsing she came, her body shivering and pressing tighter to his. Her low moans were stifled by his shirt as she burrowed her face into his chest. He felt her thighs squeezing around his as she rode out the waves.

He kissed her cheek and jaw with the same amount of affection he held for her at that moment and his overbearing desire to calm her. He didn't want her to get overwhelmed again.

"Are you okay this time?" Ash whispered. "How do you feel?"

"I'm okay," she whispered back. "Thank you."

"Do you wanna stop?"

"No," she said, and then he felt her lips on his chest again. Her breath against his skin. Her tongue tracing a tattoo she couldn't possibly see in the dark. He shivered.

He was frozen at first, not sure whether or not he should stop her, just in case it was too far for her after last time, but all thoughts turned to nothingness in his head when she closed her mouth around a nipple again.

"*God*, fuck. *Fuck*," he practically sobbed, sinking down a bit until the blanket covered them both. "That's so fucking *good*."

Tayshia seemed to hesitate for a moment, and then her hand was in his pants, right beneath his boxers. He was stunned into a choked silence as she wrapped her fingers around him. With her other hand and both of his, they worked his clothing down until he was freed. Then, she began to move her hand up and down.

It felt so good he was seeing white stars blooming against the darkness under the blanket.

"Am I doing it right?" Her breath in his ear almost made him moan again. "I've only done it twice."

Ash breathed a laugh. "Uh, yeah. Mm—y-yeah."

Her mouth descended upon his chest again, rendering him a complete mess beneath her. He whimpered again, his head falling back. His hips began to buck upward when she tightened her hold and began to twist.

"F-Fuck," he whined below his breath, his hips jerking up into her hand. There was too much going on, too many things to feel. Her hands, her lips, her tongue. It had been so fucking long for him. "Shit, it's so good."

He clenched his thighs, feeling electricity and fire building in his spine as she took him higher and higher, until he was barely breathing. The heat of their bodies, trapped beneath the blanket. The wet slick of her tongue against his chest. The firm, velvet-softness of her hand around him. It was too much.

"I'm gonna come," he groaned as quietly as he could, through tightly-gritted teeth. His hands curled around her head, holding her mouth firmly to his chest. He could barely stand it. "*Please*, I—I'm gonna *fucking* come. Please, please, please."

One more swipe of her tongue over his nipple, several more quick movements of her hand, and he was coming into it with a quiet, whimpering series of *fuck*s. The euphoric state that washed over him rendered him an incoherent mess as she continued to touch him, sending shivers running along his body like they were trying to crawl and fill every bit of available space in his body.

Ash turned his face to the right when Tayshia did and their lips crashed together. He moaned into her mouth, their tongues caressing one another's in the midst of their heated, frenzied kiss. He felt like worshipping her.

"Are you still okay?" he asked, breathless as he furrowed his brow. His hands stroked gently down her back. His mind reeled and he kissed her again. "Huh? Are you okay?"

"I'm fine," she said, and then she laughed a little. "I'm just really tired now. And... Need a towel."

"*Shit.* Right. Fuck, that's my bad."

Cool air rushed to greet them as he pushed the blanket down. She helped him tuck himself back into his jeans, and then he got up. He leaned down to kiss her one more time, just like he would any other girl he hooked up with.

But it felt different with her.

Ash stumbled to the bathroom to clean up and grab a towel for her. Once inside the room, he leaned over the sink, hanging his head. He needed a second. Just one fucking second to catch his breath. This was Tayshia. Tayshia Cole. He'd hooked up with Tayshia *fucking* Cole.

Twice.

And he felt so guilty.

Lifting his gaze to the mirror, he looked at the way his blond hair fell into his eyes, sticking up in haphazard directions like he'd been thoroughly fucked. Stared at the places where her lips had been, where he felt like he could still feel them ghosting along his flesh. Watched his crystal swinging away from his chest, glinting as though it had a life of it own.

What the Hell was he getting himself into?

CHAPTER EIGHTEEN

The Eiffel Tower.

Ash stood before a window that overlooked parts of Paris that he recognized from books and movies. The tower, standing lone and forlorn in the distance. The sun setting on the mountains behind it giving glow to the leaves of the trees at its base. Pale, multicolored buildings stretching as far as he could see.

Why was he in Paris?

"Are you really going to wear that?"

Ash turned, shocked to see Kieran O'Connell standing in the doorway of what looked to be a small hotel room. The décor was modern, cobalt and white in color. The carpet was a patterned navy blue and the wallpaper an oceanic cerulean. It was by no means a suite, but it was every bit as nice as what the O'Connell family could afford.

Why was he in a hotel room with Kieran?

Confused, he tried to speak, but found that he couldn't. In fact, he couldn't do much of anything. He tried to move his hands and feet, but nothing happened.

"Kieran." The voice was coming from his mouth, but it wasn't his and he wasn't moving his lips. It was a woman's voice — one that he recognized. "I've told you multiple times that all of us girls agreed to dress up. It's our last night in the city, and we want to have fun with it."

Kieran walked into the room and plopped down on the end of the bed, his elbows on his thighs and fingers laced in front of his face. His white skin was tanned by the sun. There was a sour expression on his face and his hair looked shorter, less wavy than Ash remembered it. Instead of curling around his ears, it was short on the sides and long on top, styled to sweep away from his forehead.

Was this the past?

Was this a dream?

What was going on?

Ash felt himself moving towards a full body mirror in the corner of the *hotel room. As he did, his reflection came into view. Except that it wasn't his reflection.*

It was Tayshia's.

Her hair had been pulled back into a sleek bun at the base of her head. The bun itself was as curly as could be, and clearly some sort of hair product had been used to slick the hair at the crown of her head down. The edges of her hair along her hairline had been styled into flat, swooping shapes from her temple to her ears.

She wore light makeup, with lips painted dark red to contrast the terracotta of her skin tone, and her dress was stunning. Red satin, off-shoulder, no brassiere, and short as can be. It ruched up the sides, giving curve to her body that Ash had never noticed before. Her black tights were sheer and she wore strappy red heels which added three or four inches to her height. When she gave herself a small, coy smile, she looked like she knew she looked good.

And she was wearing the crystal.

Ash had never been this speechless inside his own head before.

"You don't think you should wear a sweater over that, or something?" Kieran said, complaining. "We're on a trip with our youth group, not in Portland with Quinn."

"No one is gonna care, Kieran," Tayshia said, turning to him. Ash felt his arms crossing — her arms. "You can't expect me to wear a sweater when literally no one else is going to be."

"Okay," he said, but the look on his face showed that it wasn't. "But don't come crying to me when someone says you look like a whore."

Ash would have lifted his eyebrows if he could. He'd been astonished to hear Kieran talking to her the way he had in the hallway at their apartment, but to hear it again was unsettling. The two of them had always presented themselves as the perfect couple. But it seemed as though things weren't so.

"Kieran!" Tayshia put her hands on her hips. "Quit acting like an outta pocket asshole and saying things like that! I'm not a whore just because I'm wearing a dress. It's literally fashionable. I bought it when we went to the promenade. For your information, Rory bought one, too."

"First of all, I highly doubt that my sister would buy something like that," Kieran said, jumping to his feet. His face had started to redden with anger. "And second, there's not a single Godly man who would be okay with their future wife walking around like — like that."

"Jamal did like it!" Tayshia cried, throwing her hands up. "Rory showed him her dress, and he liked it!"

"Hers was probably not as short as that. There's no way — "

"Hers was not as short, no, but it's just as revealing. And yes, he was *okay with it."*

This had to be a dream. It had to be.

But if it was a dream, why was it so clear? So vivid and present? Why wasn't it presenting like a movie, like her dreams usually did?

What the fuck was going on?

It was truly as though Ash were physically there, trapped inside of Tayshia's skin as she put one foot in front of the other. He could feel what she felt — he just couldn't hear her thoughts.

"Look," Tayshia said, walking across the room to grab a purse off of the dresser. It was black with a long strap, which she crossed over her body and hung off of one shoulder. Then, she snatched her phone up and shoved it into the purse. "It's just a dress, and we're going to be late. We're in Paris, Kieran. This is normal Parisian fashion. We're going to a damn bar. No one will think less of me for wearing this dress. Now, let's go."

Kieran grumbled to himself but did as he was told.

As they exited the room, Ash saw there was a daily calendar on the bedside table, right beside the alarm clock.

August 17ᵗʰ, 2018.

☼☼☼

They'd been at the bar for an hour.

It was dark outside, and not as warm as it had been earlier. It was cool enough to where Ash had a feeling Tayshia was regretting not bringing a sweater after all. The pub they were in was only a mile or two away from the hotel. The bartenders were fast, so it was easy for everyone to get completely ripped within the first thirty minutes. Everyone there — a mix of twenty-some youth groupers from Tayshia and Kieran's church in Medford — was drunk. Everyone except Tayshia.

Ash had gleaned as much information as he could, trying to hang in there by the moment and just go with the flow, instead of wondering why and how he was literally walking in her dream.

It was indeed August. This was a church trip put together by youth group members in college, and they were in Paris, France. They'd gone to some sort of special Christian seminar thing the first day they'd been here and it was now two weeks later. This was their last day before they flew home tomorrow evening.

They'd spent the extra time sightseeing, seeing everything from Disneyland to the Louvre, and they'd had as much fun as they could possibly have. Photographs had been taken, laughter had been shared, and many of the girls had gotten trigger-happy with either their parents' or their own credit cards.

College loomed on the horizon for some of them and for others, they were already in college. Some of the youth group members were engaged to one another. Everyone knew where they were headed and what they were going to do with their lives. They had visions for their futures.

Everyone except Tayshia.

She'd been fielding questions left and right for hours, seeming more preoccupied with the fact that her boyfriend was eyeing a blonde girl nearby who wore an even shorter dress than she did. Even though Ash couldn't hear her thoughts, he could feel her heart splintering in her chest like charred wood. He could feel her confusion and her stress, and he could feel that she was sad.

Why was it attractive to Kieran when other girls dressed this way, but not when Tayshia did it?

Ash thought Kieran was blind as fuck, but he couldn't exactly tell Tayshia that.

This was a dream. Undoubtedly. And in dreams, there were no repercussions. There were supposed to be no repercussions. If he had the ability to use his words or thoughts to talk to her, he would have told her something much different than what Kieran had.

Because Ash wasn't blind.

She was gorgeous, and he had a feeling that Kieran knew that. He had a feeling that he was so insecure about it that all he could do was look elsewhere. Other girls, other toys, other shiny things. Anything to take his mind off of that fact that he wasn't good enough for someone like Tayshia. Anything to show himself that he was thousands of leagues below her on the scale. By using behaviors that made him into as bad of a person as he felt inside, he was making himself feel better, but hurting Tayshia irreparably in the process.

It wasn't as if Ash was good enough for her, either. The difference was he'd rather internalize his insecurities than externalize them. If he was with Tayshia, the last thing Ash would do is hurt her.

He'd rather hurt himself.

They were now sitting at a table full of every youth group member that had come on the trip. Everyone was chattering amiably, drinking with leisure.

"What about taking some Science courses?" a boy said from Tayshia's right. His hair was braided in rows all over his head.

Ash felt Tayshia turning her head. Her hand tightened around the one cup of water that she'd had all night. She hadn't ordered any drinks or food, and her stomach had been twisted into a tight coil ever since she'd caught sight of Kieran ogling the blonde girl.

"That's an option, Jamal," she'd said, her voice covering up the emptiness he could feel inside of her. "I thought about it. But I can't really think about it until I finish the pre-requisite program."

"Are you sure you want to do that?" Jamal replied before taking a swig of his alcoholic beverage. "University classes are so much harder than junior college courses. What if you get there and it's too hard to keep up with the homework?"

Ash felt Tayshia's stress levels rising, filling her chest like a heavy storm cloud.

"I know," she said. "I have some ideas for time management. Don't worry."

"What's your major gonna be? Like, what classes are you gonna take?"

She sipped the water. Ash could feel that her mouth remained dry. "General Studies for now, and there's too many to name."

"So, just name one of them." It was a girl that Ash now knew to be Kieran's older sister, Rory, from Jamal's right. Her hair was a wavy brown bob with blunt bangs that looked very French, in Ash's opinion. "Maybe we can help you cross it off the list if it doesn't seem very you, you know?"

Ash felt a panic spiking in Tayshia's body.

"Well – I had actually... Um..." She cleared her throat, and to Ash, it was obvious she didn't have any ideas at all. "The classes are like, niche. It would take too long for me to explain them. But Rory – are you excited to start your Master's?"

Jamal gave her a suspicious look, but Rory lit up and began talking almost immediately. She took over the conversation at the full table and soon, everyone was asking her questions instead of Tayshia.

Inside, Ash felt her relief.

Yes. This had to be a dream.

The dreams had never been this vivid, nor this imprisoning. He'd never walked inside of Tayshia's mind before. The dreams were always flashes, temporary bursts of things that he'd been unable to discern. Yet here he was, and he could feel it when Tayshia had an itch on her nose.

The nightmare that he'd had of Tayshia's screaming – the nightmare he'd had on the night of August 17th – was the dream he was walking inside of right now.

"Who wants to hit that dance club down the street one last time?" Rory said before downing the last of her mixed drink.

Several of the girls and boys raised their hands and voiced their excitement at doing just that. Ash felt an equally-enthusiastic flutter in Tayshia's heart. She wanted to go, too. She shot an expectant look over to

Kieran, but he was shaking his head.

"I wanted to bar hop. Some of us were gonna take a ride share to that part of the city we went to a few days back. The one with all the bars." He snapped his fingers. "Bastille! That's the area."

"Yeah, I'd rather do that than dance," another guy said. "Drinking's more my style."

Everyone began talking and arguing, and then Rory looked at her fiancé. She gestured to her dress, which was only about an inch longer than Tayshia's, bright glittering blue, and had short sleeves.

"Please tell me we're going dancing," she said. "I don't want to waste this dress."

"Same," Jamal said, and then he laid a large kiss against the brunette's lips.

"Can you not, and say you did?" Kieran said, balling up a napkin and tossing it at Jamal's head. "That's legit my sister."

Jamal began to tear into him, starting a back-and-forth bantering session that not even Ash could keep up with. While they did so, Rory hopped off of her stool and patted Tayshia on the arm.

"Let's go outside for a second so I can — " She pantomimed smoking and then shot a surreptitious glance towards the door.

Tayshia nodded, and then handed her purse to Kieran. "Kieran, can you watch my bag for me? We're just going to — "

"Yeah," he said, voice curt as he took the black purse from her before resuming his conversation with Jamal and the guy who had agreed with him about the bar. Ash felt like he had snatched it, but Tayshia's emotions showed no acknowledgment of his rudeness.

Tayshia followed Rory out the door. Rory wasn't wearing as high of heels as she was, but the two girls seemed able to keep up with one another as they stepped out of a side door and into a small alley.

The alley was lit only by the streetlights at either end of it and one light above their heads. On the road, automobiles trundled back and forth. The sidewalks were full, young people prancing from bar to bar, or to the many dance clubs that Paris was known for.

Rory withdrew a cigarette from her purse and lit it, crossing one arm under her chest as she leaned against the brick wall. Her brown eyes managed to remain bright, though the lighting cast a sickly-pale pallor over her white skin.

"I thought out of all of us, you would have figured out what you wanna do," she said, blowing smoke out of the corner of her glossed lips. "Even Kieran knows what he's going to do."

Ash felt Tayshia's heart plummeting to the pit of her stomach.

"I know," she said with a false laugh. "It's just a lot more difficult to choose than I thought."

"Well, you have a lot of options," Rory said, taking another drag. She tapped the ashes out onto the ground. "Or you could marry my brother early, move back to Medford to live with our parents, and wait for him to finish school so you can start popping out babies."

The two girls burst into a series of giggles.

"No, but seriously," Rory said. "You have a lot of options, but usually, you know what you wanna do deep down. There's usually just something holding you back and making you think you can't do it. Have you prayed about it?"

Ash felt irritation plaguing Tayshia's heart at that.

"Uh, not really," Tayshia replied, and her anxiety started to rise inside of her chest. It felt like it was difficult to breathe. "I have a lot to think about, but I think I'll know once school starts. The first year of the pre-req program went really well for me. I think this year will be even better."

Rory nodded, and the two of them stood staring at one another while she smoked. Then, Rory tilted her head to the side.

"Are you doing okay, Tayshia?"

"Yeah," Tayshia said. "I'm good. Why do you ask?"

"I dunno." Rory frowned, a cloud of smoke misting out of her mouth. "You just seem... Off. Is everything all right with you and Kieran?"

"For real, Rory," Tayshia said, and Ash felt her plastering a smile onto her face. "You worry too much. Everything's fine with us, and I'm okay. As for my future, I'll figure out what I want to do when I get back to Christ Rising. I'm not worried about it at all."

Ash knew she was lying. Her heart was racing much too fast for her to be telling the truth. He could feel her cheeks aching from how fake her smile was.

He just didn't understand why.

Tayshia had always seemed like the one to have her shit together. If he could have picked anyone in the entirety of their school who was more prepared for life than anyone ever before, he would have picked her. She had the best grades, the most extracurriculars, and had been involved in every school function since ninth grade.

She just didn't know what she wanted to do for a career.

By now, Ash knew without a doubt that this was more than just a dream — more than a possible nightmare. The puzzle pieces had started to fall into place and things were making sense. It was the crystal, but it was more than that. Something had happened when Tayshia let her guard down *with him on the couch. It had taken his mind and melded it with hers. Something had pulled him in and drowned him in it, forcing him to see.*

He always saw her dreaming about her day, like movies and film strips. But that's not what this was.

This was a memory.

The girls chatted for a while and then went back inside. Back at the table, everyone was starting to pay their tabs and stand up. Rory went to Jamal's side, who told her that half of the group was going to the club because it was down a few blocks; the other half was off to Bastille. Tayshia went to Kieran's side, but for some reason, he was glaring down at her.

Everyone filed outside and started walking down the street, but Kieran's hand on Tayshia's wrist stopped them on the sidewalk. They stood at the mouth of the alley that Rory had smoked in, half-shrouded in shadows. Tayshia looked up at her boyfriend, and Ash thought his expression was one of disgust.

"You're not gonna ask to go to the club, are you?" Kieran asked, tone bitter. "Because I'm going to Bastille."

"You ain't gotta have me with you," Tayshia said, sounding confused. "I can go dancing by myself."

His upper lip curled and he leaned closer, lowering his voice so none of the youth group members could hear him. "So, you're going to go to the club by yourself, looking like a whore?"

"What the actual — Kieran." She hissed the words out, her hands in fists at her sides. "Stop calling me that. It's just a dress."

"Except on you, it's not. You have curves and when you dress like that, it looks like you're a prostitute. It's not Godly."

Ash felt her anger like a torrential storm. He felt helpless to it, and at the same time, just as angry as she did.

"I'm going to that club," Tayshia snapped.

"No, you're not. You're my girlfriend, and you're coming with me."

"No. I'm. Not."

"I can't believe you." Kieran shook his head, scowling with revulsion. "I can't believe you. You actually want to go by yourself, don't you? What, you want guys grinding on you and dancing with you? You want everyone to see how slutty you look? You're such a freaking embarrassment to me."

Before she could reply, he followed the youth group out onto the sidewalk. Everyone milled about for a moment, saying their goodbyes, and then half of the group walked on down the street. That was the group going to the club. After agreeing on the address, the other half of the group started getting into ride shares that they had already ordered from inside the pub. Kieran and Tayshia stood on the sidewalk, forcing other passerby to have to walk around them.

Tayshia didn't seem to care. She folded her arms and glared up at her sorry excuse for a boyfriend.

"Why are you acting like this? Why are you trying to hurt me?"

"I'm angry with you, Tayshia. You not only convinced my sister to dress like a slut, but now you're basically okay with dancing and looking like a whore? I don't know how you expect us to get married when you're completely ruined already."

"Completely...?" Her ire expanded and exploded inside of her chest. "Whoa, whoa, whoa. I've never done anything with anyone but you, and we haven't even had sex, Kieran. This is just a dress. And if you'd come with me to the club, then maybe I wouldn't have to — "

"Yeah, whatever. I'm starting to get sick of this. You're manipulating me."

Kieran turned and walked away, likely out of anger and without thinking about where he was going, or the fact that he had yet to call a car.

Ash hoped he fell over and died for no reason.

"Manipulating you?!" Tayshia's heels clicked against the sidewalk as she sped up. She grabbed his sleeve and glared up at him. "How could you say something like that? I have never once even attempted to manipulate you! I'm telling you the truth. I wore this dress because it makes me feel good, and I have no desire to pick up guys. I just want you to — Kieran, slow down — to come with me!"

"You think I'm stupid," he shot back, also glaring. "You've always thought I was stupid, and you've always found ways to manipulate my opinion of you."

"How so? Kieran! How so?!"

"You really think I believe you're a virgin? We started dating when we were fourteen, and the first time we messed around, we were fifteen. And you seemed to already know what you were doing, didn't you?"

Ash felt Tayshia's heart splintering in her chest again, cracks spiderwebbing outward from the rift. She was heartbroken.

She exploded.

"Are you kidding me? On God, Kieran, I'm going to slap the shit out of you. What the Hell is wrong with you? I had no clue what I was doing! I was just listening to you! And if I wasn't a virgin, do you really think I'd make you wait this long?"

"You're making me wait because you're trying to keep up with the lie you told," Kieran hissed, eyes blazing. "Because if you were a Godly woman, you wouldn't dress like that."

Or maybe she was making him wait because he was a fucking asshole and no girl would ever want to lose her virginity to that piece of shit.

Ash had never felt this angry before.

"You really believe what you're saying," Tayshia said, sounding in awe. "You really think I'm a slut."

"I have yet to meet a Black girl who isn't." He spread his arms wide and gave her a nasty look. "I don't know why I thought you'd be different."

If this was a memory, that meant that this had really happened. Kieran had really said this bullshit to her. It didn't matter whether or not Tayshia was his friend – she didn't deserve to be treated like this. This wasn't some random possible employer in the mall. This was someone who claimed to love her.

But he was just a run-of-the-mill loser with a reprehensible fetish. Someone who enjoyed tearing her down to make her feel bad simply because he was insecure about how beautiful she was.

When he woke up, Ash was gonna slit Kieran's throat with his fingernails.

At the street corner, Tayshia leapt ahead and moved in front of Kieran. Ash felt her put her hands on her hips and stop him in his tracks.

"No. We're going to talk about this."

Kieran's eyes narrowed. "There's nothing to talk about. Just know that I don't trust you."

"What's there not to trust? What have I ever done to warrant you not trusting me?!"

"I'm just – look, you don't get it," Kieran snapped, trying to go around her. "You're not gonna get it, so just drop it and let's go to the stupid club. You're getting your way."

Tayshia moved into his way again and again, left and right, and then Kieran lost control.

"Just fucking forget it, Tayshia!" he yelled, causing several passersby to look their way. "Forget it! It's always been like this with you! You talk to me like I can't understand anything, and like I should just know things. And when I tell you something that pisses me off, you treat me like I'm crazy!"

Ash felt her widening her eyes. "Because you called me a slut for wearing this dress while Black, you dumbass!"

"Because it makes you look like you threw away all of your morals!"

"My morals?!" Tayshia threw back her head in a mirthless laugh of incredulity. "My morals have nothing to do with my body and the way I dress. There's nothing wrong with showing skin, and just because you don't know how to control yourself, doesn't mean that women need to cover up."

"Oh, Hell," Kieran spat with audible disgust. "Don't give me that.

Don't you give me that feminist shit. It has nothing to do with men and women and gender."

"Yes, it certainly does. The only reason why you don't want me in this dress is because you're afraid you can't control yourself when you see me in it. You sexualize my body just by looking at it, and that is not my fault. I shouldn't have to change my clothing and cover myself up when I want to feel sexy, just because you think it's an invitation."

Ash was stunned.

"As if you'd let me," Kieran said as he sneered, his lip curling upward. "All you ever want to do is kiss and your idea of messing around has gotten less and less interesting."

"Says Mr. Godly. Where in the Bible does it say I can't be a whore unless I'm your whore?"

They glared at one another for a long moment, during which Ash was sure the argument was over. They were in love. So, this would be the moment where the apology was given. If it were Ash, he knew he would have apologized by now, whether out of remorse or obligation.

Of course, he would never in a million years talk to Tayshia like this.

Yes, Kieran would apologize. It was the right —

"There are plenty of girls who aren't as frigid as you. So, whose fault is it if I or any other man feels like they can't control himself when you dress like that?"

— or maybe not.

Sorrow.

Ash felt it spreading inside of Tayshia's body, from her heart to her stomach to the rest of her body. It was the same sort of pain he'd felt the entire eleven months he'd been in jail. The pain he'd felt when he laid awake at night with his gaze fixed on the bottom of his cellmate's mattress, silent tears melting into the hair near his temples, and wished he could trade places with his mom.

When he'd felt like he wasn't good enough.

How the fuck could Tayshia think she wasn't good enough for him? She was so far out of Kieran's league that she was in the sun and he was far, far below the surface of the Earth. Hell, Ash was somewhere a few inches above Kieran. Everyone was. No one was good enough for her.

How could she not see how bright she shone?

But Tayshia — strong, confident Tayshia Cole — didn't let this vulnerability show on her face. Instead, Ash felt her pulling her brows together in a glare. She pointed up at Kieran.

"You kissed that girl in Portland last month and I forgave you. Don't

make me regret it."

Quinn hadn't been his first mistake. She had been his last.

"And there it is again!" Kieran threw one hand up and tangled it in his hair. "You're never gonna let it go, are you? You're never gonna let me forget it. I was drunk, Tayshia!"

"I know, and that's why I forgave you!"

"But you didn't forget."

Tayshia's heart stopped in her chest for a moment, drumming a few rapid beats to catch up on itself. She straightened her back and Ash saw concrete as she looked down. When she lifted her gaze again, he felt a measure of resignation inside of her.

"No. I haven't. And I won't."

"Clearly," he said as he pulled his phone out. He ranted while his thumb flew across the screen. "Clearly, and now you're trying to change me to make me into the person you wish I was. You've always done this to me. If it wasn't trying to get me to do my homework earlier, it was trying to get me to follow all the stupid rules just because you were obsessed with doing everything your parents told you to do."

"Kieran, that's not true!" Tayshia cried, and Ash felt it. She was right — she truly liked him exactly as he was. "I only want you to be who you are. You're the person I fell for."

"Literally I cannot do this anymore tonight." Kieran turned away. "I'm going to Bastille."

"Why? Can't we just talk — "

"No. Stop smothering me," he snapped. "I'm pissed off and if I don't leave now, I'm going to break up with you."

As if on cue, a ride share car pulled up. He didn't say anything to her as he got inside. The car pulled away and drove off.

The sadness that sunk into Tayshia's bones the second he was gone was almost enough to throw Ash into his own despair. It was like she'd been carrying it for years and just needed to set it down for a moment so she could breathe. But the sheer magnitude of it overwhelmed her. She was suffocating.

Now, so was he.

Suddenly, Tayshia gasped and whispered aloud to herself.

"My purse."

She turned to look over her shoulder, as though Kieran hadn't just driven away. As if he would be standing there. As if he would come back.

To the left and right of her, girls in sparkling dresses and platform heels skirted her. Men in fancy shirts and tight pants jumped around her, saying flirtatious things to her in French. Ash knew anyone else would be afraid, but inside of her heart, he felt only annoyance.

He would be annoyed, too, if his phone had gotten taken away from him in a foreign city.

"I guess I'll just wait until he figures it out and comes back," she whispered. "I just hope he does."

☼☼☼

Tayshia stood there for a solid forty-five minutes.

Ash felt the defeat in her chest as she looked to the left and to the right. He couldn't read her mind, but he assumed she was torn between going to the club where her friends were or doing something else. Perhaps going back to the hotel...?

She began to walk.

And walk.

And walk.

Ash remembered because he'd always been good with directions. When they left the hotel, they'd walked down the street, around the corner, three blocks down, left, one block, and crossed the street to get to the bar. If only there were some way for him to speak or to tell her. To think the words to her.

Silent prisoner inside her mind and her memory, all he could do was watch.

Tayshia took all the wrong turns. She went in circles. She stood on curbs and chewed her lower lip until she made another bad choice. Another bad decision. Soon, she was in an area that he knew for a fact she didn't recognize because he didn't either. It was dark, with hardly any streetlights that weren't covered in dust and grime.

His nerves began to shift, uncomfortable.

Ash realized with sinking, stonelike dismay that she was lost. She was lost, and this was August 17th. The night of the one nightmare that he'd ever had about her. The nightmare full of darkness, shadows, and screams. He hadn't known what happened to her, nor if it were real.

He was about to find out.

The street Tayshia walked onto was empty save for one person leaning against a street sign, lighting a cigarette. He wore plainclothes and a hat, and was grizzled and burly. As he looked up and locked eyes with Tayshia, Ash felt the first hint of fear sparking inside of her. She shoved it away, batting it like an insect, and marched across the pavement to get to him.

Brave.

"Excuse me," Tayshia said. "I'm – uh – I can't find my hotel."

"You speak English?" the man said, his voice accented. He pushed away from the streetlight and took a step toward her.

Tayshia's fingers flexed at her side, like she wanted to reach for her phone but realized she couldn't.

"Yes," she said. "Can you help me find my hotel? I'm staying at one over near the promenade. It's really tall, painted bright blue, and sort of near the — "

"I know where that is," the man said, smiling as he blew smoke out. He looked friendly enough, but then again, Ash wasn't the best judge of character after growing up with Gabriel for a father. "You're not too far away from it. Do you know what part of the city this is?"

"N — Yes," Tayshia said, and Ash felt her heart thumping to the beat of her lie. "But I just need some general directions."

"It's better if I walk you," the man said, nonchalant as he flicked ashes onto the ground and slipped one hand into the pocket of his slacks. His teeth were disarming in how white they were. "You'll just keep getting lost around here. The streets are old and winding."

The apprehension reared high in Tayshia's throat as she protested, backing away.

"Really, I'm fine. If you could just tell me which direction to go, I can find my way."

"Are you sure?" The tip of the cigarette glowed in the dark. "Someone as pretty as you shouldn't be alone tonight."

She's not alone, Ash wanted to say, feeling his hackles rising. Because she wasn't. He was here, inside of her mind. She didn't know it, but he was.

He wished she knew.

"Please," she said, tone polite, "if you could just tell me where to go, I can find my way just fine."

The man grunted, shook more ashes out, and allowed his smile to fade into nothingness. It added years to his face, bringing out the lines around his frowning mouth. Tayshia's muscles tightened.

It felt like she was ready to run.

"If you go back the way you came, there's an alley that shortcuts all the way there. You're not actually that far — you're just on the backside of it. It's two blocks that way." The man pointed with the cigarette to a bakery with dark windows. "Take a left there and walk all the way down. You'll have a perfect view of the Tower, and then you'll recognize the promenade. It's always lit up."

"Thank you," Tayshia said.

She turned and hurried across the street, her heels clacking against the pavement. The further she got from the man, the more her fear faded, and the better Ash felt.

Tayshia followed the instructions and sure enough, they found *themselves at the mouth of an alley that was so long that the lights on the other side looked small. Tayshia squinted. Ash could see automobiles whizzing past. It would take a good couple of minutes to get to the other side, but it didn't look like anyone was in the alleyway.*

A couple of minutes to home free.

She set off at a brisk pace, the sound of her heels echoing up along the tall buildings to either side of her. She kept her arms hugged around her against the light chill that had settled in.

Ash felt the same relief within him that he could feel within her. Soon, she'd be back at the hotel and maybe then, she would sleep. He hoped that the nightmare he'd had had been just that. He hoped this was just some fluke with the crystal – because that's the only thing that made this make any sense – and that nothing was going to happen.

It would be awkward to go back to the present knowing he'd experienced an entire night in Tayshia's body and memory, but not as awkward as reliving a nightmare with her. None of this made any sense. Because if it did, that meant the legend plastered on signs all over those stupid caverns was in some way true.

If that was the case, then what the fuck?

The end of the alley loomed closer. The car engines were so loud that Ash couldn't hear anything else. The sidewalks were moderately full. About ten or eleven yards, and then –

A hand.

A man's hand around Tayshia's left shoulder.

A man's heavy hand yanking her backward, away from the lights and the people. Tayshia twisting around. Her hand, reaching for nothing. A second hand, big and meaty, wrapping around her left wrist and pulling so hard that Ash feared her arm would come out of its socket. She started to scream.

The hand moved from her shoulder to her mouth, and then the connecting forearm slammed into part of her throat. The sound was choked into silence right as her back hit the brick. Her head cracked against the stone.

Fear that Ash had only felt in the face of his father exploded inside of Tayshia's body, vibrating like electrical pulses as she looked up into the dark eyes of the grizzled man with the cigarette that had given her the directions.

It became apparent that he still had that cigarette when he lifted it to his lips, took a drag, and then ground the lit end into the center of Tayshia's chest.

The pain was excruciating and concentrated. It was visceral and real.

Unbearable.

Her scream was stifled by his palm.

Gasping, Tayshia's hands clawed at the man's, knocking the cigarette away. He pressed his forearm into her more firmly, allowing no air to escape past his fingers as they gripped her face tighter. As her lungs begged for air, he took his finger and pressed it into the wound. When he twisted his nail into her tender, weeping flesh, Ash truly felt imprisoned.

Blood trickled down underneath the neckline of her dress, in-between her breasts.

"You were so rude," the man said, like it was important that she remember what he had to say. "Let's see if you fuck rude, too."

He hauled back and slammed his fist into Tayshia's gut, right beneath her ribcage. There was no air to rush outward, so all she could do was go limp. She wheezed behind the man's hand and Ash saw her vision beginning to swim. Acute pain twisted sharp and crippling in her torso. There was panic, blooming like dead flowers. Gardenias with white petals dissolving into brown. Roses with red petals fading to black.

The man — who smelled strongly of cigarette smoke and sweat — spun her around and smashed her into the wall. She tried to fight, but his entire girth overwhelmed her. Her fingernails scrabbled at the wall, pushing against it to try and get some space so she could breathe. He pressed and pressed, until her attempted sob became a mere squeak.

The panic increased the longer she went without air.

Ash's mind was blank. For the first time in the duration of this experience, he felt like he wasn't inside of Tayshia's mind anymore. He felt like he was floating somewhere outside of space and time, watching from afar.

Was this really happening?

The man seemed to have nothing more to say. His hands did all of the talking, the left one stroking the outside of Tayshia's thigh and pulling the hem of her ruched dress upward. Cool air rushed to touch her bottom outside of her nylons. The man's right hand wrapped around her throat from behind and squeezed, pulling backward.

She gasped, sucking in precious air that tasted sweet in spite of the rankness of the man's scent.

Just like that, Ash was back. Back inside her mind, feeling everything once more. Her fear. Her confusion. Her anguish.

"Please," Tayshia managed to whisper past the suffocation. As the man's other hand traveled inward, squeezing between her legs over the nylons, he felt her heart breaking into thousands of pieces. Both of her hands moved against his, pushing weakly down on his wrist. "P-Please stop."

Ash didn't care about a lot of things, but hearing Tayshia beg?
He cared about that.

The seconds ticked by, during which Ash thought something might happen. That someone might come down the sidewalk, or might chance a look into the shadows of the alleyway. That Tayshia might produce her phone out of midair, having not realized it was tucked inside a hidden pocket in the side of her dress.

But he felt it when the man's hands slipped into her nylons. He felt it when she realized that there was nothing she could do. He felt it when she gave up. He felt it when the man sunk his fingers into her bun and yanked her head back so far that it hurt.

He felt it when the man tore the flimsy sleeve of her dress and exposed her breast.

Another pretty dress turned sad.

Ash didn't want to see this.

"Oh, God," Tayshia said, sounding terrified — like she had only just realized what was going on. "Oh — okay. Okay, do you want money? I can get money."

Silence.

"You want me on my knees?" Her voice sounded sensual and breathy, a disguise masking the fear burning in her blood. "I'll do whatever you want me to do to you. I will, okay?"

Fuck, why was she fucking saying that? Why couldn't she scream as loudly as she could, instead of trying to reason with him? If she screamed between passing automobiles, then someone would hear and help her. Someone would help, because Ash couldn't. Why was she trying to talk her way out of —

The man's fingers probed inside of her, having slipped beneath the waistband of her underwear. Tayshia yelped when his fingernails scratched her. She tried to lift up on her toes to get away.

"Please," she said, her breaths nearing hyperventilation. Another sob. "Please, okay? Please. I can get you any amount of money. Anything you want."

The man said nothing. Abso-fucking-lutely nothing.

Tayshia didn't realize it, but Ash did: this man was not someone who could be bought with anything but the currency of flesh.

Another tearing sound. The man had withdrawn his hand from her body — without letting go of her hair, which was causing an ache in her neck — and was now tearing a hole in her nylons.

"Wait," she said, sounding almost confused. It made Ash want to punch

a wall. "Wait, wait, wait. Wait, all right? Please, wait!"

Ash felt everything.

When the man dragged her panties down and shoved his slacks and boxers down, Ash felt it.

When the man shoved himself inside of her and the pain rocketed upward through her entire body, Ash felt it.

When the man pressed her so hard into the wall that she couldn't breathe again, bravery failed her. She was forced to redirect all of her focus into struggling for breath past the agony.

And Ash felt it.

If he had the ability to use his fucking hands, that man would be fucking dead.

She screamed, but it choked off into a series of strangled sobs cut in half by the lack of air as the man tugged harder on her hair bun, causing curls to fall loose. Her neck was at an awful backward angle, her eyes only able to stare upwards at the starry sky as she was violated with violent, painful accuracy.

The man knew what he was doing – it was clear he'd had these intentions the moment he'd given her the directions. And with the way he was forcing Tayshia's head back, the way her skin was stretched – any scream she managed to give wouldn't be loud enough.

They were loud enough for Ash.

He remembered the way those screams had echoed in his head when he'd had the nightmare. He remembered the fear and desperation in them, and he'd known that they were her even though he hadn't been able to see past the darkness.

He'd been asleep while she was being assaulted.

"Please – stop," she whispered between gasps, and Ash felt the man twisting her hair and moving faster. It increased the pain, shoved her onto her tip-toes in her heels again. Regret washed through her for something Ash couldn't possibly know without asking her. "Just – plea – "

But when she tried and failed again to get a solid breath in, Ash realized with an aching clarity that she couldn't breathe. Her lungs were spasming. The pain in her chest was unbearable.

Ash felt like he couldn't breathe, either.

Tayshia's panic pulled back like the tide and crashed into the shore as despair.

She thought she was going to die.

"I – " A gasp. " – can't – " Another gasp. " – breathe."

Ash tried to take a step forward. Tried to break free of the confines of the memory and force himself into reality. Tried to do anything to help.

To do anything other than just stand there and watch. To let her know she wasn't alone.

Nothing worked.

He fucking despised himself.

She took one last gasp and then couldn't take another. Her heart beat wildly in her chest. Her fingers clawed so hard into the brick wall that Ash though she might tear her nails off.

Ash felt it all.

Everything. He felt everything she felt as though he were physically there. It was like a cage had been locked around both of his lungs, keeping them from expanding just as hers were unable to. It was horrifying. It was worse than a nightmare. It was like sticking his head underwater and inhaling.

He couldn't breathe.

It lasted for two more minutes, during which Ash tried his best to embrace the pain because he couldn't shoulder it for her. Her vision had long ago started to bleed with spots of black as darkness threatened to take over. The sickening grunts the man was eliciting would have made Ash ill if he had a corporeal form — he was certain he would never forget them.

The man staggered backward, putting himself to rights again.

Finally.

Air.

Tayshia pulled her panties up in a stupor. Her vision was slow to refocus as she took deep breaths, fixed her dress as best she could with the way it was torn, and futilely smoothed her hair. On the verge of her anxiety, walking a tight rope between anguish and numbness, she turned to face the man.

Ash felt strength inside of her, holding her upright as she looked her attacker directly in the eyes.

The man's eyebrows shot up — like he was astonished she was actually looking at him — and he took a step backward.

She stared him down until he turned and dashed off into the darkness.

Tayshia stumbled out onto the busy street, holding the front of her dress up as she did. She nearly ran into a group of college-age girls in scant dresses as she did so. They cheered — because they were drunk — and kept walking. Tayshia said nothing to them, instead choosing to look around.

She focused on the promenade, which was a series of shops lit up with lights that twinkled on and off in patterns. After looking both ways, she crossed the street to the buildings and went to the right.

Ash could feel it. The shame.

She was trying to hold it together.

It took only a couple of minutes to locate the hotel.

The right side of Tayshia's face was scraped almost raw on her cheekbone and temple. It stung like a burn. Her fingernails ached from how hard she'd been scratching at the wall, desperately pushing to get some air. Between her legs hurt. Her lungs hurt. Everything hurt.

Ash didn't know how to explain the way it felt, how absolutely destroyed her heart was — he just knew. *She felt ruined.*

Her hair had come half undone, the bun still present but barely hanging on. Parts of her curls on the bottom were hanging limp and sweaty past her shoulders. There were several pieces that had flown loose from the styling, sticking up in haphazard directions. As she limped the short distance down the sidewalk, up to the lobby entrance, Ash could see people staring at her.

If Ash were there, he'd comb it back for her so she didn't have to worry about it. She already had enough to worry about.

If Ash were there, none of this would ever have happened. He wouldn't have taken her phone. He would have treated her right. He would have taken care of her.

He felt ruined, too.

Tayshia floated in and up to the concierge like a haunt, with a feigned smile on her face and a tremble to her voice. She told them she'd lost her purse, gave them the name of the youth leader, and they called him for identity confirmation. Ash had no clue why the guy wasn't at the bar with them that night and didn't care. He couldn't understand why the employees didn't seem perturbed by her physical state.

The hotel employees gave her a new key after informing her of the charge for the lost one, and then she went into the elevator. When the doors slid shut, Ash caught sight of her appearance in the reflective surface.

She looked defeated.

Inside, Ash could feel her heart beating too fast to track. *Her muscles shook, tremulous with adrenaline and lingering fear. She was jittery — even the slight jolt of the elevator had her jumping. She was in agony.*

She couldn't breathe.

The hotel room was dark, empty of Kieran. But he'd been there. Her purse was on the bed, open. Beside it was her phone.

Ash felt his anger burning hot and acidic. *O'Connell, that fucking weak-ass bitch.*

Kieran had taken her phone out of her purse, held it, and then left it on the bed. He'd likely contemplated bringing it back to her and then had purposefully left it behind. And he wasn't even here in the room. Who knew where he was?

An inhuman sound left Tayshia's body.

She clutched a hand to her stomach, which ached as viciously as the bruises in-between her legs, and she sobbed. The sobs wrenched their way out of her gut, hurting on their way out. Her knees buckled and she collapsed on the carpeted floor against the end of the bed. Her other hand was wrapped around her phone, clutching it tight as her heart screamed in desperation. Her mouth agape, she sobbed in the dark with her unhurt cheek pressed to the edge of the mattress.

"*I can't,*" *was all she kept saying.* "*I can't, I can't, I can't. I can't.*"

Fuck. What the... Fuck.

Just — Fuck.

The last time Ash had felt this helpless, Elijah had just told him his mother was dead.

He wished he could hold Tayshia's hand. Or her. Anything. He just wanted to embrace her. He didn't care about the past. He didn't care about the bickering or the fighting or the dishes.

He wished he were in that hotel room with her so she didn't have to deal with this by herself.

He wished he were there so he could find that man and eviscerate him. Tayshia was the strongest girl he knew, yet all it had taken was Kieran keeping her phone from her to bring her down.

Kieran.

Fucking Kieran.

He was dead. He was dead as Hell when Ash got to him.

Tayshia wept herself into catatonia, until all she could do was breathe. Afterward, she moved like a specter through the hotel room, shedding her clothing and dropping it into the trash can by the dresser. She got into a shower that was ice-cold. Ash felt the water like daggers against her skin, but he accepted the pain. He could feel her accepting it, too.

With a cloth, she scrubbed between her legs not once, not twice, and not thrice — but five times. She dug her fingernails inside of her body, doing her best to be meticulous as she cleaned herself up. She stopped even though he could feel that she wasn't satisfied with her cleanliness, and went about the rest of her shower activities as normal.

Ash simply existed within her mind, trying his best to stay present in the moment and not flash back to everything he'd seen and felt. He stayed present as she smoothed conditioner along the curls, staring at the floor while it soaked into her hair. She washed it out, and then stepped out and into a towel.

When she walked past the mirror, she didn't look at herself.

Minutes later, swathed in an oversized tee shirt as pajamas, she got into bed. She curled up on her side in the darkness. Her body ached.

She looked at her phone.

An international text from her father.

Hi, baby girl. I just wanted to make sure you knew your mom and I are excited for you to come home! We're gonna be there at the airport before you even get there. Love you – Dad.

Tayshia clutched her phone to her chest with trembling hands and stared at the floral wallpaper until she grew too drowsy to keep her eyes open. Only when her breathing evened out did her muscles relax. Only then was she able to take a deep breath.

Only then did she feel safe.

CHAPTER NINETEEN

Ash woke.

Like a bolt of lightning cracking through the darkness, his body went rigid and his eyes snapped open. He gasped as he felt air entering his lungs, relief flooding his body as though he hadn't tasted oxygen in millennia. He sat up, clutching a hand to his chest as he glanced around in bewilderment.

Andre's living room was a disastrous mess, but it was empty. He, Ji Hyun, and Tayshia had all gone to school already. When Ash checked his phone on the coffee table where he'd left it, Andre had texted him to tell him to lock the door on his way out with his extra key, which Ash still had.

There was also a text from Ryo. Another one.

Ash ignored it.

It was nearly lunchtime, so that was great. It was going to be so *fun* explaining to his probation officer why he missed two classes. Thank God he hadn't done anything other than drink.

He remembered passing out after hooking up with Tayshia but everything before and after that was a hazy blur. His mind felt muddy with confusion as he went to use the bathroom and steal one of Andre's extra unopened toothbrushes. The ocean inside of him was swirling, the waters rising up to the top of his heart, making him feel too full. After spitting the toothpaste out into the sink, he squeezed his eyes shut and tried to breathe through the acuteness of it.

Ash felt panic surging through his system, and he didn't know why. His memory felt shrouded. Confused. Like it was thousands of miles away. He dug the heel of his palm into his left eye socket, feeling a headache coming on.

There was a flash of something solid. Lights. A black purse. Glittering red fabric, clinging. A tower.

The Eiffel Tower.

Right as Ash stood up straight, the memories slammed into his head like a speeding car. He cried out in pain and staggered to the side, crashing into the half-open door. He hung his head in his hands, trembling as image after image hurtled past.

Lights, twinkling on the promenade in Paris.

The Eiffel Tower in the distance, like a dark sentinel of metal and stone.

Blue wallpaper, blue décor, blue everything, and a window that overlooked the city.

A ruched red dress that sparkled like a star field, sheer black nylons, strappy high heels.

Kieran, with his face stained with rage.

"There are plenty of girls who aren't as frigid as you. So, whose fault is it if I or any other man feels like they can't control himself when you dress like that?"

Cigarettes. A pub. A dark alley.

The man with the hat and the heavy hands.

"Let's see if you fuck rude, too."

The pungency of sweat. Probing fingers. A torn dress strap.

"I'll do whatever you want me to do to you. I will, okay?"

A phone on a blue bed.

"I can't breathe."

Blood on terracotta thighs.

"I can't, I can't, I can't."

Tayshia.

Ash turned and booked it out of the room. He pulled his shoes on as fast as he could, grabbed his jacket and keys, and ran out of the house. Nearly forgetting to lock the door, he doubled back and did so, then dashed down to his car.

He had to find her. He had no idea what he was going to say, or what he could possibly do to make any of this better. He didn't know if she was going to be angry, mortified, or in despair. He didn't know if they were even going to be able to look each other in the eye.

Ash just knew he had to go to her.

✧✧✧

Nurse Pritchard wouldn't let him into her office.

Apparently, Tayshia had passed out in the bathroom during lunch period for reasons unknown. She'd had to be carried by another teacher up to the nurse's office, which is where she was now located. Ash only found out because Ji Hyun told him.

So, Ash had rushed over, only to find out that Nurse Pritchard was a fucking bitch.

"You don't understand," Ash said, speaking the words slowly. "When she wakes up, she's going to need someone there, and I am the only one who—"

"The only one who what, Mr. Robards?" Pritchard cut him off, her voice shrewd as she eyed him from her much shorter height. Her grey hair was pulled back into a long braid that ran down to her lower back and she wore a dress that belonged on the prairie. "The only one who could cause Tayshia the most distress? No, I don't think so. No one is entering my office for visitation."

"Fuck," Ash cursed, his hands balled into fists at his sides.

"Mr. Robards!" Pritchard said, her brow furrowing with ire. "Watch your language! Do I need to tell the principal that you're being this disrespectful? I'm sure your *probation* officer would love to hear it."

Ash's anger, panic, and desperation were pushing his sanity out of orbit. If she remembered—if Tayshia *remembered*—and she knew Ash had been there, then who was she going to want to see? A stuffy old nurse, or the only other person on the planet who knew what she'd been through?

"I don't give a flying *fuck* what you do, okay?" he said, eyes wide as he steepled his fingers and pointed at her. "I'm here because Tayshia is my friend, and she needs my help. If she opens her damn eyes and I'm not there? She's going to lose her *fucking* mind. Do you understand me?"

Pritchard stood there, staring at him with her jaw agape. He saw the decisions flying past in her eyes. He knew he had to be seconds away from a world of hurt.

But Ash was done messing things up where people were involved. He was done standing by and watching everyone suffer. He hadn't gone for help when he'd had the chance. He hadn't stepped forward to stop his father, nor to help Tayshia when she was begging for him to help her save her dad. He hadn't helped support his mother when she was drowning her sorrows and emotions in food.

He was done taking the coward's path.

Pritchard put her hands on her hips and fixed Ash with a withering stare.

"Thank you, Mr. Robards, but you may leave."

With a sweeping of her skirt, she turned and stormed back into her office, slamming the door shut behind her. There was a click, signifying that she had locked it.

Ash glared at the door and conceded defeat. He was fortunate he hadn't gotten detention for his outburst. If Pritchard didn't tell the principal, he'd be surprised. He tangled his fingers in his hair, tipping his head back to scowl at the ceiling.

This was fucked. This was all so fucked.

Had Tayshia realized he was there in the memory? He feared she might be ashamed and that made him want to be sick. She had nothing to be ashamed of. If it was a memory and not a nightmare, then he needed her to understand that it wasn't her fault. It was the man's and it was Kieran's.

Beneath all the surface questions lay the biggest ones.

How was it possible for an amethyst to put him into her dreams? And why couldn't she enter his?

Why did she dream in memories?

He slipped his hands into the pockets of his jeans and trudged back down the hallway, past lockers and signs telling everyone about Homecoming for the younger students. It was infuriating, seeing everything look so normal when he felt so completely and utterly changed by what he'd experienced.

Even if it *was* only a dream, it was horrific.

But then again, Ash had been seeing her dreams every night since he got out of jail, and every night before he was arrested, He knew what she dreamed and what she didn't dream — provided the legend of the crystals was real.

If it wasn't a memory, then why would she have only dreamt of this once?

There were too many emotions in his heart. Emotions he wasn't used to dealing with. Before his arrest, Ash had felt nothing but a conceited sense of pride in himself based purely upon his ill-conceived belief in teenage invincibility. He didn't feel things because he could drown them. He could hold them under the water and drown them until he didn't feel them anymore.

In jail, it was different. The emotions became all-encompassing. Fear plagued him, shadowed by grief at night and painted during the day with shame at having failed her. He knew she was hurting, his mother. He knew she needed help. But he'd made the wrong choices.

Now, he felt angry. Frantic. Needy.

He didn't want to think about the awkwardness or the consequences or the explanations that would need to be given. Ash wanted to be there when she left the nurse's office. He wanted her to know that he'd been there in the memory—that he'd seen everything and he'd seen how strong she was.

Because when he thought about it, that was what he'd always admired about her, and it was what had made him feel threatened whenever they fought. It was like there was nothing he could say that could scare her. If she were a heroine in a fantasy novel, she'd be offering gold to dragons and saving faeries from iron traps. She'd be figuring out the weaknesses and strengths of her enemies and knowing when to use them. Even in the memory, in the face of danger—while she was being attacked—she was thinking on her feet. He liked that. He'd always liked that.

He wanted to be her friend.

Tayshia needed friends. She needed people around her who weren't going to hurt her and cheat on her. Needed people who weren't gonna take her phone and then purposely leave it in the hotel room, instead of going back for her to try and make sure she was okay.

Kieran.

Kieran fucking O'Connell.

Crackling his knuckles in an absentminded manner, Ash turned and headed back for the cafeteria to get his things.

As he was stepping off the staircase between the hallway and the one that led there, Ash was surprised to see Elijah coming towards him at full speed. He looked nervous, terrified, and panicked, all at once.

"Ash!" Elijah called, skidding to a halt in front of him. "Are you— was she—"

"I didn't get to go in," Ash said, carding an angry hand through his hair. It caused it to fall about and stick up in random directions, some still hanging into his eyes. "Nurse Pritchard says no one's allowed."

Elijah shot a frown behind Ash, towards the nurse's office. "What do you—I mean—what—what happened? Like, what happened? Did she—is she okay?"

"Calm down," Ash said, even though he was anything but. "If

she was badly hurt, I think Pritchard would have told me."

"Well, what happened?"

"I have no idea. Someone outside the cafeteria said she passed out in the bathroom. That's all. She got sick last night so she's probably just dehydrated. She'll be fine."

"No offense, but maybe Nurse Pritchard thought you were lying." Elijah walked around him. "Maybe she'll let me in."

Something Ash didn't recognize — something acidic and biting — rose up like a tidal wave inside of him. His hand shot out, pressing flat to the center of Elijah's chest, and he turned his head to give him a once-over.

"Don't," he said. "Pritchard said no one goes in. If she said no to me, then she'll say no to you."

Elijah looked away and when their eyes met again, he was glowering up at him.

"You're here at school by luck, and you know it," he said.

Ash's mood flashed toward a fiery place. Elijah was his best friend, but ever since the incidents on Tayshia's birthday with Kieran, something had soured between them. Something that wasn't entirely irreparable, but that felt like one wrong step could make it so.

Which part was luck? Ash failed to see how his mother dying was good fortune. The only reason why the school took sympathy on him was for that reason, and everyone in town knew it. But Elijah seemed to know exactly how to word his question to make Ash think along those lines.

Did he know that Ash and Tayshia had hooked up?

"Whether I'm here by luck or not? I said..." Ash held Elijah's gaze, raising his eyebrows. "... What the fuck I said."

"I don't care." Elijah wrenched himself away. "I'm sorry Nurse Pritchard won't let you in to see her, but the rules that apply to you don't apply to the rest of us. I'm your best friend and I'm happy to be your best friend, but I can't keep pretending like I don't know who you are and what you did. You were a drug dealer in high school, man. A drug dealer, and you robbed an ice cream shop at gunpoint. You are a *felon*. Of course she's not gonna trust *you* to go into the room. You made the wrong choices and these are the consequences."

Ash felt Elijah's betrayal like a thorn in his heart. His already-volatile anger began to boil.

"The consequences?" he bit out through clenched teeth. "What consequences? Not being able to see my friend when she might be hurt?"

Elijah shook his head. "For someone who a while ago was adamant that he didn't care about her, it sure seems like you care now. You can't do that—you can't just hold people at arm's-length for later. You hated her two weeks ago and now it's almost October, and she's suddenly your friend? And yeah. These *are* the consequences. You chose to break the law, and now you don't get to go into the nurse's office and see Tayshia."

Ash opened his mouth, about to respond, but Elijah was already walking past him. He watched him go with ire burning hot inside of him.

Elijah didn't get it. Nurse Pritchard didn't get it. They didn't understand what Tayshia had been through. They didn't know what Ash had seen in her memory.

Neither of them could possibly know what it felt like to share her breath but not be able to breathe.

Ash waited there by the end of the hallway, expecting Elijah to come trundling back out with his tail between his legs. But when the minutes went on and on, Ash realized with a sinking feeling that Elijah might have been right.

Maybe these *were* the consequences.

And when he marched back down the hall and around the corner, he saw that no one was there. Pritchard had allowed Elijah inside. Tayshia would wake to him by her bedside, and not Ash.

It him so fucking sad.

✵✵✵

Ash fell asleep on the couch in the living room.

He hadn't meant to but for some reason, the moment his head hit the pillows, exhaustion barrelled into him. It was in his mind, weighing him down into the cushions.

There were no dreams this time.

He woke in the darkness of the Fall evening to the sound of the front door closing. His eyes fluttered open. The small measure of surprise he felt at the fact that it was dark faded when he remembered that he'd taken a nap.

And then he remembered everything else.

He sat up, his hair falling into his eyes as he did so. He could just barely make out Tayshia's form in the shadows, lingering near the door.

The silence felt heavy.

"Hi," she said.

"Hey."

Ash looked at her shadowy form, wondering if she knew what had happened. Wondering if her memories were as dark as his. Wondering if the only reason why he was present in her memory was because of the dreams he'd been having of her, and if that meant that she was having them, too.

He stood up.

Who was he kidding? Her memories were darker. Tayshia was the one who had lived through it. He had only watched, a prisoner trapped.

"Are you —" he started.

"Have you —"

They stopped and began again.

"I was —"

"Did they —"

Another longer pause.

"Are you okay?" Ash asked, hands on his hips. "I heard you fainted."

"I'm good. I was just exhausted."

"Okay."

"I'm just going to get something to eat," Tayshia said in a monotone. She turned the light on, adding a familiar ambiance to the living room. Ash watched as she traipsed into the kitchen. He heard her opening the refrigerator and then getting a dish out of the cupboard.

Ash looked at the carpeted floor and contemplated confronting her, but what could he possibly say? What could he say to someone whose mind he had been trapped within while she was being attacked? There was no comfort he could offer her for a bad memory. No solace from a past nightmare.

But that was the thing, wasn't it?

The past and the fact that he couldn't do anything about it.

If he could, he'd go back to the day that everything had gone wrong and he'd make the right choice. He'd stop his father. He'd help Tayshia. He'd go all the way back to the day that his father offered him money to sell at school, and he'd choose to tell him no.

If he could mend the past, he'd bring his mother back.

The past was certain. But the present was ever-changing. Tumultuous. Something he could influence. And in the present, he had power and control over his decisions. He knew that things could never be the same between him and Tayshia after what they'd experienced together, regardless of what happened in the present and regardless of whether or not she knew she'd been harbouring his consciousness inside of her own.

Well, things could stay the same. If he wanted them to.

But did he want them to stay the same? Could they? Could he walk the halls of Christ Rising knowing that no matter how safe they were, Tayshia would never be able to feel that same measure of safety? Fuck, did she even feel safe with him in the apartment?

That made his stomach churn. He could never — would never — hurt her like that. He'd done some reprehensible things in his life, but nothing like that.

No wonder she'd wanted to stop when they were hooking up.

His thoughts were all over the place. He wasn't sure how much Tayshia remembered but he knew he couldn't waste any time. He needed to talk to her about it. Tonight. Now.

He needed her to know she didn't have to feel as alone as he did.

Ash sighed and dragged his hands through his sleep-ruffled hair, heading towards the kitchen. He shouldered the edge of the wall across from the counter, crossing his arms over his chest and watching her stir leftover pasta in a bowl. He was six-foot-four, but he felt like he was eight feet tall. Tayshia was so much shorter than him.

Perhaps she just looked that way now that he worried about her. "Tayshia."

Her shoulders jumped. She whirled around, spoon dripping red sauce in hand. With a hard swallow, she nodded to him.

"Did you need the kitchen? I'll be done in a sec."

"No," he murmured, studying her face and trying not to remember the feeling of her cheek scraping against the brick wall of that building. "I wanted to talk."

Something shifted in her eyes, which she averted from his. She turned back to the pasta.

"About me fainting? I was dehydrated, and Nurse Pritchard said—"

"Not about that."

She cleared her throat. "Uh, well... I heard that she wouldn't let you in to the nurse's office. I mean, no cap—I didn't believe her when she said you were out there."

"Why?" Ash said, his voice a bit hoarse from slumber. "And which part was unbelievable?"

"The part where you came to visit," she said, lifting the bowl and putting it into the microwave. She turned and crossed her arms, too. "Why would you visit me?"

Ash raised one brow. "I just wanted to make sure you were all right."

Tayshia snorted and took her food out, setting the hot bowl on the counter. She picked up her fork and stuck it into the pasta, twirling it. Her lips pursed to blow cool air on the bite, and then she stuck it into her mouth and chewed.

"What does it matter to you?" she said around a mouthful. She took another bite before she'd even finished the first. "You guys made it seem like it was no big deal."

"Well, it was." He narrowed his eyes. "You ate two shroom brownies."

"Boy, stop playin' with me." She took a third bite, chewing fast and sloppy. "You guys said I would be fine."

"You threw them up so yeah, you were supposed to be fine."

"And...?"

"You passed out in the bathroom and went to the nurse's office!" he said, raising his voice a bit in annoyance. "Excuse me for giving a shit."

"Oh, whatever." She rolled her eyes. "Anyway, sorry she wouldn't let you in."

"It's an unfortunate side effect of the I-have-a-felony disease," Ash said, forcing himself not to snap the words out. "Have a nice visit with Elijah, though?"

"Yes, he was *lovely*," she said with sarcasm in her tone. "I'm just sorry you couldn't come in. I don't think it's believable to anyone that we would be friends, to be honest."

Something inside of Ash's stomach jerked. He didn't know what to name the emotion—he just knew he was more than a bit pissed off at Elijah. They weren't seeing eye-to-eye.

"Well, we are," he said, the words falling out of his lips before he could stop them. It wasn't until he said them that he realized it was true. He supposed it hadn't felt as real when they were still just thoughts, or when he was saying them to disarm Elijah. But now, it was real.

They were friends.

"Oh. I'm sorry."

"Stop that." He frowned. "Stop apologizing."

Her response was to eat more. The waves of her weave looked limper than usual and her clothes were rumpled. It was impossible to tell if she remembered the dream, memory, or whatever it was just by looking at her.

She sure could eat.

Ash didn't know how to broach the subject of August 17th, 2018. What if she didn't know he'd been in her memory? What if him bringing it up just made things worse? Maybe she knew she'd relived the memory but wasn't aware that he'd been there?

"I've gotta use the bathroom," Tayshia said, setting her empty bowl into the sink. "Have a good night."

Ash eyed the bowl. Before today, he would have reamed her out for not putting it into the dishwasher. But now, he couldn't bring himself to do it. She'd been through enough, hadn't she? He could wash the damn bowl.

The sound of the bathroom door shutting echoed into the room.

As he washed the one dish, he realized how conflicted he felt. He couldn't just go into his room and pretend like nothing happened. He couldn't pretend he didn't know.

He couldn't look at her without remembering it—remembering how she'd tried to reason with the man by offering herself up to him in other ways. How she pleaded with the man to wait, as though she understood there was no way out and just wanted to gain some sort of control back. How she couldn't breathe and how that terror had exploded in her chest like fire.

Ash couldn't act like everything wasn't completely fucking upside-down now. How could he? How could he when he just wanted to...

He wanted to hold her.

It felt like a release to admit it. He'd never before wanted to hold anyone other than his mother, but he wanted to hold Tayshia. If she would let him, he'd hold her for as long as she needed to understand that no one was ever going to do that to her again.

Because Ash would never take someone's phone from them, let alone a woman's in a foreign country. The fact that Kieran had not only gone back to the hotel room to drop off her bag, but had opened it, held the phone to acknowledge its presence, and then left it there?

His fingers pressed into the sink, hard.

He wanted to find that fucker and show him what it felt like to be without his phone. He wanted to rip his own phone out of his hands and smash his face in with it. Then, Ash wanted to slam his fist into Kieran's face over and over again, until his wasn't recognizable. He wanted Kieran to suffer ten thousand years for every time Tayshia had to wash herself in the shower that night. For every minute she spent lying awake, staring at the blue wallpaper with her phone clutched to her chest like a security blanket.

He was so fucking angry.

Ash dried his hands with a towel by the sink. He went to his room and changed into a pair of grey joggers and a white V-neck tee, and then he sat down on the edge of his bed. He traced the outlines of some of the tattoos on his right arm with his fingertips, gazing at his dresser until it blurred.

He had to talk to her.

Standing up, he went back out into the hall. The door to the bathroom was still closed, yellow light filtering out beneath it. He could hear the shower running. She'd only been in there for fifteen minutes and according to her track record, she had at least twenty more to go.

Ash sat down on the floor with his back to the wall beside the door. He pulled his knees to his chest, rested his forearms on his kneecaps, and gripped the opposite wrist with one hand. Tipping his head back against the plaster, he closed his eyes.

Forty minutes later, the door opened and the light clicked off.

Ash, who had been dozing, jolted awake. He looked up at her, his hair in his eyes.

"Hey," he said.

"Hi." Her brow furrowed. "What are you doing? Did you need to use the bathroom?"

"Nah," he said, yawning and rubbing his eye with the side of one fist. He stood up, towering over her in the small hallway. "I told you I wanted to talk to you."

Her curls were piled atop her head. She looked exhausted. But something in her eyes told him she knew what he wanted to talk about.

"There's nothing to talk about," she said. "I want to go to bed."

Ash felt the last vestiges of his drowsiness dissipating.

Did she remember?

"I don't *want* you to go to bed," he said, trying to make eye contact with her. "I want you to talk to me."

Her eyes widened, gaze darting down to take in the sight of his tattoos—his neck, his exposed chest above the low neckline of his shirt, his biceps and forearms—and then it lifted back up again.

"I know you're used to getting what you want, Ash," she said, tone icy, "but I need to go to bed. I don't have anything to say to you."

She turned to go and without thinking, Ash's hand shot out and grabbed her wrist. There was a moment where he was surprised at how cold her skin was under his own, and then she was whipping around with her other hand up.

Crack.

She slapped him.

"Don't *touch* me!" she shrieked, her voice shrill. "Don't touch me, don't talk to me, and don't be my friend!"

Ash blinked down at her, his cheek stinging. He rubbed his chin, letting out a mirthless laugh. He was angry. Angry that she'd slapped him. Angry at how helpless he felt. But mostly, angry that he was right.

She remembered.

"All right," he said, nodding. "Okay. Okay."

Tayshia hesitated, lifting one hand as though she were going to reach for him. Then, she placed her hand on the center of his chest, covering the crystal with her palm. He knew she could feel how wildly his heart was beating, but he didn't move. He simply stood there as she slid her palm up until her fingers curved over the top of his right shoulder.

In her eyes, he saw the same shame that he'd felt within her during the memory.

"I'm sorry," she whimpered, her face pinching and eyes watering. She shook her head. "You were never... No one was ever supposed to know."

Ash took a step toward her, his fingers tingling and the space beneath his diaphragm aching. She let out a harsh breath. It shuddered like she was seconds away from falling into despair. He took another step, her head lowering the closer he got, like she couldn't look at him.

He felt like he was suffocating again.

"I just wanna hold you," he whispered. His hands hovered over her waist, itching to pull her against him. "Just let me hold you, okay?"

Her gaze flickered back and forth between his face and his chest, fearful lifts and falls. Her shoulders rose, as if they could protect her if he chose to hurt her.

Ash's hands trembled as they slid past her elbows, gently traversing the planes of her upper arms. She trembled, too, her eyes squeezed shut against whatever it was she didn't want to see. She didn't move, didn't breathe, didn't speak as he wrapped his arms around her and pulled her closer.

It felt like she was made of starlight.

Ash felt tears welling up in his eyes, felt the memories of Paris beginning to attack him from all sides. The pain, the trauma, the terror. His emotions were overwhelming, ripping his heart into shreds like a black hole tearing through his galaxy.

"I'm so sorry," he whispered, dropping his head to the junction of her shoulder and neck. He buried his face into her throat and folded his arms around her as tightly as he could. "I'm so fucking sorry."

Tayshia let out a sob, her hands clutching at the back of his shirt. Her fingers clawed as she fell into her anguish, sagging against him so that he was the only thing holding her up.

"I don't wanna talk about it," she kept saying. "Please don't make me talk about it."

"I won't," he whispered, fighting against his own desire to break down. He held her so tight he thought he might consume her. "I just want to hold you."

He felt her hands traveling upward, sliding up his arms, up to the back of his neck. Her fingers dug into his hair, twisting, dragging his head back.

Ash didn't know how it happened. He was unsure what it was. Maybe it was the look of desperation on her face, or the way his heart felt shattered in his chest. But in the next moment, they were kissing.

They were kissing, their tongues pressing together and hands grasping at each other's faces and shoulders and bodies as though they were each other's lifelines. Ash had never before felt so emotional during a kiss and he was certain he would never feel this way about anyone else ever again. He would never share this type of pain with another person.

Her kiss burned him from the inside-out.

"I won't hurt you," he murmured against her lips. "I'll never hurt you. I promise. I swear."

Her response was to whimper as she kissed him back, dancing on the tips of her toes as she struggled to get to him, to get closer. She was like a woman in the desert, drinking the water of his body like it could keep her from drying out.

Ash's heart was pounding so hard that he was dizzy.

He broke the kiss to take a breath, and their eyes met. Within them, he saw the broken pieces that had been there all along. The ones she masked with anger. He saw the reason for all of their arguments, for everything that had gone wrong since they'd moved into this apartment. He saw her pain and how heavy the burden of carrying it had become.

He saw another reason to feel guilty.

Ash moved away from her, averting his eyes as he ran his fingers through his hair. He shouldn't have kissed her. He shouldn't have *ever* kissed her.

"I'm sorry," Tayshia whispered, panting softly as she wiped the tears off of her cheeks. "I shouldn't—I'm not—"

"Don't apologize to me," he said, a fierceness to his tone that he'd never heard himself use before. It felt almost protective. His eyes snapped back to meet hers again. "Don't you ever apologize to me for anything ever again, do you hear me?"

Tayshia drew her hand back to her chest, where it curled around her half of the crystal. A crestfallen look that Ash couldn't place marred her face. She lowered her gaze and when she spoke, her voice sounded defeated.

"Good night."

He sighed. "Wait. I—"

"Please," she whispered, sounding broken. "I want to go to sleep."

"Fine. But if you have any nightmares, my door's unlocked. Or you can call my name. I'm a light sleeper."

She nodded, so he went towards his room.

"Ash?"

"Yeah?"

He looked over his shoulder. She stood in front of her bedroom door, her hand still clutching her amethyst and her brows pulling together in an expression of remorse.

"There's one thing I should apologize to you for. I'm sorry that I hit you."

Ash felt it lingering on the horizon—a distant anger that felt like it was decades or even centuries old.

"You're sorry?"

"Yes," she whispered, gaze cutting across the shadows of the hallway towards him. "I am."

"Good," he said, and then he sighed. The fire of his anger left him. It wasn't the talk he'd imagined, but it was something. He scratched the back of his head and then curved his hand around his neck to massage it. "That's good. Go to bed."

She stared at him like a deer caught in headlights, and then practically threw herself into her bedroom.

Ash laid awake that night for a long time. Until the stars and the moon turned to sunlight shrouded by brewing rain clouds. Until he realized that he could still feel the man's hands on Tayshia's body, even though it had just been a memory. A dream.

A nightmare.

His life was a mess.

He didn't know what was going to happen with Elijah. He didn't know what was going to happen with Ryo. He didn't know what was going to happen with Tayshia. It was the fear of the unknown that kept him up clear into the next day, kept him floating through his classes like a wandering haunt for the entire week.

Fear kept him suspended in the midst of a life that felt as cold as Winter without the fire of Tayshia Cole in it. And there was no fire without her.

Ash feared how cold eternity would be if he had to spend it alone.

THE APRICITY SERIES

MOONLIGHT
upon the Sea

The stars were silver.

They always were in Ash's dreams. Ever since he was a kid, the stars in his dreams were silver, and the sky was whatever color his mind seemed to think mattered the most. It didn't matter what he was doing in the dream — whether playing medieval knight or flying on the back of a dragon — the sky was always the color that made him the happiest.

But when Ash opened his eyes and saw a lavender sky and silver cosmos, he wasn't happy. He was confused.

He hadn't been inside one of his own dreams in months.

Sitting up, he saw sprawling hills, distant mountains, and white flowers. Gardenias littering the grass that were drifting back and forth with the wind, bathed in faint silvery moonlight. The mountains were tipped in snow, but it wasn't cold on the hill he sat atop. When he got to his feet, in the distance to the left he could see the ocean stretching the length of the horizon. He glanced to the right and saw more hills and fields of thick, lush grass covered in glowing white flowers.

Ash.

Well, this was odd. He'd been watching Tayshia's dreams for so long that he'd forgotten what it was like to have one of his own.

Tayshia's dreams were always memories. Pieces of her experiences with the people around her each day. They could be arbitrary, like studying in her bedroom or doing cornrow braids in her hair. Or they could be a little more exciting, like the time that Tayshia and her friends had driven to Seattle for a shopping trip right after graduation.

The only thing that was certain was that they were flashes. Never her entire day – only the things that felt safe to see.

Ash's dreams were more whimsical, which was in sharp contrast to the way he felt when he was awake. He dreamed of things like flying, doing magical things, or sitting and watching the sunset. Peaceful things that didn't cause him fear or concern. He was always alone, with no other humans or civilization nearby, and that was something he'd always liked.

It felt almost alien to be inside his own head for a change, but he was glad for it.

Ash.

He decided to head down the hill towards the white flowers.

Ash always had liked flowers. Especially gardenias. They were his mother's favorites, and they were the only thing he missed about his home. The only part of Gabriel that Ash liked. At any given time, fresh gardenias could be found in every windowsill, on every shelf, and in every vase just for the family.

At least, until his father fell apart.

Kneeling down, he plucked a flower out of the ground with a quiet snap. Eyelids fluttering shut, he inhaled the scent of the flower in his hand and a sense of calm washed over him. Perhaps he would take the flower to the seashore. It would feel like his mother was there with him, watching the water crash along the sand. They used to go to the Oregon coast sometimes, but not as much as they should have. His mother loved it.

Standing, he turned and headed west across the field.

ASH!

Ash nearly leapt out of his skin, the hairs on the back of his neck standing up. He whirled around to look behind him.

Tayshia.

She was here.

"Can you hear me?" *she said.*

Ash stared down at her. She wore the same pajamas she'd been wearing when she came into his room that night, and the breeze was playing with her curls. There was a strange curiosity in her eyes that didn't match the fearful frown on her lips. Around her neck was the crystal.

269

"I guess you can't," she said. "But you can see me."

"No, I – " He cleared his throat, the sound of his voice a little jarring. His dreams were usually devoid of words. "I can hear you. Can you hear me?"

She nodded. "Is this a memory?"

"No, it's – " His brow furrowed. "Tayshia, the sky is purple and the stars are silver. I mean, bruh. Come on."

"Well, I didn't notice!" she said, throwing her hands up into the air. "I was a little busy wondering how the Hell I got into your dream!"

Ash bit his lower lip, reaching up with his free hand to touch his crystal.

Was now the perfect time to tell her? He wanted to. He was just scared what she would think. Months of walking her dreams, watching her life unfold and progress, and he'd never said a thing to her. Not that they were on speaking terms, but... He knew he'd be irritated if someone was invading his privacy like that, willing or unwilling.

If he was ever going to win her trust, he needed to start somewhere.

"Well, given that I've been watching your dreams for four-and-a-half months now, I'm not as surprised to see you as I probably should be," he said. "I'm trying to figure out what's different."

Her jaw dropped. "You've been doing what?"

Ash twirled the flower stem vertically between his forefinger and thumb, grimacing. "Dreamwalking in your dreams for four-and-a-half months?"

AVAILABLE NOW

ACKNOWLEDGMENTS

Amelia, thank you so much for not only taking *the Apricity series* to the next level, but for taking my visions and making them into a reality. *Starlight* would be flat and lifeless without you. Your talent has turned my dream into something tangible and real. I love you. This book is dedicated to you.

Mayghaen, thank you for being my point person on not only this novel, but all of my stories. My writing would be nothing without your expertise, knowledge, and honesty. I cherish our friendship. I love you. This book is dedicated to you.

Julie, thank you for being the person to help me with my ideas, see reason when my plot is getting crazy, and being my number one hype-man while I was working on this book. You're always there for me. Our friendship is very dear to me. I love you. This book is dedicated to you.

Sara, thank you very much for being the feisty, energetic, supportive person in my corner, cheering me on every step of the way. No matter how down I got, no matter how tough things were, you were always positive. You always believed in me. I am so glad I met you and I value our friendship. I love you. This book is dedicated to you.

Jillian, thank you so much for being the person to really get the beginning of this narrative nailed down. I was floating all over the place before you pinned me the Hell down. I love your bubbliness and your positive energy. I truly enjoy our friendship and feel lucky to have met you. I love you. This book is dedicated to you.

And finally, to all of my readers on Wattpad,

To my followers on TikTok,

To the members of my fan group, HoneySweetReaders,

It took a village.

This book is dedicated to you.

LOVED THE BOOK?

If you enjoyed this novel, if it spoke to you on an emotional level, or if you feel compelled to tell me your thoughts, please don't hesitate to leave me a review when you've completed it. I want to hear your opinions and most of all: I want to hear your stories. Every review means the world to me. I read each and every single one that I get.

To leave a review, you need only go to your Amazon orders, scroll to the purchase of this book, and click: *Write a Product Review.*

Alternatively, you can review on Goodreads.

www.goodreads.com/author/show/20655146.Mariah_L_Stevens

Thank you so much!

Mariah L. Stevens is a half-Black Autistic author and artist who lives in the PNW. She is a survivor of eating disorders, abuse, and sexual assault. She advocates for recovery and a life worth living. As someone diagnosed with BiPolar 1, she supports mental health awareness, as well as eating disorder awareness in Black individuals, and weaves all of these elements into her work with the sole purpose of helping others seek recovery.

Mariah has been writing since she was 13 years old, and she plans to use her passion and life experience to help other survivors through the power of prose. She loves Japanese fashion, *Kingdom Hearts*, Disneyland, and her cat.

Website: **www.starlightwriting.com**
Tiktok: **@theapricityseries**
Instagram: **@starlight.writing**
Facebook: **Starlight Readers**

Amelia Louise Carter (Meialoue) is a full time graphic designer and freelance illustrator from the UK. She's massively inspired by manga and anime, but also has a unique style all of her own. Completely self-taught, she's incredibly passionate about creating artwork and strives to be better one step at a time, every day.

"If you can't see the end of the tunnel right now, or you feel like everything is just hopeless, please don't give up. Get help, keep going, because if you keep trying and fight for your dreams, whether they're small or large I promise you, if you fight, you'll accomplish them."
✧✧✧ Meialoue, ever the imperfectionist.

Website: **www.meialoue.com**
Tiktok: **@meialoue**
Instagram: **@meialoue**
Etsy: **www.etsy.com/uk/shop/Meialoue**

Printed in Great Britain
by Amazon

72212721R00168